Praise for Robert E. Howard

"I adore these books. Howard had a gritty, vibrant style—broadsword writing that cut its way to the heart, with heroes who are truly larger than life. I heartily recommend them to anyone who loves fantasy."

—David Gemmell,
author of *Legend* and *White Wolf*

"The voice of Robert E. Howard still resonates after decades with readers—equal parts ringing steel, thunderous horse hooves, and spattered blood. Far from being a stereotype, his creation of Conan is the high heroic adventurer. His raw muscle and sinews, boiling temper, and lusty laughs are the gauge by which all modern heroes must be measured."

—Eric Nylund,
author of *Halo: The Fall of Reach* and *Signal to Noise*

"That teller of marvelous tales, Robert Howard, did indeed create a giant [Conan] in whose shadow other 'hero tales' must stand."

—John Jakes,
New York Times bestselling author
of the North and South trilogy

"For stark, living fear . . . what other writer is even in the running with Robert E. Howard?" —H. P. Lovecraft

"Howard . . . painted in the broadest strokes imaginable. A mass of glimmering black for the menace, an ice-blue cascade for the hero, between them a swath of crimson for battle, passion, blood."

—Fritz Lieber

The Conquering Sword of CONAN

THE FULLY ILLUSTRATED ROBERT E. HOWARD LIBRARY
from Del Rey Books

The Conquering Sword *of* CONAN

ROBERT E. HOWARD

ILLUSTRATED BY GREGORY MANCHESS

BALLANTINE BOOKS DEL REY NEW YORK

A Del Rey Trade Paperback Original

Published in the United States by Del Rey Books, an imprint of The Random House Publishing Group, a division of Random House, Inc., New York.

DEL REY is a registered trademark and the Del Rey colophon is a trademark of Random House, Inc.

This edition published by arrangement with Wandering Star Books, Ltd., London.

Library of Congress Control Number: 2005935622

ISBN 978-0-345-46153-7

Printed in the United States of America

www.delreybooks.com

Design: Marcelo Anciano
Typography: Stuart Williams
Editor: Patrice Louinet
Series editor: Rusty Burke

*This is for Brodie Goheen and Cody Goheen,
my models for Conan and his world. Your excitement about this
book and enthusiasm about my work continues to inspire me.*

Gregory Manchess

The Servants of Bit-Yakin
first published *Weird Tales*, March 1935 (as *Jewels of Gwahlur*)

Beyond the Black River
first published *Weird Tales*, May and June 1935

The Black Stranger
original version first published *Echoes of Valor*, Tor, 1987

The Man-Eaters of Zamboula
first published *Weird Tales*, November 1935 (as *Shadows in Zamboula*)

Red Nails
first published *Weird Tales*, July, August–September and October 1936

Contents

Plates

Foreword

I never knew Conan. Oh, I saw the movies and studied the paintings and thought I knew all about Conan's character. Then I read the stories presented here.

I knew next to nothing until then. And neither does anyone else who hasn't read Howard. Because locked within these flights of fury, these vaults of untamed male fantasy, is the actual persona of the character so many have captured on canvas.

And now it was my turn and I leapt at the chance. I believed that the real character would come to life in my mind's eye in a different way than what I had been exposed to. Intuitively, I knew I was not understanding the full picture.

I began reading with the daunting task before me of trying to capture a view of Conan that was entirely my own approach. As I read I was struck by Howard's wordsmithing. The words with which he chose to describe certain passages were themselves descriptive and visual. It sent me running for the dictionary.

The farther I read, the more I realized that these stories were becoming classic in a broader sense than the pulp genre. I viewed them in a way that N. C. Wyeth may have absorbed *Treasure Island* or Mead Schaeffer visualized *Lorna Doone*. A grand adventure scale with all the seriousness that the Golden Age illustrators embued their pictures. A classic illustrated adventure book. I wanted to own Conan the way those guys owned their presentations of beloved characters.

There was so much to choose from. The images were cascading and overlapping in waves of postures, lighting, and movement. As I sketched away into many nights, out came the Conan bouldering through a creek bed, on his way to or from so many of the actions in this collection. It became the slipcase, presenting Conan's essential portrait. Alert, confident, and solitary.

I wanted a range of his emotions. The next painting to appear stemmed from my desire to portray the stealthy, panther-like side of the Cimmerian. And so he strides atop the wall at night in *The Man-Eaters of Zamboula*, on a mission to educate someone about the way the world works. I added another night scene because I wanted to see those streets in Zamboula and find Conan rescuing Nafertari, sneaking about, ever watchful for dangerous cannibals.

Then the pirate story. As adventurous and mythical as Sabatini's *Captain Blood*, Conan steps into the story of *The Black Stranger* in full-on pirate gear. I had to show him as no one is likely to have seen him portrayed. Finest pirate regalia, as if Howard had just discovered an old trunk of his grandfather's in the dusty attic. The portrait of Black Sarono is in the Golden Age mode of limited colors: red, black, and white, and executed with the same spirit. Each black-and-white chapter painting was an excuse to capture my chance of illustrating an old pirate tale. And I reveled in it.

I also knew that I had to present Conan as the flat out, berserker warrior that instantly comes to mind at the mention of the stories. I wasn't against showing him this way, indeed, I had to find my particular point of view for the battle madness. It came as two pieces. One was Conan one on one with an equally corded Pict. This became the dustjacket. I wanted to show a bit of tension in the exchange, not a clear view of Conan conquering. And I needed to present his dynamic physique. This led to the second battle scene with Conan surrounded and exploding into a killing machine. The bodies work as a swirling, upward element toward Conan, captured in mid-flash of some offstage lightning. I added the background bolt to charge the scene and the sharpness of the melee. Another chance to capture Conan's great musculature came in *The Servants of Bit-Yakin*. I could see him rushing up those stairs for Muriela, light glistening off his sweaty back, so many archways to race over.

Beyond the Black River was especially visual in a classic Conan way, but again I chose a night scene of warriors in a stealth assault mode. I was there on the hillside as those malevolent mercenaries, like black ops of today, climbed the embankment on their mission of mayhem. In contrast, I chose a bright and sunny day to see the Picts getting pelted with anything that would fit in a catapult. It seemed ironic tragedy to be killed on such a beautiful day.

Red Nails could be painted over and over again. (And I hope it will be by many others!) But even though I steered away from showing too many monsters for fear of taking away from the readers' own exaggerated manifestation, I just had to see that decrepit old man and his bizarre instrument of death. Besides, it was an excuse to paint that babe, Tascela.

I saved the final piece for the title page. I wanted it to be an icon of the character of Conan the Cimmerian: adventurer, warrior, and explorer of the weird ways of Hyperboria. Several influences of mine cried out, but I listened to a particular voice from Leyendecker and proceeded to design with his efficiency in mind. It was a fun and fitting way for me to indulge my heroes and end my own adventure into Howard's world.

Gregory Manchess
2005

Introduction

This volume completes the Wandering Star collection of Robert E. Howard's tales of Conan of Cimmeria. Every story, fragment, synopsis, and note that Robert E. Howard ever committed to paper about the Cimmerian (even including some of the drafts) – and only those written by Howard himself – can now be found in the pages of the three volumes comprising this collection. Incredible as it may seem, it is a world premiere: Howard's complete Conan stories had never before appeared in a uniform collection free from revision, rearrangement, and interpolations by others. For the first time, Howard's Conan series can be judged on its own merits.

It is also the first time the stories are published, not arranged according to the character's "biography," but in the order Howard wrote them, as seems to have been his intention: "That's why they skip about so much, without following a regular order. The average adventurer, telling tales of a wild life at random, seldom follows any ordered plan, but narrates episodes widely separated by space and years, as they occur to him."

Previously, any conclusion one was tempted to draw regarding Howard's achievement with his Conan series could only be based upon a presentation which not only didn't show Howard's growth as a writer, but presented the stories according to Conan's "career," in a manner which, I would argue, was meant to bolster an interpretation of that career alien to Howard's original conception. The interpolation of non–Howard Conan stories into the series, the altering and rewriting of certain passages in Howard's texts (notably in *The Black Stranger*), the adding of introductory paragraphs before every story, and even the retitling of Howard's novel from the original *The Hour of the Dragon* to *Conan the Conqueror*, all worked toward presenting the whole series not as the life of "the average adventurer," as Howard would have it, but as a cohesive saga, with a beginning, a middle, and an end, a kind of Tolkienesque quest in which each story represented yet another step up a ladder from penniless thief (as depicted in *Tower of the Elephant*) to mighty monarch of a civilized empire (*The Hour of the Dragon*).

Conan's haphazard and carefree life was artificially transformed into a "career." What made the series so wonderful – that intense sentiment of freedom resulting from the complete independence of each story from its predecessor and successor (almost no recurring character other than Conan in these tales!) – was undone, and Conan's adventurous life became a "manifest destiny," so to speak. It then became easy enough to see in Conan nothing more than a superman who would rise from poverty to kingship through his physical might (as exemplified in the Hollywood version of the Cimmerian).

That Conan eventually became king of Aquilonia is not in question, of course: he was king in the very first story Howard wrote about him. But nowhere in the stories as Howard wrote them do we detect a hint of a plan to become king one day. In *Beyond the Black River*, Conan comments: "I've been a mercenary captain, a corsair, a kozak, a penniless vagabond, a general – hell, I've been everything except a king, and I may be that, before I die." In *Red Nails*, he is no more precise: "I've never been king of an Hyborian kingdom. . . . But I've dreamed of being even that. I may be too, some day. Why shouldn't I?" Conan became a king simply because the situation presented itself to him at a particular moment of his life, not because of any predetermined plan.

As to Howard's conception of kingship, it was not an imperialistic one, but rather an Arthurian one, in which the king is first and foremost at the service of his people and not the reverse, so much so that in fact King Conan's only ambition at times would be not to be a king anymore: "Prospero . . . these matters of statecraft weary me as all the fighting I have done never did. . . . I wish I might ride with you to Nemedia. . . . It seems ages since I had a horse between my knees – but Publius says that affairs in the city require my presence. Curse him! . . . I did not dream far enough, Prospero. When King Numedides lay dead at my feet and I tore the crown from his gory head and set it on my own, I had reached the ultimate border of my dreams. I had prepared myself to take the crown, not to hold it. In the old free days all I wanted was a sharp sword and a straight path to my enemies. Now no paths are straight and my sword is useless." When his supporters propose that he conquer another kingdom after having been dispossessed of Aquilonia, in *The Hour of the Dragon*, Conan's answer is unequivocal: "Let others dream imperial dreams. I but wish to hold what is mine. I have no desire to rule an empire welded together by blood and fire. It's one thing to seize a throne with the aid of its subjects and rule them with their consent. It's another to subjugate a foreign realm and rule it by fear. I don't wish to be another Valerius. No, Trocero, I'll rule all Aquilonia and no more, or I'll rule nothing."

We are here very far from the perception the general public has of Conan, that of a fur-clad, semi-illiterate brute (for Conan in the media suffered the same fate as Burroughs' Tarzan: both mysteriously lost their ability for articulate speech), bent only on raping, slaying, and conquering. The tales of Conan as a king, the last ones chronologically speaking, should thus in no way be considered as the culmination of a lifelong saga that leads to becoming the most powerful ruler of the Hyborian Age. After all, these tales of King Conan were penned rather early in the history of the series (*The Phoenix on the Sword* and *The Scarlet Citadel* were among the very first Conan stories written by Howard in 1932, and *The Hour of the Dragon*, written in 1934, was essentially a cannibalization of earlier efforts).

All the tales in this third volume were written well after *The Hour of the Dragon*.

It is therefore in these that we will find Howard's final words on Conan, the conclusion to his four-year stint with the character that brought him fame. They do not represent any sort of conclusion whatsoever to the character's life (how could they when Howard himself pleaded ignorance: "As for Conan's eventual fate – frankly I can't predict it. In writing these yarns I've always felt less as creating them than as if I were simply chronicling his adventures as he told them to me."), but they are the conclusion to the series: *Red Nails* was completed in July 1935, eleven months before Howard's suicide. No evidence exists that Howard ever wrote anything about the character after that date.

Weird Tales' inability to pay Howard regularly probably played a great part in this, and it could be said that Howard was forced by circumstances to abandon the character. The fact that he submitted only one story to Weird Tales after *Red Nails* supports the idea. However, by late 1934, Howard was clearly branching out from fantasy fiction, and was more and more interested in the history and lore of his own country, the American Southwest, and in its potential as a subject for fiction. It is this growing passion which colored the last Conan tales: for the first time, Howard's interest was something with which he was in touch in his everyday life. His knowledge of the Celts, which had permeated many of the early Conan stories, was gained from books only. The last Conan stories – those contained in this volume – were tales in which Howard would continue, as he had in all the stories to date, to explore his theme of "barbarism versus civilization," but for the first time he was in a position to add much more sincerity and firsthand knowledge of his subject.

Three of the tales contained in this volume are among Howard's best Conan stories: *Beyond the Black River*, *Red Nails*, and *The Black Stranger*. The first two are overwhelmingly considered by Howard scholars and connoisseurs alike to be among the best tales of the entirety of Howard's fiction. Here was a writer at the peak of his talent producing the tales which would eventually propel him beyond the status of exceptional storyteller, to that of an author who also had a message to deliver. With these last Conan tales, Howard proved that he was indeed worthy of critical attention.

It is in that sense that we can consider the last Conan stories as a conclusion to the series, but also as a form of literary testament. The events depicted in *Beyond the Black River* were nothing especially new in Howard's fiction, replete with tales depicting successful forays of savages against civilized settlements and cities that had grown too weak to defend themselves. In *Beyond the Black River*, as in those other tales, it is the inevitable division of the civilized people and the weakening that goes with it which brings about their defeat. What sets *Beyond the Black River* apart, however, is that the background and characters ring true, because all were drawn from sources that were so much closer to Howard than his usual pseudo-Celtic or pseudo-Assyrian settings. The settlers, farmers, and workers that people this particular story are not cardboard characters, but are as alive and vibrant as Conan himself. Few are the writers of fantasy stories who have succeeded in mingling fantasy with realism with such mastery. The story is a masterpiece because Howard didn't let any damsel in distress get in the way, because he subdued the more fantastic elements of the tale, and refused to resort to pulp magazine conventions: he carried his grim opening predicament through to its bitter end, and didn't let melodrama get in the way. The last Conan stories are much more realistic than fantastic, and it is that realism which sets them apart. Howard was very much aware of this. Just after he had sold *Red Nails* he commented to Clark Ashton Smith: "Too much raw meat, maybe, but I merely portrayed what I honestly believe would be the reactions of certain types of people in the situations on which the plot of the story hung. It may sound fantastic to link the term 'realism' with Conan; but as a matter of fact – his supernatural adventures aside – he is the most realistic character I ever evolved."

If *Beyond the Black River* represents Howard's definitive statement of his views concerning barbarism, he chose, in *Red Nails*, the other Conan masterpiece, to explore the other side of the coin: decaying civilizations. Once again, it was definitely not a new theme for the Texan. For example, Conan's predecessor, Kull of Atlantis, was the king of the decadent empire of Valusia, and countless Howard stories are set in locales that usually were somewhere between decadent and decayed. The situation inevitably led to a final destruction, usually at the hands of the barbarians who were always, conveniently, at the gates, waiting for such a moment. In *Red Nails*, however, Howard dispensed with the barbarians and made sure his city was utterly isolated. *Red Nails* would thus be the story of a decaying process that would be carried to its logical conclusion. Written at a time when Howard's mother's health was declining at an alarming rate, her body slowly decaying under her son's eyes toward a conclusion that was as inevitable as it was obvious, the last Conan story is a tale which is particularly rich in resonance with the terrible events that were happening in Howard's life and mind at the time he was composing the story. (For a fuller explanation of the background to each story, see "Hyborian Genesis Part III" at the end of this volume.)

With the Conan stories, Howard ensured his literary legacy. His suicide at age thirty cut short a career that had promised to be an exceptional one. Less than a month before his death, he wrote Lovecraft: "I find it more and more difficult to write anything but western yarns. . . . I have always felt that if I ever accomplished anything worthwhile in the literary field, it would be with stories dealing of the central and western frontier." Howard would probably have become an important writer in that field, but fate decided otherwise. However, the Conan stories transcend by their very nature the genre they are derived from, whether it be western, history, or high-adventure. By displacing them from their historical context and cloaking them in a Hyborian guise, Howard gave those stories a universality they would not have had in another form. They became timeless, as truthful today as they were seventy years ago.

"Scratch the veneer at your own risk," I wrote concerning the stories found in the first volume. You are about to discover that the veneer is almost nonexistent in most of the tales of this last opus.

This is Howard at his rawest.

At his best.

Patrice Louinet
2005

The Servants of Bit-Yakin

The Servants of Bit-Yakin

I

PATHS OF INTRIGUE

The cliffs rose sheer from the jungle, towering ramparts of stone that glinted jade blue and dull crimson in the rising sun, and curved away and away to east and west above the waving emerald ocean of fronds and leaves. It looked insurmountable, that giant palisade with its sheer curtains of solid rock in which bits of quartz winked dazzlingly in the sunlight. But the man who was working his tedious way upward was already half way to the top.

He came of a race of hillmen, accustomed to scaling forbidding crags, and he was a man of unusual strength and agility. His only garment was a pair of short red silk breeks, and his sandals were slung to his back, out of his way, as were his sword and dagger.

He was a powerfully built man, supple as a panther. His skin was brown, bronzed by the sun, his square-cut black mane confined by a silver band about his temples. His iron muscles, quick eye and sure foot served him well here, for it was a climb to test these qualities to the utmost. A hundred and fifty feet below him waved the jungle. An equal distance above him the rim of the cliffs was etched clear-cut against the morning sky.

He labored like one driven by the necessity of haste, yet he was forced to move at a snail's pace, clinging like a fly on a wall. His groping hands and feet found niches and knobs, precarious holds at best, and sometimes he virtually hung by his finger

3

nails. Yet upward he went, clawing, squirming, fighting for every foot. At times he paused to rest his aching muscles, and, shaking the sweat out of his eyes, twisted his head to stare searchingly out over the jungle, combing the green expanse for any trace of human life or motion.

Now the summit was not far above him, and he observed, only a few feet above his head, a break in the sheer stone of the cliff. An instant later he had reached it – a small cavern, just below the edge of the rim. As his head rose above the lip of its floor, he grunted. He clung there, his elbows hooked over the lip. The cave was so tiny that it was little more than a niche cut in the stone, but it held an occupant. A shrivelled brown mummy, cross-legged, arms folded on the withered breast upon which the shrunken head was sunk, sat in the little cavern. The limbs were bound in place with rawhide thongs which had become mere rotted wisps. If the form had ever been clothed, the ravages of time had long reduced the garments to dust. But thrust between the crossed arms and the shrunken breast there was a roll of parchment, yellowed with age to the color of old ivory.

The climber stretched forth a long arm and wrenched away this cylinder. Without investigation he thrust it into his girdle and hauled himself up until he was standing in the opening of the niche. A spring upward and he caught the rim of the cliffs and pulled himself up and over almost with the same motion.

There he halted, panting, and stared downward.

It was like looking into the interior of a vast bowl, rimmed by a circular stone wall. The floor of the bowl was covered with trees and denser vegetation, though nowhere did the growth duplicate the jungle denseness of the outer forest. The cliffs marched around it without a break and of uniform height. It was a freak of nature, not to be paralleled, perhaps, in the whole world: a vast natural amphitheater, a circular bit of forested plain, three or four miles in diameter, cut off from the rest of the world, and confined within the ring of those palisaded cliffs.

But the man on the cliffs did not devote his thoughts to marvelling at the topographical phenomenon. With tense eagerness he searched the tree-tops below him, and exhaled a gusty sigh when he caught the glint of marble domes amidst the twinkling green. It was no myth, then; below him lay the fabulous and deserted palace of Alkmeenon.

Conan the Cimmerian, late of the Barachan Isles, of the Black Coast, and of many other climes where life ran wild, had come to the kingdom of Keshan following the lure of a fabled treasure that outshone the hoard of the Turanian kings.

Keshan was a barbaric kingdom lying in the eastern hinterlands of Kush where the broad grass lands merge with the forests that roll up from the south. The people were a mixed race, a dusky nobility ruling a population that was largely pure negro. The rulers – princes and high priests – claimed descent from a white race which, in a mythical age, had ruled a kingdom whose capital city was Alkmeenon. Conflicting legends sought to explain the reason for that race's eventual downfall, and the abandonment of the city by the survivors. Equally nebulous were the tales of the Teeth of Gwahlur, the treasure of Alkmeenon. But these misty legends had been enough to bring Conan to Keshan, over vast distances of plain, river-laced jungle, and mountains.

He had found Keshan, which in itself was considered mythical by many northern and western nations, and he had heard enough to confirm the rumors of the treasure that men called the Teeth of Gwahlur. But its hiding place he could not learn, and he was confronted with the necessity of explaining his presence in Keshan. Unattached strangers were not welcome there.

But he was not nonplused. With cool assurance he made his offer to the stately, plumed, suspicious grandees of the barbarically magnificent court. He was a professional fighting man. In search of employment (he said) he had come to Keshan. For a price he would train the armies of Keshan and lead them against Punt, their hereditary enemy, whose recent successes in the field had roused the fury of Keshan's irascible king.

This proposition was not as audacious as it might seem. Conan's fame had preceded him, even into distant Keshan; his exploits as a chief of the black corsairs, those wolves of the southern coasts, had made his name known, admired and feared throughout the black kingdoms. He did not refuse tests devised by the dusky lords. Skirmishes along the borders were incessant, affording the Cimmerian plenty of opportunities to demonstrate his ability at hand-to-hand fighting. His reckless ferocity impressed the lords of Keshan, already aware of his reputation as a leader of men, and the prospects seemed favourable. All Conan secretly desired was employment to give him legitimate excuse for remaining in Keshan long enough to locate the hiding place of the Teeth of Gwahlur. Then there came an interruption. Thutmekri came to Keshan at the head of an embassy from Zembabwei.

Thutmekri was a Stygian, an adventurer and a rogue whose wits had recommended him to the twin kings of the great hybrid trading kingdom which lay many days' march to the east. He and the Cimmerian knew one another of old, and without love. Thutmekri likewise had a proposition to make to the king of Keshan, and it also concerned the conquest of Punt – which kingdom, incidentally, lying east of Keshan, had recently expelled the Zembabwan traders and burned their fortresses.

His offer outweighed even the prestige of Conan. He pledged himself to invade Punt from the east with a host of black spearmen, Shemitish archers, and mercenary swordsmen, and to aid the king of Keshan to annex the hostile kingdom. The benevolent kings of Zembabwei desired only the monopoly of the trade of Keshan and her tributaries – and, as a pledge of good faith, some of the Teeth of Gwahlur. These would be put to no base usage, Thutmekri hastened to explain to the suspicious chieftains; they would be placed in the temple of Zembabwei beside the squat gold idols of Dagon and Derketo, sacred guests in the holy shrine of the kingdom, to seal the covenant between Keshan and Zembabwei. This statement brought a savage grin to Conan's hard lips.

The Cimmerian made no attempt to match wits and intrigue with Thutmekri and his Shemitish partner, Zargheba. He knew that if Thutmekri won his point, he would insist on the instant banishment of his rival. There was but one thing for Conan to do: find the jewels before the king of Keshan made up his mind, and flee with them. But by this time he was certain that they were not hidden in Keshia, the royal city, which was a swarm of thatched huts crowding about a mud wall that enclosed a palace of stone and mud and bamboo.

While he fumed with nervous impatience, the high priest Gorulga announced that before any decision could be reached, the will of the gods must be ascertained concerning the proposed alliance with Zembabwei and the pledge of objects long held holy and inviolate. The oracle of Alkmeenon must be consulted.

This was an awesome thing, that caused tongues to wag excitedly in palace and bee-hive hut. Not for a century had the priests visited the silent city. The oracle, men said, was the Princess Yelaya, the last ruler of Alkmeenon, who had died in the full bloom of her youth and beauty, and whose body had miraculously remained unblemished throughout the ages. Of old priests had made their way into the haunted city, and she had taught them wisdom. The last priest to seek the oracle had been a wicked man, who had sought to steal for himself the curiously-cut jewels that men called the Teeth of Gwahlur. But some doom had come upon him in the deserted palace, from which his acolytes, fleeing, had told tales of horror that had for a hundred years frightened the priests from the city and the oracle.

But Gorulga, the present high priest, as one confident in his knowledge of his own integrity, announced that he would go with a handful of followers to revive the ancient custom. And in the excitement tongues buzzed indiscreetly, and Conan caught the clue for which he had sought for weeks — the overheard whisper of a lesser priest that sent the Cimmerian stealing out of Keshia the night before the dawn when the priests were to start.

Riding hard as he dared for a night and a day and a night, he came in the early dawn to the cliffs of Alkmeenon, which stood in the southwestern corner of the kingdom, amidst uninhabited jungle which was taboo to common men. None but the priests dared approach the haunted city within a distance of many miles. And not even a priest had entered Alkmeenon for a hundred years.

No man had ever climbed these cliffs, legends said, and none but the priests knew the secret entrance into the valley. Conan did not waste time looking for it. Steeps that balked these black people, horsemen and dwellers of plain and level forest, were not impossible for a man born in the rugged hills of Cimmeria.

Now on the summit of the cliffs he looked down into the circular valley and wondered what plague, war or superstition had driven the members of that ancient white race forth from their stronghold to mingle with and be absorbed by the black tribes that hemmed them in.

This valley had been their citadel. There the palace stood, and there only the royal family and their court dwelt. The real city stood outside the cliffs. Those waving masses of green jungle vegetation hid its ruins. But the domes that glistened in the leaves below him were the unbroken pinnacles of the royal palace of Alkmeenon which had defied the corroding ages.

Swinging a leg over the rim he went down swiftly. The inner side of the cliffs was more broken, not quite so sheer. In less than half the time it had taken him to ascend the outer side, he dropped to the swarded valley floor.

With one hand on his sword, he looked alertly about him. There was no reason to suppose men lied when they said that Alkmeenon was empty and deserted, haunted only by the ghosts of the dead past. But it was Conan's nature to be suspicious and wary. The silence was primordial; not even a leaf quivered on a branch. When he bent to peer under the trees, he saw nothing but the marching rows of trunks, receding and receding into the blue gloom of the deep woods.

Nevertheless he went warily, sword in hand, his restless eyes combing the shadows from side to side, his springy tread making no sound on the sward. All about him he saw signs of an ancient civilization; marble fountains, voiceless and crumbling, stood in circles of slender trees whose patterns were too symmetrical to have been a chance of nature. Forest-growth and underbrush had invaded the evenly-planned groves, but their outlines were still visible. Broad pavements ran away under the trees, broken, and with grass growing through the wide cracks. He glimpsed walls with ornamental copings, lattices of carven stone that might once have served as the walls of pleasure pavilions.

Ahead of him, through the trees, the domes gleamed and the bulk of the structure supporting them became more apparent as he advanced. Presently, pushing through a screen of vine-tangled branches, he came into a comparatively open space where the trees straggled, unencumbered by undergrowth, and saw before him the wide, pillared portico of the palace.

As he mounted the broad marble steps, he noted that the building was in far better state of preservation than the lesser structures he had glimpsed. The thick walls and massive pillars seemed too powerful to crumble before the assault of time and the elements. The same enchanted quiet brooded over all. The catlike pad of his sandalled feet seemed startlingly loud in the stillness.

Somewhere in this palace lay the effigy or image which had in times past served as oracle for the priests of Keshan. And somewhere in the palace, unless that indiscreet priest had babbled a lie, was hidden the treasure of the forgotten kings of Alkmeenon.

Conan passed into a broad, lofty hall, lined with tall columns, between which arches gaped, their doors long rotted away. He traversed this in a twilight dimness, and at the other end passed through great double-valved bronze doors which stood partly open, as they might have stood for centuries. He emerged into a vast domed chamber which must have served as audience hall for the kings of Alkmeenon.

It was octagonal in shape, and the great dome up to which the lofty ceiling curved obviously was cunningly pierced, for the chamber was much better lighted than the hall which led to it. At the further side of the great room there rose a dais with broad lapis-lazuli steps leading up to it, and on that dais there stood a massive chair with ornate arms and a high back which once doubtless supported a cloth-of-gold canopy. Conan grunted explosively and his eyes lit. The golden throne of Alkmeenon, named in immemorial legendry! He weighed it with a practised eye. It represented a fortune in itself, if he were but able to bear it away. Its richness fired his imagination concerning the treasure itself, and made him burn with eagerness. His fingers itched to plunge among the gems he had heard described by story-tellers in the market squares of Keshia, who repeated tales handed down from mouth to mouth through the centuries — jewels not to be duplicated in the world, rubies, emeralds, diamonds, bloodstones, opals, sapphires, the loot of the ancient world.

He had expected to find the oracle-effigy seated on the throne, but since it was not, it was probably placed in some other part of the palace, if, indeed, such a thing really existed. But since he had turned his face toward Keshan so many myths had proven realities that he did not doubt that he would find some kind of image or god.

Behind the throne there was a narrow arched doorway which doubtless had been masked by hangings in the days of Alkmeenon's life. He glanced through it and saw that it let into an alcove, empty, and with a narrow corridor leading off from it at right angles. Turning away from it, he spied another arch to the left of the dais, and it, unlike the others, was furnished with a door. Nor was it any common door. The portal was of the same rich metal as the throne, and carved with many curious arabesques.

At his touch it swung open so readily that its hinges might recently have been oiled. Inside he halted, staring.

He was in a square chamber of no great dimensions, whose marble walls rose to an ornate ceiling, inlaid with gold. Gold friezes ran about the base and the top of the walls, and there was no door other than the one through which he had entered. But he noted these details mechanically. His whole attention was centered on the shape which lay on an ivory dais before him.

He had expected an image, probably carved with the skill of a forgotten art. But no art could mimic the perfection of the figure which lay before him.

It was no effigy of stone or metal or ivory. It was the actual body of a woman, and by what dark art the ancients had preserved that form unblemished for so many ages Conan could not even guess. The very garments she wore were intact — and Conan scowled at that, a vague uneasiness stirring at the back of his mind. The arts that preserved the body should not have affected the garments. Yet there they were — gold breast-plates set with concentric circles of small gems, gilded sandals, and a short silken skirt upheld by a jeweled girdle. Neither cloth nor metal showed any signs of decay.

Yelaya was coldly beautiful, even in death. Her body was like alabaster, slender yet voluptuous; a great crimson jewel gleamed against the darkly piled foam of her hair.

Conan stood frowning down at her, and then tapped the dais with his sword. Possibilities of a hollow containing the treasure occurred to him, but the dais rang solid. He turned and paced the chamber in some indecision. Where should he search first, in the limited time at his disposal? The priest he had overheard babbling to a courtesan had said the treasure was hidden in the palace. But that included a space of considerable vastness. He wondered if he should hide himself until the priests had come and gone, and then renew the search. But there was a strong chance that they might take the jewels with them when they returned to Keshia. For he was convinced that Thutmekri had corrupted Gorulga.

Conan could predict Thutmekri's plans, from his knowledge of the man. He knew that it had been Thutmekri who had proposed the conquest of Punt to the kings of Zembabwei, which conquest was but one move toward their real goal — the capture of the Teeth of Gwahlur. Those wary kings would demand proof that the treasure really existed before they made any move. The jewels Thutmekri asked as a pledge would furnish that proof.

With positive evidence of the treasure's reality, the kings of Zembabwei would move. Punt would be invaded simultaneously from the east and the west, but the Zembabwans would see to it that the Keshani did most of the fighting and then, when both Punt and Keshan were exhausted from the struggle, the Zembabwans would crush both races, loot Keshan and take the treasure by force, if they had to destroy every building and torture every living human in the kingdom.

But there was always another possibility: if Thutmekri could get his hands on the hoard, it would be characteristic of the man to cheat his employers, steal the jewels for himself and decamp, leaving the Zembabwan emissaries holding the sack.

Conan believed that this consulting of the oracle was but a ruse to persuade the king of Keshan to accede to Thutmekri's wishes — for he never for a moment doubted that Gorulga was as subtle and devious as all the rest mixed up in this grand swindle. Conan had not approached the high priest himself, because in the game of bribery he would have no chance against Thutmekri, and to attempt it would be to play directly into the Stygian's hands. Gorulga could denounce the Cimmerian to the people, establish a reputation for integrity, and rid Thutmekri of his rival at one stroke. He wondered how Thutmekri had corrupted the high priest, and just what could be offered as a bribe to a man who had the greatest treasure in the world under his fingers.

At any rate he was sure that the oracle would be made to say that the gods willed it that Keshan should follow Thutmekri's wishes, and he was sure too, that it would drop a few pointed remarks concerning himself. After that Keshia would be too hot for the Cimmerian, nor had Conan had any intention of returning when he rode away in the night.

The oracle chamber held no clue for him. He went forth into the great throne-room and laid his hands on the throne. It was heavy, but he could tilt it up. The floor beneath, a thick marble dais, was solid. Again he sought the alcove. His mind clung to a secret crypt near the oracle. Painstakingly he began to tap along the walls, and presently his taps rang hollow at a spot opposite the mouth of the narrow corridor. Looking more closely he saw that the crack between the marble panel at that point and the next was wider than usual. He inserted a dagger point and pried.

Silently the panel swung open, revealing a niche in the wall, but nothing else. He swore feelingly. The aperture was empty, and it did not look like it had ever served as a crypt for treasure. Leaning into the niche he saw a system of tiny holes in the wall, about on a level with a man's mouth. He peered through, and grunted understandingly. That was the wall that formed the partition between the alcove and the oracle-chamber. Those holes had not been visible in the chamber. Conan grinned. This explained the mystery of the oracle, but it was a bit cruder than he had expected. Gorulga would plant either himself or some trusted minion in that niche, to talk through the holes, and the credulous acolytes, black men all, would accept it as the veritable voice of Yelaya.

Remembering something, the Cimmerian drew forth the roll of parchment he had taken from the mummy and unrolled it carefully, as it seemed ready to fall to pieces with age. He scowled over the dim characters with which it was covered. In his roaming about the world the giant adventurer had picked up a wide smattering of knowledge, particularly including the speaking and reading of many alien tongues. Many a sheltered scholar would have been astonished at the Cimmerian's linguistic abilities, for he had experienced many adventures where knowledge of a strange language had meant the difference between life and death.

These characters were puzzling, at once familiar and unintelligible, and presently he discovered the reason. They were the characters of archaic Pelishtim, which possessed many points of difference from the modern script, with which he was familiar, and which, three centuries ago, had been modified by conquest by a nomad tribe. This older, purer script baffled him. He made out a recurrent phrase, however, which he recognized as a proper name: Bit-Yakin. He gathered it was the name of the writer.

Scowling, his lips unconsciously moving as he struggled with the task, he blundered through the manuscript, finding much of it untranslatable and most of the rest of it obscure.

He gathered that the writer, the mysterious Bit-Yakin, had come from afar with his servants, and entered the valley of Alkmeenon. Much that followed was meaningless, interspersed as it was with unfamiliar phrases and characters. Such as he could translate seemed to indicate the passing of a very long period of time. The name of Yelaya was repeated frequently, and toward the last part of the manuscript it became apparent that Bit-Yakin knew that death was upon him. With a slight start Conan realized that the mummy in the cavern must be the remains of the writer of the manuscript, the mysterious Pelishtim, Bit-Yakin. The man had died, as he had prophesied, and his servants, obviously, had placed him in that open crypt, high up on the cliffs, according to his instructions before his death.

It was strange that Bit-Yakin was not mentioned in any of the legends of Alkmeenon. Obviously he had come to the valley after it had been deserted by the original inhabitants – the manuscript indicated as much – but it seemed peculiar that the priests who came in the old days to consult the oracle had not seen the man or his servants. Conan felt sure that the mummy and this parchment were more than a hundred years old. Bit-Yakin had dwelt in the valley when the priests came of old to bow before dead Yelaya. Yet concerning him the legends were silent, telling only of a deserted city, haunted only by the dead.

Why had the man dwelt in this desolate spot, and to what unknown destination had his servants departed after disposing of their master's corpse?

Conan shrugged his shoulders and thrust the parchment back into his girdle – he started violently, the skin on the backs of his hands tingling. Startlingly, shockingly in the slumberous stillness, there had boomed the deep strident clangor of a great gong!

He wheeled, crouching like a great cat, sword in hand, glaring down the narrow corridor from which the sound had seemed to come. Had the priests of Keshia arrived? This was improbable, he knew; they would not have had time to reach the valley. But that gong was indisputable evidence of human presence.

Conan was basically a direct actionist. Such subtlety as he possessed had been acquired through contact with the more devious races. When taken off guard by some unexpected occurrence, he reverted instinctively to type. So now, instead of hiding or slipping away in the opposite direction as the average man might have done, he ran straight down the corridor in the direction of the sound. His sandals made no more sound than the pads of a panther would have made; his eyes were slits, his lips unconsciously asnarl. Panic had momentarily touched his soul at the shock of that unexpected reverberation, and the red rage of the primitive that is wakened by threat of peril, always lurked close to the surface of the Cimmerian.

He emerged presently from the winding corridor into a small open court. Something glinting in the sun caught his eye. It was the gong, a great gold disk, hanging from a gold arm extending from the crumbling wall. A brass mallet lay near, but there was no sound or sight of humanity. The surrounding arches gaped emptily. Conan crouched inside the doorway for what seemed a long time. There was no sound or movement throughout the great palace. His patience exhausted at last, he glided around the curve of the court, peering into the arches, ready to leap either way like a flash of light, or to strike right or left as a cobra strikes.

He reached the gong, stared into the arch nearest it. He saw only a dim chamber, littered with the debris of decay. Beneath the gong the polished marble flags showed no footprint, but there was a scent in the air – a faintly fetid odor he could not classify; his nostrils dilated like those of a wild beast as he sought in vain to identify it.

He turned toward the arch – with appalling suddenness the seemingly solid flags splintered and gave way under his feet. Even as he fell he spread wide his arms and caught the edges of the aperture that gaped beneath him. The edges crumbled off under his clutching fingers. Down into utter darkness he shot, into black icy water that gripped him and whirled him away with breathless speed.

II

A Goddess Awakens

The Cimmerian at first made no attempt to fight the current that was sweeping him through lightless night. He kept himself afloat, gripping between his teeth the sword which he had not relinquished, even in his fall, and did not even seek to guess to what doom he was being borne. But suddenly a beam of light lanced the darkness ahead of him. He saw the surging, seething black surface of the water, in turmoil as if disturbed by some monster of the deep, and he saw the sheer stone walls of the channel curved up to a vault overhead. On each side ran a narrow ledge, just below the arching roof, but they were far out of his reach. At one point this roof had been broken, probably fallen in, and the light was streaming through the aperture. Beyond that shaft of light was utter blackness, and panic assailed the Cimmerian as he saw he would be swept on past that spot of light, and into the unknown blackness again.

Then he saw something else: bronze ladders extended from the ledges to the water's surface at regular intervals and there was one just ahead of him. Instantly he struck out for it, fighting the current that would have held him to the middle of the stream. It dragged at him as with tangible, animate slimy hands, but he buffeted the rushing surge with the strength of desperation and drew closer and closer inshore, fighting furiously for every inch. Now he was even with the ladder and with a fierce, gasping plunge he gripped the bottom rung and hung on, breathless.

A few seconds later he struggled up out of the seething water, trusting his great weight dubiously to the corroded rungs. They sagged and bent, but they held, and he clambered up onto the narrow ledge which ran along the wall scarcely a man's length below the curving roof. The tall Cimmerian was forced to bend his head as he stood up. A heavy bronze door showed in the stone at a point even with the head of the ladder, but it did not give to Conan's efforts. He transferred his sword from his teeth to its scabbard, spitting blood – for the edge had cut his lips in that fierce fight with the river – and turned his attention to the broken roof.

He could reach his arms up through the crevice and grip the edge, and careful testing told him it would bear his weight. An instant later he had drawn himself up through the hole, and found himself in a wide chamber, in a state of extreme disrepair. Most of the roof had fallen in, as well as a great section of the floor, which was laid over the vault of subterranean river. Broken arches opened into other chambers and corridors, and Conan believed he was still in the great palace. He wondered uneasily how many chambers in that palace had underground water directly under them, and when the ancient flags or tiles might give way again and precipitate him back into the current from which he had just crawled.

And he wondered just how much of an accident that fall had been. Had those rotten flags simply chanced to give way beneath his weight, or was there a more sinister explanation? One thing at least was obvious: he was not the only living thing in that palace. That gong had not sounded of its own accord, whether the noise had been meant to lure him to his death, or not. The silence of the palace became suddenly sinister, fraught with crawling menace.

Could it be some one on the same mission as himself? A sudden thought occurred to him, at the memory of the mysterious Bit-Yakin. Was it not possible that this man had found the Teeth of Gwahlur in his long residence in Alkmeenon – that his servants had taken them with them when they departed? The possibility that he might be following a will-of-the-wisp infuriated the Cimmerian.

Choosing a corridor which he believed led back toward the part of the palace he had first entered, he hurried along it, stepping gingerly as he thought of that black river that seethed and foamed somewhere below his feet.

His speculations recurrently revolved about the oracle chamber and its cryptic occupant. Somewhere in that vicinity must be the clue to the mystery of the treasure, if indeed it still remained in its immemorial hiding place.

The great palace lay silent as ever, disturbed only by the swift passing of his sandalled feet. The chambers and halls he traversed were crumbling into ruin, but as he advanced the ravages of decay became less apparent. He wondered briefly for what purpose the ladders had been suspended from the ledges over the subterranean river, but dismissed the matter with a shrug. He was little interested in speculating over unremunerative problems of antiquity.

He was not sure just where the oracle chamber lay, from where he was, but presently he emerged into a corridor which led back into the great throne room under one of the arches. He had reached a decision; it was useless for him to wander aimlessly about the palace, seeking the hoard. He would conceal himself somewhere here, wait until the Keshani priests came, and then, after they had gone through the farce of consulting the oracle, he would follow them to the hiding place of the gems, to which he was certain they would go. Perhaps they would take only a few of the jewels with them. He would content himself with the rest.

Drawn by a morbid fascination, he re-entered the oracle chamber and stared down again at the motionless figure of the princess who was worshipped as a goddess, entranced by her frigid beauty. What cryptic secret was locked in that marvelously molded form?

He started violently. The breath sucked through his teeth, the short hairs prickled at the back of his scalp. The body still lay as he had first seen it, silent, motionless, in breast-plates of jeweled gold, gilded sandals and silken skirt. But now there was a subtle difference. The lissome limbs were not rigid, a peach-bloom touched the cheeks, the lips were red —

With a panicky curse Conan ripped out his sword.

"Crom! She's alive!"

At his words the long dark lashes lifted; the eyes opened and gazed up at him inscrutably, dark, lustrous, mystical. He glared in frozen speechlessness.

She sat up with a supple ease, still holding his ensorcelled stare.

He licked his dry lips and found voice.

"You — are — are you Yelaya?" he stammered.

"I am Yelaya!" The voice was rich and musical, and he stared with new wonder. "Do not fear. I will not harm you if you do my bidding."

"How can a dead woman come to life after all these centuries?" he demanded, as if skeptical of what his senses told him. A curious gleam was beginning to smolder in his eyes.

She lifted her arms in a mystical gesture.

"I am a goddess. A thousand years ago there descended upon me the curse of the greater gods, the gods of darkness beyond the borders of light. The mortal in me died; the goddess in me could never die. Here I have lain for so many centuries, to awaken each night at sunset and hold my court of yore, with spectres drawn from the shadows of the past. Man, if you would not view that which will blast your soul for ever, get hence quickly! I command you! Go!" The voice became imperious, and her slender arm lifted and pointed.

Conan, his eyes burning slits, slowly sheathed his sword, but he did not obey her order. He stepped closer, as if impelled by a powerful fascination — without the slightest warning he grabbed her up in a bearlike grasp. She screamed, a very ungoddesslike scream, and there was a sound of ripping silk, as with one ruthless wrench he tore off her skirt.

"Goddess! Ha!" His bark was full of angry contempt. He ignored the frantic writhings of his captive. "I thought it was strange that a princess of Alkmeenon would speak with a Corinthian accent! As soon as I'd gathered my wits I knew I'd seen you somewhere. You're Muriela, Zargheba's Corinthian dancing girl. This crescent-shaped birth-mark on your hip proves it. I saw it once when Zargheba was whipping you. Goddess! Bah!" He smacked the betraying hip contemptuously and resoundingly with his open hand, and the girl yelped piteously.

All her imperiousness had gone out of her. She was no longer a mystical figure of antiquity, but a terrified and humiliated dancing girl, such as can be bought at almost any Shemitish market-place. She lifted up her voice and wept unashamedly. Her captor glared down at her with angry triumph.

"Goddess! Ha! So you were one of the veiled women Zargheba brought to Keshia with him. Did you think you could fool me, you little idiot? A year ago I saw you in Akbitana with that swine, Zargheba, and I don't forget faces — or women's figures. I think I'll —"

Squirming about in his grasp she threw her slender arms about his massive neck in an abandon of terror; tears coursed down her cheeks, and her sobs quivered with a note of hysteria.

"Oh, please don't hurt me! Don't! I had to do it! Zargheba brought me here to act as the oracle!"

"Why, you sacrilegious little hussy!" rumbled Conan. "Do you not fear the gods? Crom, is there no honesty anywhere?"

"Oh, please!" she begged, quivering with abject fright. "I couldn't disobey Zargheba. Oh, what shall I do? I shall be cursed by these heathen gods!"

"What do you think the priests will do to you if they find out you're an imposter?" he demanded.

At the thought her legs refused to support her, and she collapsed in a shuddering heap, clasping Conan's knees and mingling incoherent pleas for mercy and protection with piteous protestations of her innocence of any malign intention. It was a vivid change from her pose as the ancient princess, but not surprising. The fear that had nerved her then was now her undoing.

"Where is Zargheba?" he demanded. "Stop yammering, damn it, and answer me."

"Outside the palace," she whimpered, "watching for the priests."

"How many men with him?"

"None. We came alone."

"Ha!" It was much like the satisfied grunt of a hunting lion. "You must have left Keshia a few hours after I did. Did you climb the cliffs?"

She shook her head, too choked with tears to speak coherently. With an impatient imprecation he seized her slim shoulders and shook her until she gasped for breath.

"Will you quit that blubbering and answer me? How did you get into the valley?"

"Zargheba knew the secret way," she gasped. "The priest Gwarunga told him, and Thutmekri. On the south side of the valley there is a broad pool lying at the foot of the cliffs. There is a cave-mouth under the surface of the water that is not visible to the casual glance. We ducked under the water and entered it. The cave slopes up out of the water swiftly and leads through the cliffs. The opening on the side of the valley is masked by heavy thickets."

"I climbed the cliffs on the east side," he muttered. "Well, what then?"

"We came to the palace and Zargheba hid me among the trees while he went to look for the chamber of the oracle. I do not think he fully trusted Gwarunga. While he was gone I thought I heard a gong sound, but I was not sure. Presently Zargheba came and took me into the palace and brought me to this chamber, where the goddess Yelaya lay upon the dais. He stripped the body and clothed me in the garments and ornaments. Then he went forth to hide the body and watch for the priests. I have been afraid. When you entered I wanted to leap up and beg you to take me away from this place, but I feared Zargheba. When you discovered I was alive, I thought I could frighten you away."

"What were you to say as the oracle?" he asked.

"I was to bid the priests to take the Teeth of Gwahlur and give some of them to Thutmekri as a pledge, as he desired, and place the rest in the palace at Keshia. I was to tell them that an awful doom threatened Keshan if they did not agree to Thutmekri's proposals. And oh, yes, I was to tell them that you were to be skinned alive immediately."

"Thutmekri wanted the treasure where he – or the Zembabwans – could lay hand on it easily," muttered Conan, disregarding the remark concerning himself. "I'll carve his liver yet – Gorulga is a party to this swindle, of course?"

"No. He believes in his gods, and is incorruptible. He knows nothing about this. He will obey the oracle. It was all Thutmekri's plan. Knowing the Keshani would consult the oracle, he had Zargheba bring me with the embassy from Zembabwei, closely veiled and secluded."

"Well, I'm damned!" muttered Conan. "A priest who honestly believes in his oracle, and can not be bribed. Crom! I wonder if it was Zargheba who banged that gong. Did he know I was here? Could he have known about that rotten flagging? Where is he now, girl?"

"Hiding in a thicket of lotus trees, near the ancient avenue that leads from the south wall of the cliffs to the palace," she answered. Then she renewed her importunities. "Oh, Conan, have pity on me! I am afraid of this evil, ancient place. I know I have heard stealthy footfalls padding about me – oh, Conan, take me away with you! Zargheba will kill me when I have served his purpose here – I know it! The priests, too, will kill me if they discover my deceit.

"He is a devil – he bought me from a slave trader who stole me out of a caravan bound through southern Koth, and has made me the tool of his intrigues ever since. Take me away from him! You can not be as cruel as he. Don't leave me to be slain here! Please! Please!"

She was on her knees, clutching at Conan hysterically, her beautiful tear-stained face upturned to him, her dark silken hair flowing in disorder over her white shoulders. Conan picked her up and set her on his knee.

"Listen to me. I'll protect you from Zargheba. The priests shall not know of your perfidy. But you've got to do as I tell you."

She faltered promises of explicit obedience, clasping his corded neck as if seeking security from the contact.

"Good. When the priests come, you'll act the part of Yelaya, as Zargheba planned – it'll be dark, and in the torchlight they'll never know the difference.

"But you'll say this to them: 'It is the will of the gods that the Stygian and his Shemitish dogs be driven from Keshan. They are thieves and traitors who plot to rob the gods. Let the Teeth of Gwahlur be placed in the care of the general Conan. Let him lead the armies of Keshan. He is beloved of the gods.'"

She shivered, with an expression of desperation, but acquiesced.

"But Zargheba?" she cried. "He'll kill me!"

"Don't worry about Zargheba," he grunted. "I'll take care of that dog. You do as I say. Here, put up your hair again. It's fallen all over your shoulders. And the gem's fallen out of it."

He replaced the great glowing gem himself, nodding approval.

"It's worth a room-full of slaves, itself alone. Here, put your skirt back on. It's torn down the side, but the priests will never notice it. Wipe your face. A goddess doesn't cry like a whipped schoolgirl. By Crom, you *do* look like Yelaya, face, hair, figure and all. If you act the goddess with the priests as well as you did with me, you'll fool them easily."

"I'll try," she shivered.

"Good; I'm going to find Zargheba."

At that she became panicky again.

"No! Don't leave me alone! This place is haunted!"

"There's nothing here to harm you," he assured her impatiently. "Nothing but Zargheba, and I'm going to look after him. I'll be back shortly. I'll be watching from close by in case anything goes wrong during the ceremony; but if you play your part properly, nothing will go wrong."

And turning, he hastened out of the oracle chamber; behind him Muriela squeaked wretchedly at his going. Twilight had fallen. The great rooms and halls were shadowy and indistinct; copper friezes glinted dully through the dusk. Conan strode like a silent phantom through the great halls, with a sensation as of being stared at from the shadowed recesses by invisible ghosts of the past. No wonder the girl was nervous amid such surroundings.

He glided down the marble steps like a slinking panther, sword in hand. Silence reigned over the valley, and above the rim of the cliffs stars were blinking out. If the priests of Keshia had entered the valley there was not a sound, not a movement in the greenery to betray them. He made out the ancient broken-paved avenue, wandering away to the south, lost amid clustering masses of fronds and thick-leaved bushes. He followed it warily, hugging the edge of the paving where the shrubs massed their shadows thick, until he saw ahead of him, dimly in the dusk, the clump of lotus-trees, the strange growth peculiar to the black lands of Kush. There, according to the girl, Zargheba should be lurking. Conan became stealth personified. A velvet-footed shadow he melted into the thickets.

He approached the lotus grove by a circuitous movement, and scarcely the rustle of a leaf proclaimed his passing. At the edge of the trees he halted suddenly, crouched like a suspicious panther among the deep shrubs. Ahead of him, among the dense leaves, showed a pallid oval, dim in the uncertain light. It might have been one of the great white blossoms which shone thickly among the branches. But Conan knew that it was a man's face. And it was turned toward him. He shrank quickly deeper into the shadows. Had Zargheba seen him? The man was looking directly toward him. Seconds passed. That dim face had not moved. Conan could make out the dark tuft below that was the short black beard.

And suddenly Conan was aware of something unnatural. Zargheba, he knew, was not a tall man. Standing erect his head would scarcely top the Cimmerian's shoulder. Yet that face was on a level with Conan's own. Was the man standing on something? Conan bent and peered toward the ground below the spot where the face showed, but his vision was blocked by undergrowth and the thick boles of the trees. But he saw something else, and he stiffened. Through a slot in the underbrush he glimpsed the stem of the tree under which, apparently, Zargheba was standing. The face was directly in line with that tree. He should have seen below that face, not the tree-trunk, but Zargheba's body – but there was no body there.

Suddenly tenser than a tiger who stalks its prey, Conan glided deeper into the thicket, and a moment later drew aside a leafy branch and glared at the face that had not moved. Nor would it ever move again, of its own volition. He looked on Zargheba's severed head, suspended from the branch of the tree by its own long black hair.

III

THE RETURN OF THE ORACLE

Conan wheeled supply, sweeping the shadows with a fiercely questing stare. There was no sign of the murdered man's body; only yonder the tall lush grass was trampled and broken down and the sward was dabbled darkly and wetly. Conan stood scarcely breathing as he strained his ears into the silence. The trees and bushes with their great pallid blossoms stood dark, still and sinister, etched against the deepening dusk.

Primitive fears whispered at the back of Conan's mind. Was this the work of the priests of Keshan? If so, where were they? Was it Zargheba, after all, who had struck the gong? Again there rose the memory of Bit-Yakin and his mysterious servants. Bit-Yakin was dead, shrivelled to a hulk of wrinkled leather and bound in his hollowed crypt to greet the rising sun for ever. But the servants of Bit-Yakin were unaccounted for. *There was no proof they had ever left the valley.*

Conan thought of the girl, Muriela, alone and unguarded in that great shadowy palace. He wheeled and ran back down the shadowed avenue, and he ran as a suspicious panther runs, poised even in full stride to whirl right or left and strike death blows.

The palace loomed through the trees, and he saw something else – the glow of fire reflecting redly from the polished marble. He melted into the bushes that lined the broken street, glided through the dense growth and reached the edge of the open space before the portico. Voices reached him; torches bobbed and their flare shone on glossy ebony shoulders. The priests of Keshan had come.

They had not advanced up the wide, over-grown avenue as Zargheba had expected them to do. Obviously there was more than one secret way into the valley of Alkmeenon.

They were filing up the broad marble steps, holding their torches high. He saw Gorulga at the head of the parade, a profile chiselled out of copper, etched in the torchglare. The rest were acolytes, giant black men from whose skins the torches struck high lights. At the end of the procession there stalked a huge negro with an unusually wicked cast of countenance, at the sight of whom Conan scowled. That was Gwarunga, whom Muriela had named as the man who had revealed the secret of the pool-entrance to Zargheba. Conan wondered how deeply the man was in the intrigues of the Stygian.

He hurried toward the portico, circling the open space to keep in the fringing shadows. They left no one to guard the entrance. The torches streamed steadily down the long dark hall. Before they had reached the double-valved door at the other end, Conan had mounted the outer steps and was in the hall behind them. Slinking swiftly along the column-lined wall, he reached the great door as they crossed the huge throne room, their torches driving back the shadows. They did not look back. In single file, their ostrich plumes nodding, their leopard skin tunics contrasting curiously with the marble and arabesqued metal of the ancient palace, they moved across the wide room and halted momentarily at the golden door to the left of the throne-dais.

Gorulga's voice boomed eerily and hollowly in the great empty space, framed in sonorous phrases unintelligible to the lurking listener; then the high priest thrust open the golden door and entered, bowing repeatedly to his waist, and behind him the torches sank and rose, showering flakes of flame, as the worshippers imitated their master. The gold door closed behind them, shutting out sound and sight, and Conan darted across the throne-chamber and into the alcove behind the throne. He made less sound than a wind blowing across the chamber.

Tiny beams of light streamed through the apertures in the wall, as he pried open the secret panel. Gliding into the niche he peered through. Muriela sat upright on the dais, her arms folded, her head leaning back against the wall, within a few inches of his eyes. The delicate perfume of her foamy hair was in his nostrils. He could not see her face, of course, but her attitude was as if she gazed tranquilly into some far gulf of space, over and beyond the shaven heads of the black giants who knelt before her. Conan grinned with appreciation. "The little slut's an actress," he told himself. He knew she was shrivelling with terror, but she showed no sign. In the uncertain flare of the torches she looked exactly like the goddess he had seen lying on that same dais, if one could imagine that goddess imbued with vibrant life.

Gorulga was booming forth some kind of a chant in an accent unfamiliar to Conan, and which was probably some invocation in the ancient tongue of Alkmeenon, handed down from generation to generation of high priests. It seemed interminable. Conan grew restless. The longer the thing lasted, the more terrific would be the strain on Muriela. If she snapped – he hitched his sword and dagger forward. He could not see the little trollop tortured and slain by black men.

But the chant – deep, low-pitched and indescribably ominous – came to a conclusion at last, and a shouted acclaim from the acolytes marked its period. Lifting his head and raising his arms toward the silent form on the dais, Gorulga cried in the deep rich resonance that was the natural attribute of the Keshani priest: "Oh, great goddess, dweller with the great ones of darkness, let thy heart be melted, thy lips opened for the ears of thy slave whose head is in the dust beneath thy feet! Speak, great goddess of the holy valley! Thou knowest the paths before us; the darkness that vexes us is as the light of the midday sun to thee. Shed the radiance of thy wisdom on the paths of thy servants! Tell us, oh mouthpiece of the gods, what is their will concerning Thutmekri the Stygian?"

The high-piled burnished mass of hair that caught the torchlight in dull bronze gleams quivered slightly. A gusty sigh rose from the blacks, half in awe, half in fear. Muriela's voice came plainly to Conan's ears in the breathless silence, and it seemed cold, detached, impersonal, though he winced at the Corinthian accent.

"It is the will of the gods that the Stygian and his Shemitish dogs be driven from Keshan!" She was repeating his exact words. "They are thieves and traitors who plot to rob the gods. Let the Teeth of Gwahlur be placed in the care of the general Conan. Let him lead the armies of Keshan. He is beloved of the gods!" There was a quiver in her voice as she ended, and Conan began to sweat, believing she was on the point of an hysterical collapse.

But the blacks did not notice, any more than they identified the Corinthian accent, of which they knew nothing. They smote their palms softly together and a murmur of wonder and awe rose from them. Gorulga's eyes glittered fanatically in the torchlight.

"Yelaya has spoken!" he cried in an exalted voice. "It is the will of the gods! Long ago, in the days of our ancestors, they were made taboo and hidden at the command of the gods, who wrenched them from the awful jaws of Gwahlur the king of darkness, in the birth of the world. At the command of the gods the Teeth of Gwahlur were hidden; at their command they shall be brought forth again. Oh star-born goddess, give us your leave to go to the secret hiding place of the Teeth to secure them for him whom the gods love!"

22

"You have my leave to go!" answered the false goddess, with an imperious gesture of dismissal that set Conan grinning again, and the priests backed out, ostrich plumes and torches rising and falling with the rhythm of their genuflexions.

The gold door closed and with a moan, the goddess fell back limply on the dais. "Conan!" she whimpered faintly. "Conan!"

"Shhh!" he hissed through the apertures, and turning, glided from the niche and closed the panel. A glimpse past the jamb of the carven door showed him the torches receding across the great throne room, but he was at the same time aware of a radiance that did not emanate from the torches. He was startled, but the solution presented itself instantly. An early moon had risen and its light slanted through the pierced dome which by some curious workmanship intensified the light. The shining dome of Alkmeenon was no fable, then. Perhaps its interior was of the curious whitely flaming crystal found only in the hills of the black countries. The light flooded the throne-room and seeped into the chambers immediately adjoining.

But as Conan made toward the door that led into the throne-room, he was brought around suddenly by a noise that seemed to emanate from the passage that led off from the alcove. He crouched at the mouth, staring into it, remembering the clangor of the gong that had echoed from it to lure him into a snare. The light from the dome filtered only a little way into that narrow corridor, and showed him only empty space. Yet he could have sworn that he had heard the furtive pad of a foot somewhere down it.

While he hesitated, he was electrified by a woman's strangled cry from behind him. Bounding through the door behind the throne, he saw an unexpected spectacle, in the crystal light.

The torches of the priests had vanished from the great hall outside – but one priest was still in the palace: Gwarunga. His wicked features were convulsed with fury, and he grasped the terrified Muriela by the throat, choking her efforts to scream and plead, shaking her brutally.

"Traitress!" Between his thick red lips his voice hissed like a cobra. "What game are you playing? Did not Zargheba tell you what to say? Aye, Thutmekri told me! Are you betraying your master, or is he betraying his friends through you? Slut! I'll twist off your false head – but first I'll –"

A widening of his captive's lovely eyes as she stared over his shoulder warned the huge black. He released her and wheeled, just as Conan's sword lashed down. The impact of the stroke knocked him headlong backwards to the marble floor where he lay twitching, blood oozing from a ragged gash in his scalp.

Conan started toward him to finish the job – for he knew that the black's sudden movement had caused the blade to strike flat – but Muriela threw her arms convulsively about him.

"I've done as you ordered!" she gasped hysterically. "Take me away! Oh, please take me away!"

"We can't go yet," he grunted. "I want to follow the priests and see where they get the jewels. There may be more loot hidden there. But you can go with me. Where's that gem you wore in your hair?"

"It must have fallen out on the dais," she stammered, feeling for it. "I was so frightened – when the priests left I ran out to find you and this big brute had stayed behind, and he grabbed me –"

"Well, go get it while I dispose of this carcass," he commanded. "Go on! That gem is worth a fortune itself."

She hesitated, as if loath to return to that cryptic chamber, then, as he grasped Gwarunga's girdle and dragged him into the alcove, she turned and entered the oracle room. Conan dumped the senseless black on the floor, and lifted his sword. The Cimmerian had lived too long in the wild places of the world to have any illusions about mercy. The only safe enemy was a headless enemy. But before he could strike, a startling scream checked the lifted blade. It came from the oracle chamber.

"Conan! Conan! *She's come back!*" The shriek ended in a gurgle and a scraping shuffle.

With an oath Conan dashed out of the alcove, across the throne dais and into the oracle-chamber, almost before the sound had ceased. There he halted, glaring bewilderedly. To all appearances Muriela lay placidly on the dais, eyes closed as if in slumber.

"What in the hell are you doing?" he demanded acidly. "Is this any time to be playing jokes –"

His voice trailed away. His gaze ran along the ivory thigh molded in the close-fitting silk skirt. That skirt should gape from girdle to hem. He knew, because it had been his own hand that tore it, as he ruthlessly stripped the garment from the dancer's writhing body. But the skirt showed no rent. A single stride brought him to the dais and he laid his hand on the ivory body – snatched away as if it had encountered hot iron instead of the cold immobility of death.

"Crom!" he muttered, his eyes suddenly slits of bale-fire. "It's not Muriela! It's Yelaya!"

He understood now that frantic scream that had burst from Muriela's lips when she entered the chamber. The goddess had returned. The body had been stripped by Zargheba to furnish the accoutrements for the pretender. Yet now it was clad in silk and jewels as Conan had first seen it. A peculiar prickling made itself manifest among the short hairs at the base of Conan's scalp.

"Muriela!" he shouted suddenly. "*Muriela!* Where the devil are you?"

The walls threw back his voice mockingly. There was no entrance that he could see except the golden door, and none could have entered or departed through that without his knowledge. This much was indisputable: Yelaya had been replaced on the dais within the few minutes that had elapsed since Muriela had first left the chamber to be seized by Gwarunga; his ears were still tingling with the echoes of Muriela's scream, yet the Corinthian had vanished as if into thin air. There was but one explanation, if he rejected the darker speculation that suggested the supernatural – somewhere in the chamber there was a secret door. And even as the thought crossed his mind, he saw it.

In what had seemed a curtain of solid marble, a thin perpendicular crack showed and in the crack hung a wisp of silk. In an instant he was bending over it. That shred was from Muriela's torn skirt. The implication was unmistakable. It had been caught in the closing door and torn off as she was borne through the opening by whatever grim beings were her captors. The bit of cloth had prevented the door from fitting perfectly into its frame.

Thrusting his dagger point into the crack, Conan exerted leverage with a corded forearm. The blade bent, but it was of unbreakable Akbitanan steel. The marble door opened. Conan's sword was lifted as he peered into the aperture beyond, but he saw no shape of menace. Light filtering into the oracle chamber revealed a short flight of steps cut out of marble. Pulling the door back to its fullest extent, he drove his dagger into a crack in the floor, propping it open. Then he went down the steps without hesitation. He saw nothing, heard nothing. A dozen steps down the stair ended in a narrow corridor which ran straight away into the gloom.

He halted suddenly, posed like a statue at the foot of the stair, staring at the paintings which frescoed the walls, half visible in the dim light which filtered down from above. The art was unmistakably Pelishtim; he had seen frescoes of identical characteristics on the walls of Asgalun. But the scenes depicted had no connection with anything Pelishtim, except for one human figure, frequently recurrent: a lean, white-bearded old man whose racial characteristics were unmistakable. They seemed to represent various sections of the palace above. Several scenes showed a chamber he recognized as the oracle chamber with the figure of Yelaya stretched upon the ivory dais and huge black men kneeling before it. And there behind the wall, in the niche, lurked the ancient Pelishtim. And there were other figures, too – figures that moved through the deserted palace, did the bidding of the Pelishtim, and dragged unnamable things out of the subterranean river. In the few seconds Conan stood frozen, hitherto unintelligible phrases in the parchment manuscript blazed in his brain with chilling clarity. The loose bits of the pattern clicked into place. The mystery of Bit-Yakin was a mystery no longer, nor the riddle of Bit-Yakin's servants.

Conan turned and peered into the darkness, an icy finger crawling along his spine. Then he went along the corridor, cat-footed, and without hesitation, moving deeper and deeper into the darkness as he drew further away from the stair. The air hung heavy with the odor he had scented in the court of the gong.

Now in utter blackness he heard a sound ahead of him – the shuffle of bare feet, or the swish of loose garments against stone, he could not tell which. But an instant later his outstretched hand encountered a barrier which he identified as a massive door of carven metal. He pushed against it fruitlessly, and his sword point sought vainly for a crack. It fitted into the sill and jambs as if molded there. He exerted all his strength, his feet straining against the floor, the veins knotting in his temples. It was useless; a charge of elephants would scarcely have shaken that titanic portal.

As he leaned there he caught a sound on the other side that his ears instantly identified – it was the creak of rusty iron, like a lever scraping in its slot. Instinctive action followed recognition so spontaneously that sound, impulse and action were practically simultaneous. And as his prodigious bound carried him backward, there was the rush of a great bulk from above, and a thunderous crash filled the tunnel with deafening vibrations. Bits of flying splinters struck him – a huge block of stone, he knew from the sound, dropped on the spot he had just quitted. An instant's slower thought or action and it would have crushed him like an ant.

Conan fell back. Somewhere on the other side of that metal door Muriela was a captive, if she still lived. But he could not pass that door and if he remained in the tunnel, another block might fall, and he might not be so lucky. It would do the girl no good for him to be crushed into a purple pulp. He could not continue his search in that direction. He must get above ground and look for some other avenue of approach.

He turned and hurried toward the stair, sighing as he emerged into comparative radiance. And as he set foot on the first step, the light was blotted out, and above him the marble door rushed shut with a resounding reverberation.

Something like panic seized the Cimmerian then, trapped in that black tunnel, and he wheeled on the stair, lifting his sword and glaring murderously into the darkness behind him, expecting a rush of ghoulish assailants. But there was no sound or movement down the tunnel. Did the men beyond the door – if they *were* men – believe that he had been disposed of by the fall of the stone from the roof, which had undoubtedly been released by some sort of machinery?

Then why had the door been shut above him? Abandoning speculation Conan groped his way up the steps, his skin crawling in anticipation of a knife in his back at every stride, yearning to drown his semi-panic in a barbarous burst of blood-letting.

He thrust against the door at the top, and cursed soulfully to find that it did not give to his efforts. Then as he lifted his sword with his right hand to hew at the marble, his groping left encountered a metal bolt that evidently slipped into place at the closing of the door. In an instant he had drawn this bolt, and then the door gave to his shove. He bounded into the chamber like a slit-eyed snarling incarnation of fury, ferociously desirous to come to grips with whatever enemy was hounding him.

The dagger was gone from the floor. The chamber was empty, and so was the dais. Yelaya had again vanished.

"By Crom!" muttered the Cimmerian. "Is she alive, after all?"

He strode out into the throne-room, baffled, and then, struck by a sudden thought, stepped behind the throne and peered into the alcove. There was blood on the smooth marble where he had cast down the senseless body of Gwarunga – that was all. The black man had vanished as completely as Yelaya.

IV

The Dome of the Teeth of Gwahlur

Baffled wrath confused the brain of Conan the Cimmerian. He knew no more how to go about searching for Muriela than he had known how to go about searching for the Teeth of Gwahlur. Only one thought occurred to him – to follow the priests. Perhaps at the hiding place of the treasure some clue would be revealed to him. It was a slim chance, but better than wandering about aimlessly.

As he hurried through the great shadowy hall that led to the portico he half expected the lurking shades to come to life behind him with rending fangs and talons. But only the beat of his own rapid heart accompanied him into the moonlight that dappled the shimmering marble.

At the foot of the wide steps he cast about in the bright moonlight for some sign to show him the direction he must go. And he found it – petals scattered on the sward told where an arm or garment had brushed against a blossom-laden branch. Grass had been pressed down under heavy feet. Conan, who had tracked wolves in his native hills, found no insurmountable difficulty in following the trail of the Keshani priests.

It led away from the palace, through masses of exotically-scented shrubbery where great pale blossoms spread their shimmering petals, through verdant, tangled bushes that showered blooms at the touch, until he came at last to a great mass of

28

rock that jutted like a titan's castle out from the cliffs at a point closest to the palace, which, however, was almost hidden from view by vine-interlaced trees. Evidently that babbling priest in Keshia had been mistaken when he said the Teeth were hidden in the palace. This trail had led him away from the place where Muriela had disappeared, but a belief was growing in Conan that each part of the valley was connected with that palace by subterranean passages.

Crouching in the deep velvet-black shadows of the bushes, he scrutinized the great jut of rock which stood out in bold relief in the moonlight. It was covered with strange, grotesque carvings, depicting men and animals, and half-bestial creatures that might have been gods or devils. The style of art differed so strikingly from that of the rest of the valley, that Conan wondered if it did not represent a different era and race, and was itself a relic of an age lost and forgotten at whatever immeasurably distant date the people of Alkmeenon had found and entered the haunted valley.

A great door stood open in the sheer curtain of the cliff, and a gigantic dragon head was carved about it so that the open door was like the dragon's gaping mouth. The door itself was of carven bronze and looked to weigh several tons. There was no lock that he could see, but a series of bolts showing along the edge of the massive portal, as it stood open, told him that there was some system of locking and unlocking – a system doubtless known only to the priests of Keshan.

The trail showed that Gorulga and his henchmen had gone through that door. But Conan hesitated. To wait until they emerged would probably mean to see the door locked in his face, and he might not be able to solve the mystery of its unlocking. On the other hand, if he followed them in, they might emerge and lock him in the cavern.

Throwing caution to the winds, he glided through the great portal. Somewhere in the cavern were the priests, the Teeth of Gwahlur, and perhaps a clue to the fate of Muriela. Personal risks had never yet deterred him from any purpose.

Moonlight illumined, for a few yards, the wide tunnel in which he found himself. Somewhere ahead of him he saw a faint glow and heard the echo of a weird chanting. The priests were not so far ahead of him as he had thought. The tunnel debouched into a wide room before the moonlight played out, an empty cavern of no great dimensions, but with a lofty, vaulted roof, glowing with a phosphorescent encrustation, which, as Conan knew, was a common phenomenon in that part of the world. It made a weird ghostly half-light, in which he was able to see a bestial image squatting on a shrine, and the black mouths of six or seven tunnels leading off from the chamber. Down the widest one of these – the one directly behind the squat image which looked toward the outer opening – he caught the gleam of torches, wavering whereas the phosphorescent glow was fixed, and heard the chanting increased in volume.

Down it he went recklessly, and was presently peering into a larger cavern than the one he had just left. There was no phosphorus here, but the light of the torches fell on a larger altar and a more obscene and repulsive god squatting toad-like upon it. Before this repugnant deity Gorulga and his ten acolytes knelt and beat their heads upon the ground, while chanting monotonously. Conan realized why their progress had been so slow. Evidently approaching the secret crypt of the Teeth was a complicated and elaborate ritual.

He was fidgeting in nervous impatience before the chanting and bowing were over, but presently they rose and passed into the tunnel which opened behind the idol. Their torches bobbed away into the nighted vault, and he followed swiftly. Not much danger of being discovered. He glided along the shadows like a creature of the night, and the black priests were completely engrossed in their ceremonial mummery. Apparently they had not even noticed the absence of Gwarunga.

Emerging into a cavern of huge proportions, about whose upward curving walls gallery-like ledges marched in tiers, they began their worship anew before an altar which was larger, and a god which was more disgusting than any encountered thus far.

Conan crouched in the black mouth of the tunnel, staring at the walls reflecting the lurid glow of the torches. He saw a carven stone stair winding up from tier to tier of the galleries; the roof was lost in darkness.

He started violently and the chanting broke off as the kneeling blacks flung up their heads. An inhuman voice boomed out high above them. They froze on their knees, their faces turned upward and a ghastly blue hue in the sudden glare of a weird light that burst blindingly up near the lofty roof, and then burned with a throbbing glow. That glare lighted a gallery and a cry went up from the high priest, echoed shudderingly by his acolytes. In the flash there had been briefly disclosed to them a slim white figure standing upright in a sheen of silk and a glint of jewel-crusted gold. Then the blaze smoldered to a throbbing, pulsing luminosity in which nothing was distinct, and that slim shape was but a shimmering blur of ivory.

"*Yelaya!*" screamed Gorulga, his brown features ashen. "Why have you followed us? What is your pleasure?"

That weird unhuman voice rolled down from the roof, re-echoing under that arching vault that magnified and altered it beyond recognition.

"Woe to the unbelievers! Woe to the false children of Keshia! Doom to them which deny their deity!"

A cry of horror went up from the priests. Gorulga looked like a shocked vulture in the glare of the torches.

"I do not understand!" he stammered. "We are faithful. In the chamber of the oracle you told us —"

"Do not heed what you heard in the chamber of the oracle!" rolled that terrible voice, multiplied until it was as though a myriad voices thundered and muttered the same warning. "Beware of false prophets and false gods! A demon in my guise spoke to you in the palace giving false prophecy. Now harken and obey, for only I am the true goddess, and I give you one chance to save yourselves from doom!

"Take the Teeth of Gwahlur from the crypt where they were placed so long ago. Alkmeenon is no longer holy, because it has been desecrated by blasphemers. Give the Teeth of Gwahlur into the hands of Thutmekri, the Stygian, to place in the sanctuary of Dagon and Derketo. Only this can save Keshan from the doom the demons of the night have plotted. Take the Teeth of Gwahlur and go; return instantly to Keshia; there give the jewels to Thutmekri, and seize the foreign devil Conan and flay him alive in the great square."

There was no hesitation in obeying. Chattering with fear the priests scrambled up and ran for the door that opened behind the bestial god. Gorulga led the flight. They jammed briefly in the doorway, yelping as wildly waving torches touched squirming black bodies; they plunged through and the patter of their speeding feet dwindled down the tunnel.

Conan did not follow. He was consumed with a furious desire to learn the truth of this fantastic affair. Was that indeed Yelaya, as the cold sweat on the backs of his hands told him, or was it that little hussy Muriela, turned traitress after all? If it was —

Before the last torch had vanished down the black tunnel he was bounding vengefully up the stone stair. The blue glow was dying down, but he could still make out that the ivory figure stood motionless on the gallery. His blood ran cold as he approached it, but he did not hesitate. He came on with his sword lifted, and towered like a threat of death over the inscrutable shape.

"Yelaya!" he snarled. "Dead as she's been for a thousand years! *Ha!*"

From the dark mouth of a tunnel behind him a dark form lunged. But the sudden, deadly rush of unshod feet had reached the Cimmerian's quick ears. He whirled like a cat and dodged the blow aimed murderously at his back. As the gleaming steel in the dark hand hissed past him, he struck back with the intent and fury of a roused python, and the long straight blade impaled his assailant and stood out a foot and a half between his shoulders.

"So!" Conan tore his sword free as the victim sagged to the floor, gasping and gurgling. The man writhed briefly and stiffened. In the dying light he saw a black body and ebony countenance, hideous in the blue glare. He had killed Gwarunga.

Conan turned from the corpse to the goddess. Thongs about her knees and breast held her upright against a stone pillar, and her thick hair, fastened to the column, held her head up. At a few yards' distance these bonds were not visible in the uncertain light.

"He must have come to after I descended into the tunnel," muttered Conan. "He must have suspected I was down there. So he pulled out the dagger —" Conan stooped and wrenched the identical weapon from the stiffening fingers, glanced at it and replaced it in his own girdle; "and shut the door. Then he took Yelaya to befool his brother idiots. That was he shouting a while ago. You couldn't recognize his voice, under this echoing roof. And that bursting blue flame — I thought it looked familiar. It's a trick of the Stygian priests. Thutmekri must have given some of it to Gwarunga."

The man could have easily reached this cavern ahead of his companions. Evidently familiar with the plan of the caverns by hearsay or by maps handed down in the priest-craft, he had entered the cave after the others, carrying the goddess, followed a circuitous route through the tunnels and chambers, and ensconced himself and his burden on the balcony while Gorulga and the other acolytes were engaged in their endless rituals.

The blue glare had faded, but now Conan was aware of another glow, emanating from the mouth of the one of the corridors that opened on the ledge. Somewhere down that corridor there was another field of phosphorus, for he recognized the faint steady radiance. The corridor led in the direction the priests had taken, and he decided to follow it, rather than descend into the darkness of the great cavern below. Doubtless it connected with another gallery in some other chamber, which might be the destination of the priests. He hurried down it, the illumination growing stronger as he advanced, until he could make out the floor and the walls of the tunnel. Ahead of him and below him he could hear the priests chanting again.

Abruptly a doorway in the left hand wall was limned in the phosphorous glow, and to his ears came the sound of soft, hysterical sobbing. He wheeled, glared through the door.

He was looking into a chamber hewed out of solid rock, not a natural cavern like the others. The domed roof shone with the phosphorous light, and the walls were almost covered with arabesques of beaten gold.

Near the further wall on a granite throne, staring for ever toward the arched doorway, sat the monstrous and obscene Pteor, the god of the Pelishtim, wrought in brass, with his exaggerated attributes reflecting the grossness of his cult. And in his lap sprawled a limp white figure —

"Well, I'll be damned!" muttered Conan. He glanced suspiciously about the chamber, seeing no other entrance or evidence of occupation, and then advanced noiselessly and looked down at the girl whose slim shoulders shook with sobs of abject misery, her face sunk in her arms. From thick bands of gold on the idol's arms slim gold chains ran to smaller bands on her wrists. He laid a hand on her naked shoulder and she started convulsively, shrieked, and twisted her tear-stained face toward him.

"*Conan!*" She made a spasmodic effort to go into the usual clinch, but the chains hindered her. He cut through the soft gold as close to her wrists as he could, grunting: "You'll have to wear these bracelets until I can find a chisel or a file. Let go of me, damn it! You actresses are too damned emotional. What happened to you, anyway?"

"When I went back into the oracle chamber," she whimpered, "I saw the goddess lying on the dais as I'd first seen her. I called out to you and started to run to the door — then something grabbed me from behind. It clapped a hand over my mouth and carried me through a panel in the wall, and down some steps and along a dark hall. I didn't see what it was that had hold of me until we passed through a big metal door and came into a tunnel whose roof was alight, like this chamber.

"Oh, I nearly fainted when I saw! They are not humans! They are grey, hairy devils that walk like men and speak a gibberish no human could understand. They stood there and seemed to be waiting, and once I thought I heard somebody trying the door. Then one of the *things* pulled a metal lever in the wall, and something crashed on the other side of the door.

"Then they carried me on and on through winding tunnels and up stone stairways, into this chamber, where they chained me on the knees of this abominable idol, and then they went away. Oh, Conan, what are they?"

"Servants of Bit-Yakin," he grunted. "I found a manuscript that told me a number of things, and then stumbled upon some frescoes that told me the rest. Bit-Yakin was a Pelishtim who wandered into the valley with his servants after the people of Alkmeenon had deserted it. He found the body of Princess Yelaya, and discovered that the priests returned from time to time to make offerings to her, for even then she was worshipped as a goddess.

"He made an oracle of her, and he was the voice of the oracle, speaking from a niche he cut in the wall behind the ivory dais. The priests never suspected, never saw him or his servants, for they always hid themselves when the men came. Bit-Yakin lived and died here without ever being discovered by the priests. Crom knows how long he dwelt here, but it must have been for centuries. The wise men of the Pelishtim know how to increase the span of their lives for hundreds of years. I've seen some of them myself. Why he lived here alone, and why he played the part of oracle no ordinary human can guess, but I believe the oracle part was to keep the city inviolate and sacred, so he could remain undisturbed. He ate the food the priests brought as an offering to Yelaya, and his servants ate other things — I've always known there was a subterranean river flowing away from the lake where the people of the Puntish highlands throw their dead. That river runs under this palace. They have ladders hung over the water where they can hang and fish for the corpses that come floating through. Bit-Yakin recorded everything on parchment and painted walls.

"But he died at last, and his servants mummified him according to instructions he gave them before his death, and stuck him in a cave in the cliffs. The rest is easy to guess. His servants, which were even more immortal than he, kept on dwelling here, but the next time a high priest came to consult the oracle, not having a master to restrain them, they tore him to pieces. So since then – until Gorulga – nobody came to talk to the oracle.

"It's obvious they've been renewing the garments and ornaments of the goddess, as they'd seen Bit-Yakin do. Doubtless there's a sealed chamber somewhere where the silks are kept from decay. They clothed the goddess and brought her back to the oracle room after Zargheba had stolen her. And, oh, by the way, they took off Zargheba's head and hung it up in a thicket."

She shivered, yet at the same time breathed a sigh of relief.

"He'll never whip me again."

"Not this side of hell," agreed Conan. "But come on. Gwarunga ruined my chances with his stolen goddess. I'm going to follow the priests and take my chance of stealing the loot from them after they get it. And you stay close to me. I can't spend all my time looking for you."

"But the servants of Bit-Yakin!" she whispered fearfully.

"We'll have to take our chance," he grunted. "I don't know what's in their minds, but so far they haven't shown any disposition to come out and fight in the open. Come on."

Taking her wrist he led her out of the chamber and down the corridor. As they advanced they heard the chanting of the priests, and mingling with the sound the low sullen rushing of waters. The light grew stronger above them as they emerged on a high-pitched gallery of a great cavern and looked down on a scene weird and fantastic.

Above them gleamed the phosphorescent roof; a hundred feet below them stretched the smooth stone floor of the cavern. On the far side this floor was cut by a deep, narrow stream brimming its rocky channel. Rushing out of impenetrable gloom, it swirled across the cavern and was lost again in darkness. The visible surface reflected the radiance above; the dark seething waters glinted as if flecked with living jewels, frosty blue, lurid red, shimmering green, an ever changing iridescence.

Conan and his companion stood upon one of the gallery-like ledges that banded the curve of the lofty wall, and from this ledge a natural bridge of stone soared in a breath-taking arch over the vast gulf of the cavern to join a much smaller ledge on the opposite side, across the river. Ten feet below it another, broader arch spanned the cave. At either end a carven stair joined the extremities of these flying arches.

Conan's gaze, following the curve of the arch that swept away from the ledge on which they stood, caught a glint of light that was not the lurid phosphorus of the cavern. On that small ledge opposite them there was an opening in the cave wall through which stars were glinting.

But his full attention was drawn to the scene beneath them. The priests had reached their destination. There in a sweeping angle of the cavern wall stood a stone altar, but there was no idol upon it. Whether there was one behind it, Conan could not ascertain, because some trick of the light, or the sweep of the wall left the space behind the altar in total darkness.

The priests had stuck their torches into holes in the stone floor, forming a semi-circle of fire in front of the altar at a distance of several yards. Then the priests themselves formed a semi-circle inside the crescent of torches, and Gorulga, after lifting his arms aloft in invocation, bent to the altar and laid hands on it. It lifted and tilted backward on its hinder edge, like the lid of a chest, revealing a small crypt.

Extending a long arm into the recess, Gorulga brought up a small brass chest. Lowering the altar back into place, he set the chest on it, and threw back the lid. To the eager watchers on the high gallery it seemed as if the action had released a blaze of living fire which throbbed and quivered about the opened chest. Conan's heart leaped and his hand caught at his hilt. The Teeth of Gwahlur at last! The treasure that would make its possessor the richest man in the world! His breath came fast between his clenched teeth.

Then he was suddenly aware that a new element had entered into the light of the torches and of the phosphorescent roof, rendering both void. Darkness stole around the altar, except for that glowing spot of evil radiance cast by the Teeth of Gwahlur, and that grew and grew. The blacks froze into basaltic statues, their shadows streaming grotesquely and gigantically out behind them.

The altar was laved in the glow now, and the astounded features of Gorulga stood out in sharp relief. Then the mysterious space behind the altar swam into the widening illumination. And slowly with the crawling light, figures became visible, like shapes growing out of the night and silence.

At first they seemed like grey stone statues, those motionless shapes, hairy, manlike, yet hideously human; but their eyes were alive, cold sparks of grey icy fire. And as the weird glow lit their bestial countenances, Gorulga screamed and fell backward, throwing up his long arms in a gesture of frenzied horror.

But a longer arm shot across the altar and a misshapen hand locked on his throat. Screaming and fighting the high priest was dragged back across the altar; a hammer-like fist smashed down, and Gorulga's cries were stilled. Limp and broken he sagged across the altar, his brains oozing from his crushed skull. And then the servants of Bit-Yakin surged like a bursting flood from hell on the black priests who stood like horror-blasted images.

Then there was slaughter, grim and appalling.

Conan saw black bodies tossed like chaff in the inhuman hands of the slayers, against whose horrible strength and agility the daggers and swords of the priests were ineffective. He saw men lifted bodily and their heads cracked open against the stony altar. He saw a flaming torch, grasped in a monstrous hand, thrust inexorably down the gullet of an agonized wretch who writhed in vain against the arms that pinioned him. He saw a man torn in two pieces, as one might tear a chicken, and the bloody fragments hurled clear across the cavern. The massacre was as short and devastating as the rush of a hurricane. In a burst of red abysmal ferocity it was over, except for one wretch who fled screaming back the way the priests had come, pursued by a swarm of blood-dabbled shapes of horror which reached out their red-smeared hands for him. Fugitive and pursuers vanished down the black tunnel, and the screams of the human came back dwindling and confused by the distance.

Muriela was on her knees clutching Conan's legs; her face pressed against his knee and her eyes tightly shut. She was a quaking, quivering mold of abject terror. But Conan was galvanized. A quick glance across at the aperture where the stars shone, a glance down at the chest that still blazed open on the blood-smeared altar, and he saw and seized the desperate gamble.

"I'm going after that chest!" he grated. "Stay here!"

"Oh Mitra, no!" In an agony of fright she fell to the floor and caught at his sandals. "Don't! Don't! Don't leave me!"

"Lie still and keep your mouth shut!" he snapped, disengaging himself from her frantic clasp.

He disregarded the tortuous stair. He dropped from ledge to ledge with reckless haste. There was no sign of the monsters as his feet hit the floor. A few of the torches still flared in their sockets, the phosphorescent glow throbbed and quivered, and the river flowed with an almost articulate muttering, scintillant with undreamed radiances. The glow that had heralded the appearance of the servants had vanished with them. Only the light of the jewels in the brass chest shimmered and quivered.

He snatched the chest, noting its contents in one lustful glance – strange curiously-shapen stones that burned with an icy, nonterrestrial fire. He slammed the lid, thrust the chest under his arm, and ran back up the steps. He had no desire to encounter the hellish servants of Bit-Yakin. His glimpse of them in action had dispelled any illusion concerning their fighting ability. Why they had waited so long before striking at the invaders he was unable to say. What human could guess the motives or thoughts of these monstrosities? That they were possessed of craft and intelligence equal to humanity had been demonstrated. And there on the cavern floor lay crimson proof of their bestial ferocity.

The Corinthian still cowered on the gallery where he had left her. He caught her wrist and yanked her to her feet, grunting: "I guess it's time to go!"

Too bemused with terror to be fully aware of what was going on, the girl suffered herself to be led across the dizzy span. It was not until they were poised over the rushing water that she looked down, voiced a startled yelp and would have fallen but for Conan's massive arm about her. Growling an objurgation in her ear, he

snatched her up under his free arm and swept her, in a flutter of limply waving arms and legs, across the arch and into the aperture that opened at the other end. Without bothering to set her on her feet, he hurried through the short tunnel into which this aperture opened. An instant later they emerged upon a narrow ledge on the outer side of the cliffs that circled the valley. Less than a hundred feet below them the jungle waved in the starlight.

Looking down, Conan vented a gusty sigh of relief. He believed that he could negotiate the descent, even though burdened with the jewels and the girl; although he doubted if even he, unburdened, could have ascended at that spot. He set the chest, still smeared with Gorulga's blood and clotted with his brains, on the ledge, and was about to remove his girdle in order to tie the box to his back, when he was galvanized by a sound behind him, a sound sinister and unmistakable.

"Stay here!" he snapped at the bewildered Corinthian. "Don't move!" And drawing his sword, he glided into the tunnel, glaring back into the cavern.

Half way across the upper span he saw a grey, deformed shape. One of the servants of Bit-Yakin was on his trail. There was no doubt that the brute had seen them and was following them. Conan did not hesitate. It might be easier to defend the mouth of the tunnel – but this fight must be finished quickly, before the other servants could return.

He ran out on the span, straight toward the oncoming monster. It was no ape, neither was it a man. It was some shambling horror spawned in the mysterious, nameless jungles of the south, where strange life teemed in the reeking rot without the dominance of man, and drums thundered in temples that had never known the tread of a human foot. How the ancient Pelishtim had gained lordship over them – and with it eternal exile from humanity – was a foul riddle about which Conan did not care to speculate, even if he had had opportunity.

Man and monster they met at the highest arch of the span, where, a hundred feet below, rushed the furious black water. As the monstrous shape with its leprous grey body and the features of a carven, unhuman idol, loomed over him, Conan struck as a wounded tiger strikes, with every ounce of thew and fury behind the blow. That stroke would have sheared a human body asunder; but the bones of the servant of Bit-Yakin were like tempered steel. Yet even tempered steel could not wholly have withstood that furious stroke. Ribs and shoulder bone parted and blood spouted from the great gash.

There was no time for a second stroke. Before the Cimmerian could lift his blade again or spring clear, the sweep of a giant arm knocked him from the span as a fly is flicked from a wall. As he plunged downward the rush of the river was like a knell in his ears, but his twisting body fell half-way across the lower arch. He wavered there precariously for one blood-chilling instant, then his clutching fingers hooked over the further edge, and he scrambled to safety, his sword still in his other hand.

As he sprang up, he saw the monster, spurting blood hideously, rush toward the cliff-side of the bridge, obviously intending to descend the stair that connected the arches and renew the battle. At the very ledge the brute paused in mid-flight – and Conan saw it too – Muriela, with the jewel chest under her arm, stood staring wildly in the mouth of the tunnel.

With a triumphant bellow the monster scooped her up under one arm, snatched the jewel chest with the other hand as she dropped it, and turning, lumbered back across the bridge. Conan cursed with passion and ran for the other side also. He doubted if he could climb the stair to the higher arch in time to catch the brute before it could plunge into the labyrinths of tunnels on the other side.

But the monster was slowing, like clock-work running down. Blood gushed in torrents from that terrible gash in his breast, and he lurched drunkenly from side to side. Suddenly he stumbled, reeled and toppled sidewise – pitched headlong from the arch and hurtled downward. Girl and jewel chest fell from his nerveless hands and Muriela's scream rang terribly above the snarl of the water below.

Conan was almost under the spot from which the creature had fallen. The monster struck the lower arch glancingly and shot off, but the writhing figure of the girl struck and clung, and the chest hit the edge of the span near her. One falling object struck on one side of Conan and one on the other. Either was within arm's length; for the fraction of a split second the chest teetered on the edge of the bridge, and Muriela clung by one arm, her face turned desperately toward Conan, her eyes dilated with the fear of death and her lips parted in a haunting cry of despair.

Conan did not hesitate, nor did he even glance toward the chest that held the wealth of an epoch. With a quickness that would have shamed the spring of a hungry jaguar, he swooped, grasped the girl's arm just as her fingers slipped from the smooth stone, and snatched her up on the span with one explosive heave. The chest toppled on over and struck the water ninety feet below, whither the body of the servant of Bit-Yakin had already vanished. A splash, a jetting flash of foam marked where the Teeth of Gwahlur disappeared for ever from the sight of man.

Conan scarcely wasted a downward glance. He darted across the span and ran up the cliff stair like a cat, carrying the limp girl as if she had been an infant. A hideous ululation caused him to glance over his shoulder as he reached the higher arch, to see the other servants streaming back into the cavern below, blood dripping from their bared fangs. They raced up the stair that wound up from tier to tier, roaring vengefully, but he slung the girl unceremoniously over his shoulder, dashed through the tunnel and went down the cliffs like an ape himself, dropping and springing from hold to hold with breakneck recklessness. When the fierce countenances looked over the ledge of the aperture, it was to see the Cimmerian and the girl disappearing into the forest that surrounded the cliffs.

"Well," said Conan, setting the girl on her feet within the sheltering screen of branches, "we can take our time now. I don't think those brutes will follow us outside the valley. Anyway, I've got a horse tied at a water-hole close by, if the lions haven't eaten him. Crom's devils! What are you crying about *now*?"

She covered her tear-stained face with her hands, and her slim shoulders shook with sobs.

"I lost the jewels for you," she wailed miserably. "It was my fault. If I'd obeyed you and stayed out on the ledge, that brute would never have seen me. You should have caught the gems and let me drown!"

"Yes, I suppose I should," he agreed. "But forget it. Never worry about what's past. And stop crying, will you? That's better. Come on."

"You mean you're going to keep me? Take me with you?" she asked hopefully.

"What else do you suppose I'd do with you?" He ran an approving glance over her voluptuous figure and grinned at the torn skirt which revealed a generous expanse of tempting ivory-tinted curves. "I can use an actress like you. There's no use going back to Keshia. There's nothing in Keshan now that I want. We'll go to Punt. The people of Punt worship an ivory woman, and they wash gold out of the rivers in wicker baskets. I'll tell them that Keshan is intriguing with Thutmekri to enslave them – which is true – and that the gods have sent me to protect them – for about a houseful of gold. If I can manage to smuggle you into their temple to exchange places with their ivory goddess, we'll skin them out of their jaw teeth before we get through with them!"

Beyond the Black River

Beyond the Black River

I

CONAN LOSES HIS AXE

The stillness of the forest trail was so primeval that the tread of a soft-booted foot was a startling disturbance. At least it seemed so to the ears of the wayfarer, though he was moving along the path with the caution that must be practised by any man who ventured beyond Thunder River. He was a young man of medium height, with an open countenance and a mop of tousled tawny hair unconfined by cap or helmet. His garb was common enough for that country – a coarse tunic, belted at the waist, short leather breeches beneath, and soft buckskin boots that came short of the knee. A knife hilt jutted from one boot-top. The broad leather belt supported a short heavy sword, and a buckskin pouch. There was no perturbation in the wide eyes that scanned the green walls which fringed the trail. Though not tall, he was well built, and the arms that the short wide sleeves of the tunic left bare were thick with corded muscle.

He tramped imperturbably along although the last settler's cabin lay miles behind him, and each step was carrying him nearer the grim peril that hung like a brooding shadow over the ancient forest.

He was not making as much noise as it seemed to him, though he well knew that the faint tread of his booted feet would be like a tocsin of alarm to the fierce ears that might be lurking in the treacherous green fastness. His careless attitude was not genuine; his eyes and ears were keenly alert; especially his ears, for no gaze could penetrate the leafy tangle for more than a few feet in either direction.

But it was instinct more than any warning by the external senses which brought him up suddenly, his hand on his hilt. He stood stock-still in the middle of the trail, unconsciously holding his breath, wondering what he had heard, and wondering if he had heard anything. The silence seemed absolute. Not a squirrel chattered or bird chirped. Then his gaze fixed itself on a mass of bushes beside the trail a few yards ahead of him. There was no breeze, yet he had seen a branch quiver. The short hairs on his scalp prickled, and he stood for an instant undecided, certain that a move in either direction would bring death streaking at him from the bushes.

A heavy chopping crunch sounded behind the leaves. The bushes were shaken violently, and simultaneously with the sound, an arrow arched erratically from among them and vanished among the trees along the trail. The wayfarer glimpsed its flight as he sprang frantically to cover.

Crouching behind a thick stem, his sword quivering in his fingers, he saw the bushes part, and a tall figure stepped leisurely into the trail. The traveller stared in surprise. The stranger was clad like himself in regard to boots and breeks, though the latter were of silk instead of leather. But he wore a sleeveless hauberk of dark mesh-mail in place of a tunic, and a helmet perched on his black mane. That helmet held the other's gaze; it was without a crest, but adorned by short bull's horns. No civilized hand ever forged that head-piece. Nor was the face below it that of a civilized man: dark, scarred, with smoldering blue eyes, it was a face as untamed as the primordial forest which formed its background. The man held a broadsword in his right hand, and the edge was smeared with crimson.

"Come on out!" he called, in an accent unfamiliar to the wayfarer. "All's safe now. There was only one of the dogs. Come on out."

The other emerged dubiously and stared at the stranger. He felt curiously helpless and futile as he gazed on the proportions of the forest man – the massive iron-clad breast, and the arm that bore the reddened sword, burned dark by the sun and ridged and corded with muscles. He moved with the dangerous ease of a panther; he was too fiercely supple to be a product of civilization, even of that fringe of civilization which composed the outer frontiers.

Turning, he stepped back to the bushes and pulled them apart. Still not certain just what had happened, the wayfarer from the east advanced and stared down into the bushes. A man lay there, a short, dark, thickly-muscled man, naked except for a loin cloth, a necklace of human teeth and a brass armlet. A short sword was thrust into the girdle of the loin cloth, and one hand still gripped a heavy black bow. The man had long black hair; that was about all the wayfarer could tell about his head, for his features were a mask of blood and brains. His skull had been split to the teeth.

"A Pict, by the gods!" exclaimed the wayfarer.

The burning blue eyes turned upon him.

"Are you surprized?"

"Why, they told me at Velitrium, and again at the settlers' cabins along the road that these devils sometimes sneaked across the border, but I didn't expect to meet one this far in the interior."

"You're only four miles east of Black River," the stranger informed him. "They've been shot within a mile of Velitrium. No settler between Thunder River and Fort Tuscelan is really safe. I picked up this dog's trail three miles south of the fort this morning, and I've been following him ever since. I came up behind him just as he was drawing an arrow on you. Another instant and there'd have been a stranger in Hell. But I spoiled his aim for him."

The wayfarer was staring wide-eyed at the larger man, dumbfounded by the realization that the man had actually tracked down one of the forest-devils and slain him unsuspected. That implied woodsmanship of a quality undreamed, even for Conajohara.

"You are one of the fort's garrison?" he asked.

"I'm no soldier. I draw the pay and rations of an officer of the line, but I do my work in the woods. Valannus knows I'm of more use ranging along the river than cooped up in the fort."

Casually the slayer shoved the body deeper into the thickets with his foot, pulled the bushes together and turned away down the trail. The other followed him.

"My name is Balthus," he offered. "I was at Velitrium last night. I haven't decided whether I'll take up a hide of land, or enter fort-service."

"The best land near Thunder River is already taken," grunted the slayer. "Plenty of good land between Scalp Creek – you crossed it a few miles back – and the fort, but that's getting too devilish close to the river. The Picts steal over to burn and murder – like that one did. They don't always come singly. Some day they'll try to sweep the settlers out of Conajohara. And they may succeed. Probably will succeed. This colonization business is mad, anyway. There's plenty of good land east of the Bossonian marches. If the Aquilonians would cut up some of the big estates of their barons, and plant wheat where now only deer are hunted, they wouldn't have to cross the border and take the land of the Picts away from them."

"That's queer talk from a man in the service of the Governor of Conajohara," objected Balthus.

"It's nothing to me," the other retorted. "I'm a mercenary. I sell my sword to the highest bidder. I never planted wheat and never will, so long as there are other harvests to be reaped with the sword. But you Hyborians have expanded as far as you'll be allowed to expand. You've crossed the marches, burned a few villages, exterminated a few clans and pushed back the frontier to Black River; but I doubt if you'll even be able to hold what you've conquered, and you'll never push the frontier any further westward.

"Your idiotic king doesn't understand conditions here. He won't send you enough reinforcements, and there are not enough settlers to withstand the shock of a concerted attack from across the river."

"But the Picts are divided into small clans," persisted Balthus. "They'll never unite. We can whip any single clan."

"Or any three or four clans," admitted the slayer. "But some day a man will rise and unite thirty or forty clans, just as was done among the Cimmerians, when the Gundermen tried to push the border northward, years ago. They tried to colonize the southern marches of Cimmeria: destroyed a few small clans, built a fort-town, Venarium, — you've heard the tale."

"So I have indeed," replied Balthus, wincing. The memory of that red disaster was a black blot in the chronicles of a proud and warlike people. "My uncle was at Venarium when the Cimmerians swarmed over the walls. He was one of the few who escaped that slaughter. I've heard him tell the tale, many a time. The barbarians swept out of the hills in a ravening horde, without warning, and stormed Venarium with such fury none could stand before them. Men, women and children were butchered. Venarium was reduced to a mass of charred ruins, as it is to this day. The Aquilonians were driven back across the marches, and have never since tried to colonize the Cimmerian country. But you speak of Venarium familiarly. Perhaps you were there?"

"I was," grunted the other. "I was one of the horde that swarmed over the walls. I hadn't yet seen fifteen snows, but already my name was repeated about the council fires."

Balthus involuntarily recoiled, staring. It seemed incredible that the man walking tranquilly at his side should have been one of those screeching, blood-mad devils that had poured over the walls of Venarium on that long-gone day to make her streets run crimson.

"Then you, too, are a barbarian!" he exclaimed involuntarily.

The other nodded, without taking offense.

"I am Conan, a Cimmerian."

"I've heard of you!" Fresh interest quickened Balthus' gaze. No wonder the Pict had fallen victim to his own sort of subtlety. The Cimmerians were barbarians as ferocious as the Picts, and much more intelligent. Evidently Conan had spent much time among civilized men, though that contact had obviously not softened him, nor weakened any of his primitive instincts. Balthus' apprehension turned to admiration as he marked the easy catlike stride, the effortless silence with which the Cimmerian moved along the trail. The oiled links of his armor did not clink, and Balthus knew Conan could glide through the deepest thicket or most tangled copse as noiselessly as any naked Pict that ever lived.

"You're not a Gunderman?" It was more assertion than question.

Balthus shook his head. "I'm from the Tauran."

"I've seen good woodsmen from the Tauran. But the Bossonians have sheltered you Aquilonians from the outer wildernesses for too many centuries. You need hardening."

That was true; the Bossonian marches, with their fortified villages filled with determined bowmen, had long served Aquilonia as a buffer against the outlying barbarians. Now among the settlers beyond Thunder River there was growing up a breed of forest-men capable of meeting the barbarians at their own game, but their numbers were still scanty. Most of the frontiersmen were like Balthus – more of the settler than the woodsman type.

The sun had not set, but it was no longer in sight, hidden as it was behind the dense forest wall. The shadows were lengthening, deepening back in the woods as the companions strode on down the trail.

"It'll be dark before we reach the fort," commented Conan casually – then: "*Listen!*"

He stopped short, half crouching, sword ready, transformed into a savage figure of suspicion and menace, poised to spring and rend. Balthus had heard it too – a wild scream that broke at its highest note. It was the cry of a man in dire fear or agony.

Conan was off in an instant, racing down the trail, each stride widening the distance between him and his straining companion. Balthus puffed a curse. Among the settlements of the Tauran he was accounted a good runner, but Conan was leaving him behind with an ease which was maddening. Then Balthus forgot his exasperation as his ears were outraged by the most frightful cry he had ever heard. It was not human, this one; it was a demoniacal caterwauling of hideous triumph that seemed to exult over fallen humanity and find echo in black gulfs beyond human ken.

Balthus faltered in his stride and clammy sweat beaded his flesh. But Conan did not hesitate; he darted around a bend in the trail and disappeared, and Balthus, panicky at finding himself alone with that awful scream still shuddering through the forest in grisly echoes, put on an extra burst of speed and plunged after him.

The Aquilonian slid to a stumbling halt, almost colliding with the Cimmerian who stood in the trail over a crumpled body. But Conan was not looking at the corpse which lay there in the crimson-soaked dust. He was glaring into the deep woods on each side of the trail.

Balthus muttered a horrified oath. It was the body of a man which lay there in the trail, a short, fat man, clad in the gilt-worked boots and (despite the heat) the ermine-trimmed tunic of a wealthy merchant. His fat, pale face was set in a stare of frozen horror; his thick throat had been slashed from ear to ear as if by a razor-sharp blade. The short sword still in its scabbard seemed to indicate that he had been struck down without a chance to fight for his life.

"A Pict?" Balthus whispered, as he turned to peer into the deepening shadows of the forest.

Conan shook his head and straightened to scowl down at the dead man.

"A forest devil. This is the fourth, by Crom!"

"What do you mean?"

"Did you ever hear of a Pictish wizard called Zogar Sag?"

Balthus shook his head uneasily.

"He dwells in Gwawela, the nearest village across the river. Three months ago he hid beside this road and stole a string of pack-mules from a pack-train bound for the fort – drugged their drivers, somehow. The mules belonged to this man –" Conan casually indicated the corpse with his foot – "Tiberias, a merchant of Velitrium. They were loaded with ale kegs and old Zogar stopped to guzzle before he got across the river. A woodsman named Soractus trailed him, and led Valannus and a couple of soldiers to where he lay dead drunk in a thicket. At the importunities of Tiberias, Valannus threw Zogar Sag into a cell, which is the worst insult you can give a Pict. He managed to kill his guard and escape, and sent back word that he meant to kill Tiberias and the four men who captured him in a way that would make Aquilonians shudder for centuries to come.

"Well, Soractus and the soldiers are dead. Soractus was killed on the river, the soldiers in the very shadow of the fort. And now Tiberias is dead. No Pict killed any of them. Each victim – except Tiberias, as you see – lacked his head – which no doubt is now ornamenting the altar of Zogar Sag's particular god."

"How do you know they weren't killed by the Picts?" demanded Balthus.

Conan pointed to the corpse of the merchant.

"You think that was done with a knife or a sword? Look closer and you'll see that only a *talon* could have made a gash like that. The flesh is ripped, not cut."

"Perhaps a panther –" began Balthus, without conviction.

Conan shook his head impatiently.

"A man from the Tauran wouldn't mistake the mark of a panther's claws. No. It's a forest devil summoned by Zogar Sag to carry out his revenge. Tiberias was a fool to start for Velitrium alone, and this close to dusk. But each one of the victims seemed to be smitten with madness just before doom overtook him. Look here; the signs are plain enough. Tiberias came riding along the trail on his mule, maybe with a bundle of choice otter pelts behind his saddle to sell in Velitrium, and the *thing* sprang on him from behind that bush. See where the branches are crushed down.

"Tiberias gave one scream, and then his throat was torn open and he was selling his otter skins in Hell. The mule ran away into the woods. Listen! Even now you can hear him thrashing about under the trees. The demon didn't have time to take Tiberias' head; it took fright as we came up."

"As you came up," amended Balthus. "It must not be a very terrible creature if it flees from one armed man. But how do you know it was not a Pict with some kind of a hook that rips instead of slicing? Did you see it?"

"Tiberias was an armed man," grunted Conan. "If Zogar Sag can bring demons to aid him, he can tell them which men to kill and which to let alone. No, I didn't see it. I only saw the bushes shake as it left the trail. But if you want further proof, look here!"

The slayer had stepped into the pool of blood in which the dead man sprawled. Under the bushes at the edge of the path there was a footprint, made in blood on the hard loam.

"Did a man make that?" demanded Conan.

Balthus felt his scalp prickle. Neither man nor any beast that he had ever seen could have left that strange, monstrous three-toed print, that was curiously combined of the bird and the reptile, yet a true type of neither. He spread his fingers above the print, careful not to touch it, and grunted explosively. He could not span the mark.

"What is it?" he whispered. "I never saw a beast that left a spoor like that."

"Nor any other sane man," answered Conan grimly. "It's a swamp demon – Hell, they're thick as bats in the swamps beyond Black River. You can hear them howling like damned souls when the wind blows strong from the south on hot nights."

"What shall we do?" asked the Aquilonian, peering uneasily into the deep blue shadows. The frozen fear on the dead countenance haunted him. He wondered what hideous head the wretch had seen thrust grinning from among the leaves to chill his blood with terror.

"No use to try to follow a demon," grunted Conan, drawing a short woodman's axe from his girdle. "I tried tracking him after he killed Soractus. I lost his trail within a dozen steps. He might have grown himself wings and flown away, or sunk down through the earth to Hell. I don't know. I'm not going after the mule, either. It'll either wander back to the fort, or to some settler's cabin."

As he spoke Conan was busy at the edge of the trail with his axe. With a few strokes he cut a pair of saplings nine or ten feet long, and denuded them of their branches. Then he cut a length from a serpent-like vine that crawled among the bushes near-by, and making one end fast to one of the poles, a couple of feet from the end, whipped the vine over the other sapling and interlaced it back and forth. In a few moments he had a crude but strong litter.

"The demon isn't going to get Tiberias' head if I can help it," he growled. "We'll carry the body into the fort. It isn't more than three miles. I never liked the fat bastard, but we can't have Pictish devils making so cursed free with white men's heads."

The Picts were a white race, though swarthy, but the border men never spoke of them as such.

Balthus took the rear end of the litter, onto which Conan unceremoniously dumped the unfortunate merchant, and they moved on down the trail as swiftly as possible. Conan made no more noise laden with their grim burden than he had made when unencumbered. He had made a loop with the merchant's belt at the end of the poles, and was carrying his share of the load with one hand, while the other gripped his naked broadsword, and his restless gaze roved the sinister walls about them. The shadows were thickening. A darkening blue mist seemed to blur the outlines of the foliage. The forest deepened in the twilight, became a blue haunt of mystery sheltering unguessed things.

They had covered more than a mile, and the muscles in Balthus' sturdy arms were beginning to ache a little, when a cry rang shudderingly from the woods whose blue shadows were deepening into purple.

Conan started convulsively, and Balthus almost let go the poles.

"A woman!" cried the younger man. "Great Mitra, a woman cried out then!"

"A settler's wife straying in the woods," snarled Conan, setting down his end of the litter. "Looking for a cow, probably, and – stay here!"

He dived like a hunting wolf into the leafy wall. Balthus' hair bristled.

"Stay here alone with this corpse and a devil hiding in the woods?" he yelped. "I'm coming with you!"

And suiting action to words, he plunged after the Cimmerian. Conan glanced back at him, but made no objection, though he did not moderate his pace to accommodate the shorter legs of his companion. Balthus wasted his wind in swearing as the Cimmerian drew away from him again, flitting like a phantom between the trees, and then Conan burst into a dim glade and halted crouching, lips snarling, sword lifted.

"What are we stopping for?" panted Balthus, dashing the sweat out of his eyes and gripping his short sword.

"That scream came from this glade, or near by," answered Conan. "I don't mistake the location of sounds, even in the woods. But where –"

Abruptly the sound rang out again – *behind them*; in the direction of the trail they had just quitted. It rose piercingly and pitifully, the cry of a woman in frantic terror – and then, shockingly, it changed to a yell of mocking laughter that might have burst from the lips of a fiend of lower Hell.

"What in Mitra's name –!" Balthus' face was a pale blur in the gloom.

With a scorching oath Conan wheeled and dashed back the way he had come, and the Aquilonian stumbled bewilderedly after him. He blundered into the Cimmerian as the latter stopped dead, and rebounded from his brawny shoulders as though from an iron statue. Gasping from the impact, he heard Conan's breath hiss through his teeth. The Cimmerian seemed frozen in his tracks. Looking over his shoulder, Balthus felt his hair stand up stiffly. Something was moving through the deep bushes that fringed the trail – something that neither walked nor flew, but seemed to glide like a serpent. But it was not a serpent. Its outlines were indistinct, but it was taller than a man, and not very bulky. It gave off a glimmer of weird light, like a faint blue flame. Indeed, the eery fire was the only tangible thing about it. It might have been an embodied flame moving with reason and purpose through the blackening woods.

Conan snarled a savage curse and hurled his axe with ferocious will. But the thing glided on without altering its course. Indeed it was only a few instants' fleeting glimpse they had of it – a tall, shadowy thing of misty flame floating through the thickets. Then it was gone and the forest crouched in breathless stillness.

With a snarl Conan plunged through the intervening foliage and into the trail. His profanity, as Balthus floundered after him, was lurid and impassioned. The Cimmerian was standing over the litter on which lay the body of Tiberias. And that body no longer possessed a head.

"Tricked us with its damnable caterwauling!" raved Conan, swinging his great sword about his head in his wrath. "I might have known! I might have guessed a trick! Now there'll be five heads to decorate Zogar's altar."

"But what thing is it that can cry like a woman and laugh like a devil, and shines like witch-fire as it glides through the trees?" gasped Balthus, mopping the sweat from his pale face.

"A swamp devil," responded Conan morosely. "Grab those poles. We'll take in the body, anyway. At least our load's a bit lighter."

With which grim philosophy he gripped the leather loop and stalked down the trail.

II

THE WIZARD OF GWAWELA

Fort Tuscelan stood on the eastern bank of Black River, the tides of which washed the foot of the stockade. The latter was of logs, as were all the buildings within, including the donjon, to dignify it by that appellation, in which were the governor's quarters, overlooking the stockade and the sullen river. Beyond that river lay a huge forest, which approached jungle-like density along the spongy shores. Men paced the runways along the log parapet day and night, watching that dense green wall. Seldom a menacing figure appeared, but the sentries knew that they too were watched, fiercely, hungrily, with the mercilessness of ancient hate. The forest beyond the river might seem desolate and vacant of life to the ignorant eye, but life teemed there, not alone of bird and beast and reptile, but also of men, the fiercest of all the hunting beasts.

There, at the fort, civilization ended. This was no empty phrase. Fort Tuscelan was indeed the last outpost of a civilized world; it represented the westernmost thrust of the dominant Hyborian races. Beyond the river the primitive still reigned in shadowy forests, brush-thatched huts where hung the grinning skulls of men, and mud-walled enclosures where fires flickered and drums rumbled, and spears were whetted in the hands of dark, silent men with tangled black hair and the eyes of serpents. Those eyes often glared through the bushes at the fort across the river. Once dark-skinned men had built their huts where that fort stood; yes, and their huts had risen where now stood the fields and log-cabins of fair-haired settlers, back beyond Velitrium, that raw, turbulent frontier town on the banks of Thunder River, to the shores of that other river that bounds the Bossonian marches. Traders had come, and priests of Mitra who walked with bare feet and empty hands, and died horribly, most of them; but soldiers had followed, and men with axes in their hands, and women and children in ox-drawn wains. Back to Thunder River, and still back, beyond Black River, the aborigines had been pushed, with slaughter and massacre. But the dark-skinned people did not forget that once Conajohara had been theirs.

The guard inside the eastern gate bawled a challenge. Through a barred aperture torch-light flickered, glinting on a steel head-piece and suspicious eyes beneath it.

"Open the gate," snorted Conan. "You see it's me, don't you?"

Military discipline put his teeth on edge.

The gate swung inward and Conan and his companion passed through. Balthus noted that the gate was flanked by a tower on each side, the summits of which rose above the stockade. He saw loop-holes for arrows.

The guardsmen grunted as they saw the burden borne between the men. Their pikes jangled against each other as they thrust shut the gate, chin on shoulder, and Conan asked testily: "Have you never seen a headless body before?"

The faces of the soldiers were pallid in the torchlight.

"That's Tiberias," blurted one. "I recognize that fur-trimmed tunic. Valerius here owes me five lunas. I told him Tiberias had heard the loon call when he rode through the gate on his mule, with his glassy stare. I wagered he'd come back without his head."

Conan grunted enigmatically, motioned Balthus to ease the litter to the ground, and then strode off toward the governor's quarters, with the Aquilonian at his heels. The tousle-headed youth stared about him eagerly and curiously, noting the rows of barracks along the walls, the stables, the tiny merchants' stalls, the towering blockhouse, and the other buildings, with the open square in the middle where the soldiers drilled, and where, now, fires danced and men off duty lounged. These were now hurrying to join the morbid crowd gathered about the litter at the gate. The rangy figures of Aquilonian pikemen and forest runners mingled with the shorter, stockier forms of Bossonian archers.

He was not greatly surprised that the governor received them himself. Autocratic society with its rigid caste laws lay east of the marches. Valannus was still a young man, well-knit, with a finely-chiselled countenance already carved into sober cast by toil and responsibility.

"You left the fort before daybreak, I was told," he said to Conan. "I had begun to fear that the Picts had caught you at last."

"When they smoke my head the whole river will know it," grunted Conan. "They'll hear Pictish women wailing their dead as far as Velitrium – I was on a lone scout. I couldn't sleep. I kept hearing drums talking across the river."

"They talk each night," reminded the governor, his fine eyes shadowed, as he stared closely at Conan. He had learned the unwisdom of discounting wild men's instincts.

"There was a difference last night," growled Conan. "There has been ever since Zogar Sag got back across the river."

"We should either have given him presents and sent him home, or else hanged him," sighed the governor. "You advised that, but —"

"But it's hard for you Hyborians to learn the ways of the outlands," said Conan. "Well, it can't be helped now, but there'll be no peace on the border so long as Zogar lives and remembers the cell he sweated in. I was following a warrior who slipped over to put a few white notches on his bow. After I split his head I fell in with this lad whose name is Balthus and who's come from the Tauran to help hold the frontier."

Valannus approvingly eyed the young man's frank countenance and strongly-knit frame.

"I am glad to welcome you, young sir. I wish more of your people would come. We need men used to forest life. Many of our soldiers and some of our settlers are from the eastern provinces and know nothing of woodcraft, or even of agricultural life."

"Not many of that breed this side of Velitrium," grunted Conan. "That town's full of them, though. But listen, Valannus, we found Tiberias dead on the trail." And in a few words he related the grisly affair.

Valannus paled.

"I did not know he had left the fort. He must have been mad!"

"He was," answered Conan. "Like the other four; each one, when his time came, went mad and rushed into the woods to meet his death like a hare running down the throat of a python. *Something* called to them from the deeps of the forest, something the men call a loon, for lack of a better name, but only the doomed ones could hear it. Zogar Sag's made a magic Aquilonian civilization can't overcome."

To this thrust Valannus made no reply; he wiped his brow with a shaky hand.

"Do the soldiers know of this?"

"We left the body by the eastern gate."

"You should have concealed the fact — hidden the corpse somewhere in the woods. The soldiers are nervous enough already."

"They'd have found it out some way. If I'd hidden the body, it would have been returned to the fort as the corpse of Soractus was — tied up outside the gate for the men to find in the morning."

Valannus shuddered. Turning, he walked to a casement and stared silently out over the river, black and shiny under the glint of the stars. Beyond the river the jungle rose like an ebony wall. The distant screech of a panther broke the stillness. The night seemed pressing in, blurring the sounds of the soldiers outside the blockhouse, dimming the fires. A wind whispered through the black branches, rippling the dusky water. On its wings came a low, rhythmic pulsing, sinister as the pad of a leopard's foot.

"After all," said Valannus, as if speaking his thoughts aloud, "what do we know — what does anyone know — of the things that jungle may hide? We have dim rumors of great swamps and rivers, and a forest that stretches on and on over everlasting plains and hills to end at last on the shores of the western ocean. But what things lie between this river and that ocean we dare not even guess. No white man has ever plunged deep into that fastness and returned alive to tell us what he found. We are wise in our civilized knowledge, but our knowledge extends just so far – to the western bank of that ancient river! Who knows what shapes earthly and unearthly may lurk beyond the dim circle of light our knowledge has cast?

"Who knows what gods are worshipped under the shadows of that heathen forest, or what devils crawl out of the black ooze of the swamps? Who can be sure that all the inhabitants of that black country are natural? Zogar Sag – a sage of the eastern cities would sneer at his primitive magic-making as the mummery of a fakir; yet he has driven mad and killed five men in a manner no man can explain. I wonder if he himself is wholly human."

"If I can get within axe-throwing distance of him I'll settle that question," growled Conan, helping himself to the governor's wine and pushing a glass toward Balthus, who took it hesitatingly, and with an uncertain glance toward Valannus.

The governor turned toward Conan and stared at him thoughtfully.

"The soldiers, who do not believe in ghosts or devils," he said, "are almost in a panic of fear. You, who believe in ghosts, ghouls, goblins, and all manner of uncanny things, do not seem to fear any of the things in which you believe."

"There's nothing in the universe cold steel won't cut," answered Conan. "I threw my axe at the demon, and he took no hurt, but I might have missed, in the dusk, or a branch deflected its flight. I'm not going out of my way looking for devils; but I wouldn't step out of my path to let one go by."

Valannus lifted his head and met Conan's gaze squarely.

"Conan, more depends on you than you realize. You know the weakness of this province – a slender wedge thrust into the untamed wilderness. You know that the lives of all the people west of the marches depend on this fort. Were it to fall, red axes would be splintering the gates of Velitrium before a horseman could cross the marches. His majesty, or his majesty's advisers, have ignored my pleas that more troops be sent to hold the frontier. They know nothing of border conditions, and are averse to expending any more money in this direction. The fate of the frontier depends upon the men who now hold it."

"You know that most of the army which conquered Conajohara has been withdrawn. You know the force left me is inadequate, especially since that devil Zogar Sag managed to poison our water supply, and forty men died in one day. Many of the others are sick, or have been bitten by serpents or mauled by wild beasts which seem to swarm in increasing numbers in the vicinity of the fort. The soldiers believe Zogar's boast that he could summon the forest beasts to slay his enemies.

"I have three hundred pikemen, four hundred Bossonian archers, and perhaps fifty men, who, like yourself, are skilled in woodcraft. They are worth ten times their number of soldiers, but there are so few of them – frankly, Conan, my situation is becoming precarious. The soldiers whisper of desertion; they are low spirited, believing Zogar Sag has loosed devils on us. They fear the black plague with which he threatened us – the terrible black death of the swamplands. When I see a sick soldier I sweat with fear of seeing him turn black and shrivel and die before my eyes.

"Conan, if the plague is loosed upon us, the soldiers will desert in a body! The border will be left unguarded and nothing will check the sweep of the dark-skinned hordes to the very gates of Velitrium – maybe beyond! If we can not hold the fort, how can they hold the town?

"Conan, Zogar Sag must die, if we are to hold Conajohara! You have penetrated the unknown deeper than any other man in the fort; you know where Gwawela stands, and something of the forest trails across the river. Will you take a band of men tonight and endeavor to kill or capture him? Oh, I know it's mad. There isn't more than one chance in a thousand that any of you will come back alive. But if we don't get him, it's death for us all. You can take as many men as you wish."

"A dozen men are better for a job like that than a regiment," answered Conan. "Five hundred men couldn't fight their way to Gwawela and back. But a dozen might slip in and out again. Let me pick my men. I don't want any soldiers."

"Let me go!" eagerly exclaimed Balthus. "I've hunted deer all my life on the Tauran."

"All right. Valannus, we'll eat at the stall where the foresters gather, and I'll pick my men. We'll start within an hour, drop down the river in a boat to a point below the village and then steal upon it through the woods. If we live, we should be back by daybreak."

III

THE CRAWLERS IN THE DARK

The river was a vague trace between walls of ebony. The paddles that propelled the long boat creeping along in the dense shadow of the eastern bank dipped softly into the water making no more noise than the beak of a heron. The broad shoulders of the man in front of Balthus were a blur in the dense gloom. He knew not even the keen eyes of the man who knelt in the prow could discern anything more than a few feet ahead of them. Conan was feeling his way by instinct and an intensive familiarity with the river.

No one spoke. Balthus had had a good look at his companions in the fort before they slipped out of the stockade and down the bank into the waiting canoe. They were of a new breed growing up in the world on the raw edge of the frontier – men whom grim necessity had taught woodcraft. Aquilonians of the western provinces to a man, they had many points in common. They dressed alike – in buckskin boots, leathern breeks and deer-skin shirts, with broad girdles that held axes and short swords; and they were all gaunt and scarred and hard-eyed; sinewy and taciturn.

They were wild men, of a sort, yet there was still a wide gulf between them and the Cimmerian. They were sons of civilization, reverted to a semi-barbarism. He was a barbarian of a thousand generations of barbarians. They had acquired stealth and craft, but he had been born to these things. He excelled them even in lithe economy of motion. They were wolves, but he was a tiger.

Balthus admired them and their leader and felt a pulse of pride that he was admitted into their company. He was proud that his paddle made no more noise than did theirs. In that respect at least he was their equal, though woodcraft learned in hunts on the Tauran could never equal that ground into the souls of men on the savage border.

Below the fort the river made a wide bend. The lights of the outpost were quickly lost, but the canoe held on its way for nearly a mile, avoiding snags and floating logs with almost uncanny precision.

Then a low grunt from their leader, and they swung its head about and glided toward the opposite shore. Emerging from the black shadows of the brush that fringed the bank and coming into the open of the mid-stream created a peculiar illusion of rash exposure. But the stars gave little light, and Balthus knew that unless one were watching for it, it would be all but impossible for the keenest eye to make out the shadowy shape of the canoe crossing the river.

They swung in under the overhanging bushes of the western shore and Balthus groped for and found a projecting root which he grasped. No word was spoken. All instructions had been given before the scouting party left the fort. As silently as a great panther Conan slid over the side and vanished in the bushes. Equally noiseless, nine men followed him. To Balthus, grasping the root with his paddle across his knees, it seemed incredible that ten men should thus fade into the tangled forest with no more sound than these made.

He settled himself to wait. No word passed between him and the other man who had been left with him. Somewhere, a mile or so to the north west, Zogar Sag's village stood girdled by the thick woods. Balthus understood his orders; he and his companion were to wait for the return of the raiding party. If Conan and his men had not returned by the first tinge of dawn, then they were to race back up the river to the fort and report that the forest had again taken its immemorial toll of the invading race.

The silence was oppressive. No sound came from the black woods, invisible beyond the ebony masses that were the overhanging bushes. Balthus no longer heard the drums. They had been silent for hours. He kept blinking, unconsciously trying to see through the deep gloom. The dank night-smells of the river and the damp forest oppressed him. Somewhere, nearby, there was a sound as if a big fish had flopped and splashed the water. Balthus thought it must have leaped so close to the canoe that it had struck the side, for a slight quiver vibrated the craft. The boat's stern began to swing slightly away from the shore. The man behind him must have let go of the projection he was gripping. Balthus twisted his head to hiss a warning, and could just make out the figure of his companion, a slightly blacker bulk in the blackness.

The man did not reply. Wondering if he had fallen asleep, Balthus reached out and grasped his shoulder. To his amazement, the man crumpled under his touch and

slumped down in the canoe. Twisting his body half about Balthus groped for him, his heart shooting into his throat. His fumbling fingers slid over the man's throat – only the youth's convulsive clenching of his jaws choked back the cry that rose in his throat. His fingers encountered a gaping, oozing wound – his companion's throat had been cut from ear to ear.

In that instant of horror and panic Balthus started up – and then a muscular arm out of the darkness locked fiercely about his throat, strangling his yell. The canoe rocked wildly. Balthus' knife was in his hand, though he did not remember jerking it out of his boot, and he stabbed fiercely and blindly. He felt the blade sink deep, and a fiendish yell rang in his ear, a yell that was horribly answered. The darkness seemed to come to life about him. A bestial clamor rose on all sides, and other arms grappled him. Borne under a mass of hurtling bodies the canoe rolled sidewise, but before he went under with it, something cracked against Balthus' head and the night was briefly illuminated by a blinding burst of fire before it gave way to a blackness where not even stars shone.

IV

The Beasts of Zogar-Sag

Fires dazzled Balthus again as he slowly recovered his senses. He blinked, shook his head. Their glare hurt his eyes. A confused medley of sound rose about him, growing more distinct as his senses cleared. He lifted his head and stared stupidly about him. Black figures hemmed him in, etched against crimson tongues of flame.

Memory and understanding came in a rush. He was bound upright to a post in an open space, ringed by fierce and terrible figures. Beyond that ring fires burned, tended by naked, dark-skinned women. Beyond the fires he saw huts of mud and wattle, thatched with brush. Beyond the huts there was a stockade with a broad gate. But he saw these things only incidentally. Even the cryptic dark women with their curious coiffures were noted by him only absently. His full attention was fixed in awful fascination on the men who stood glaring at him.

Short men, broad-shouldered, deep-chested, lean-hipped. They were naked except for scanty loin clouts. The firelight brought out the play of their swelling muscles in bold relief. Their dark faces were immobile, but their narrow eyes glittered with the fire that burns in the eyes of a stalking tiger. Their tangled manes were bound back with bands of copper. Swords and axes were in their hands. Crude bandages banded the limbs of some, and smears of blood were dried on their dark skins. There had been fighting, recent and deadly.

His eyes wavered away from the steady glare of his captors, and he repressed a cry of horror. A few feet away there rose a low, hideous pyramid: it was built of gory human heads. Dead eyes glared glassily up at the black sky. Numbly he recognized the countenances which were turned toward him. They were the heads of the men who had followed Conan into the forest. He could not tell if the Cimmerian's head were among them. Only a few faces were visible to him. It looked to him as if there must be ten or eleven heads at least. A deadly sickness assailed him. He fought a desire to retch. Beyond the heads lay the bodies of half a dozen Picts, and he was aware of a fierce exultation at the sight. The forest runners had taken toll, at least.

Twisting his head away from the ghastly spectacle, he became aware that another post stood near him – a stake painted black as was the one to which he was bound. A man sagged in his bonds there, naked except for his leathern breeks, whom Balthus recognized as one of Conan's woodsmen. Blood trickled from his mouth, oozed sluggishly from a gash in his side. Lifting his head he licked his livid lips and muttered, making himself heard with difficulty above the fiendish clamor of the Picts: "So they got you, too!"

"Sneaked up in the water and cut the other fellow's throat," groaned Balthus. "We never heard them till they were on us. Mitra, how can anything move so silently?"

"They're devils," mumbled the frontiersman. "They must have been watching us from the time we left mid-stream. We walked into a trap. Arrows from all sides were ripping into us before we knew it. Most of us dropped the first fire. Three or four broke through the bushes and came to hand-grips. But there were too many. Conan might have gotten away. I haven't seen his head. Been better for you and me if they'd killed us outright. I can't blame Conan. Ordinarily we'd have gotten to the village without being discovered. They don't keep spies on the river bank as far down as we landed. We must have stumbled into a big party coming up the river from the south. Some devilment is up. Too many Picts here. These aren't all Gwaweli; men from the western tribes here and from up and down the river."

Balthus stared at the ferocious shapes. Little as he knew of Pictish ways, he was aware that the number of men clustered about them was out of proportion to the size of the village. There were not enough huts to have accommodated them all. Then he noticed that there was a difference in the barbaric tribal designs painted on their faces and breasts.

"Some kind of devilment," muttered the forest runner. "They might have gathered here to watch Zogar's magic-making. He'll make some rare magic with our carcasses. Well, a border-man doesn't expect to die in bed. But I wish we'd gone out along with the rest."

The wolfish howling of the Picts rose in volume and exultation, and from a movement in their ranks, an eager surging and crowding, Balthus deduced that someone of importance was coming. Twisting his head about he saw that the stakes were set before a long building, larger than the other huts, decorated by human skulls dangling from the eaves. Through the door of that structure now danced a fantastic figure.

"Zogar!" muttered the woodsman, his bloody countenance set in wolfish lines as he unconsciously strained at his cords. Balthus saw a lean figure of middle height, almost hidden in ostrich plumes set on a harness of leather and copper. From amidst the plumes peered a hideous and malevolent face. The plumes puzzled Balthus. He knew their source lay half the width of a world to the south. They fluttered and rustled evilly as the shaman leaped and cavorted.

With fantastic bounds and prancings he entered the ring and whirled before his bound and silent captives. With another man it would have seemed ridiculous – a foolish savage prancing meaninglessly in a whirl of feathers. But that ferocious face glaring out from the billowing mass gave the scene a grim significance. No man with a face like that could seem ridiculous or like anything except the devil he was.

Suddenly he froze to statuesque stillness; the plumes rippled once and sank about him. The howling warriors fell silent. Zogar Sag stood erect and motionless, and he seemed to increase in height – to grow and expand. Balthus experienced the illusion that the Pict was towering above him, staring contemptuously down from a great height, though he knew the shaman was not as tall as himself. He shook off the illusion with difficulty.

The shaman was talking now, a harsh, guttural intonation that yet carried the hiss of a cobra. He thrust his head on his long neck toward the wounded man on the stake; his eyes shone red as blood in the firelight. For answer the frontiersman spat full in his face.

With a fiendish howl Zogar bounded convulsively into the air, and the warriors gave tongue to a yell that shuddered up to the stars that peered over the tops of the great trees girdling the village. They rushed toward the man on the stake, but the shaman beat them back. A snarled command sent men running to the gate. They hurled it open, turned and raced back to the circle. The ring of men split, divided with desperate haste to right and left. Balthus saw the women and naked children scurrying to the huts. They peeked out of doors and windows. A broad lane was left to the open gate beyond which loomed the black forest, crowding sullenly in upon the clearing, unlighted by the fires.

A tense silence reigned as Zogar Sag turned toward the forest, raised on his tip-toes and sent a weird inhuman call shuddering out into the night. Somewhere, far out in the black forest, a deeper cry answered him. Balthus shuddered. From the timbre of that cry he knew it never came from a human throat. He remembered what Valannus had said – that Zogar boasted that he could summon wild beasts to do his bidding. The woodsman was livid beneath his mask of blood. He licked his lips spasmodically.

The village held its breath. Zogar Sag stood still as a statue, his plumes trembling faintly about him. But suddenly the gate was no longer empty.

A shuddering gasp swept over the village and men crowded hastily back, jamming each other between the huts. Balthus felt the short hair stir on his scalp. The creature that stood in the gate was like the embodiment of nightmare legend. Its color was of a curious pale quality which made it seem ghostly and unreal in the dim light. But there was nothing unreal about the low-hung savage head, and the great curved fangs that glistened in the firelight. On noiseless padded feet it approached like a phantom out of the past. It was a survival of an older, grimmer age, the ogre of many an ancient legend – a saber-tooth tiger. No Hyborian hunter had looked upon one of those primordial brutes for centuries. Immemorial myths lent the creatures a supernatural quality, induced by their ghostly color and their fiendish ferocity.

The beast that glided toward the men on the stakes was longer and heavier than a common, striped tiger, almost as bulky as a bear. Its shoulders and forelegs were so massive and mightily muscled as to give it a curiously top-heavy look, though its hind-quarters were more powerful than those of a lion. Its jaws were massive, but its head was brutishly shaped. Its brain capacity was small. It had room for no instincts except those of destruction. It was a freak of carnivorous development; evolution run amuck in a horror of fangs and talons.

This was the monstrosity Zogar Sag had summoned out of the forest. Balthus no longer doubted the actuality of the shaman's magic. Only the black arts could establish a domination over that tiny-brained, mightily-thewed monster. Like a whisper at the back of his consciousness rose the vague memory of the name of an ancient, ancient god of darkness and primordial fear, to whom once both men and beasts bowed and whose children – men whispered – still lurked in dark corners of the world. New horror tinged the glare he fixed on Zogar Sag.

The monster moved past the heap of bodies and the pile of gory heads without appearing to notice them. He was no scavenger. He hunted only the living, in a life dedicated solely to slaughter. An awful hunger burned greenly in the wide, unwinking eyes; the hunger not alone of belly-emptiness, but the lust of death-dealing. His gaping jaws slavered. The shaman stepped back; his hand waved toward the woodsman.

The great cat sank into a crouch and Balthus numbly remembered tales of its appalling ferocity: of how it would spring upon an elephant and drive its sword-like fangs so deeply into the titan's skull that they could never be withdrawn, but would keep it nailed to its victim, to die by starvation. The shaman cried out shrilly – and with an ear-shattering roar the monster sprang.

Balthus had never dreamed of such a spring, such a hurtling of incarnated destruction embodied in that giant bulk of iron thews and ripping talons. Full on the woodsman's breast it struck, and the stake splintered and snapped at the base, crashing to the earth under the impact. Then the saber-tooth was gliding toward the gate, half dragging, half carrying a hideous crimson hulk that only faintly resembled a man. Balthus glared almost paralyzed, his brain refusing to credit what his eyes had seen.

In that leap the great beast had not only broken off the stake, it had ripped the mangled body of its victim from the post to which it was bound. The huge talons in that instant of contact had disembowelled and partially dismembered the man, and the giant fangs had torn away the whole top of his head, shearing through the skull as easily as through flesh. Stout rawhide thongs had given way like paper; where the thongs had held, flesh and bones had not. Balthus retched suddenly. He had hunted bears and panthers, but he had never dreamed the beast lived which could make such a red ruin of a human frame in the flicker of an instant.

The saber-tooth vanished through the gate and a few moments later a deep roar sounded through the forest, receding in the distance. But the Picts still shrank back against the huts, and the shaman still stood facing the gate that was like a black opening to let in the night.

Cold sweat burst suddenly out on Balthus' skin. What new horror would come through that gate to make carrion-meat of *his* body? Sick panic assailed him and he strained futilely at his thongs. The night pressed in very black and horrible outside the firelight. The fires themselves glowed lurid as the fires of hell. He felt the eyes of the Picts upon him — hundreds of hungry, cruel eyes that reflected the lust of souls utterly without humanity as he knew it. They no longer seemed men; they were devils of this black jungle, as inhuman as the creatures to which the fiend in the nodding plumes screamed through the darkness.

Zogar sent another call shuddering through the night, and it was utterly unlike the first cry. There was a hideous sibilance in it — Balthus turned cold at the implication. If a serpent could hiss that loud, it would make just such a sound.

This time there was no answer — only a period of breathless silence in which the pound of Balthus' heart strangled him; and then there sounded a swishing outside the gate, a dry rustling that sent chills down Balthus' spine. Again the fire-lit gate held a hideous occupant.

Again Balthus recognized the monster from ancient legends. He saw and knew the ancient and evil serpent which swayed there, its wedge-shaped head, huge as that of a horse, as high as a tall man's head, and its palely gleaming barrel rippling out behind it. A forked tongue darted in and out, and the firelight glittered on bared fangs.

Balthus became incapable of emotion. The horror of his fate paralyzed him. That was the reptile that the ancients called Ghost Snake, the pale, abominable terror that of old glided into huts by night to devour whole families. Like the

python it crushed its victim, but unlike other constrictors its fangs bore venom that carried madness and death. It too had long been considered extinct. But Valannus had spoken truly. No white man knew what shapes haunted the great forests beyond Black River.

It came on silently, rippling over the ground, its hideous head on the same level, its neck curving back slightly for the stroke. Balthus gazed with glazed, hypnotized stare into that loathsome gullet down which he would soon be engulfed, and he was aware of no sensation except a vague nausea.

And then something that glinted in the firelight streaked from the shadows of the huts, and the great reptile whipped about and went into instant convulsions. As in a dream Balthus saw a short throwing spear transfixing the mighty neck, just below the gaping jaws; the shaft protruded from one side, the steel head from the other.

Knotting and looping hideously, the maddened reptile rolled into the circle of men who strove back from him. The spear had not severed its spine, but merely transfixed its great neck muscles. Its furiously lashing tail mowed down a dozen men and its jaws snapped convulsively, splashing others with venom that burned like liquid fire. Howling, cursing, screaming, frantic, they scattered before it, knocking each other down in their flight, trampling the fallen, bursting through the huts. The giant snake rolled into a fire, scattering sparks and brands, and the pain lashed it to more frenzied efforts. A hut wall buckled under the ram-like impact of its flailing tail, disgorging howling people.

Men stampeded through the fires, knocking the logs right and left. The flames sprang up, then sank. A reddish dim glow was all that lighted that nightmare scene where the giant reptile whipped and rolled and men clawed and shrieked in frantic flight.

Balthus felt something jerk at his wrists and then, miraculously, he was free, and a strong hand dragged him behind the post. Dazedly he saw Conan, felt the forest man's iron grip on his arm.

There was blood on the Cimmerian's mail, dried blood on the sword in his right hand; he loomed dim and gigantic in the shadowy light.

"Come on! Before they get over their panic!"

Balthus felt the haft of an axe shoved into his hand. Zogar Sag had disappeared. Conan dragged Balthus after him until the youth's numb brain awoke, and his legs began to move of their own accord. Then Conan released him and ran into the building where the skulls hung. Balthus followed him. He got a glimpse of a grim stone altar, faintly lighted by the glow outside; five human heads grinned on that altar, and there was a grisly familiarity about the features of the freshest; it was the head of the merchant Tiberias. Behind the altar was an idol, dim, indistinct, bestial, yet vaguely man-like in outline. Then fresh horror choked Balthus as the shape heaved up suddenly with a rattle of chains, lifting long misshapen arms in the gloom.

Conan's sword flailed down, crunching through flesh and bone, and then the Cimmerian was dragging Balthus around the altar, past a huddled shaggy bulk on the floor, to a door at the back of the long hut. Through this they burst, out into the enclosure again. But a few yards beyond them loomed the stockade.

It was dark behind the altar-hut. The mad stampede of the Picts had not carried them in that direction. At the wall Conan halted, gripped Balthus and heaved him at arms' length in the air as he might have lifted a child. Balthus grasped the points of the upright logs set in the sun-dried mud and scrambled up on them, ignoring the havoc done his skin. He lowered a hand to the Cimmerian, when around the corner of the altar-hut sprang a fleeing Pict. He halted short, glimpsing the man on the wall in the faint glow of the fires. Conan hurled his axe with deadly aim, but the warrior's mouth was already open for a yell of warning, and it rang loud above the din, cut short as he dropped with a shattered skull.

Blind terrors had not submerged all ingrained instincts. As that wild yell rose above the clamor, there was an instant's lull, and then a hundred throats bayed ferocious answer and warriors came leaping to repel the attack presaged by the warning.

Conan leaped high, caught, not Balthus' hand but his arm near the shoulder, and swung himself up. Balthus set his teeth against the strain, and then the Cimmerian was on the wall beside him, and the fugitives dropped down on the other side.

V

THE CHILDREN OF JHEBBAL SAG

"Which way is the river?" Balthus was confused.

"We don't dare try for the river now," grunted Conan. "The woods between the village and the river are swarming with warriors. Come on! We'll head in the last direction they'll expect us to go – west!"

Looking back as they entered the thick growth, Balthus beheld the wall dotted with black heads as the savages peered over. The Picts were bewildered. They had not gained the wall in time to see the fugitives take cover. They had rushed to the wall expecting to repel an attack in force. They had seen the body of the dead warrior. But no enemy was in sight.

Balthus realized that they did not yet know their prisoner had escaped. From other sounds he believed that the warriors, directed by the shrill voice of Zogar Sag, were destroying the wounded serpent with arrows. The monster was out of the shaman's control. A moment later the quality of the yells was altered. Screeches of rage rose in the night.

Conan laughed grimly. He was leading Balthus along a narrow trail that ran west under the black branches, stepping as swiftly and surely as if he trod a well-lighted thoroughfare. Balthus stumbled after him, guiding himself by feeling the dense wall on either hand.

"They'll be after us now. Zogar's discovered you're gone, and he knows my head wasn't in the pile before the altar-hut. The dog! If I'd had another spear I'd have thrown it through him before I struck the snake. Keep to the trail. They can't track us by torchlight, and there are a score of paths leading from the village. They'll follow those leading to the river first – throw a cordon of warriors for miles along the bank, expecting us to try to break through. We won't take to the woods until we have to. We can make better time on this trail. Now buckle down to it and run as you never ran before."

"They got over their panic cursed quick!" panted Balthus, complying with a fresh burst of speed.

"They're not afraid of anything, very long," grunted Conan.

For a space nothing was said between them. The fugitives devoted all their attention to covering distance. They were plunging deeper and deeper into the wilderness and getting further away from civilization at every step, but Balthus did not question Conan's wisdom. The Cimmerian presently took time to grunt: "When we're far enough away from the village we'll swing back to the river in a big circle. No other village within miles of Gwawela. All the Picts are gathered in that vicinity. We'll circle wide around them. They can't track us until daylight. They'll pick up our path then, but before dawn we'll leave the trail and take to the woods."

They plunged on. The yells died out behind them. Balthus' breath was whistling through his teeth. He felt a pain in his side. Running became torture. He blundered against the bushes on each side of the trail. Conan pulled up suddenly, turned and stared back down the dim path.

Somewhere the moon was rising, a dim white glow amidst a tangle of branches.

"Shall we take to the woods?" panted Balthus.

"Give me your axe," murmured Conan softly. "Something is close behind us."

"Then we'd better leave the trail!" exclaimed Balthus.

Conan shook his head and drew his companion into a dense thicket. The moon rose higher, making a dim light in the path.

"We can't fight the whole tribe!" whispered Balthus.

"No human being could have found our trail so quickly, or followed us so swiftly," muttered Conan. "Keep silent."

There followed a tense silence in which Balthus felt that his heart could be heard pounding for miles away. Then abruptly, without a sound to announce its coming, a savage head appeared in the dim path. Balthus' heart jumped into his throat; at first glance he feared to look upon the awful head of the saber-tooth. But this head was smaller, more narrow; it was a leopard which stood there, snarling silently and glaring down the trail. What wind there was was blowing toward the hiding men, concealing their scent. The beast lowered his head and snuffed the trail, then moved forward uncertainly. A chill played down Balthus' spine. The brute was undoubtedly trailing them.

And it was suspicious. It lifted its head, its eyes glowing like balls of fire, and growled low in its throat. And at that instant Conan hurled the axe.

All the weight of arm and shoulder was behind the throw, and the axe was a streak of silver in the dim moon. Almost before he realized what had happened, Balthus saw the leopard rolling on the ground in its death-throes, the handle of the axe standing up from its head. The head of the weapon had split its narrow skull.

Conan bounded from the bushes, wrenched his axe free and dragged the limp body in among the trees, concealing it from the casual glance.

"Now let's go and go fast!" he grunted, leading the way southward, away from the trail. "There'll be warriors coming after that cat. As soon as he got his wits back Zogar sent him after us. The Picts would follow him, but he'd leave them far behind. He'd circle the village until he hit our trail and then come after us like a streak. They couldn't keep up with him, but they'll have an idea as to our general direction. They'd follow, listening for his cry. Well, they won't hear that, but they'll find the blood on the trail, and look around and find the body in the brush. They'll pick up our spoor there, if they can. Walk with care."

He avoided clinging briars and low hanging branches effortlessly, gliding between trees without touching the stems and always planting his feet in the places calculated to show less evidence of his passing; but with Balthus it was slower, more laborious work.

No sound came from behind them. They had covered more than a mile when Balthus said: "Does Zogar Sag catch leopard-cubs and train them for blood-hounds?"

Conan shook his head. "That was a leopard he called out of the woods."

"But," Balthus persisted, "if he can order the beasts to do his bidding, why doesn't he rouse them all and have them after us? The forest is full of leopards; why send only one after us?"

Conan did not reply for a space, and when he did it was with a curious reticence.

"He can't command all the animals. Only such as remember Jhebbal Sag."

"Jhebbal Sag?" Balthus repeated the ancient name hesitantly. He had never heard it spoken more than three or four times in his whole life.

"Once all living things worshipped him. That was long ago, when beasts and men spoke one language. Men have forgotten him; even the beasts forget. Only a few remember. The men who remember Jhebbal Sag and the beasts who remember are brothers and speak the same tongue."

Balthus did not reply; he had strained at a Pictish stake and seen the nighted jungle give up its fanged horrors at a shaman's call.

"Civilized men laugh," said Conan. "But not one can tell me how Zogar Sag can call pythons and tigers and leopards out of the wilderness and make them do his bidding. They would say it is a lie, if they dared. That's the way with civilized men.

When they can't explain something by their half-baked science, they refuse to believe it."

The people on the Tauran were closer to the primitive than most Aquilonians; superstitions persisted, whose sources were lost in antiquity. And Balthus had seen that which still prickled his flesh. He could not refute the monstrous thing which Conan's words implied.

"I've heard that there's an ancient grove sacred to Jhebbal Sag somewhere in this forest," said Conan. "I don't know. I've never seen it. But more beasts *remember* in this country than any I've ever seen."

"Then others will be on our trail?"

"They are now," was Conan's disquieting answer. "Zogar would never leave our tracking to one beast alone."

"What are we to do, then?" asked Balthus uneasily, grasping his axe as he stared at the gloomy arches above them. His flesh crawled with the momentary expectation of ripping talons and fangs leaping from the shadows.

"Wait!"

Conan turned, squatted and with his knife began scratching a curious symbol in the mold. Stooping to look at it over his shoulder, Balthus felt a crawling of the flesh along his spine, he knew not why. He felt no wind against his face, but there was a rustling of leaves above them and a weird moaning swept ghostlily through the branches. Conan glanced up inscrutably, then rose and stood staring somberly down at the symbol he had drawn.

"What is it?" whispered Balthus. It looked archaic and meaningless to him. He supposed that it was his ignorance of artistry which prevented his identifying it as one of the conventional designs of some prevailing culture. But had he been the most erudite artist in the world, he would have been no nearer the solution.

"I saw it carved in the rock of a cave no human had visited for a million years," muttered Conan. "In the uninhabited mountains beyond the Sea of Vilayet, half a world away from this spot. Later I saw a black witch-finder of Kush scratch it in the sand of a nameless river. He told me part of its meaning – it's sacred to Jhebbal Sag and the creatures which worship him. Watch!"

They drew back among the dense foliage some yards away and waited in tense silence. To the east drums muttered and somewhere to north and west other drums answered. Balthus shivered, though he knew long miles of black forest separated him from the grim beaters of those drums whose dull pulsing was a sinister overture that set the dark stage for bloody drama.

Balthus found himself holding his breath. Then with a slight shaking of the leaves, the bushes parted and a magnificent panther came into view. The moonlight dappling through the leaves shone on its glossy coat rippling with the play of the great muscles beneath it.

With its head held low it glided toward them. It was smelling out their trail. Then it halted as if frozen, its muzzle almost touching the symbol cut in the mold. For a long space it crouched motionless; it flattened its long body and laid its head on the ground before the mark. And Balthus felt the short hairs stir on his scalp. For the attitude of the great carnivore was one of awe and adoration.

Then the panther rose and backed away carefully, belly almost to the ground. With his hind-quarters among the bushes he wheeled as if in sudden panic and was gone like a flash of dappled light.

Balthus mopped his brow with a trembling hand and glanced at Conan.

The barbarian's eyes were smoldering with fires that never lit the eyes of men bred to the ideas of civilization. In that instant he was all wild, and had forgotten the man at his side. In his burning gaze Balthus glimpsed and vaguely recognized pristine images and half-embodied memories, shadows from Life's dawn, forgotten and repudiated by sophisticated races – ancient, primeval phantasms unnamed and nameless.

Then the deeper fires were masked and Conan was silently leading the way deeper into the forest.

"We've no more to fear from the beasts," he said after awhile. "But we've left a sign for men to read. They won't follow our trail very easily, and until they find that symbol they won't know for sure we've turned south. Even then it won't be easy to smell us without the beasts to aid them. But the woods south of the trail will be full of warriors looking for us. If we keep moving after daylight, we'll be sure to run into some of them. As soon as we find a good place we'll hide and wait until another night to swing back and make the river. We've got to warn Valannus, but it won't help him any if we get ourselves killed."

"Warn Valannus?"

"Hell, the woods along the river are swarming with Picts! That's why they got us. Zogar's brewing war-magic; no mere raid this time. He's done something no Pict has done in my memory – united as many as fifteen or sixteen clans. His magic did it; they'll follow a wizard farther than they will a war-chief. You saw the mob in the village; and there were hundreds hiding along the river bank that you didn't see. More coming, from the farther villages. He'll have at least three thousand fighting men. I lay in the bushes and heard their talk as they went past. They mean to attack the fort. When, I don't know, but they won't delay long. Zogar doesn't dare. He's gathered them and whipped them into a frenzy. If he doesn't lead them into battle quickly, they'll fall to quarreling with each other. They're like blood-mad tigers.

"I don't know whether they can take the fort or not. Anyway, we've got to get back across the river and give the warning. The settlers on the Velitrium road must either get into the fort or back to Velitrium. While the Picts are besieging the fort, war-parties will range the road far to the east – might even cross Thunder River and raid the thickly settled country behind Velitrium."

As he talked he was leading the way deeper and deeper into the ancient wilderness. Presently he grunted with satisfaction. They had reached a spot where the underbrush was more scattered, and an outcropping of stone was visible, wandering off southward. Balthus felt more secure as they followed it. Not even a Pict could trail them over naked rock.

"How did you get away?" he asked presently.

Conan tapped his mail shirt and helmet.

"If more borderers would wear harness there'd be fewer skulls hanging on the altar-huts. But most men make noise if they wear armor. They were waiting on each side of the path, without moving. And when a Pict stands motionless, the very beasts of the forest pass him without seeing him. They'd seen us crossing the river and got in their places. If they'd gone into ambush after we left the bank, I'd have had some hint of it. But they were waiting and not even a leaf trembled. The devil himself couldn't have suspected anything. The first suspicion I had was when I heard a shaft rasp against a bow as it was pulled back. I dropped and yelled for the men behind me to drop, but they were too slow – taken by surprize like that.

"Most of them fell at the first volley that raked us from both sides. Some of the arrows crossed the trail and struck Picts on the other side. I heard them howl." He grinned with vicious satisfaction. "Such of us as were left plunged into the woods and closed with them. When I saw the others were all down or taken, I broke through and outfooted the painted devils through the darkness. They were all around me. I ran and crawled and sneaked and sometimes I lay on my belly under the bushes while they passed me on all sides.

"I tried for the shore and found it lined with them, waiting for just such a move. But I'd have cut my way through and taken a chance on swimming, only I heard the drums pounding in the village and knew they'd taken somebody alive.

"They were all so engrossed in Zogar's magic that I was able to climb the wall behind the altar-hut. There was a warrior supposed to be watching at that point, but he was squatting behind the hut and peering around the corner at the ceremony. I came up behind him and broke his neck with my hands before he knew what was happening. It was his spear I threw into the snake, and that's his axe you're carrying."

"But what was that – that thing you killed in the altar-hut?" asked Balthus, with a shiver at the memory of the dim-seen horror.

"One of Zogar's gods. One of Jhebbal's children that didn't remember and had to be kept chained to the altar. A bull ape. The Picts think they're sacred to the Hairy One who lives on the moon – the gorilla-god of Gullah.

"It's getting light. Here's a good place to hide until we see how close they're on our trail. Probably have to wait until night to break back to the river."

A low hill pitched upward, girdled and covered by thick trees and bushes. Near the crest Conan slid into a tangle of jutting rocks, crowned by dense bushes. Lying among them they could see the jungle below without being seen. It was a good place to hide or defend. Balthus did not believe that even a Pict could have trailed them over the rocky ground for the past four or five miles, but he was afraid of the beasts that obeyed Zogar Sag. His faith in the curious symbol wavered a little now. But Conan had dismissed the possibility of beasts tracking them.

A ghostly whiteness spread through the dense branches; the patches of sky visible altered in hue – grew from pink to blue. Balthus felt the gnawing of hunger, though he had slaked his thirst at a stream they had skirted. There was complete silence, except for an occasional chirp of a bird. The drums were no longer to be heard. Balthus' thoughts reverted to the grim scene before the altar-hut.

"Those were ostrich plumes Zogar Sag wore," he said. "I've seen them on the helmets of knights who rode from the East to visit the barons of the marches. There are no ostriches in this forest, are there?"

"They came from Kush," answered Conan. "West of here, many marches, lies the sea-shore. Ships from Zingara occasionally come and trade weapons and ornaments and wine to the coastal tribes for skins and copper ore and gold dust. Sometimes they trade ostrich plumes they got from the Stygians, who in turn got them from the black tribes of Kush, which lies south of Stygia. The Pictish shamans place great store by them. But there's much risk in such trade. The Picts are too likely to try to seize the ship. And the coast is dangerous to ships. I've sailed along it when I was with the pirates of the Barachan Isles, which lie southwest of Zingara."

Balthus looked at his companion with admiration.

"I knew you hadn't spent your life on this frontier. You've mentioned several far places. You've travelled widely?"

"I've roamed far; farther than any other man of my race ever wandered. I've seen all the great cities of the Hyborians, the Shemites, the Stygians and the Hyrkanians. I've roamed in the unknown countries south of the black kingdoms of Kush, and east of the Sea of Vilayet. I've been mercenary captain, a corsair, a *kozak*, a penniless vagabond, a general – hell, I've been everything except a king, and I may be that, before I die." The fancy pleased him, and he grinned hardly. Then he shrugged his shoulders and stretched his mighty figure on the rocks. "This is as good life as any. I don't know how long I'll stay on the frontier; a week, a month, a year. I have a roving foot. But it's as well on the border as anywhere."

Balthus set himself to watch the forest below them. Momentarily he expected to see fierce painted faces thrust through the leaves. But as the hours passed no stealthy footfall disturbed the brooding quiet. Balthus believed the Picts had missed their trail and given up the chase. Conan grew restless.

"We should have sighted parties scouring the woods for us. If they've quit the chase it's because they're after bigger game. They may be gathering to cross the river and storm the fort."

"Would they come this far south if they lost the trail?"

"They've lost the trail, all right; otherwise they'd have been on our necks before now. Under ordinary circumstances they'd scour the woods for miles in every direction. Some of them should have passed within sight of this hill. They must be preparing to cross the river. We've got to take a chance and make for the river."

Creeping down the rocks Balthus felt his flesh crawl between his shoulders as he momentarily expected a withering blast of arrows from the green masses about them. He feared that the Picts had discovered them and were lying about in ambush. But Conan was convinced no enemies were near, and the Cimmerian was right.

"We're miles to the south of the village," grunted Conan. "We'll hit straight through for the river. I don't know how far down the river they've spread. We'll hope to hit it below them."

With haste that seemed reckless to Balthus they hurried eastward. The woods seemed empty of life. Conan believed that all the Picts were gathered in the vicinity of Gwawela, if, indeed, they had not already crossed the river. He did not believe they would cross in the daytime, however.

"Some woodsman would be sure to see them and give the alarm. They'll cross above and below the fort, out of sight of the sentries. Then others will get in canoes and make straight across for the river wall. As soon as they attack, those hidden in the woods on the east shore will assail the fort from the other sides. They've tried that before, and got the guts shot and hacked out of them. But this time they've got enough men to make a real onslaught of it."

They pushed on without pausing, though Balthus gazed longingly at the squirrels flitting among the branches, which he could have brought down with a cast of his axe. With a sigh he drew up his broad belt. The everlasting silence and gloom of the primitive forest was beginning to depress him. He found himself thinking of the open oak groves and sun-dappled meadows of the Tauran, of the bluff cheer of his father's steep-thatched, diamond-paned house, of the fat cows browsing through the deep, lush grass, and the hearty fellowship of the brawny, bare-armed ploughmen and herdsmen.

He felt lonely, in spite of his companion. Conan was as much a part of this wilderness as Balthus was alien to it. The Cimmerian might have spent years among the great cities of the world; he might have walked with the rulers of civilization; he might even achieve his wild whim some day and rule as king of a civilized nation; stranger things had happened. But he was no less a barbarian. He was concerned only with the naked fundamentals of life. The warm intimacies of small, kindly things, the sentiments and delicious trivialities that make up so much of civilized men's lives were meaningless to him. A wolf was no less a wolf because a whim of chance caused him to run with the watch-dogs. Bloodshed and violence and savagery were the natural elements of the life Conan knew; he could not, and would never understand the little things that are so dear to the souls of civilized men and women.

The shadows were lengthening when they reached the river and peered through the masking bushes. They could see up and down the river for about a mile each way. The sullen stream lay bare and empty. Conan scowled across at the other shore.

"We've got to take another chance here. We've got to skirt the river. We don't know whether they've crossed or not. The woods over there may be alive with them. We've got to risk it. We're about six miles south of Gwawela."

He wheeled and ducked as a bowstring twanged. Something like a white flash of light streaked through the bushes. Balthus knew it was an arrow. Then with a tigerish bound Conan was through the bushes. Balthus caught the gleam of steel as he whirled his sword, and heard a death scream. The next instant he had broken through the bushes after the Cimmerian.

A Pict with a shattered skull lay face-down on the ground, his fingers spasmodically clawing at the grass. Half a dozen others were swarming about Conan, swords and axes lifted. They had cast away their bows, useless at such deadly close quarters. Their lower jaws were painted white contrasting vividly with their dark faces, and the designs on their muscular breasts differed from any Balthus had ever seen.

One of them hurled his axe at Balthus and rushed after it with lifted knife. Balthus ducked and then caught the wrist that drove the knife licking at his throat. They went to the ground together, rolling over and over. The Pict was like a wild beast, his muscles hard as steel strings.

Balthus was striving to maintain his hold on the wild man's wrist and bring his own axe into play, but so fast and furious was the struggle that each attempt to strike was blocked. The Pict was wrenching furiously to free his knife hand, was clutching at Balthus' axe, and driving his knees at the youth's groin. Suddenly he attempted to shift his knife to his free hand, and in that instant Balthus, struggling up on one knee, split the painted head with a desperate blow of his axe.

He sprang up and glared wildly about for his companion, expecting to see him overwhelmed by numbers. Then he realized the full strength and ferocity of the Cimmerian. Conan bestrode two of his attackers, shorn half asunder by that terrible broadsword. As Balthus looked he saw the Cimmerian beat down a thrusting short sword, avoid the stroke of an axe with a cat-like sidewise spring which brought him within arm's length of a squat savage stooping for a bow. Before the Pict could straighten the red sword flailed down and clove him from shoulder to mid-breastbone where the blade stuck. The remaining warriors rushed in, one from each side. Balthus hurled his axe with an accuracy that reduced the attackers to one, and Conan, abandoning his efforts to free his sword, wheeled and met the remaining Pict with his bare hands. The stocky warrior, a head shorter than his tall enemy, leaped in striking with his axe, at the same time stabbing murderously with his knife. The knife broke on the Cimmerian's mail, and the axe checked in mid-air as

Conan's fingers locked like iron on the descending arm. A bone snapped loudly, and Balthus saw the Pict wince and falter. The next instant he was swept off his feet, lifted high above the Cimmerian's head – he writhed in mid-air for an instant, kicking and thrashing, and then was dashed headlong to the earth with such force that he rebounded, and then lay still, his limp posture telling of splintered limbs and a broken spine.

"Come on!" Conan wrenched his sword free and snatched up an axe. "Grab a bow and a handful of arrows, and hurry! We've got to trust to our heels again. That yell was heard. They'll be here in no time. If we tried to swim across now, they'd feather us with arrows before we reached mid-stream!"

Up the river sounded a fierce howling. Balthus shuddered to think that it came from human mouths. Grasping the weapons he had snatched he followed Conan who plunged into the thickets away from the bank, and ran like a flying shadow.

VI

RED AXES OF THE BORDER

Conan did not plunge deeply into the forest. A few hundred yards from the river, he altered his slanting course and ran parallel with it. Balthus recognized a grim determination not to be hunted away from the river which they must cross if they were to warn the men in the fort. Behind them rose more loudly the yells of the forest men. Balthus believed the Picts had reached the glade where the bodies of the slain men lay. Then further yells seemed to indicate that the savages were streaming into the woods in pursuit. They had left a trail any Pict could follow.

Conan increased his speed and Balthus grimly set his teeth and kept on his heels, though he felt he might collapse any time. It seemed centuries since he had eaten last. He kept going more by an effort of will than anything else. His blood was pounding so furiously in his ear drums that he was not aware when the yells died out behind them.

Conan halted suddenly. Balthus leaned against a tree and panted.

"They've quit!" grunted the Cimmerian, scowling.

"Sneaking – up – on – us!" gasped Balthus. Conan shook his head.

"A short chase like this they'd yell every step of the way. No. They've gone back. I thought I heard somebody yelling behind them a few seconds before the noise began to get dimmer. They've been recalled. And that's good for us, but damned bad for the men in the fort. It means the warriors are being summoned out of the woods for the attack. Those men we ran into were warriors from a tribe down the river. They were undoubtedly headed for Gwawela to join in the assault on the fort. Damn it, we're further away than ever, now. We've *got* to get across the river."

Turning east he hurried through the thickets with no attempt at concealment. Balthus followed him, for the first time feeling the sting of lacerations on his breast and shoulder where the Pict's savage teeth had scored him. He was pushing through the thick bushes that fringed the bank when Conan pulled him back. Then he heard a rhythmic splashing and peering through the leaves, saw a dug-out canoe coming up the river, its single occupant paddling hard against the current. He was a strongly built Pict with a white heron feather thrust in a copper band that confined his square-cut mane.

"That's a Gwawela man," muttered Conan. "Emissary from Zogar. White plume shows that. He's carried a peace talk to the tribes down the river and now he's trying to get back and take a hand in the slaughter."

The lone ambassador was now almost even with their hiding place, and suddenly Balthus almost jumped out of his skin. At his very ear had sounded the harsh gutturals of a Pict. Then he realized that Conan had called to the paddler in his own tongue. The man started, scanned the bushes and called back something. Then cast a startled glance across the river, bent low and sent the canoe shooting in toward the western bank. Not understanding, Balthus saw Conan take from his hand the bow he had picked up in the glade, and notch an arrow.

The Pict had run his canoe in close to the shore, and staring up into the bushes, called out something. His answer came in the twang of the bow-string, the streaking flight of the arrow that sank to the feathers in his broad breast. With a choking gasp he slumped sidewise and rolled into the shallow water. In an instant Conan was down the bank and wading into the water to grasp the drifting canoe. Balthus stumbled after him, somewhat dazedly crawled into the canoe. Conan scrambled in, seized the paddle and sent the craft shooting toward the eastern shore. Balthus noted with envious admiration the play of the great muscles beneath the sun-burnt skin. The Cimmerian seemed an iron man, who never knew fatigue.

"What did you say to the Pict?" asked Balthus.

"Told him to pull into shore; said there was a white forest runner on the other bank who was trying to get a shot at him."

"That doesn't seem fair," Balthus objected. "He thought a friend was speaking to him. You mimicked a Pict perfectly –"

"We needed his boat," grunted Conan, not pausing in his exertions. "Only way to lure him to the bank. Which is worse – to betray a Pict who'd enjoy skinning us both alive, or betray the men across the river whose lives depend on our getting over?"

Balthus mulled over this delicate ethical question for a moment, then shrugged his shoulder and asked: "How far are we from the fort?"

Conan pointed to a creek which flowed into Black River from the east, a few hundred yards below them.

"That's South Creek; it's ten miles from its mouth to the fort. It's the southern boundary of Conajohara. Marshes miles wide south of it. No danger of a raid from across them. Nine miles above the fort North Creek forms the other boundary. Marshes beyond that, too. That's why an attack must come from the west, across Black River. Conajohara's just like a spear, with a point nineteen miles wide, thrust into the Pictish wilderness."

"Why don't we keep to the canoe and make the trip by water?"

"Because, considering the current we've got to brace, and the bends in the river, we can go faster afoot. Besides, remember Gwawela is south of the fort; if the Picts are crossing the river we'd run right into them."

Dusk was gathering as they stepped upon the eastern bank. Without pause Conan pushed on northward, at a pace that made Balthus' sturdy legs ache.

"Valannus wanted a fort built at the mouths of North and South Creeks," grunted the Cimmerian. "Then the river could be patrolled constantly. But the government wouldn't do it.

"Soft bellied fools sitting on velvet cushions with naked girls offering them iced wine on their knees – I know the breed. They can't see any further than their palace wall. Diplomacy – hell! They'd fight Picts with theories of territorial expansion. Valannus and men like him have to obey the orders of a set of damned fools. They'll never grab any more Pictish land, any more than they'll ever rebuild Venarium. The time may come when they'll see the barbarians swarming over the walls of the Eastern cities!"

A week before Balthus would have laughed at any such preposterous suggestion. Now he made no reply. He had seen the unconquerable ferocity of the men who dwelt beyond the frontiers.

He shivered, casting glances at the sullen river, just visible through the bushes, at the arches of the trees which crowded close to its banks. He kept remembering that the Picts might have crossed the river and be lying in ambush between them and the fort. It was growing dark fast.

A slight sound ahead of them jumped his heart into his throat and Conan's sword gleamed in the air. He lowered it when a dog, a great, gaunt, scarred beast, slunk out of the bushes and stood staring at them.

"That dog belonged to a settler who tried to build his cabin on the bank of the river a few miles south of the fort," grunted Conan. "The Picts slipped over and killed him, of course, and burned his cabin. We found him dead among the embers, and the dog lying senseless among three Picts he'd killed. He was almost cut to pieces. We took him to the fort and dressed his wounds, but after he recovered he took to the woods and turned wild. What now, Slasher, are you hunting the men who killed your master?"

The massive head swung from side to side and his eyes glowed greenly. He did not growl or bark. Silently as a phantom he slid in behind them.

"Let him come," muttered Conan. "He can smell the devils before we can see them."

Balthus smiled and laid his hand caressingly on the dog's head. The lips involuntarily writhed back to display the gleaming fangs, then the great beast bent his head sheepishly, and his tail moved with jerky uncertainty, as if the owner had almost forgotten the emotions of friendliness. Balthus mentally compared the great gaunt hard body with the fat sleek hounds tumbling vociferously over one another in his father's kennel yard. He sighed. The frontier was no less hard for beasts than for men. This dog had almost forgotten the meaning of kindness and friendliness.

Slasher glided ahead and Conan let him take the lead. The last tinge of dusk faded into stark darkness. The miles fell away under their steady feet. Slasher seemed voiceless. Suddenly he halted, tense, ears lifted. An instant later the men heard it — a demoniac yelling up the river ahead of them, faint as a whisper.

Conan swore like a madman.

"They've attacked the fort! We're too late! Come on!"

He increased his pace, trusting to the dog to smell out ambushes ahead. In a flood of tense excitement Balthus forgot his hunger and weariness. The yells grew louder as they advanced, and above the devilish screaming they could hear the deep shouts of the soldiers. Just as Balthus began to fear they would run into the savages who seemed to be howling just ahead of them, Conan swung away from the river in a wide semi-circle that carried them to a low rise from which they could look over the forest. They saw the fort, lighted with torches thrust over the parapets on long poles. These cast a flickering uncertain light over the clearing, and in that light they saw throngs of naked, painted figures along the fringe of the clearing. The river swarmed with canoes. The Picts had the fort completely surrounded.

An incessant hail of arrows rained against the stockade from the woods and the river. The deep twanging of the bow-strings rose above the howling. Yelling like wolves several hundred naked warriors with axes in their hands ran from under the trees and raced toward the eastern gate. They were within a hundred and fifty yards of their objective when a withering blast of arrows from the wall littered the ground with corpses and sent the survivors fleeing back to the trees. The men in the canoes rushed their boats toward the river-wall, and were met by another shower of cloth-yard shafts and a volley from the small balistas mounted on towers on that side of the stockade. Stones and logs whirled through the air and splintered and sank half a dozen canoes, killing their occupants, and the other boats drew back out of range. A deep roar of triumph rose from the walls of the fort, answered by bestial howling from all quarters.

"Shall we try to break through?" asked Balthus, trembling with eagerness.

Conan shook his head. He stood with his arms folded, his head slightly bent, a somber and brooding figure.

"The fort's doomed. The Picts are blood-mad, and won't stop until they're all killed. And there are too many of them for the men in the fort to kill. We couldn't break through, and if we did, we could do nothing but die with Valannus."

"There's nothing we can do but save our own hides, then?"

"Yes. We've got to warn the settlers. Do you know why the Picts are not trying to burn the fort with fire-arrows? Because they don't want a flame that might warn the people to the east. They plan to stamp out the fort, and then sweep east before anyone knows of its fall. They may cross Thunder River and take Velitrium before the people know what's happened. At least they'll destroy every living thing between the fort and Thunder River.

"We've failed to warn the fort, and I see now it would have done no good if we hadn't. The fort's too poorly manned. A few more charges and the Picts will be over the walls and breaking down the gates. But we can start the settlers toward Velitrium. Come on! We're outside the circle the Picts have thrown around the fort. We'll keep clear of it."

They swung out in a wide arc, hearing the rising and falling of the volume of the yells, marking each charge and repulse. The men in the fort were holding their own; but the shrieks of the Picts did not diminish in savagery. They vibrated with a timbre that held assurance of ultimate victory.

Before Balthus realized they were close to it, they broke into the road leading east.

"Now run!" grunted Conan. Balthus set his teeth. It was nineteen miles to Velitrium, a good five to Scalp Creek beyond which began the settlements. It seemed to the Aquilonian that they had been fighting and running for centuries. But the nervous excitement that rioted through his blood stimulated him to superhuman efforts.

Slasher ran ahead of them, his head to the ground, snarling low, the first sound they had heard.

"Picts ahead of us!" snarled Conan, dropping to one knee and scanning the ground in the starlight. He shook his head, baffled. "I can't tell how many. Probably only a small party. Some that couldn't wait to take the fort. They've gone ahead to butcher the settlers in their beds! Come on!"

Ahead of them presently they saw a small blaze through the trees, and heard a wild and ferocious chanting. The trail bent there, and leaving it, they cut across the bend, through the thickets. A few moments later they were looking on a hideous sight. An ox wain stood in the road piled with meager household furnishings; it was burning; the oxen lay near with their throats cut. A man and a woman lay in the road, stripped and mutilated. Five Picts were dancing about them with fantastic leaps and bounds, waving bloody axes; one of them brandished the woman's red-smeared gown.

At the sight a red haze swam before Balthus. Lifting his bow he lined the prancing figure, black against the fire, and loosed. The slayer leaped convulsively and fell dead with the arrow through his heart. Then the two white men and the dog were upon the startled survivors. Conan was animated merely by his fighting spirit and an old, old racial hate, but Balthus was afire with new-kindled wrath.

He met the first Pict to oppose him with a ferocious swipe that split the painted skull, and sprang over his falling body to grapple with the others. But Conan had already killed one of the two he had chosen, and the leap of the Aquilonian was a second late. The warrior was down with the long sword through him even as Balthus' axe was lifted. Turning toward the remaining Pict, Balthus saw Slasher rise from his victim, his great jaws dripping blood.

Balthus said nothing as he looked down at the pitiful forms in the road beside the burning wain. Both were young, the woman little more than a girl. By some whim of chance the Picts had left her face unmarred, and even in the agonies of an awful death it was beautiful. But her soft young body had been hideously slashed with many knives — a mist clouded Balthus' eyes and he swallowed chokingly. The tragedy momentarily overcame him. He felt like falling upon the ground and weeping and biting the earth.

"Some young couple just hitting out on their own," Conan was saying as he wiped his sword unemotionally. "On their way to the fort when the Picts met them. Maybe the boy was going to enter the service; maybe take up land on the river. Well, that's what will happen to every man, woman and child this side of Thunder River if we don't get them into Velitrium in a hurry."

His knees trembled with nausea as Balthus followed Conan. There was no hint of weakness in the long easy stride of the Cimmerian. There was a kinship between him and the great gaunt brute that glided beside him. Slasher no longer growled

with his head to the trail. The way was clear before them. The yelling on the river came faintly to them, but Balthus believed the fort was still holding. Conan halted suddenly, with an oath.

He showed Balthus a trail that led north from the road. It was an old trail, partly grown with new young growth, and this growth had recently been broken down. Balthus realized this fact more by feel than sight, though Conan seemed to see like a cat in the dark. The Cimmerian showed him where broad wagon tracks turned off the main trail, deeply indented in the forest mold.

"Settlers going to the licks after salt," he grunted. "They're at the edges of the marsh, about nine miles from here. Blast it! They'll be cut off and butchered to a man! Listen! One man can warn the people on the road. Go ahead and wake them up and herd them into Velitrium. I'll go and get the men gathering the salt. They'll be camped by the licks. We won't come back to the road. We'll head straight through the woods."

With no further comment Conan turned off the trail and hurried down the dim path, and Balthus, after staring after him for a few moments, set down along the road. The dog had remained with him, and glided softly at his heels. When Balthus had gone a few rods he heard the animal growl. Whirling, he glared back the way he had come, and was startled to see a vague ghostly glow vanishing into the forest in the direction Conan had taken. Slasher rumbled deep in his throat, his hackles stiff and his eyes balls of green fire. Balthus remembered the grim apparition that had taken the head of the merchant Tiberias not far from that spot, and he hesitated. The thing must be following Conan. But the giant Cimmerian had repeatedly demonstrated his ability to take care of himself, and Balthus felt his duty lay toward the helpless settlers who slumbered in the path of the red hurricane. The horror of the fiery phantom was overshadowed by the horror of those limp, violated bodies beside the burning ox wain.

He hurried down the road, crossed Scalp Creek and came in sight of the first settlers' cabin – a long, low structure of axe-hewn logs. In an instant he was pounding on the door. A sleepy voice inquired his pleasure.

"Get up! The Picts are over the river!"

That brought instant response. A low cry echoed his words and then the door was thrown open by a woman in a scanty shift. Her hair hung over her bare shoulders in disorder; she held a candle in one hand and an axe in the other. Her face was colorless, her eyes wide with terror.

"Come in!" she begged. "We'll hold the cabin."

"No. We must make for Velitrium. The fort can't hold them back. It may have fallen already. Don't stop to dress. Get your children and come on."

"But my man's gone with the others after salt!" she wailed, wringing her hands. Behind her peered three tousled youngsters, blinking and bewildered.

"Conan's gone after them. He'll fetch them through safe. We must hurry up the road to warn the other cabins."

Relief flooded her countenance.

"Mitra be thanked!" she cried. "If the Cimmerian's gone after them, they're safe if mortal man can save them!"

In a whirlwind of activity she snatched up the smallest child and herded the others through the door ahead of her. Balthus took the candle and ground it out under his heel. He listened an instant. No sound came up the dark road.

"Have you got a horse?"

"In the stable," she groaned. "Oh, hurry!"

He pushed her aside as she fumbled with shaking hands at the bars. He led the horse out and lifted the children on its back, telling them to hold to its mane and to each other. They stared at him seriously, making no outcry. The woman took the horse's halter and set out up the road. She still gripped her axe and Balthus knew that if cornered she would fight with the desperate courage of a she-panther.

He held behind, listening. He was oppressed by the belief that the fort had been stormed and taken; that the dark-skinned hordes were already streaming up the road toward Velitrium, drunken on slaughter and mad for blood. They would come with the speed of starving wolves.

Presently they saw another cabin looming ahead. The woman started to shriek a warning, but Balthus stopped her. He hurried to the door and knocked. A woman's voice answered him. He repeated his warning, and soon the cabin disgorged its occupants – an old woman, two young women and four children. Like the other woman's husband, their men had gone to the salt licks the day before, unsuspecting of any danger. One of the young women seemed dazed, the other prone to hysteria. But the old woman, a stern old veteran of the frontier, quieted them harshly; she helped Balthus get out the two horses that were stabled in a pen behind the cabin and put the children on them. Balthus urged that she herself mount with them, but she shook her head and made one of the younger women ride.

"She's with child," grunted the old woman. "I can walk – and fight, too, if it comes to that."

As they set out one of the young women said: "A young couple passed along the road about dusk; we advised them to spend the night at our cabin, but they were anxious to make the fort tonight – did – did – "

"They met the Picts," answered Balthus briefly; the woman sobbed in horror.

They were scarcely out of sight of the cabin when some distance behind them quavered a long high-pitched yell.

"A wolf!" exclaimed one of the women.

"A painted wolf with an axe in his hand," muttered Balthus. "Go! Rouse the other settlers along the road and take them with you. I'll scout along behind."

Without a word the old woman herded her charges ahead of her. As they faded into the darkness, Balthus could see the pale ovals that were the faces of the children twisted back over their shoulders to stare toward him. He remembered his own people on the Tauran and a moment's giddy sickness swam over him. With momentary weakness he groaned and sank down in the road; his muscular arm fell over Slasher's massive neck and he felt the dog's warm moist tongue touch his face.

He lifted his head and grinned with a painful effort.

"Come on, boy," he mumbled, rising. "We've got work to do."

A red glow suddenly became evident through the trees. The Picts had fired the last hut. He grinned. How Zogar Sag would froth if he knew his warriors had let their destructive natures get the better of them. The fire would warn the people further up the road. They would be awake and alert when the fugitives reached them. But his face grew grim. The women were travelling slowly, on foot and on the overloaded horses. The swift-footed Picts would run them down within a mile, unless – he took his position behind a tangle of fallen logs beside the trail. The road west of him was lighted by the burning cabin, and when the Picts came he saw them first – black, furtive figures etched against the distant glare.

Drawing a shaft to the head he loosed and one of the figures crumpled. The rest melted into the woods on either side of the road. Slasher whimpered with the killing lust beside him. Suddenly a figure appeared at the fringe of the trail, under the trees, and began gliding toward the fallen timbers. Balthus' bow-string twanged and the Pict yelped, staggered and fell into the shadows with the arrow through his thigh. Slasher cleared the timbers with a bound and leaped into the bushes. They were violently shaken and then the dog slunk back to Balthus' side, his jaws crimson.

No more appeared in the trail; Balthus began to fear they were stealing past his position through the woods, and when he heard a faint sound to his left he loosed blindly. He cursed as he heard the shaft splinter against a tree, but Slasher glided away as silently as a phantom, and presently Balthus heard a thrashing and a gurgling, and then Slasher came like a ghost through the bushes, snuggling his great, crimson-stained head against Balthus' arm. Blood oozed from a wound in his shoulder, but the sounds in the wood had ceased forever.

The men lurking on the edges of the road evidently sensed the fate of their companion, and decided that an open charge was preferable to being dragged down in the dark by a devil-beast they could not see nor hear. Perhaps they realized that only one man lay behind the logs. They came with a sudden rush, breaking cover from both sides of the trail. Three dropped with arrows through them – and the remaining pair hesitated. One turned and ran back down the road, but the other lunged over the breastwork, his eyes and teeth gleaming in the dim light, his axe lifted. Balthus' foot slipped as he sprang up, but the slip saved his life. The descending axe shaved a lock of hair from his head and the Pict rolled down the logs from the force of his wasted blow. Before he could regain his feet Slasher tore his throat out.

Then followed a tense period of waiting, in which time Balthus wondered if the man who had fled had been the only survivor of the party. Obviously it had been a small band who had either left the fighting at the fort, or was scouting ahead of the main body. Each moment that passed increased the chances for safety of the women and children hurrying toward Velitrium.

Then without warning a shower of arrows whistled over his retreat. A wild howling rose from the woods along the trail. Either the survivor had gone after aid, or another party had joined the first. The burning cabin still smoldered, lending a little light. Then they were after him, gliding through the trees beside the trail. He shot three arrows and threw the bow away. As if sensing his plight, they came on, not yelling now, but in deadly silence except for a swift pad of many feet.

He fiercely hugged the head of the great dog growling at his side, muttered: "All right, boy, give 'em hell!" and sprang to his feet, drawing his axe. Then the dark figures flooded over the breastworks and closed in a storm of flailing axes, stabbing knives and ripping fangs.

VII
The Devil in the Fire

When Conan turned from the Velitrium road he expected a run of some nine miles and set himself to the task. But he had not gone four when he heard the sounds of a party of men ahead of him. From the noise they were making in their progress he knew they were not Picts. He hailed them.

"Who's there?" challenged a harsh voice. "Stand where you are until we know you, or you'll get an arrow through you."

"You couldn't hit an elephant in this darkness," answered Conan impatiently. "Come on, fool; it's me – Conan. The Picts are over the river."

"We suspected as much," answered the leader of the men, as they strode forward – tall, rangy men, stern-faced, with bows in their hands. "One of our party wounded an antelope and tracked it nearly to Black River. He heard them yelling down the river and ran back to our camp. We left the salt and the wagons, turned the oxen loose and came as swiftly as we could. If the Picts are besieging the fort, war-parties will be ranging up the road toward our cabins."

"Your families are safe," grunted Conan. "My companion went ahead to take them to Velitrium. If we go back to the main road we may run into the whole horde. We'll strike southeast, through the timber. Go ahead. I'll scout behind."

A few moments later the whole band was hurrying southeastward. Conan followed more slowly, keeping just within ear-shot. He cursed the noise they were making; that many Picts or Cimmerians would have moved through the woods with no more noise than the wind makes as it blows through the black branches.

He had just crossed a small glade when he wheeled, answering the conviction of his primitive instincts that he was being followed. Standing motionless among the bushes he heard the sounds of the retreating settlers fade away. Then a voice called faintly back along the way he had come: "Conan! Conan! Wait for me, Conan!"

"Balthus!" he swore bewilderedly. Cautiously he called: "Here I am!"

"Wait for me, Conan!" the voice came more distinctly.

Conan moved out of the shadows, scowling. "What the devil are you doing here – *Crom!*"

He half crouched, the flesh prickling along his spine. It was not Balthus who was emerging from the other side of the glade. A weird glow burned through the trees. It moved toward him, shimmering weirdly – a green witch-fire that moved with purpose and intent.

It halted some feet away and Conan glared at it, trying to distinguish its fire-misted outlines. The quivering flame had a solid core; the flame was but a green garment that masked some animate and evil entity; but the Cimmerian was unable to make out its shape or likeness. Then, shockingly, a voice spoke to him from amidst the fiery column.

"Why do you stand like a sheep waiting for the butcher, Conan?"

The voice was human but carried strange vibrations that were not human.

"Sheep?" Conan's wrath got the best of his momentary awe. "Do you think I'm afraid of a damned Pictish swamp devil? A friend called me."

"I called in his voice," answered the other. "The men you follow belong to my brother; I would not rob his knife of their blood. But you are mine. Oh, fool, you have come from the far grey hills of Cimmeria to meet your doom in the forests of Conajohara."

"You've had your chance at me before now," snorted Conan. "Why didn't you kill me then, if you could?"

"My brother had not painted a skull black for you and hurled it into the fire that burns for ever on Gullah's black altar. He had not whispered your name to the black ghosts that haunt the uplands of the Dark Land. But a bat has flown over the Mountains of the Dead and drawn your image in blood on the white tiger's hide that hangs before the long hut where sleep the Four Brothers of the Night. The great serpents coil about their feet and the stars burn like fire-flies in their hair."

"Why have the gods of darkness doomed me to death?" growled Conan.

Something – a hand, foot or talon, he could not tell which, thrust out from the fire and marked swiftly on the mold. A symbol blazed there, marked with fire, and faded, but not before he recognized it.

"You dared make the sign which only a priest of Jhebbal Sag dare make. Thunder rumbled through the black Mountains of the Dead and the altar-hut of Gullah was thrown down by a wind from the Gulf of Ghosts. The loon which is messenger to the Four Brothers of the Night flew swiftly and whispered your name in my ear. Your race is run. You are a dead man already. Your head will hang in the altar-hut of my brother. Your body will be eaten by the black-winged, sharp-beaked Children of Jhil."

"Who the devil is your brother?" demanded Conan. His sword was naked in his hand, and he was subtly loosening the axe in his belt.

"Zogar Sag; a child of Jhebbal Sag who still visits his sacred groves at times. A woman of Gwawela slept in a grove holy to Jhebbal Sag. Her babe was Zogar Sag. I too am a son of Jhebbal Sag, out of a fire-being of a far realm. Zogar Sag summoned me out of the Misty Lands. With incantations and sorcery and his own blood he materialized me in the flesh of his own planet. We are one, tied together by invisible threads. His thoughts are my thoughts; if he is struck, I am bruised. If I am cut, he bleeds. But I have talked enough. Soon your ghost will talk with the ghosts of the Dark Land, and they will tell you of the old gods which are not dead, but sleep in the outer abysses, and from time to time awake."

"I'd like to see what you look like," muttered Conan, working his axe free; "you who leave a track like a bird, who burn like a flame and yet speak with a human voice."

"You shall see," answered the voice from the flame; "see, and carry the knowledge with you into the Dark Land."

The flames leaped and sank, dwindling and dimming. A face began to take shadowy form; at first Conan thought it was Zogar Sag himself who stood wrapped in green fire. But the face was higher than his own, and there was a demoniac aspect about it – Conan had noted various abnormalities about Zogar Sag's features – an obliqueness of the eyes, a sharpness of the ears, a wolfish thinness of the lips in the apparition which swayed before him. The eyes were red as coals of living fire.

More details came into view: a slender torso, covered with snaky scales, which was yet manlike in shape, with man-like arms, from the waist upward; below, long crane-like legs ended in splay, three-toed feet like those of some huge bird. Along the monstrous limbs the green fire fluttered and ran. He saw it as through a glistening mist.

Then suddenly it was towering over him, though he had not seen it move toward him. A long arm, which for the first time he noticed was armed with curving, sickle-like talons, swung high and swept down at his neck. With a fierce cry he broke the spell and bounded aside, hurling his axe. The demon avoided the cast with an unbelievably quick movement of its narrow head and was on him again with a hissing rush of leaping flames.

But fear had fought for it when it slew its other victims, and Conan was not afraid. He knew that any being clothed in material flesh can be slain by material weapons, however grisly its form may be.

One flailing talon-armed limb knocked his helmet from his head. A little lower and it would have decapitated him. But fierce joy surged through him as his savagely driven sword sank deep in the monster's groin. He bounded backward from a flailing stroke, tearing his sword free as he leaped. The talons raked his breast, ripping through mail-links as if they had been cloth. But his return spring was like that of a starving wolf. He was inside the lashing arms and driving his sword deep in the monster's belly – felt the arms lock about him and the talons ripping the mail from his back as they sought his vitals – he was lapped and dazzled by blue flame that was chill as ice – then he had torn fiercely away from the weakening arms and his sword cut the air in a tremendous swipe.

The demon staggered and fell sprawling sidewise, its head hanging only by a shred of flesh. The fires that veiled it leaped fiercely upward, now red as gushing blood, hiding the figure from view. A scent of burning flesh filled Conan's nostrils. Shaking the blood and sweat from his eyes, he wheeled and ran staggeringly through the woods. Blood trickled down his limbs. Somewhere, miles to the south, he saw the faint glow of flames that might mark a burning cabin. Behind him, toward the road, rose a distant howling that spurred him to greater efforts.

VIII
Conajohara No More

There had been fighting on Thunder River; fierce fighting before the walls of Velitrium; axe and torch had been plied up and down the bank, and many a settler's cabin lay in ashes before the painted horde was rolled back.

A strange quiet followed the storm, in which people gathered and talked in hushed voices, and men with red-stained bandages drank their ale silently in the taverns along the river bank.

There, to Conan the Cimmerian, moodily quaffing from a leathern jack, came a gaunt forester with a bandage about his head and his arm in a sling. He was the one survivor of Fort Tuscelan.

"You went with the soldiers to the ruins of the fort?"

Conan nodded.

"I wasn't able," murmured the other. "There was no fighting?"

"The Picts had fallen back across Black River. Something must have broken their nerve, though only the Devil who made them knows what."

The woodsman glanced at his bandaged arm and sighed.

"They say there were no bodies worth disposing of."

Conan shook his head. "Ashes. The Picts had piled them in the fort and set fire to the fort before they crossed the river. Their own dead and the men of Valannus."

"Valannus was killed among the last – in the hand-to-hand fighting when they broke the barriers. They tried to take him alive, but he made them kill him. They took ten of the rest of us prisoners when we were so weak from fighting we could fight no more. They butchered nine of us then and there. It was when Zogar Sag died that I got my chance to break free and run for it."

"Zogar Sag's dead?" ejaculated Conan.

"Aye. I saw him die. That's why the Picts didn't press the fight against Velitrium as fiercely as they did against the fort. It was strange. He took no wounds in battle. He was dancing among the slain, waving an axe with which he'd just brained the last of my comrades. He came at me, howling like a wolf – and then he staggered and dropped the axe, and began to reel in a circle screaming as I never heard a man or beast scream before. He fell between me and the fire they'd built to roast me, gagging and frothing at the mouth, and all at once he went rigid and the Picts shouted that he was dead. It was during the confusion that I slipped my cords and ran for the woods."

He hesitated, leaned closer to Conan and lowered his voice.

"I saw him lying in the firelight. No weapon had touched him. Yet there were red marks like the wounds of a sword in groin, belly and neck – the last as if his head had been almost severed from his body. What do you make of that?"

Conan made no reply, and the forester, aware of the reticence of barbarians on certain matters, continued: "He lived by magic, and somehow, he died by magic. It was the mystery of his death that took the heart out of the Picts. Not a man who saw it was in the fighting before Velitrium. They hurried back across Black River. Those that struck Thunder River were warriors who had come on before Zogar Sag died. They were not enough to take the city by themselves.

"I came along the road, behind their main force, and I know none followed me from the fort. I sneaked through their lines and got into the town. You brought the settlers through all right, but their women and children got into Velitrium just ahead of those painted devils. If the youth Balthus and old Slasher hadn't held them up awhile, they'd have butchered every woman and child in Conajohara. I passed the place where Balthus and the dog made their last stand. They were lying amid a heap of dead Picts – I counted seven, brained by his axe, or disembowelled by the dog's fangs, and there were others in the road with arrows sticking in them. Gods, what a fight that must have been."

"He was a man," said Conan. "I drink to his shade, and to the shade of the dog, who knew no fear." He quaffed part of the wine, then emptied the rest upon the floor, with a curious heathen gesture, and smashed the goblet. "The heads of ten Picts shall pay for his, and seven heads for the dog, who was a better warrior than many a man."

And the forester, staring into the moody, smoldering blue eyes knew the barbaric oath would be kept.

"They'll not rebuild the fort."

"No; Conajohara is lost to Aquilonia. The frontier has been pushed back. Thunder River will be the new border."

The woodsman sighed and stared at his calloused hand, worn from contact with axe haft and sword hilt. Conan reached his long arm for the wine jug. The forester stared at him, comparing him with the men about them, the men who had died along the lost river; comparing him with those other wild men over that river. Conan did not seem aware of his gaze.

"Barbarism is the natural state of mankind," the borderer said, still staring somberly at the Cimmerian. "Civilization is unnatural. It is a whim of circumstance. And barbarism must always ultimately triumph."

The Black Stranger

The Black Stranger

I

THE PAINTED MEN

One moment the glade lay empty; the next, a man stood poised warily at the edge of the bushes. There had been no sound to warn the grey squirrels of his coming. But the gay-hued birds that flitted about in the sunshine of the open space took fright at his sudden appearance and rose in a clamoring cloud. The man scowled and glanced quickly back the way he had come, as if fearing their flight had betrayed his position to some one unseen. Then he stalked across the glade placing his feet with care. For all his massive, muscular build he moved with the supple certitude of a panther. He was naked except for a rag twisted about his loins, and his limbs were criss-crossed with scratches from briars, and caked with dried mud. A brown-crusted bandage was knotted about his thickly-muscled left arm. Under his matted black mane his face was drawn and gaunt, and his eyes burned like the eyes of a wounded panther. He limped slightly as he followed the dim path that led across the open space.

Half-way across the glade he stopped short and whirled, catlike, facing back the way he had come, as a long-drawn call quavered out across the forest. To another man it would have seemed merely the howl of a wolf. But this man knew it was no wolf. He was a Cimmerian and understood the voices of the wilderness as a city-bred man understands the voices of his friends.

Rage burned redly in his bloodshot eyes as he turned once more and hurried along the path, which, as it left the glade, ran along the edge of a dense thicket that rose in a solid clump of greenery among the trees and bushes. A massive log, deeply embedded in the grassy earth, paralleled the fringe of the thicket, lying between it and the path. When the Cimmerian saw this log he halted and looked back across the glade. To the average eye there were no signs to show that he had passed; but there was evidence visible to his wilderness-sharpened eyes, and therefore to the equally keen eyes of those who pursued him. He snarled silently, the red rage growing in his eyes – the berserk fury of a hunted beast which is ready to turn at bay.

He walked down the trail with comparative carelessness, here and there crushing a grass-blade beneath his foot. Then, when he had reached the further end of the great log, he sprang upon it, turned and ran lightly back along it. The bark had long been worn away by the elements. He left no sign to show the keenest forest-eyes that he had doubled on his trail. When he reached the densest point of the thicket he faded into it like a shadow, with hardly the quiver of a leaf to mark his passing.

The minutes dragged. The grey squirrels chattered again on the branches – then flattened their bodies and were suddenly mute. Again the glade was invaded. As silently as the first man had appeared, three other men materialized out of the eastern edge of the clearing. They were dark-skinned men of short stature, with thickly-muscled chests and arms. They wore beaded buckskin loin-cloths, and an eagle's feather was thrust into each black mane. They were painted in hideous designs, and heavily armed.

They had scanned the glade carefully before showing themselves in the open, for they moved out of the bushes without hesitation, in close single-file, treading as softly as leopards, and bending down to stare at the path. They were following the trail of the Cimmerian, but it was no easy task even for these human bloodhounds. They moved slowly across the glade, and then one stiffened, grunted and pointed with his broad-bladed stabbing spear at a crushed grass-blade where the path entered the forest again. All halted instantly and their beady black eyes quested the forest walls. But their quarry was well hidden; they saw nothing to awake their suspicion, and presently they moved on, more rapidly, following the faint marks that seemed to indicate their prey was growing careless through weakness or desperation.

They had just passed the spot where the thicket crowded closest to the ancient trail when the Cimmerian bounded into the path behind them and plunged his knife between the shoulders of the last man. The attack was so quick and unexpected the Pict had no chance to save himself. The blade was in his heart before he knew he was in peril. The other two whirled with the instant, steel-trap quickness of savages, but even as his knife sank home, the Cimmerian struck a tremendous blow with the war-axe in his right hand. The second Pict was in the act of turning as the axe fell. It split his skull to the teeth.

The remaining Pict, a chief by the scarlet tip of his eagle-feather, came savagely to the attack. He was stabbing at the Cimmerian's breast even as the killer wrenched his axe from the dead man's head. The Cimmerian hurled the body against the chief and followed with an attack as furious and desperate as the charge of a wounded tiger. The Pict, staggering under the impact of the corpse against him, made no attempt to parry the dripping axe; the instinct to slay submerging even the instinct to live, he drove his spear ferociously at his enemy's broad breast. The Cimmerian had the advantage of a greater intelligence, and a weapon in each hand. The hatchet, checking its downward sweep, struck the spear aside, and the knife in the Cimmerian's left hand ripped upward into the painted belly.

An awful howl burst from the Pict's lips as he crumpled, disembowelled – a cry not of fear or of pain, but of baffled, bestial fury, the death-screech of a panther. It was answered by a wild chorus of yells some distance east of the glade. The Cimmerian started convulsively, wheeled, crouching like a wild thing at bay, lips asnarl, shaking the sweat from his face. Blood trickled down his forearm from under the bandage.

With a gasping, incoherent imprecation he turned and fled westward. He did not pick his way now, but ran with all the speed of his long legs, calling on the deep and all but inexhaustible reservoirs of endurance which are Nature's compensation for a barbaric existence. Behind him for a space the woods were silent, then a demoniacal howling burst out at the spot he had recently left, and he knew his pursuers had found the bodies of his victims. He had no breath for cursing the blood drops that kept spilling to the ground from his freshly opened wound, leaving a trail a child could follow. He had thought that perhaps these three Picts were all that still pursued him of the war-party which had followed him for over a hundred miles. But he might have known these human wolves never quit a blood-trail.

The woods were silent again, and that meant they were racing after him, marking his path by the betraying blood-drops he could not check. A wind out of the west blew against his face, laden with a salty dampness he recognized. Dully he was amazed. If he was that close to the sea the long chase had been even longer than he had realized. But it was nearly over. Even his wolfish vitality was ebbing under the terrible strain. He gasped for breath and there was a sharp pain in his side. His legs trembled with weariness and the lame one ached like the cut of a knife in the tendons each time he set the foot to earth. He had followed the instincts of the wilderness which bred him, straining every nerve and sinew, exhausting every subtlety and artifice to survive. Now in his extremity he was obeying another instinct, looking for a place to turn at bay and sell his life at a bloody price.

He did not leave the trail for the tangled depths on either hand. He knew that it was futile to hope to evade his pursuers now. He ran on down the trail while the blood pounded louder and louder in his ears and each breath he drew was a racking, dry-lipped gulp. Behind him a mad baying broke out, token that they were close on his heels and expected to overhaul their prey swiftly. They would come as fleet as starving wolves now, howling at every leap.

Abruptly he burst from the denseness of the trees and saw, ahead of him, the ground pitching upward, and the ancient trail winding up rocky ledges between jagged boulders. All swam before him in a dizzy red mist, but it was a hill he had come to, a rugged crag rising abruptly from the forest about its foot. And the dim trail wound up to a broad ledge near the summit.

That ledge would be as good a place to die as any. He limped up the trail, going on hands and knees in the steeper places, his knife between his teeth. He had not yet reached the jutting ledge when some forty painted savages broke from among the trees, howling like wolves. At the sight of their prey their screams rose to a devil's crescendo, and they raced toward the foot of the crag, loosing arrows as they came. The shafts showered about the man who doggedly climbed upward, and one stuck in the calf of his leg. Without pausing in his climb he tore it out and threw it aside, heedless of the less accurate missiles which splintered on the rocks about him. Grimly he hauled himself over the rim of the ledge and turned about, drawing his hatchet and shifting knife to hand. He lay glaring down at his pursuers over the rim, only his shock of hair and blazing eyes visible. His chest heaved as he drank in the air in great shuddering gasps, and he clenched his teeth against a tendency toward nausea.

Only a few arrows whistled up at him. The horde knew its prey was cornered. The warriors came on howling, leaping agilely over the rocks at the foot of the hill, war-axes in their hand. The first to reach the crag was a brawny brave whose eagle feather was stained scarlet as a token of chieftainship. He halted briefly, one foot on the sloping trail, arrow notched and drawn half-way back, head thrown back and lips parted for an exultant yell. But the shaft was never loosed. He froze into motionlessness, and the blood-lust in his black eyes gave way to a look of startled recognition. With a whoop he gave back, throwing his arms wide to check the rush of his howling braves. The man crouching on the ledge above them understood the Pictish tongue, but he was too far away to catch the significance of the staccato phrases snapped at the warriors by the crimson-feathered chief.

But all ceased their yelping, and stood mutely staring up – not at the man on the ledge, it seemed to him, but at the hill itself. Then without further hesitation, they unstrung their bows and thrust them into buckskin cases at their girdles; turned their backs and trotted across the open space, to melt into the forest without a backward look.

The Cimmerian glared in amazement. He knew the Pictish nature too well not to recognize the finality expressed in the departure. He knew they would not come back. They were heading for their villages, a hundred miles to the east.

But he could not understand it. What was there about his refuge that would cause a Pictish war-party to abandon a chase it had followed so long with all the passion of hungry wolves? He knew there were sacred places, spots set aside as sanctuaries by the various clans, and that a fugitive, taking refuge in one of these sanctuaries, was safe from the clan which raised it. But the different tribes seldom respected sanctuaries of other tribes; and the men who had pursued him certainly had no sacred spots of their own in this region. They were the men of the Eagle, whose villages lay far to the east, adjoining the country of the Wolf-Picts.

It was the Wolves who had captured him, in a foray against the Aquilonian settlements along Thunder River, and they had given him to the Eagles in return for a captured Wolf chief. The Eagle-men had a red score against the giant Cimmerian, and now it was redder still, for his escape had cost the life of a noted war-chief. That was why they had followed him so relentlessly, over broad rivers and hills and through long leagues of gloomy forest, the hunting grounds of hostile tribes. And now the survivors of that long chase turned back when their enemy was run to earth and trapped. He shook his head, unable to understand it.

He rose gingerly, dizzy from the long grind, and scarcely able to realize that it was over. His limbs were stiff, his wounds ached. He spat dryly and cursed, rubbing his burning, bloodshot eyes with the back of his thick wrist. He blinked and took stock of his surroundings. Below him the green wilderness waved and billowed away and away in a solid mass, and above its western rim rose a steel-blue haze he knew hung over the ocean. The wind stirred his black mane, and the salt tang of the atmosphere revived him. He expanded his enormous chest and drank it in.

Then he turned stiffly and painfully about, growling at the twinge in his bleeding calf, and investigated the ledge whereon he stood. Behind it rose a sheer rocky cliff to the crest of the crag, some thirty feet above him. A narrow ladder-like stair of hand-holds had been niched into the rock. And a few feet from its foot there was a cleft in the wall, wide enough and tall enough for a man to enter.

He limped to the cleft, peered in, and grunted. The sun, hanging high above the western forest, slanted into the cleft, revealing a tunnel-like cavern beyond, and rested a revealing beam on the arch at which this tunnel ended. In that arch was set a heavy iron-bound oaken door!

This was amazing. This country was howling wilderness. The Cimmerian knew that for a thousand miles this western coast ran bare and uninhabited except by the villages of the ferocious sea-land tribes, who were even less civilized than their forest-dwelling brothers.

The nearest outposts of civilization were the frontier settlements along Thunder River, hundreds of miles to the east. The Cimmerian knew he was the only white man ever to cross the wilderness that lay between that river and the coast. Yet that door was no work of Picts.

Being unexplainable, it was an object of suspicion, and suspiciously he approached it, axe and knife ready. Then as his blood-shot eyes became more accustomed to the soft gloom that lurked on either side of the narrow shaft of sunlight, he noticed something else – thick iron-bound chests ranged along the walls. A blaze of comprehension came into his eyes. He bent over one, but the lid resisted his efforts. He lifted his hatchet to shatter the ancient lock, then changed his mind and limped toward the arched door. His bearing was more confident now, his weapons hung at his sides. He pushed against the ornately carved door and it swung inward without resistance.

Then his manner changed again, with lightning-like abruptness; he recoiled with a startled curse, knife and hatchet flashing as they leaped to positions of defense. An instant he poised there, like a statue of fierce menace, craning his massive neck to glare through the door. It was darker in the large natural chamber into which he was looking, but a dim glow emanated from the great jewel which stood on a tiny ivory pedestal in the center of the great ebony table about which sat those silent shapes whose appearance had so startled the intruder.

They did not move, they did not turn their heads toward him.

"Well," he said harshly; "are you all drunk?"

There was no reply. He was not a man easily abashed, yet now he felt disconcerted.

"You might offer me a glass of that wine you're swigging," he growled, his natural truculence roused by the awkwardness of the situation. "By Crom, you show damned poor courtesy to a man who's been one of your own brotherhood. Are you going to –" his voice trailed into silence, and in silence he stood and stared awhile at those bizarre figures sitting so silently about the great ebon table.

"They're not drunk," he muttered presently. "They're not even drinking. What devil's game is this?" He stepped across the threshold and was instantly fighting for his life against the murderous, unseen fingers that clutched his throat.

II

Men From the Sea

Belesa idly stirred a sea-shell with a daintily slippered toe, mentally comparing its delicate pink edges to the first pink haze of dawn that rose over the misty beaches. It was not dawn now, but the sun was not long up, and the light, pearl-grey clouds which drifted over the waters had not yet been dispelled.

Belesa lifted her splendidly shaped head and stared out over a scene alien and repellent to her, yet drearily familiar in every detail. From her dainty feet the tawny sands ran to meet the softly lapping waves which stretched westward to be lost in the blue haze of the horizon. She was standing on the southern curve of the wide bay, and south of her the land sloped upward to the low ridge which formed one horn of that bay. From that ridge, she knew, one could look southward across the bare waters – into infinities of distance as absolute as the view to the westward and to the northward.

Glancing listlessly landward, she absently scanned the fortress which had been her home for the past year. Against a vague pearl and cerulean morning sky floated the golden and scarlet flag of her house – an ensign which awakened no enthusiasm in her youthful bosom, though it had flowed triumphantly over many a bloody field in the far South. She made out the figures of men toiling in the gardens and fields that huddled near the fort, seeming to shrink from the gloomy rampart of the forest which fringed the open belt on the east, stretching north and south as far as she could see. She feared that forest, and that fear was shared by every one in that tiny settlement. Nor was it an idle fear – death lurked in those whispering depths, death swift and terrible, death slow and hideous, hidden, painted, tireless, unrelenting.

She sighed and moved listlessly toward the water's edge, with no set purpose in mind. The dragging days were all of one color, and the world of cities and courts and gaiety seemed not only thousands of miles but long ages away. Again she sought in vain for the reason that had caused a Count of Zingara to flee with his retainers to this wild coast, a thousand miles from the land that bore him, exchanging the castle of his ancestors for a hut of logs.

Her eyes softened at the light patter of small bare feet across the sands. A young girl came running over the low sandy ridge, quite naked, her slight body dripping, and her flaxen hair plastered wetly on her small head. Her wistful eyes were wide with excitement.

"Lady Belesa!" she cried, rendering the Zingaran words with a soft Ophirean accent. "Oh, Lady Belesa!"

Breathless from her scamper, she stammered and made incoherent gestures with her hands. Belesa smiled and put an arm about the child, not minding that her silken dress came in contact with the damp, warm body. In her lonely, isolated life Belesa bestowed the tenderness of a naturally affectionate nature on the pitiful waif she had taken away from a brutal master encountered on that long voyage up from the southern coasts.

"What are you trying to tell me, Tina? Get your breath, child."

"A ship!" cried the girl, pointing southward. "I was swimming in a pool that the sea-tide left in the sand, on the other side of the ridge, and I saw it! A ship sailing up out of the south!"

She tugged timidly at Belesa's hand, her slender body all a-quiver. And Belesa felt her own heart beat faster at the mere thought of an unknown visitor. They had seen no sail since coming to that barren shore.

Tina flitted ahead of her over the yellow sands, skirting the tiny pools the out-going tide had left in shallow depressions. They mounted the low-undulating ridge, and Tina poised there, a slender white figure against the clearing sky, her wet flaxen hair blowing about her thin face, a frail quivering arm outstretched.

"Look, my Lady!"

Belesa had already seen it – a billowing white sail, filled with the freshening south wind, beating up along the coast, a few miles from the point. Her heart skipped a beat. A small thing can loom large in colorless and isolated lives; but Belesa felt a premonition of strange and violent events. She felt that it was not by chance that this sail was beating up this lonely coast. There was no harbor town to the north, though one sailed to the ultimate shores of ice; and the nearest port to the south was a thousand miles away. What brought this stranger to lonely Korvela Bay?

Tina pressed close to her mistress, apprehension pinching her thin features.

"Who can it be, my Lady?" she stammered, the wind whipping color to her pale cheeks. "Is it the man the Count fears?"

Belesa looked down at her, her brow shadowed.

"Why do you say that, child? How do you know my uncle fears any one?"

"He must," returned Tina naively, "or he would never have come to hide in this lonely spot. Look, my Lady, how fast it comes!"

"We must go and inform my uncle," murmured Belesa. "The fishing boats have not yet gone out, and none of the men have seen that sail. Get your clothes, Tina. Hurry!"

The child scampered down the low slope to the pool where she had been bathing when she sighted the craft, and snatched up the slippers, tunic and girdle she had left lying on the sand. She skipped back up the ridge, hopping grotesquely as she donned her scanty garments in mid-flight.

Belesa, anxiously watching the approaching sail, caught her hand, and they hurried toward the fort. A few moments after they had entered the gate of the log palisade which enclosed the building, the strident blare of a trumpet startled the workers in the gardens, and the men just opening the boat-house doors to push the fishing boats down their rollers to the water's edge.

Every man outside the fort dropped his tool or abandoned whatever he was doing and ran for the stockade without pausing to look about for the cause of the alarm. The straggling lines of fleeing men converged on the opened gate, and every head was twisted over its shoulder to gaze fearfully at the dark line of woodland to the east. Not one looked seaward.

They thronged through the gate, shouting questions at the sentries who patrolled the firing-ledges built below the up-jutting points of the upright palisade logs.

"What is it? Why are we called in? Are the Picts coming?"

For answer one taciturn man-at-arms in worn leather and rusty steel pointed southward. From his vantage point the sail was now visible. Men began to climb up on the ledges, staring toward the sea.

On a small lookout tower on the roof of the manor house, which was built of logs like the other buildings, Count Valenso watched the onsweeping sail as it rounded the point of the southern horn. The Count was a lean, wiry man of medium height and late middle age. He was dark, somber of expression. Trunk-hose and doublet were of black silk, the only color about his costume the jewels that twinkled on his sword hilt, and the wine-colored cloak thrown carelessly over his shoulder. He twisted his thin black mustache nervously, and turned his gloomy eyes on his seneschal – a leather-featured man in steel and satin.

"What do you make of it, Galbro?"

"A carack," answered the seneschal. "It is a carack trimmed and rigged like a craft of the Barachan pirates – look there!"

A chorus of cries below them echoed his ejaculation; the ship had cleared the point and was slanting inward across the bay. And all saw the flag that suddenly broke forth from the masthead – a black flag, with a scarlet skull gleaming in the sun.

The people within the stockade stared wildly at that dread emblem; then all eyes turned up toward the tower, where the master of the fort stood somberly, his cloak whipping about him in the wind.

"It's a Barachan, all right," grunted Galbro. "And unless I am mad, it's Strom's 'Red Hand'. What is he doing on this naked coast?"

"He can mean no good for us," growled the Count. A glance below showed him that the massive gates had been closed, and that the captain of his men-at-arms, gleaming in steel, was directing his men to their stations, some to the ledges, some to the lower loop-holes. He was massing his main strength along the western wall, in the midst of which was the gate.

Valenso had been followed into exile by a hundred men: soldiers, vassals and serfs. Of these some forty were men-at-arms, wearing helmets and suits of mail, armed with swords, axes and crossbows. The rest were toilers, without armor save for shirts of toughened leather, but they were brawny stalwarts, and skilled in the use of their hunting bows, woodsmen's axes, and boar-spears. They took their places, scowling at their hereditary enemies. The pirates of the Barachan Isles, a tiny archipelago off the southwestern coast of Zingara, had preyed on the people of the mainland for more than a century.

The men on the stockade gripped their bows or boar-spears and stared somberly at the carack which swung inshore, its brass work flashing in the sun. They could see the figures swarming on the deck, and hear the lusty yells of the seamen. Steel twinkled along the rail.

The Count had retired from the tower, shooing his niece and her eager protégée before him, and having donned helmet and cuirass, he betook himself to the palisade to direct the defense. His subjects watched him with moody fatalism. They intended to sell their lives as dearly as they could, but they had scant hope of victory, in spite of their strong position. They were oppressed by a conviction of doom. A year on that naked coast, with the brooding threat of that devil-haunted forest looming for ever at their backs, had shadowed their souls with gloomy forebodings. Their women stood silently in the doorways of their huts, built inside the stockade, and quieted the clamor of their children.

Belesa and Tina watched eagerly from an upper window in the manor house, and Belesa felt the child's tense little body all aquiver within the crook of her protecting arm.

"They will cast anchor near the boat-house," murmured Belesa. "Yes! There goes their anchor, a hundred yards off-shore. Do not tremble so, child! They can not take the fort. Perhaps they wish only fresh water and supplies. Perhaps a storm blew them into these seas."

"They are coming ashore in long boats!" exclaimed the child. "Oh, my Lady, I am afraid! They are big men in armor! Look how the sun strikes fire from their pikes and burganets! Will they eat us?"

Belesa burst into laughter in spite of her apprehension.

"Of course not! Who put that idea into your head?"

"Zingelito told me the Barachans eat women."

"He was teasing you. The Barachans are cruel, but they are no worse than the Zingaran renegades who call themselves buccaneers. Zingelito was a buccaneer once."

"He was cruel," muttered the child. "I'm glad the Picts cut his head off."

"Hush, child." Belesa shuddered slightly. "You must not speak that way. Look, the pirates have reached the shore. They line the beach, and one of them is coming toward the fort. That must be Strom."

"Ahoy, the fort there!" came a hail in a voice gusty as the wind. "I come under a flag of truce!"

The Count's helmeted head appeared over the points of the palisade; his stern face, framed in steel, surveyed the pirate somberly. Strom had halted just within good ear-shot. He was a big man, bare-headed, his tawny hair blowing in the wind. Of all the sea-rovers who haunted the Barachans, none was more famed for deviltry than he.

"Speak!" commanded Valenso. "I have scant desire to converse with one of your breed."

Strom laughed with his lips, not with his eyes.

"When your galleon escaped me in that squall off the Trallibes last year I never thought to meet you again on the Pictish Coast, Valenso!" said he. "Although at the time I wondered what your destination might be. By Mitra, had I known, I would have followed you then! I got the start of my life a little while ago when I saw your scarlet falcon floating over a fortress where I had thought to see naught but bare beach. You have found it, of course?"

"Found what?" snapped the Count impatiently.

"Don't try to dissemble with me!" the pirate's stormy nature showed itself momentarily in a flash of impatience. "I know why you came here — and I have come for the same reason. I don't intend to be balked. Where is your ship?"

"That is none of your affair."

"You have none," confidently asserted the pirate. "I see pieces of a galleon's masts in that stockade. It must have been wrecked, some how, after you landed here. If you'd had a ship you'd have sailed away with your plunder long ago."

"What are you talking about, damn you?" yelled the Count. "My plunder? Am I a Barachan to burn and loot? Even so, what would I loot on this naked coast?"

"That which you came to find," answered the pirate coolly. "The same thing I'm after — and mean to have. But I'll be easy to deal with — just give me the loot and I'll go my way and leave you in peace."

"You must be mad," snarled Valenso. "I came here to find solitude and seclusion, which I enjoyed until you crawled out of the sea, you yellow-headed dog.

Begone! I did not ask for a parley, and I weary of this empty talk. Take your rogues and go your ways."

"When I go I'll leave that hovel in ashes!" roared the pirate in a transport of rage. "For the last time – will you give me the loot in return for your lives? I have you hemmed in here, and a hundred and fifty men ready to cut your throats at my word."

For answer the Count made a quick gesture with his hand below the points of the palisade. Almost instantly a shaft hummed venomously through a loophole and splintered on Strom's breastplate. The pirate yelled ferociously, bounded back and ran toward the beach, with arrows whistling all about him. His men roared and came on like a wave, blades gleaming in the sun.

"Curse you, dog!" raved the Count, felling the offending archer with his iron-clad fist. "Why did you not strike his throat above the gorget? Ready with your bows, men – here they come!"

But Strom had reached his men, checked their headlong rush. The pirates spread out in a long line that overlapped the extremities of the western wall, and advanced warily, loosing their shafts as they came. Their weapon was the longbow, and their archery was superior to that of the Zingarans. But the latter were protected by their barrier. The long arrows arched over the stockade and quivered upright in the earth. One struck the window-sill over which Belesa watched, wringing a cry of fear from Tina, who cringed back, her wide eyes fixed on the venomous vibrating shaft.

The Zingarans sent their bolts and hunting arrows in return, aiming and loosing without undue haste. The women had herded the children into their huts and now stoically awaited whatever fate the gods had in store for them.

The Barachans were famed for their furious and headlong style of battling, but they were wary as they were ferocious, and did not intend to waste their strength vainly in direct charges against the ramparts. They maintained their wide-spread formation, creeping along and taking advantage of every natural depression and bit of vegetation – which was not much, for the ground had been cleared on all sides of the fort against the threat of Pictish raids.

A few bodies lay prone on the sandy earth, back-pieces glinting in the sun, quarrel shafts standing up from arm-pit or neck. But the pirates were quick as cats, always shifting their position, and were protected by their light armor. Their constant raking fire was a continual menace to the men in the stockade. Still, it was evident that as long as the battle remained an exchange of archery, the advantage must remain with the sheltered Zingarans.

But down at the boat-house on the beach, men were at work with axes. The Count cursed sulphurously when he saw the havoc they were making among his boats, which had been built laboriously of planks sawn out of solid logs.

"They're making a mantlet, curse them!" he raged. "A sally now, before they complete it – while they're scattered –"

Galbro shook his head, glancing at the bare-armed henchmen with their clumsy pikes.

"Their arrows would riddle us, and we'd be no match for them in hand-to-hand fighting. We must keep behind our walls and trust to our archers."

"Well enough," growled Valenso. "If we can keep *them* outside our walls."

Presently the intention of the pirates became apparent to all, as a group of some thirty men advanced, pushing before them a great shield made out of the planks from the boats, and the timbers of the boat-house itself. They had found an ox-cart, and mounted the mantlet on the wheels, great solid disks of oak. As they rolled it ponderously before them it hid them from the sight of the defenders except for glimpses of their moving feet.

It rolled toward the gate, and the straggling line of archers converged toward it, shooting as they ran.

"Shoot!" yelled Valenso, going livid. "Stop them before they reach the gate!"

A storm of arrows whistled across the palisade, and feathered themselves harmlessly in the thick wood. A derisive yell answered the volley. Shafts were finding loop-holes now, as the rest of the pirates drew nearer, and a soldier reeled and fell from the ledge, gasping and choking, with a clothyard shaft through his throat.

"Shoot at their feet!" screamed Valenso; and then – "Forty men at the gate with pikes and axes! The rest hold the wall!"

Bolts ripped into the sand before the moving shield. A blood-thirsty howl announced that one had found its target beneath the edge, and a man staggered into view, cursing and hopping as he strove to withdraw the quarrel that skewered his foot. In an instant he was feathered by a dozen hunting arrows.

But, with a deep-throated shout, the mantlet was pushed to the wall, and a heavy, iron-tipped boom, thrust through an aperture in the center of the shield, began to thunder on the gate, driven by arms knotted with brawny muscles and backed with blood-thirsty fury. The massive gate groaned and staggered, while from the stockade bolts poured in a steady hail and some struck home. But the wild men of the sea were afire with the fighting-lust.

With deep shouts they swung the ram, and from all sides the others closed in, braving the weakened fire from the walls, and shooting fast and hard.

Cursing like a madman the Count sprang from the wall and ran to the gate, drawing his sword. A clump of desperate men-at-arms closed in behind him, gripping their spears. In another moment the gate would cave in and they must stop the gap with their living bodies.

Then a new note entered the clamor of the melee. It was a trumpet, blaring stridently from the ship. On the cross-trees a figure waved his arms and gesticulated wildly.

That sound registered on Strom's ears, even as he lent his strength to the swinging ram. Exerting his mighty thews he resisted the surge of the other arms, bracing his legs to halt the ram on its backward swing. He turned his head, sweat dripping from his face.

"Wait!" he roared. "Wait, damn you! *Listen!*"

In the silence that followed that bull's bellow, the blare of the trumpet was plainly heard, and a voice that shouted something unintelligible to the people inside the stockade.

But Strom understood, for his voice was lifted again in profane command. The ram was released, and the mantlet began to recede from the gate as swiftly as it had advanced.

"Look!" cried Tina at her window, jumping up and down in her wild excitement. "They are running! All of them! They are running to the beach! Look! They have abandoned the shield just out of range! They are leaping into the boats and rowing for the ship! Oh, my Lady, have we won?"

"I think not!" Belesa was staring sea-ward. "Look!"

She threw the curtains aside and leaned from the window. Her clear young voice rose above the amazed shouts of the defenders, turned their heads in the direction she pointed. They sent up a deep yell as they saw another ship swinging majestically around the southern point. Even as they looked she broke out the royal golden flag of Zingara.

Strom's pirates were swarming up the sides of their carack, heaving up the anchor. Before the stranger had progressed half-way across the bay, *The Red Hand* was vanishing around the point of the northern horn.

III
The Coming of the Black Man

"Out, quick!" snapped the Count, tearing at the bars of the gate. "Destroy that mantlet before these strangers can land!"

"But Strom has fled," expostulated Galbro, "and yonder ship is Zingaran."

"Do as I order!" roared Valenso. "My enemies are not all foreigners! Out, dogs! Thirty of you, with axes, and make kindling wood of that mantlet. Bring the wheels into the stockade."

Thirty axemen raced down toward the beach, brawny men in sleeveless tunics, their axes gleaming in the sun. The manner of their lord had suggested a possibility of peril in that oncoming ship, and there was panic in their haste. The splintering of the timbers under their flying axes came plainly to the people inside the fort, and the axemen were racing back across the sands, trundling the great oaken wheels with them, before the Zingaran ship had dropped anchor where the pirate ship had stood.

"Why does not the Count open the gate and go down to meet them?" wondered Tina. "Is he afraid that the man he fears might be on that ship?"

"What do you mean, Tina?" Belesa demanded uneasily. The Count had never vouchsafed a reason for this self-exile. He was not the sort of a man to run from an enemy, though he had many. But this conviction of Tina's was disquieting; almost uncanny.

Tina seemed not to have heard her question.

"The axemen are back in the stockade," she said. "The gate is closed again and barred. The men still keep their places along the wall. If that ship was chasing Strom, why did it not pursue him? But it is not a war-ship. It is a carack, like the other. Look, a boat is coming ashore. I see a man in the bow, wrapped in a dark cloak."

The boat having grounded, this man came pacing leisurely up the sands, followed by three others. He was a tall, wiry man, clad in black silk and polished steel.

"Halt!" roared the Count. "I will parley with your leader, alone!"

The tall stranger removed his morion and made a sweeping bow. His companions halted, drawing their wide cloaks about them, and behind them the sailors leaned on their oars and stared at the flag floating over the palisade.

When he came within easy call of the gate: "Why, surely," said he, "there should be no suspicion between gentlemen in these naked seas!"

Valenso stared at him suspiciously. The stranger was dark, with a lean, predatory face, and a thin black mustache. A bunch of lace was gathered at his throat, and there was lace on his wrists.

"I know you," said Valenso slowly. "You are Black Zarono, the buccaneer."

Again the stranger bowed with stately elegance.

"And none could fail to recognize the red falcon of the Korzettas!"

"It seems this coast has become the rendezvous of all the rogues of the southern seas," growled Valenso. "What do you wish?"

"Come, come, sir!" remonstrated Zarono. "This is a churlish greeting to one who has just rendered you a service. Was not that Argossean dog, Strom, just thundering at your gate? And did he not take to his sea-heels when he saw me round the point?"

"True," grunted the Count grudgingly. "Though there is little to choose between a pirate and a renegade."

Zarono laughed without resentment and twirled his mustache.

"You are blunt in speech, my lord. But I desire only leave to anchor in your bay, to let my men hunt for meat and water in your woods, and perhaps, to drink a glass of wine myself at your board."

"I see not how I can stop you," growled Valenso. "But understand this, Zarono: no man of your crew comes within this palisade. If one approaches closer than a hundred feet, he will presently find an arrow through his gizzard. And I charge you do no harm to my gardens or the cattle in the pens. Three steers you may have for fresh meat, but no more. And we can hold this fort against your ruffians, in case you think otherwise."

"You were not holding it very successfully against Strom," the buccaneer pointed out with a mocking smile.

"You'll find no wood to build mantlets unless you chop down trees, or strip it from your own ship," assured the Count grimly. "And your men are not Barachan archers; they're no better bowmen than mine. Besides, what little loot you'd find in this castle would not be worth the price."

"Who speaks of loot and warfare?" protested Zarono. "Nay, my men are sick to stretch their legs ashore, and nigh to scurvy from chewing salt pork. I guarantee their good conduct. May they come ashore?"

Valenso grudgingly signified his consent, and Zarono bowed, a thought sardonically, and retired with a tread as measured and stately as if he trod the polished crystal floor of the Kordava royal court, where indeed, unless rumor lied, he had once been a familiar figure.

"Let no man leave the stockade," Valenso ordered Galbro. "I do not trust that renegade dog. Because he drove Strom from our gate is no guarantee that he would not cut our throats."

Galbro nodded. He was well aware of the enmity which existed between the pirates and the Zingaran buccaneers. The pirates were mainly Argossean sailors, turned outlaw; to the ancient feud between Argos and Zingara was added, in the case of the freebooters, the rivalry of opposing interests. Both breeds preyed on the shipping and the coastal towns; and they preyed on one another with equal rapacity.

So no one stirred from the palisade while the buccaneers came ashore, dark-faced men in flaming silk and polished steel, with scarfs bound about their heads and gold hoops in their ears. They camped on the beach, a hundred and seventy-odd of them, and Valenso noticed that Zarono posted lookouts on both points. They did not molest the gardens, and only the three beeves designated by Valenso, shouting from the palisade, were driven forth and slaughtered. Fires were kindled on the strand, and a wattled cask of ale was brought ashore and broached.

Other kegs were filled with water from the spring that rose a short distance south of the fort, and men began to straggle toward the woods, crossbows in their hands. Seeing this, Valenso was moved to shout to Zarono, striding back and forth through the camp: "Don't let your men go into the forest. Take another steer from the pens if you haven't enough meat. If they go trampling into the woods they may fall foul of the Picts.

"Whole tribes of the painted devils live back in the forest. We beat off an attack shortly after we landed, and since then six of my men have been murdered in the forest, at one time or another. There's peace between us just now, but it hangs by a thread. Don't risk stirring them up."

Zarono shot a startled glance at the lowering woods, as if he expected to see hordes of savage figures lurking there. Then he bowed and said: "I thank you for the warning, my lord." And he shouted for his men to come back, in a rasping voice that contrasted strangely with his courtly accents when addressing the Count.

If Zarono could have penetrated the leafy mask he would have been more apprehensive, if he could have seen the sinister figure that lurked there, watching the strangers with inscrutable black eyes – a hideously painted warrior, naked but for a doe-skin breech-clout, with a toucan feather drooping over his left ear.

As evening drew on a thin skim of grey crawled up from the sea-rim and overcast the sky. The sun sank in a wallow of crimson, touching the tips of the black waves with blood. Fog crawled out of the sea and lapped at the feet of the forest, curling about the stockade in smoky wisps. The fires on the beach shone dull crimson through the mist, and the singing of the buccaneers seemed deadened and far away. They had brought old sail-canvas from the carack and made them shelters along the strand, where beef was still roasting, and the ale granted them by their captain was doled out sparingly.

The great gate was shut and barred. Soldiers stolidly tramped the ledges of the palisade, pike on shoulder, beads of moisture glistening on their steel caps. They glanced uneasily at the fires on the beach, stared with greater fixity toward the forest, now a vague dark line in the crawling fog. The compound lay empty of life, a bare, darkened space. Candles gleamed feebly through the cracks of the huts, and light streamed from the windows of the manor. There was silence except for the tread of the sentries, the drip of water from the eaves, and the distant singing of the buccaneers.

Some faint echo of this singing penetrated into the great hall where Valenso sat at wine with his unsolicited guest.

"Your men make merry, sir," grunted the Count.

"They are glad to feel the sand under their feet again," answered Zarono. "It has been a wearisome voyage – yes, a long, stern chase." He lifted his goblet gallantly to the unresponsive girl who sat on his host's right, and drank ceremoniously.

Impassive attendants ranged the walls, soldiers with pikes and helmets, servants in satin coats. Valenso's household in this wild land was a shadowy reflection of the court he had kept in Kordava.

The manor house, as he insisted on calling it, was a marvel for that coast. A hundred men had worked night and day for months building it. Its log-walled exterior was devoid of ornamentation, but within it was as nearly a copy of Korzetta Castle as was possible. The logs that composed the walls of the hall were hidden with heavy silk tapestries, worked in gold. Ship beams, stained and polished, formed the beams of the lofty ceiling. The floor was covered with rich carpets. The broad stair that led up from the hall was likewise carpeted, and its massive balustrade had once been a galleon's rail.

A fire in the wide stone fireplace dispelled the dampness of the night. Candles in the great silver candelabrum in the center of the broad mahogany board lit the hall, throwing long shadows on the stair. Count Valenso sat at the head of that table, presiding over a company composed of his niece, his piratical guest, Galbro, and the captain of the guard. The smallness of the company emphasized the proportions of the vast board, where fifty guests might have sat at ease.

"You followed Strom?" asked Valenso. "You drove him this far afield?"

"I followed Strom," laughed Zarono, "but he was not fleeing from me. Strom is not the man to flee from anyone. No; he came seeking for something; something I too desire."

"What could tempt a pirate or a buccaneer to this naked land?" muttered Valenso, staring into the sparkling contents of his goblet.

"What could tempt a count of Kordava?" retorted Zarono, and an avid light burned an instant in his eyes.

"The rottenness of a royal court might sicken a man of honor," remarked Valenso.

"Korzettas of honor have endured its rottenness with tranquility for several generations," said Zarono bluntly. "My lord, indulge my curiosity – why did you sell your lands, load your galleon with the furnishings of your castle and sail over the horizon out of the knowledge of the king and the nobles of Zingara? And why settle here, when your sword and your name might carve out a place for you in any civilized land?"

Valenso toyed with the golden seal-chain about his neck.

"As to why I left Zingara," he said, "that is my own affair. But it was chance that left me stranded here. I had brought all my people ashore, and much of the furnishings you mentioned, intending to build a temporary habitation. But my ship, anchored out there in the bay, was driven against the cliffs of the north point and wrecked by a sudden storm out of the west. Such storms are common enough at certain times of the year. After that there was naught to do but remain and make the best of it."

"Then you would return to civilization, if you could?"

"Not to Kordava. But perhaps to some far clime – to Vendhya, or Khitai –"

"Do you not find it tedious here, my Lady?" asked Zarono, for the first time addressing himself directly to Belesa.

Hunger to see a new face and hear a new voice had brought the girl to the great hall that night. But now she wished she had remained in her chamber with Tina. There was no mistaking the meaning in the glance Zarono turned on her. His speech was decorous and formal, his expression sober and respectful; but it was but a mask through which gleamed the violent and sinister spirit of the man. He could not keep the burning desire out of his eyes when he looked at the aristocratic young beauty in her low-necked satin gown and jeweled girdle.

"There is little diversity here," she answered in a low voice.

"If you had a ship," Zarono bluntly asked his host, "you would abandon this settlement?"

"Perhaps," admitted the Count.

"I have a ship," said Zarono. "If we could reach an agreement —"

"What sort of an agreement?" Valenso lifted his head to stare suspiciously at his guest.

"Share and share alike," said Zarono, laying his hand on the board with the fingers wide spread. The gesture was curiously reminiscent of a great spider. But the fingers quivered with curious tension, and the buccaneer's eyes burned with a new light.

"Share what?" Valenso stared at him in evident bewilderment. "The gold I brought with me went down in my ship, and unlike the broken timbers, it did not wash ashore."

"Not that!" Zarono made an impatient gesture. "Let us be frank, my lord. Can you pretend it was chance which caused you to land at this particular spot, with a thousand miles of coast from which to choose?"

"There is no need for me to pretend," answered Valenso coldly. "My ship's master was one Zingelito, formerly a buccaneer. He had sailed this coast, and persuaded me to land here, telling me he had a reason he would later disclose. But this reason he never divulged, because the day after we landed he disappeared into the woods, and his headless body was found later by a hunting party. Obviously he was ambushed and slain by the Picts."

Zarono stared fixedly at Valenso for a space.

"Sink me," quoth he at last, "I believe you, my lord. A Korzetta has no skill at lying, regardless of his other accomplishments. And I will make you a proposal. I will admit when I anchored out there in the bay I had other plans in mind. Supposing you to have already secured the treasure, I meant to take this fort by strategy and cut all your throats. But circumstances have caused me to change my mind —" he cast a glance at Belesa that brought the color into her face, and made her lift her head indignantly.

"I have a ship to carry you out of exile," said the buccaneer, "with your household and such of your retainers as you shall choose. The rest can fend for themselves."

The attendants along the walls shot uneasy glances side-long at each other. Zarono went on, too brutally cynical to conceal his intentions.

"But first you must help me secure the treasure for which I've sailed a thousand miles."

"What treasure, in Mitra's name?" demanded the Count angrily. "You are yammering like that dog Strom, now."

"Did you ever hear of Bloody Tranicos, the greatest of the Barachan pirates?" asked Zarono.

"Who has not? It was he who stormed the island castle of the exiled prince Tothmekri of Stygia, put the people to the sword and bore off the treasure the prince had brought with him when he fled from Khemi."

"Aye! And the tale of that treasure brought the men of the Red Brotherhood swarming like vultures after a carrion – pirates, buccaneers, even the black corsairs from the South. Fearing betrayal by his captains, he fled northward with one ship, and vanished from the knowledge of men. That was nearly a hundred years ago.

"But the tale persists that one man survived that last voyage, and returned to the Barachans, only to be captured by a Zingaran war-ship. Before he was hanged he told his story and drew a map in his own blood, on parchment, which he smuggled somehow out of his captor's reach. This was the tale he told: Tranicos had sailed far beyond the paths of shipping, until he came to a bay on a lonely coast, and there he anchored. He went ashore, taking his treasure and eleven of his most trusted captains who had accompanied him on his ship. Following his orders, the ship sailed away, to return in a week's time, and pick up their admiral and his captains. In the meantime Tranicos meant to hide the treasure somewhere in the vicinity of the bay. The ship returned at the appointed time, but there was no trace of Tranicos and his eleven captains, except the rude dwelling they had built on the beach.

"This had been demolished, and there were tracks of naked feet about it, but no sign to show there had been any fighting. Nor was there any trace of the treasure, or any sign to show where it was hidden. The pirates plunged into the forest to search for their chief and his captains, but were attacked by wild Picts and driven back to their ship. In despair they heaved anchor and sailed away, but before they raised the Barachans, a terrific storm wrecked the ship and only that one man survived.

"That is the tale of the Treasure of Tranicos, which men have sought in vain for nearly a century. That the map exists is known, but its whereabouts have remained a mystery.

"I have had one glimpse of that map. Strom and Zingelito were with me, and a Nemedian who sailed with the Barachans. We looked upon it in a hovel in a certain Zingaran sea-port town, where we were skulking in disguise. Somebody knocked over the lamp, and somebody howled in the dark, and when we got the light on again, the old miser who owned the map was dead with a dirk in his heart, and the map was gone, and the night-watch was clattering down the street with their pikes to investigate the clamor. We scattered, and each went his own way.

"For years thereafter Strom and I watched one another, each supposing the other had the map. Well, as it turned out, neither had it, but recently word came to me that

Strom had departed northward, so I followed him. You saw the end of that chase.

"I had but a glimpse at the map as it lay on the old miser's table, and could tell nothing about it. But Strom's actions show that he knows this is the bay where Tranicos anchored. I believe that they hid the treasure somewhere in that forest and returning, were attacked and slain by the Picts. The Picts did not get the treasure. Men have traded up and down this coast a little, knowing nothing of the treasure, and no gold ornament or rare jewel has ever been seen in the possession of the coastal tribes.

"This is my proposal: let us combine our forces. Strom is somewhere within striking distance. He fled because he feared to be pinned between us, but he will return. But allied, we can laugh at him. We can work out from the fort, leaving enough men here to hold it if he attacks. I believe the treasure is hidden nearby. Twelve men could not have conveyed it far. We will find it, load it in my ship, and sail for some foreign port where I can cover my past with gold. I am sick of this life. I want to go back to a civilized land, and live like a noble, with riches, and slaves, and a castle – and a wife of noble blood."

"Well?" demanded the Count, slit-eyed with suspicion.

"Give me your niece for my wife," demanded the buccaneer bluntly.

Belesa cried out sharply and started to her feet. Valenso likewise rose, livid, his fingers knotting convulsively about his goblet as if he contemplated hurling it at his guest. Zarono did not move; he sat still, one arm on the table and the fingers hooked like talons. His eyes smoldered with passion, and a deep menace.

"You dare!" ejaculated Valenso.

"You seem to forget you have fallen from your high estate, Count Valenso," growled Zarono. "We are not at the Kordavan court, my lord. On this naked coast nobility is measured by the power of men and arms. And there I rank you. Strangers tread Korzetta Castle, and the Korzetta fortune is at the bottom of the sea. You will die here, an exile, unless I give you the use of my ship.

"You will have no cause to regret the union of our houses. With a new name and a new fortune you will find that Black Zarono can take his place among the aristocrats of the world and make a son-in-law of which not even a Korzetta need be ashamed."

"You are mad to think of it!" exclaimed the Count violently. "You – who is that?"

A patter of soft-slippered feet distracted his attention. Tina came hurriedly into the hall, hesitated when she saw the Count's eyes fixed angrily on her, curtsied deeply, and sidled around the table to thrust her small hands into Belesa's fingers. She was panting slightly, her slippers were damp, and her flaxen hair was plastered down on her head.

"Tina!" exclaimed Belesa anxiously. "Where have you been? I thought you were in your chamber, hours ago."

"I was," answered the child breathlessly, "but I missed my coral necklace you gave me —" she held it up, a trivial trinket, but prized beyond all her other possessions because it had been Belesa's first gift to her. "I was afraid you wouldn't let me go if you knew — a soldier's wife helped me out of the stockade and back again — please, my Lady, don't make me tell who she was, because I promised not to. I found my necklace by the pool where I bathed this morning. Please punish me if I have done wrong."

"Tina!" groaned Belesa, clasping the child to her. "I'm not going to punish you. But you should not have gone outside the palisade, with these buccaneers camped on the beach, and always a chance of Picts skulking about. Let me take you to your chamber and change these damp clothes —"

"Yes, my Lady," murmured Tina, "but first let me tell you about the black man —"

"What?" The startling interruption was a cry that burst from Valenso's lips. His goblet clattered to the floor as he caught the table with both hands. If a thunderbolt had struck him, the lord of the castle's bearing could not have been more subtly or horrifyingly altered. His face was livid, his eyes almost starting from his head.

"What did you say?" he panted, glaring wildly at the child who shrank back against Belesa in bewilderment. "What did you say, wench?"

"A black man, my lord," she stammered, while Belesa, Zarono and the attendants stared at him in amazement. "When I went down to the pool to get my necklace, I saw him. There was a strange moaning in the wind, and the sea whimpered like a thing in fear, and then he came. I was afraid, and hid behind a little ridge of sand. He came from the sea in a strange black boat with blue fire playing all about it, but there was no torch. He drew his boat up on the sands below the south point, and strode toward the forest, looking like a giant in the fog — a great, tall man, black like a Kushite —"

Valenso reeled as if he had received a mortal blow. He clutched at his throat, snapping the golden chain in his violence. With the face of a madman he lurched about the table and tore the child screaming from Belesa's arms.

"You little slut!" he panted. "You lie! You have heard me mumbling in my sleep and have told this lie to torment me! Say that you lie before I tear the skin from your back!"

"Uncle!" cried Belesa, in outraged bewilderment, trying to free Tina from his grasp. "Are you mad? What are you about?"

With a snarl he tore her hand from his arm and spun her staggering into the arms of Galbro who received her with a leer he made little effort to disguise.

"Mercy, my lord!" sobbed Tina. "I did not lie!"

"I said you lied!" roared Valenso. "Gebbrelo!"

The stolid serving man seized the trembling youngster and stripped her with one brutal wrench that tore her scanty garments from her body. Wheeling, he drew her slender arms over his shoulders, lifting her writhing feet clear of the floor.

"Uncle!" shrieked Belesa, writhing vainly in Galbro's lustful grasp. "You are mad! You can not – oh, you can not –!" The voice choked in her throat as Valenso caught up a jewel-hilted riding whip and brought it down across the child's frail body with a savage force that left a red weal across her naked shoulders.

Belesa moaned, sick with the anguish in Tina's shriek. The world had suddenly gone mad. As in a nightmare she saw the stolid faces of the soldiers and servants, beast-faces, the faces of oxen, reflecting neither pity nor sympathy. Zarono's faintly sneering face was part of the nightmare. Nothing in that crimson haze was real except Tina's naked white body, criss-crossed with red welts from shoulders to knees; no sound real except the child's sharp cries of agony, and the panting gasps of Valenso as he lashed away with the staring eyes of a madman, shrieking: "You lie! You lie! Curse you, you lie! Admit your guilt, or I will flay your stubborn body! *He could not have followed me here* –"

"Oh, have mercy, my lord!" screamed the child, writhing vainly on the brawny servant's back, too frantic with fear and pain to have the wit to save herself by a lie. Blood trickled in crimson beads down her quivering thighs. "I saw him! I do not lie! Mercy! Please! Ahhhh!"

"You fool! *Tou fool!*" screamed Belesa, almost beside herself. "Do you not see she is telling the truth? Oh, you beast! Beast! Beast!"

Suddenly some shred of sanity seemed to return to the brain of Count Valenso Korzetta. Dropping the whip he reeled back and fell up against the table, clutching blindly at its edge. He shook as with an ague. His hair was plastered across his brow in dank strands, and sweat dripped from his livid countenance which was like a carven mask of Fear. Tina, released by Gebbrelo, slipped to the floor in a whimpering heap. Belesa tore free from Galbro, rushed to her, sobbing, and fell on her knees, gathering the pitiful waif into her arms. She lifted a terrible face to her uncle, to pour upon him the full vials of her wrath – but he was not looking at her. He seemed to have forgotten both her and his victim. In a daze of incredulity, she heard him say to the buccaneer: "I accept your offer, Zarono; in Mitra's name, let us find this accursed treasure and begone from this damned coast!"

At this the fire of her fury sank to sick ashes. In stunned silence she lifted the sobbing child in her arms and carried her up the stair. A glance backward showed Valenso crouching rather than sitting at the table, gulping wine from a huge goblet he gripped in both shaking hands, while Zarono towered over him like a somber predatory bird – puzzled at the turn of events, but quick to take advantage of the shocking change that had come over the Count. He was talking in a low, decisive voice, and Valenso nodded mute agreement, like one who scarcely heeds what is being said. Galbro stood back in the shadows, chin pinched between forefinger and thumb, and the attendants along the walls glanced furtively at each other, bewildered by their lord's collapse.

Up in her chamber Belesa laid the half-fainting girl on the bed and set herself to wash and apply soothing ointments to the weals and cuts on her tender skin. Tina gave herself up in complete submission to her mistress's hands, moaning faintly. Belesa felt as if her world had fallen about her ears. She was sick and bewildered, overwrought, her nerves quivering from the brutal shock of what she had witnessed. Fear of and hatred for her uncle grew in her soul. She had never loved him; he was harsh and apparently without natural affection, grasping and avid. But she had considered him just, and fearless. Revulsion shook her at the memory of his staring eyes and bloodless face. It was some terrible fear which had roused this frenzy; and because of this fear Valenso had brutalized the only creature she had to love and cherish; because of that fear he was selling her, his niece, to an infamous outlaw. What was behind this madness? Who was the black man Tina had seen?

The child muttered in semi-delirium.

"I did not lie, my Lady! Indeed I did not! It was a black man, in a black boat that burned like blue fire on the water! A tall man, black as a negro, and wrapped in a black cloak! I was afraid when I saw him, and my blood ran cold. He left his boat on the sands and went into the forest. Why did the Count whip me for seeing him?"

"Hush, Tina," soothed Belesa. "Lie quietly. The smarting will soon pass."

The door opened behind her and she whirled, snatching up a jeweled dagger. The Count stood in the door, and her flesh crawled at the sight. He looked years older; his face was grey and drawn, and his eyes stared in a way that roused fear in her bosom. She had never been close to him; now she felt as though a gulf separated them. He was not her uncle who stood there, but a stranger come to menace her.

She lifted the dagger.

"If you touch her again," she whispered from dry lips, "I swear before Mitra I will sink this blade in your breast."

He did not heed her.

"I have posted a strong guard about the manor," he said. "Zarono brings his men into the stockade tomorrow. He will not sail until he has found the treasure. When he finds it we shall sail at once for some port not yet decided upon."

"And you will sell me to him?" she whispered. "In Mitra's name —"

He fixed upon her a gloomy gaze in which all considerations but his own self-interest had been crowded out. She shrank before it, seeing in it the frantic cruelty that possessed the man in his mysterious fear.

"You will do as I command," he said presently, with no more human feeling in his voice than there is in the ring of flint on steel. And turning, he left the chamber. Blinded by a sudden rush of horror, Belesa fell fainting beside the couch where Tina lay.

IV

A Black Drum Droning

Belesa never knew how long she lay crushed and senseless. She was first aware of Tina's arms about her and the sobbing of the child in her ear. Mechanically she straightened herself and drew the girl into her arms; and she sat there, dry-eyed, staring unseeingly at the flickering candle. There was no sound in the castle. The singing of the buccaneers on the strand had ceased. Dully, almost impersonally she reviewed her problem.

Valenso was mad, driven frantic by the story of the mysterious black man. It was to escape this stranger that he wished to abandon the settlement and flee with Zarono. That much was obvious. Equally obvious was the fact that he was ready to sacrifice her in exchange for that opportunity to escape. In the blackness of spirit which surrounded her she saw no glint of light. The serving men were dull or callous brutes, their women stupid and apathetic. They would neither dare nor care to help her. She was utterly helpless.

Tina lifted her tear-stained face as if she were listening to the prompting of some inner voice. The child's understanding of Belesa's inmost thoughts was almost uncanny, as was her recognition of the inexorable drive of Fate and the only alternative left to the weak.

"We must go, my Lady!" she whispered. "Zarono shall not have you. Let us go far away into the forest. We shall go until we can go no further, and then we shall lie down and die together."

The tragic strength that is the last refuge of the weak entered Belesa's soul. It was the only escape from the shadows that had been closing in upon her since that day when they fled from Zingara.

"We shall go, child."

She rose and was fumbling for a cloak, when an exclamation from Tina brought her about. The girl was on her feet, a finger pressed to her lips, her eyes wide and bright with terror.

"What is it, Tina?" The child's expression of fright induced Belesa to pitch her voice to a whisper, and a nameless apprehension crawled over her.

"Someone outside in the hall," whispered Tina, clutching her arm convulsively. "He stopped at our door, and then went on, toward the Count's chamber at the other end."

"Your ears are keener than mine," murmured Belesa. "But there is nothing strange in that. It was the Count himself, perchance, or Galbro." She moved to open the door, but Tina threw her arms frantically about her neck, and Belesa felt the wild beating of her heart.

"No, no, my Lady! Do not open the door! I am afraid! I do not know why, but I feel that some evil thing is skulking near us!"

Impressed, Belesa patted her reassuringly, and reached a hand toward the gold disk that masked the tiny peep-hole in the center of the door.

"He is coming back!" shivered the girl. "I hear him!"

Belesa heard something too – a curious stealthy pad which she knew, with a chill of nameless fear, was not the step of anyone she knew. Nor was it the step of Zarono, or any booted man. Could it be the buccaneer gliding along the hallway on bare, stealthy feet, to slay his host while he slept? She remembered the soldiers who would be on guard below. If the buccaneer had remained in the manor for the night, a man-at-arms would be posted before his chamber door. But who was that sneaking along the corridor? None slept upstairs besides herself, Tina and the Count, except Galbro.

With a quick motion she extinguished the candle so it would not shine through the hole in the door, and pushed aside the gold disk. All the lights were out in the hall, which was ordinarily lighted by candles. Someone was moving along the darkened corridor. She sensed rather than saw a dim bulk moving past her doorway, but she could make nothing of its shape except that it was manlike. But a chill wave of terror swept over her so she crouched dumb, incapable of the scream that froze behind her lips. It was not such terror as her uncle now inspired in her, or fear like her fear of Zarono, or even of the brooding forest. It was blind unreasoning terror that laid an icy hand on her soul and froze her tongue to her palate.

The figure passed on to the stairhead, where it was limned momentarily against the faint glow that came up from below, and at the glimpse of that vague black image against the red, she almost fainted.

She crouched there in the darkness, awaiting the outcry that would announce that the soldiers in the great hall had seen the intruder. But the manor remained silent; somewhere a wind wailed shrilly. That was all.

Belesa's hands were moist with perspiration as she groped to relight the candle. She was still shaken with horror, though she could not decide just what there had been about that black figure etched against the red glow that had roused this frantic loathing in her soul. It was manlike in shape, but the outline was strangely alien – abnormal – though she could not clearly define that abnormality. But she knew that it was no human being that she had seen, and she knew that the sight had robbed her of all her new-found resolution. She was demoralized, incapable of action.

The candle flared up, limning Tina's white face in the yellow glow.

"It was the black man!" whispered Tina. "I know! My blood turned cold, just as it did when I saw him on the beach. There are soldiers downstairs; why did they not see him? Shall we go and inform the Count?"

Belesa shook her head. She did not care to repeat the scene that had ensued upon Tina's first mention of the black man. At any event, she dared not venture out into that darkened hallway.

"We dare not go into the forest!" shuddered Tina. "He will be lurking there –"

Belesa did not ask the girl how she knew the black man would be in the forest; it was the logical hiding-place for any evil thing, man or devil. And she knew Tina was right; they dared not leave the fort now. Her determination which had not faltered at the prospect of certain death, gave way at the thought of traversing those gloomy woods with that black shambling creature at large among them. Helplessly she sat down and sank her face in her hands.

Tina slept, presently, on the couch, whimpering occasionally in her sleep. Tears sparkled on her long lashes. She moved her smarting body uneasily in her restless slumber. Toward dawn Belesa was aware of a stifling quality in the atmosphere. She heard a low rumble of thunder somewhere off to sea-ward. Extinguishing the candle, which had burned to its socket, she went to a window whence she could see both the ocean and a belt of the forest behind the fort.

The fog had disappeared, but out to sea a dusky mass was rising from the horizon. From it lightning flickered and the low thunder growled. An answering rumble came from the black woods. Startled she turned and stared at the forest, a brooding black rampart. A strange rhythmic pulsing came to her ears – a droning reverberation that was not the roll of a Pictish drum.

"The drum!" sobbed Tina, spasmodically opening and closing her fingers in her sleep. "The black man – beating on a black drum – in the black woods! Oh, save us –!"

Belesa shuddered. Along the eastern horizon ran a thin white line that presaged dawn. But that black cloud on the western rim writhed and billowed, swelling and expanding. She stared in amazement, for storms were practically unknown on that coast at that time of the year, and she had never seen a cloud like that one.

It came pouring up over the world-rim in great boiling masses of blackness, veined with fire. It rolled and billowed with the wind in its belly. Its thundering made the air vibrate. And another sound mingled awesomely with the reverberations of the thunder – the voice of the wind, that raced before its coming. The inky horizon was torn and convulsed in the lightning flashes; afar to sea she saw the white-capped waves racing before the wind. She heard its droning roar, increasing in volume as it swept shoreward. But as yet no wind stirred on the land. The air was hot, breathless. There was a sensation of unreality about the contrast: out there wind and thunder and chaos sweeping inland; but here stifling stillness. Somewhere below her a shutter slammed, startling in the tense silence, and a woman's voice was lifted, shrill with alarm. But most of the people of the fort seemed sleeping, unaware of the oncoming hurricane.

She realized that she still heard that mysterious droning drum-beat and she stared toward the black forest, her flesh crawling. She could see nothing, but some obscure instinct or intuition prompted her to visualize a black hideous figure squatting under black branches and enacting a nameless incantation on something that sounded like a drum –

Desperately she shook off the ghoulish conviction, and looked sea-ward, as a blaze of lightning fairly split the sky. Outlined against its glare she saw the masts of Zarono's ship; she saw the tents of the buccaneers on the beach, the sandy ridges of the south point and the rock cliffs of the north point as plainly as by midday sun. Louder and louder rose the roar of the wind, and now the manor was awake. Feet came pounding up the stair, and Zarono's voice yelled, edged with fright.

Doors slammed and Valenso answered him, shouting to be heard above the roar of the elements.

"Why didn't you warn me of a storm from the west?" howled the buccaneer. "If the anchors don't hold –"

"A storm never came from the west before, at this time of year!" shrieked Valenso, rushing from his chamber in his night-shirt, his face livid and his hair standing stiffly on end. "This is the work of –" His words were drowned as he raced madly up the ladder that led to the lookout tower, followed by the swearing buccaneer.

Belesa crouched at her window, awed and deafened. Louder and louder rose the wind, until it drowned all other sound – all except that maddening droning that now rose like an inhuman chant of triumph. It roared inshore, driving before it a foaming league-long crest of white – and then all hell and destruction was loosed on that coast. Rain fell in driving torrents, sweeping the beaches with blind frenzy. The wind hit like a thunder-clap, making the timbers of the fort quiver. The surf roared over the sands drowning the coals of the fires the seamen had built. In the glare of lightning Belesa saw, through the curtain of the slashing rain, the tents of the buccaneers whipped to ribbons and washed away, saw the men themselves staggering toward the fort, beaten almost to the sands by the fury of torrent and blast.

And limned against the blue glare she saw Zarono's ship, ripped loose from her moorings, driven headlong against the jagged cliffs that jutted up to receive her.........

V

A MAN FROM THE WILDERNESS

The storm had spent its fury. Full dawn rose in a clear blue rain-washed sky. As the sun rose in a blaze of fresh gold, bright-hued birds lifted a swelling chorus from the trees on whose broad leaves beads of water sparkled like diamonds, quivering in the gentle morning breeze.

At a small stream which wound over the sands to join the sea, hidden beyond a fringe of trees and bushes, a man bent to lave his hands and face. He performed his ablutions after the manner of his race, grunting lustily and splashing like a buffalo. But in the midst of these splashings he lifted his head suddenly, his tawny hair dripping and water running in rivulets over his brawny shoulders. He crouched in a listening attitude for a split second, then was on his feet and facing inland, sword in hand, all in one motion. And there he froze, glaring wide-mouthed.

A man as big as himself was striding toward him over the sands, making no attempt at stealth; and the pirate's eyes widened as he stared at the close-fitting silk breeches, high flaring-topped boots, wide-skirted coat and head-gear of a hundred years ago. There was a broad cutlass in the stranger's hand and unmistakable purpose in his approach.

The pirate went pale, as recognition blazed in his eyes.

"You!" he ejaculated unbelievingly. "By Mitra! *You!*"

Oaths streamed from his lips as he heaved up his cutlass. The birds rose in flaming showers from the trees as the clang of steel interrupted their song. Blue sparks flew from the hacking blades, and the sand grated and ground under the stamping boot heels. Then the clash of steel ended in a chopping crunch, and one man went to his knees with a choking gasp. The hilt escaped his nerveless hand and he slid full-length on the sand which reddened with his blood. With a dying effort he fumbled at his girdle and drew something from it, tried to lift it to his mouth, and then stiffened convulsively and went limp.

The conqueror bent and ruthlessly tore the stiffening fingers from the object they crumpled in their desperate grasp.

ZARONO and Valenso stood on the beach, staring at the drift wood their men were gathering — spars, pieces of masts, broken timbers. So savagely had the storm hammered Zarono's ship against the low cliffs that most of the salvage was matchwood. A short distance behind them stood Belesa, listening to their conversation, one arm about Tina. The girl was pale and listless, apathetic to whatever Fate held in store for her. She heard what the men said, but with little interest. She was crushed by the realization that she was but a pawn in the game, however it was to be played out — whether it was to be a wretched life dragged out on that desolate coast, or a return, effected somehow, to some civilized land.

Zarono cursed venomously, but Valenso seemed dazed.

"This is not the time of year for storms from the west," he muttered, staring with haggard eyes at the men dragging the wreckage up on the beach. "It was not chance that brought that storm out of the deep to splinter the ship in which I meant to escape. Escape? I am caught like a rat in a trap, as it was meant. Nay, we are all trapped rats —"

"I don't know what you're talking about," snarled Zarono, giving a vicious yank at his mustache. "I've been unable to get any sense out of you since that flaxen-haired slut upset you so last night with her wild tale of black men coming out of the sea. But I do know that I'm not going to spend my life on this cursed coast. Ten of my men went to hell in the ship, but I've got a hundred and sixty more. You've got a hundred. There are tools in your fort, and plenty of trees in yonder forest. We'll build a ship. I'll set men to cutting down trees as soon as they get this drift dragged up out of the reach of the waves."

"It will take months," muttered Valenso.

"Well, is there any better way in which we could employ our time? We're here — and unless we build a ship we'll never get away. We'll have to rig up some kind of a sawmill, but I've never encountered anything yet that balked me long. I hope that storm smashed Strom to bits — the Argossean dog! While we're building the ship we'll hunt for old Tranicos's loot."

"We will never complete your ship," said Valenso somberly.

"You fear the Picts? We have enough men to defy them."

"I do not speak of the Picts. I speak of a black man."

Zarono turned on him angrily.

"Will you talk sense? *Who* is this accursed black man?"

"Accursed indeed," said Valenso, staring sea-ward. "A shadow of mine own red-stained past risen up to hound me to hell. Because of him I fled Zingara, hoping to lose my trail in the great ocean. But I should have known he would smell me out at last."

"If such a man came ashore he must be hiding in the woods," growled Zarono. "We'll rake the forest and hunt him out."

Valenso laughed harshly.

"Seek for a shadow that drifts before a cloud that hides the moon; grope in the dark for a cobra; follow a mist that steals out of the swamp at midnight."

Zarono cast him an uncertain look, obviously doubting his sanity.

"Who is this man? Have done with ambiguity."

"The shadow of my own mad cruelty and ambition; a horror come out of the lost ages; no man of mortal flesh and blood, but a —"

"Sail ho!" bawled the lookout on the north point.

Zarono wheeled and his voice slashed the wind.

"Do you know her?"

"Aye!" the reply came back faintly. "It's *The Red Hand*!"

Zarono cursed like a wild man.

"Strom! The devil takes care of his own! How could he ride out that blow?" The buccaneer's voice rose to a yell that carried up and down the strand. "Back to the fort, you dogs!"

Before *The Red Hand*, somewhat battered in appearance, nosed around the point, the beach was bare of human life, the palisade bristling with helmets and scarf-bound heads. The buccaneers accepted the alliance with the easy adaptability of adventurers, the henchmen with the apathy of serfs.

Zarono ground his teeth as a longboat swung leisurely in to the beach, and he sighted the tawny head of his rival in the bow. The boat grounded, and Strom strode toward the fort alone.

Some distance away he halted and shouted in a bull's bellow that carried clearly in the still morning. "Ahoy, the fort! I want to parley!"

"Well, why in hell don't you?" snarled Zarono.

"The last time I approached under a flag of truce an arrow broke on my brisket!" roared the pirate. "I want a promise it won't happen again!"

"You have my promise!" called Zarono sardonically.

"Damn your promise, you Zingaran dog! I want Valenso's word."

A measure of dignity remained to the Count. There was an edge of authority to his voice as he answered: "Advance, but keep your men back. You will not be fired upon."

"That's enough for me," said Strom instantly. "Whatever a Korzetta's sins, once his word is given, you can trust him."

He strode forward and halted under the gate, laughing at the hate-darkened visage Zarono thrust over at him.

"Well, Zarono," he taunted, "you are a ship shorter than you were when last I saw you! But you Zingarans never were sailors."

"How did you save your ship, you Messantian gutter-scum?" snarled the buccaneer.

"There's a cove some miles to the north protected by a high-ridged arm of land that broke the force of the gale," answered Strom. "I was anchored behind it. My anchors dragged, but they held me off the shore."

Zarono scowled blackly. Valenso said nothing. He had not known of that cove. He had done scant exploring of his domain. Fear of the Picts and lack of curiosity had kept him and his men near the fort. The Zingarans were by nature neither explorers nor colonists.

"I come to make a trade," said Strom, easily.

"We've naught to trade with you save sword-strokes," growled Zarono.

"I think otherwise," grinned Strom, thin-lipped. "You tipped your hand when you murdered Galacus, my first mate, and robbed him. Until this morning I supposed that Valenso had Tranicos's treasure. But if either of you had it, you wouldn't have gone to the trouble of following me and killing my mate to get the map."

"The map?" Zarono ejaculated, stiffening.

"Oh, don't dissemble!" laughed Strom, but anger blazed blue in his eyes. "I know you have it. Picts don't wear boots!"

"But —" began the Count, nonplused, but fell silent as Zarono nudged him.

"And if we have the map," said Zarono, "what have you to trade that we might require?"

"Let me come into the fort," suggested Strom. "There we can talk."

He was not so obvious as to glance at the men peering at them from along the wall, but his two listeners understood. And so did the men. Strom had a ship. That fact would figure in any bargaining, or battle. But it would carry just so many, regardless of who commanded; whoever sailed away in it, there would be some left behind. A wave of tense speculation ran along the silent throng at the palisade.

"Your men will stay where they are," warned Zarono, indicating both the boat drawn up on the beach, and the ship anchored out in the bay.

"Aye. But don't get the idea that you can seize me and hold me for a hostage!" He laughed grimly. "I want Valenso's word that I'll be allowed to leave the fort alive and unhurt within the hour, whether we come to terms or not."

"You have my pledge," answered the Count.

"All right, then. Open that gate and let's talk plainly."

The gate opened and closed, the leaders vanished from sight, and the common men of both parties resumed their silent surveillance of each other: the men on the palisade, and the men squatting beside their boat, with a broad stretch of sand between; and beyond a strip of blue water, the carack, with steel caps glinting all along her rail.

On the broad stair, above the great hall, Belesa and Tina crouched, ignored by the men below. These sat about the broad table: Valenso, Galbro, Zarono and Strom. But for them the hall was empty.

Strom gulped wine and set the empty goblet on the table. The frankness suggested by his bluff countenance was belied by the dancing lights of cruelty and treachery in his wide eyes. But he spoke bluntly enough.

"We all want the treasure old Tranicos hid somewhere near this bay," he said abruptly. "Each has something the others need. Valenso has laborers, supplies, and a stockade to shelter us from the Picts. You, Zarono, have my map. I have a ship."

"What I'd like to know," remarked Zarono, "is this: if you've had that map all these years, why haven't you come after the loot sooner?"

"I didn't have it. It was that dog, Zingelito, who knifed the old miser in the dark and stole the map. But he had neither ship nor crew, and it took him more than a year to get them. When he did come after the treasure, the Picts prevented his landing, and his men mutinied and made him sail back to Zingara. One of them stole the map from him, and recently sold it to me."

"That was why Zingelito recognized the bay," muttered Valenso.

"Did that dog lead you here, Count? I might have guessed it. Where is he?"

"Doubtless in hell, since he was once a buccaneer. The Picts slew him, evidently while he was searching in the woods for the treasure."

"Good!" approved Strom heartily. "Well, I don't know how you knew my mate was carrying the map. I trusted him, and the men trusted him more than they did me, so I let him keep it. But this morning he wandered inland with some of the others, got separated from them, and we found him sworded to death near the beach, and the map gone. The men were ready to accuse me of killing him, but I showed the fools the tracks left by his slayer, and proved to them that my feet wouldn't fit them. And I knew it wasn't any one of the crew, because none of them wear boots that make that sort of track. And Picts don't wear boots at all. So it had to be a Zingaran.

"Well, you've got the map, but you haven't got the treasure. If you had it, you wouldn't have let me inside the stockade. I've got you penned up in this fort. You can't get out to look for the loot, and even if you did get it, you have no ship to get away in.

"Now here's my proposal: Zarono, give me the map. And you, Valenso, give me fresh meat and other supplies. My men are nigh to scurvy after the long voyage. In return I'll take you three men, the Lady Belesa and her girl, and set you ashore within reach of some Zingaran port – or I'll put Zarono ashore near some buccaneer rendezvous if he prefers, since doubtless a noose awaits him in Zingara. And to clinch the bargain I'll give each of you a handsome share in the treasure."

The buccaneer tugged his mustache meditatively. He knew that Strom would not keep any such pact, if made. Nor did Zarono even consider agreeing to his proposal. But to refuse bluntly would be to force the issue into a clash of arms. He sought his agile brain for a plan to outwit the pirate. He wanted Strom's ship as avidly as he desired the lost treasure.

"What's to prevent us from holding you captive and forcing your men to give us your ship in exchange for you?" he asked.

Strom laughed at him.

"Do you think I'm a fool? My men have orders to heave up the anchors and sail hence if I don't reappear within the hour, or if they suspect treachery. They wouldn't give you the ship, if you skinned me alive on the beach. Besides I have the Count's word."

"My pledge is not straw," said Valenso somberly. "Have done with threats, Zarono."

Zarono did not reply, his mind wholly absorbed in the problem of getting possession of Strom's ship; of continuing the parley without betraying the fact that he did not have the map. He wondered who in Mitra's name *did* have the accursed map.

"Let me take my men away with me on your ship when we sail," he said. "I can not desert my faithful followers –"

Strom snorted.

"Why don't you ask for my cutlass to slit my gullet with? Desert your faithful – bah! You'd desert your brother to the devil if you could gain anything by it. No! You're not going to bring enough men aboard to give you a chance to mutiny and take my ship."

"Give us a day to think it over," urged Zarono, fighting for time.

Strom's heavy fist banged on the table, making the wine dance in the glasses.

"No, by Mitra! Give me my answer now!"

Zarono was on his feet, his black rage submerging his craftiness.

"You Barachan dog! I'll give you your answer – in your guts –"

He tore aside his cloak, caught at his sword-hilt. Strom heaved up with a roar, his chair crashing backward to the floor. Valenso sprang up, spreading his arms between them as they faced one another across the board, jutting jaws close together, blades half drawn, faces convulsed.

"Gentlemen, have done! Zarono, he has my pledge –"

"The foul fiend gnaw your pledge!" snarled Zarono.

"Stand from between us, my lord," growled the pirate, his voice thick with the killing lust. "Your word was that I should not be treacherously entreated. It shall be considered no violation of your pledge for this dog and me to cross swords in equal play."

"Well spoken, Strom!" It was a deep, powerful voice behind them, vibrant with grim amusement. All wheeled and glared, open-mouthed. Up on the stair Belesa started up with an involuntary exclamation.

A man strode out from the hangings that masked a chamber door, and advanced toward the table without haste or hesitation. Instantly he dominated the group, and all felt the situation subtly charged with a new, dynamic atmosphere.

The stranger was as tall as either of the freebooters, and more powerfully built than either, yet for all his size he moved with pantherish suppleness in his high, flaring-topped boots. His thighs were cased in close-fitting breeches of white silk, his wide-skirted sky-blue coat open to reveal an open-necked white silken shirt beneath, and the scarlet sash that girdled his waist. There were silver acorn-shaped buttons on the coat, and it was adorned with gilt-worked cuffs and pocket-flaps, and a satin collar. A lacquered hat completed a costume obsolete by nearly a hundred years. A heavy cutlass hung at the wearer's hip.

"Conan!" ejaculated both freebooters together, and Valenso and Galbro caught their breath at that name.

"Who else?" The giant strode up to the table, laughing sardonically at their amazement.

"What – what do you here?" stuttered the seneschal. "How come you here, uninvited and unannounced?"

"I climbed the palisade on the east side while you fools were arguing at the gate," Conan answered. "Every man in the fort was craning his neck westward. I entered the manor while Strom was being let in at the gate. I've been in that chamber there ever since, eavesdropping."

"I thought you were dead," said Zarono slowly. "Three years ago the shattered hull of your ship was sighted off a reefy coast, and you were heard of on the Main no more."

"I didn't drown with my crew," answered Conan. "It'll take a bigger ocean than that one to drown me."

Up on the stair Tina was clutching Belesa in her excitement and staring through the balustrades with all her eyes.

"Conan! My Lady, it is Conan! Look! Oh, look!"

Belesa was looking; it was like encountering a legendary character in the flesh. Who of all the sea-folk had not heard the wild, bloody tales told of Conan, the wild rover who had once been a captain of the Barachan pirates, and one of the greatest scourges of the sea? A score of ballads celebrated his ferocious and audacious exploits. The man could not be ignored; irresistibly he had stalked into the scene, to form another, dominant element in the tangled plot. And in the midst of her frightened fascination, Belesa's feminine instinct prompted the speculation as to Conan's attitude toward her – would it be like Strom's brutal indifference, or Zarono's violent desire?

Valenso was recovering from the shock of finding a stranger within his very hall. He knew Conan was a Cimmerian, born and bred in the wastes of the far north, and therefore not amenable to the physical limitations which controlled civilized men. It was not so strange that he had been able to enter the fort undetected, but Valenso flinched at the reflection that other barbarians might duplicate that feat – the dark, silent Picts, for instance.

"What do you want here?" he demanded. "Did you come from the sea?"

"I came from the woods," the Cimmerian jerked his head toward the east.

"You have been living with the Picts?" Valenso asked coldly.

A momentary anger flickered bluely in the giant's eyes.

"Even a Zingaran ought to know there's never been peace between Picts and Cimmerians, and never will be," he retorted with an oath. "Our feud with them is older than the world. If you'd said that to one of my wilder brothers, you'd have found yourself with a split head. But I've lived among you civilized men long enough to understand your ignorance and lack of common courtesy – the churlishness that demands his business of a man who appears at your door out of a thousand-mile wilderness. Never mind that." He turned to the two freebooters who stood staring glumly at him.

"From what I overheard," quoth he, "I gather there is some dissention over a map!"

"That is none of your affair," growled Strom.

"Is this it?" Conan grinned wickedly and drew from his pocket a crumpled object – a square of parchment, marked with crimson lines.

Strom started violently, paling.

"My map!" he ejaculated. "Where did you get it?"

"From your mate, Galacus, when I killed him," answered Conan with grim enjoyment.

"You dog!" raved Strom, turning on Zarono. "You never had the map! You lied –"

"I didn't say I had it," snarled Zarono. "You deceived yourself. Don't be a fool.

Conan is alone. If he had a crew he'd have already cut our throats. We'll take the map from him —"

"You'll never touch it!" Conan laughed fiercely.

Both men sprang at him, cursing. Stepping back he crumpled the parchment and cast it into the glowing coals of the fireplace. With an incoherent bellow Strom lunged past him, to be met with a buffet under the ear that stretched him half-senseless on the floor. Zarono whipped out his sword but before he could thrust, Conan's cutlass beat it out of his hand.

Zarono staggered against the table, with all hell in his eyes. Strom dragged himself erect, his eyes glazed, blood dripping from his bruised ear. Conan leaned slightly over the table, his outstretched cutlass just touched the breast of Count Valenso.

"Don't call for your soldiers, Count," said the Cimmerian softly. "Not a sound out of you — or from you, either, dog-face!" His name for Galbro, who showed no intention of braving his wrath. "The map's burned to ashes, and it'll do no good to spill blood. Sit down, all of you."

Strom hesitated, made an abortive gesture toward his hilt, then shrugged his shoulders and sank sullenly into a chair. The others followed suit. Conan remained standing, towering over the table, while his enemies watched him with bitter eyes of hate.

"You were bargaining," he said. "That's all I've come to do."

"And what have you to trade?" sneered Zarono.

"The treasure of Tranicos!"

"What?" All four men were on their feet, leaning toward him.

"Sit down!" he roared, banging his broad blade on the table. They sank back, tense and white with excitement.

He grinned in huge enjoyment of the sensation his words had caused.

"Yes! I found it before I got the map. That's why I burned the map. I don't need it. And now nobody will ever find it, unless I show him where it is."

They stared at him with murder in their eyes.

"You're lying," said Zarono without conviction. "You've told us one lie already. You said you came from the woods, yet you say you haven't been living with the Picts. All men know this country is a wilderness, inhabited only by savages. The nearest outposts of civilization are the Aquilonian settlements on Thunder River, hundreds of miles to eastward."

"That's where I came from," replied Conan imperturbably. "I believe I'm the first white man to cross the Pictish Wilderness. I crossed Thunder River to follow a raiding party that had been harrying the frontier. I followed them deep into the wilderness, and killed their chief, but was knocked senseless by a stone from a sling during the melee, and the dogs captured me alive. They were Wolfmen, but they traded me to the Eagle clan in return for a chief of theirs the Eagles had captured. The Eagles carried me nearly a hundred miles westward to burn me in their chief village, but I killed their war-chief and three or four others one night, and broke away.

"I couldn't turn back. They were behind me, and kept herding me westward. A few days ago I shook them off, and by Crom, the place where I took refuge turned out to be the treasure trove of old Tranicos! I found it all: chests of garments and weapons – that's where I got these clothes and this blade – heaps of coins and gems and gold ornaments, and in the midst of all, the jewels of Tothmekri gleaming like frozen starlight! And old Tranicos and his eleven captains sitting about an ebon table and staring at the hoard, as they've stared for a hundred years!"

"What?"

"Aye!" he laughed. "Tranicos died in the midst of his treasure, and all with him! Their bodies have not rotted nor shrivelled. They sit there in their high boots and skirted coats and lacquered hats, with their wine glasses in their stiff hands, just as they have sat for a century!"

"That's an unchancy thing!" muttered Strom uneasily, but Zarono snarled: "What boots it? It's the treasure we want. Go on, Conan."

Conan seated himself at the board, filled a goblet and quaffed it before he answered.

"The first wine I've drunk since I left Conawaga, by Crom! Those cursed Eagles hunted me so closely through the forest I had hardly time to munch the nuts and roots I found. Sometimes I caught frogs and ate them raw because I dared not light a fire."

His impatient hearers informed him profanely that they were not interested in his adventures prior to finding the treasure.

He grinned hardly and resumed: "Well, after I stumbled onto the trove I lay up and rested a few days, and made snares to catch rabbits, and let my wounds heal. I saw smoke against the western sky, but thought it some Pictish village on the beach. I lay close, but as it happens, the loot's hidden in a place the Picts shun. If any spied on me, they didn't show themselves.

"Last night I started westward, intending to strike the beach some miles north of the spot where I'd seen the smoke. I wasn't far from the shore when that storm hit. I took shelter under the lee of a rock and waited until it had blown itself out. Then I climbed a tree to look for Picts, and from it I saw your carack at anchor, Strom, and your men coming in to shore. I was making my way toward your camp on the beach when I met Galacus. I shoved a sword through him because there was an old feud between us. I wouldn't have known he had a map, if he hadn't tried to eat it before he died.

"I recognized it for what it was, of course, and was considering what use I could make of it, when the rest of you dogs came up and found the body. I was lying in a thicket not a dozen yards from you while you were arguing with your men over the matter. I judged the time wasn't ripe for me to show myself then!"

He laughed at the rage and chagrin displayed in Strom's face.

"Well, while I lay there, listening to your talk, I got a drift of the situation, and learned, from the things you let fall, that Zarono and Valenso were a few miles south on the beach. So when I heard you say that Zarono must have done the killing and taken the map, and that you meant to go and parley with him, seeking an opportunity to murder him and get it back —"

"Dog!" snarled Zarono. Strom was livid, but he laughed mirthlessly.

"Do you think I'd play fairly with a treacherous dog like you? – Go on, Conan."

The Cimmerian grinned. It was evident that he was deliberately fanning the fires of hate between the two men.

"Nothing much, then. I came straight through the woods while you tacked along the coast, and raised the fort before you did. Your guess that the storm had destroyed Zarono's ship was a good one – but then, you knew the configuration of this bay.

"Well, there's the story. I have the treasure, Strom has a ship, Valenso has supplies. By Crom, Zarono, I don't see where you fit into the scheme, but to avoid strife I'll include you. My proposal is simple enough.

"We'll split the treasure four ways. Strom and I will sail away with our shares aboard *The Red Hand*. You and Valenso take yours and remain lords of the wilderness, or build a ship out of tree trunks, as you wish."

Valenso blenched and Zarono swore, while Strom grinned quietly.

"Are you fool enough to go aboard *The Red Hand* alone with Strom?" snarled Zarono. "He'll cut your throat before you're out of sight of land!"

Conan laughed with genuine enjoyment.

"This is like the problem of the sheep, the wolf and the cabbage," he admitted. "How to get them across the river without their devouring each other!"

"And that appeals to your Cimmerian sense of humor," complained Zarono.

"I will not stay here!" cried Valenso, a wild gleam in his dark eyes. "Treasure or no treasure, I must go!"

Conan gave him a slit-eyed glance of speculation.

"Well, then," said he, "how about this plan: we divide the loot as I suggested. Then Strom sails away with Zarono, Valenso, and such members of the Count's household as he may select, leaving me in command of the fort and the rest of Valenso's men, and all of Zarono's. I'll build my own ship."

Zarono looked slightly sick.

"I have the choice of remaining here in exile, or abandoning my crew and going alone on *The Red Hand* to have my throat cut?"

Conan's laughter rang gustily through the hall, and he smote Zarono jovially on the back, ignoring the black murder in the buccaneer's glare.

"That's it, Zarono!" quoth he. "Stay here while Strom and I sail away, or sail away with Strom, leaving your men with me."

"I'd rather have Zarono," said Strom frankly. "You'd turn my own men against me, Conan, and cut my throat before I raised the Barachans."

Sweat dripped from Zarono's livid face.

"Neither I, the Count, nor his niece will ever reach the land alive if we ship with that devil," said he. "You are both in my power in this hall. My men surround it. What's to prevent me cutting you both down?"

"Not a thing," Conan admitted cheerfully. "Except the fact that if you do Strom's men will sail away and leave you stranded on this coast where the Picts will presently cut all your throats; and the fact that with me dead you'd never find the treasure; and the fact that I'll split your skull down to your chin if you try to summon your men."

Conan laughed as he spoke, as if at some whimsical situation, but even Belesa sensed that he meant what he said. His naked cutlass lay across his knees, and Zarono's sword was under the table, out of the buccaneer's reach. Galbro was not a fighting man, and Valenso seemed incapable of decision or action.

"Aye!" said Strom with an oath. "You'd find the two of us no easy prey. I'm agreeable to Conan's proposal. What do you say, Valenso?"

"I must leave this coast!" whispered Valenso, staring blankly. "I must hasten – I must go – go far – quickly!"

Strom frowned, puzzled at the Count's strange manner, and turned to Zarono, grinning wickedly: "And you, Zarono?"

"What can I say?" snarled Zarono. "Let me take my three officers and forty men aboard *The Red Hand*, and the bargain's made."

"The officers and thirty men!"

"Very well."

"Done!"

There was no shaking of hands, or ceremonial drinking of wine to seal the pact. The two captains glared at each other like hungry wolves. The Count plucked his mustache with a trembling hand, rapt in his own somber thoughts. Conan stretched like a great cat, drank wine, and grinned on the assemblage; but it was the sinister grin of a stalking tiger. Belesa sensed the murderous purposes that reigned there, the treacherous intent that dominated each man's mind. Not one had any intention of keeping his part of the pact, Valenso possibly excluded. Each of the freebooters intended to possess both the ship and the entire treasure. Neither would be satisfied with less. But how? What was going on in each crafty mind? Belesa felt oppressed and stifled by the atmosphere of hatred and treachery. The Cimmerian, for all his ferocious frankness, was no less subtle than the others – and even fiercer. His domination of the situation was not physical alone, though his gigantic shoulders and massive limbs seemed too big even for the great hall. There was an iron vitality about the man that overshadowed even the hard vigor of the other freebooters.

"Lead us to the treasure!" Zarono demanded.

"Wait a bit," answered Conan. "We must keep our power evenly balanced, so one can't take advantage of the others. We'll work it this way: Strom's men will come ashore, all but half a dozen or so, and camp on the beach. Zarono's men will come out of the fort, and likewise camp on the strand, within easy sight of them. Then each crew can keep a check on the other, to see that nobody slips after us who go after the treasure, to ambush either of us. Those left aboard *The Red Hand* will take her out into the bay out of reach of either party. Valenso's men will stay in the fort, but will leave the gate open. Will you come with us, Count?"

"Go into that forest?" Valenso shuddered, and drew his cloak about his shoulders. "Not for all the gold of Tranicos!"

"All right. It'll take about thirty men to carry the loot. We'll take fifteen from each crew and start as soon as possible."

Belesa, keenly alert to every angle of the drama being played out beneath her, saw Zarono and Strom shoot furtive glances at one another, then lower their gaze quickly as they lifted their glasses to hide the murky intent in their eyes. Belesa saw the fatal weakness in Conan's plan, and wondered how he could have overlooked it. Perhaps he was too arrogantly confident in his personal prowess. But she knew that he would never come out of that forest alive. Once the treasure was in their grasp, the others would form a rogues' alliance long enough to rid themselves of the man both hated. She shuddered, staring morbidly at the man she knew was doomed; strange to see that powerful fighting man sitting there, laughing and swilling wine, in full prime and power, and to know that he was already doomed to a bloody death.

The whole situation was pregnant with dark and bloody portents. Zarono would trick and kill Strom if he could, and she knew that Strom had already marked Zarono for death, and doubtless, also, her uncle and herself. If Zarono won the final battle of cruel wits, their lives were safe — but looking at the buccaneer as he sat there chewing his mustache, with all the stark evil of his nature showing naked in his dark face, she could not decide which was more abhorrent — death or Zarono.

"How far is it?" demanded Strom.

"If we start within the hour we can be back before midnight," answered Conan. He emptied his glass, rose, adjusted his girdle, and glanced at the Count.

"Valenso," he said, "are you mad, to kill a Pict in his hunting paint?"

Valenso started.

"What do you mean?"

"Do you mean to say you don't know that your men killed a Pict hunter in the woods last night?"

The Count shook his head.

"None of my men was in the woods last night."

"Well, somebody was," grunted the Cimmerian, fumbling in a pocket. "I saw his head nailed to a tree near the edge of the forest. He wasn't painted for war. I didn't find any boot-tracks, from which I judged that it had been nailed up there before the storm. But there were plenty of other signs – moccasin tracks on the wet ground. Picts have been there and seen that head. They were men of some other clan, or they'd have taken it down. If they happen to be at peace with the clan the dead man belonged to, they'll make tracks to his village to tell his tribe."

"Perhaps they killed him," suggested Valenso.

"No, they didn't. But they know who did, for the same reason that I know. This chain was knotted about the stump of the severed neck. You must have been utterly mad, to identify your handiwork like that."

He drew forth something and tossed it on the table before the Count who lurched up, choking, as his hand flew to his throat. It was the gold seal-chain he habitually wore about his neck.

"I recognized the Korzetta seal," said Conan. "The presence of that chain would tell any Pict it was the work of a foreigner."

Valenso did not reply. He sat staring at the chain as if at a venomous serpent.

Conan scowled at him, and glanced questioningly at the others. Zarono made a quick gesture to indicate the Count was not quite right in the head.

Conan sheathed his cutlass and donned his lacquered hat.

"All right; let's go."

The captains gulped down their wine and rose, hitching at their sword-belts. Zarono laid a hand on Valenso's arm and shook him slightly. The Count started and stared about him, then followed the others out, like a man in a daze, the chain dangling from his fingers. But not all left the hall.

Belesa and Tina, forgotten on the stair, peeping between the balusters, saw Galbro fall behind the others, loitering until the heavy door closed after them. Then he hurried to the fireplace and raked carefully at the smoldering coals. He sank to his knees and peered closely at something for a long space. Then he straightened and with a furtive air, stole out of the hall by another door.

"What did Galbro find in the fire?" whispered Tina. Belesa shook her head, then, obeying the promptings of her curiosity, rose and went down to the empty hall. An instant later she was kneeling where the seneschal had knelt, and she saw what he had seen.

It was the charred remnant of the map Conan had thrown into the fire. It was ready to crumble at a touch, but faint lines and bits of writing were still discernable upon it. She could not read the writing, but she could trace the outlines of what seemed to be the picture of a hill or crag, surrounded by marks evidently representing dense trees. She could make nothing of it, but from Galbro's actions, she believed he recognized it as portraying some scene or topographical feature familiar to him. She knew the seneschal had penetrated inland further than any other man of the settlement.

VI

THE PLUNDER OF THE DEAD

Belesa came down the stair and paused at the sight of Count Valenso seated at the table, turning the broken chain about in his hands. She looked at him without love, and with more than a little fear. The change that had come over him was appalling; he seemed to be locked up in a grim world all his own, with a fear that flogged all human characteristics out of him.

The fortress stood strangely quiet in the noonday heat that had followed the storm of the dawn. Voices of people within the stockade sounded subdued, muffled. The same drowsy stillness reigned on the beach outside where the rival crews lay in armed suspicion, separated by a few hundred yards of bare sand. Far out in the bay *The Red Hand* lay at anchor with a handful of men aboard her, ready to snatch her out of reach at the slightest indication of treachery. The carack was Strom's trump card, his best guarantee against the trickery of his associates.

Conan had plotted shrewdly to eliminate the chances of an ambush in the forest by either party. But as far as Belesa could see, he had failed utterly to safeguard himself against the treachery of his companions. He had disappeared into the woods, leading the two captains and their thirty men, and the Zingaran girl was positive that she would never see him alive again.

Presently she spoke, and her voice was strained and harsh to her own ear.

"The barbarian has led the captains into the forest. When they have the gold in their hands, they'll kill him. But when they return with the treasure, what then? Are we to go aboard the ship? Can we trust Strom?"

Valenso shook his head absently.

"Strom would murder us all for our shares of the loot. But Zarono whispered his intentions to me secretly. We will not go aboard *The Red Hand* save as her masters. Zarono will see that night overtakes the treasure-party, so they are forced to camp in the forest. He will find a way to kill Strom and his men in their sleep. Then the buccaneers will come on stealthily to the beach. Just before dawn I will send some of my fishermen secretly from the fort to swim out to the ship and seize her. Strom never thought of that, neither did Conan. Zarono and his men will come out of the forest and with the buccaneers encamped on the beach, fall upon the pirates in the dark, while I lead my men-at-arms from the fort to complete the rout. Without their captain they will be demoralized, and outnumbered, fall easy prey to Zarono and me. Then we will sail in Strom's ship with all the treasure."

"And what of me?" she asked with dry lips.

"I have promised you to Zarono," he answered harshly. "But for my promise he would not take us off."

"I will never marry him," she said helplessly.

"You will," he responded gloomily, and without the slightest touch of sympathy. He lifted the chain so it caught the gleam of the sun, slanting through a window. "I must have dropped it on the sand," he muttered. "*He* has been that near — on the beach —"

"You did not drop it on the strand," said Belesa, in a voice as devoid of mercy as his own; her soul seemed turned to stone. "You tore it from your throat, by accident, last night in this hall, when you flogged Tina. I saw it gleaming on the floor before I left the hall."

He looked up, his face grey with a terrible fear.

She laughed bitterly, sensing the mute question in his dilated eyes.

"Yes! The black man! He was here! In this hall! He must have found the chain on the floor. The guardsmen did not see him. But he was at your door last night. I saw him, padding along the upper hallway."

For an instant she thought he would drop dead of sheer terror. He sank back in his chair, the chain slipping from his nerveless fingers and clinking on the table.

"In the manor!" he whispered. "I thought bolts and bars and armed guards could keep him out, fool that I was! I can no more guard against him than I can escape him! At my door! At my door!" The thought overwhelmed him with horror. "Why did he not enter?" he shrieked, tearing at the lace upon his collar as though it strangled him. "Why did he not end it? I have dreamed of waking in my darkened chamber to see him squatting above me and the blue hell-fire playing about his horned head! Why —"

The paroxysm passed, leaving him faint and trembling.

"I understand!" he panted. "He is playing with me, as a cat with a mouse. To have slain me last night in my chamber were too easy, too merciful. So he destroyed the ship in which I might have escaped him, and he slew that wretched Pict and left my chain upon him, so that the savages might believe I had slain him – they have seen that chain upon my neck many a time.

"But why? What subtle deviltry has he in mind, what devious purpose no human mind can grasp or understand?"

"Who is this black man?" asked Belesa, chill fear crawling along her spine.

"A demon loosed by my greed and lust to plague me throughout eternity!" he whispered. He spread his long thin fingers on the table before him, and stared at her with hollow, weirdly-luminous eyes that seemed to see her not at all, but to look through her and far beyond to some dim doom.

"In my youth I had an enemy at court," he said, as if speaking more to himself than to her. "A powerful man who stood between me and my ambition. In my lust for wealth and power I sought aid from the people of the black arts – a black magician, who, at my desire, raised up a fiend from the outer gulfs of existence and clothed it in the form of a man. It crushed and slew my enemy; I grew great and wealthy and none could stand before me. But I thought to cheat my fiend of the price a mortal must pay who calls *the black folk* to do his bidding.

"By his grim arts the magician tricked the soulless waif of darkness and bound him in hell where he howled in vain – I supposed for eternity. But because the sorcerer had given the fiend the form of a man, he could never break the link that bound it to the material world, never completely close the cosmic corridors by which it had gained access to this planet.

"A year ago in Kordava word came to me that the magician, now an ancient man, had been slain in his castle, with marks of demon fingers on his throat. Then I knew that the black one had escaped from the hell where the magician had bound him, and that he would seek vengeance upon me. One night I saw his demon face leering at me from the shadows in my castle hall –

"It was not his material body, but his spirit sent to plague me – his spirit which could not follow me over the windy waters. Before he could reach Kordava in the flesh, I sailed to put broad seas between me and him. He has his limitations. To follow me across the seas he must remain in his man-like body of flesh. But that flesh is not human flesh. He can be slain, I think, by fire, though the magician, having raised him up, was powerless to slay him – such are the limits set upon the powers of sorcerers.

"But the black one is too crafty to be trapped or slain. When he hides himself no man can find him. He steals like a shadow through the night, making naught of bolts and bars. He blinds the eyes of guardsmen with sleep. He can raise storms and command the serpents of the deep, and the fiends of the night. I hoped to drown my trail in the blue rolling wastes — but he has tracked me down to claim his grim forfeit."

The weird eyes lit palely as he gazed beyond the tapestried walls to far, invisible horizons.

"I'll trick him yet," he whispered. "Let him delay to strike this night — dawn will find me with a ship under my heels and again I will cast an ocean between me and his vengeance."

"HELL'S fire!"

Conan stopped short, glaring upward. Behind him the seamen halted — two compact clumps of them, bows in their hands, and suspicion in their attitude. They were following an old path made by Pictish hunters which led due east, and though they had progressed only some thirty yards, the beach was no longer visible.

"What is it?" demanded Strom suspiciously. "What are you stopping for?"

"Are you blind? Look there!"

From the thick limb of a tree that overhung the trail a head grinned down at them — a dark painted face, framed in thick black hair, in which a toucan feather drooped over the left ear.

"I took that head down and hid it in the bushes," growled Conan, scanning the woods about them narrowly. "What fool could have stuck it back up there? It looks as if somebody was trying his damndest to bring the Picts down on the settlement."

Men glanced at each other darkly, a new element of suspicion added to the already seething caldron.

Conan climbed the tree, secured the head and carried it into the bushes where he tossed it into a stream and saw it sink.

"The Picts whose tracks are about this tree weren't Toucans," he growled, returning through the thicket. "I've sailed these coasts enough to know something about the sea-land tribes. If I read the prints of their moccasins right, they were Cormorants. I hope they're having a war with the Toucans. If they're at peace, they'll head straight for the Toucan village, and there'll be hell to pay. I don't know how far away that village is — but as soon as they learn of this murder, they'll come through the forest like starving wolves. That's the worst insult possible to a Pict — kill a man not in war-paint and stick his head up in a tree for the vultures to eat. Damn peculiar things going on along this coast. But that's always the way when civilized men come into the wilderness. They're all crazy as hell. Come on."

Men loosened blades in their scabbards and shafts in their quivers as they strode deeper into the forest. Men of the sea, accustomed to the rolling expanses of grey water, they were ill at ease with the green mysterious walls of trees and vines hemming them in. The path wound and twisted until most of them quickly lost their sense of direction, and did not even know in which direction the beach lay.

Conan was uneasy for another reason. He kept scanning the trail and finally grunted: "Somebody's passed along here recently — not more than an hour ahead of us. Somebody in boots, with no woods-craft. Was he the fool who found that Pict's head and stuck it back up in that tree? No, it couldn't have been him. I didn't find his tracks under the tree. But who was it? I didn't find any tracks there, except those of the Picts I'd seen already. And who's this fellow hurrying ahead of us? Did either of you bastards send a man ahead of us for any reason?"

Both Strom and Zarono loudly disclaimed any such act, glaring at each other with mutual disbelief. Neither man could see the signs Conan pointed out; the faint prints which he saw on the grassless, hard-beaten trail were invisible to their untrained eyes.

Conan quickened his pace and they hurried after him, fresh coals of suspicion added to the smoldering fire of distrust. Presently the path veered northward, and Conan left it, and began threading his way through the dense trees in a southeasterly direction. Strom stole an uneasy glance at Zarono. This might force a change in their plans. Within a few hundred feet from the trail both were hopelessly lost, and convinced of their inability to find their way back to the path. They were shaken by the fear that, after all, the Cimmerian had a force at his command, and was leading them into an ambush.

This suspicion grew as they advanced, and had almost reached panic-proportions when they emerged from the thick woods and saw just ahead of them a gaunt crag that jutted up from the forest floor. A dim path leading out of the woods from the east ran among a cluster of boulders and wound up the crag on a ladder of stony shelves to a flat ledge near the summit.

Conan halted, a bizarre figure in his piratical finery.

"That trail is the one I followed, running from the Eagle-Picts," he said. "It leads up to a cave behind that ledge. In that cave are the bodies of Tranicos and his captains, and the treasure he plundered from Tothmekri. But a word before we go up after it: if you kill me here, you'll never find your way back to the trail we followed from the beach. I know you sea-faring men. You're helpless in the deep woods. Of course the beach lies due west, but if you have to make your way through the tangled woods, burdened with the plunder, it'll take you not hours, but days. And I don't think these woods will be very safe for white men, when the Toucans learn about their hunter." He laughed at the ghastly, mirthless smiles with which they greeted his recognition of their intentions regarding him. And he also comprehended the thought that sprang in the mind of each: let the barbarian secure the loot for them, and lead them back to the beach-trail before they killed him.

"All of you stay here except Strom and Zarono," said Conan. "We three are enough to pack the treasure down from the cave."

Strom grinned mirthlessly.

"Go up there alone with you and Zarono? Do you take me for a fool? One man at least comes with me!" And he designated his boatswain, a brawny, hard-faced giant, naked to his broad leather belt, with gold hoops in his ears, and a crimson scarf knotted about his head.

"And my executioner comes with me!" growled Zarono. He beckoned to a lean sea-thief with a face like a parchment-covered skull, who carried a two-handed scimitar naked over his bony shoulder.

Conan shrugged his shoulders. "Very well. Follow me."

They were close on his heels as he strode up the winding path and mounted the ledge. They crowded him close as he passed through the cleft in the wall behind it, and their breath sucked greedily between their teeth as he called their attention to the iron-bound chests on either side of the short tunnel-like cavern.

"A rich cargo there," he said carelessly. "Silks, laces, garments, ornaments, weapons – the loot of the southern seas. But the real treasure lies beyond that door."

The massive door stood partly open. Conan frowned. He remembered closing that door before he left the cavern. But he said nothing of the matter to his eager companions as he drew aside to let them look through.

They looked into a wide cavern, lit by a strange blue glow that glimmered through a smoky mist-like haze. A great ebon table stood in the midst of the cavern, and in a carved chair with a high back and broad arms, that might once have stood in the castle of some Zingaran baron, sat a giant figure, fabulous and fantastic – there sat Bloody Tranicos, his great head sunk on his bosom, one brawny hand still gripping a jeweled goblet in which wine still sparkled; Tranicos, in his lacquered hat, his gilt-embroidered coat with jeweled buttons that winked in the blue flame, his flaring boots and gold-worked baldric that upheld a jewel-hilted sword in a golden sheath.

And ranging the board, each with his chin resting on his lace-bedecked breast, sat the eleven captains. The blue fire played weirdly on them and on their giant admiral, as it flowed from the enormous jewel on the tiny ivory pedestal, striking glints of frozen fire from the heaps of fantastically cut gems which shone before the place of Tranicos – the plunder of Khemi, the jewels of Tothmekri! The stones whose value was greater than the value of all the rest of the known jewels in the world put together!

The faces of Zarono and Strom showed pallid in the blue glow; over their shoulders their men gaped stupidly.

"Go in and take them," invited Conan, drawing aside, and Zarono and Strom crowded avidly past him, jostling one another in their haste. Their followers were treading on their heels. Zarono kicked the door wide open – and halted with one foot on the threshold at the sight of a figure on the floor, previously hidden from view by the partly-closed door. It was a man, prone and contorted, head drawn back between his shoulders, white face twisted in a grin of mortal agony, gripping his own throat with clawed fingers.

"Galbro!" ejaculated Zarono. "Dead! What —" With sudden suspicion he thrust his head over the threshold, into the bluish mist that filled the inner cavern. And he screamed, chokingly: "There is death in the smoke!"

Even as he screamed, Conan hurled his weight against the four men bunched in the doorway, sending them staggering – but not headlong into the mist-filled cavern as he had planned. They were recoiling at the sight of the dead man and the realization of the trap, and his violent push, while it threw them off their feet, yet failed of the result he desired. Strom and Zarono sprawled half over the threshold on their knees, the boatswain tumbling over their legs, and the executioner caromed against the wall. Before Conan could follow up his ruthless intention of kicking the fallen men into the cavern and holding the door against them until the poisonous mist did its deadly work, he had to turn and defend himself against the frothing onslaught of the executioner who was the first to regain his balance and his wits.

The buccaneer missed a tremendous swipe with his headsman's sword as the Cimmerian ducked, and the great blade banged against the stone wall, spattering blue sparks. The next instant his skullfaced head rolled on the cavern-floor under the bite of Conan's cutlass.

In the split seconds this swift action consumed the boatswain regained his feet, and he fell on the Cimmerian, raining blows with a cutlass that would have overwhelmed a lesser man. Cutlass met cutlass with a ring of steel that was deafening in the narrow cavern. The two captains rolled back across the threshold, gagging and gasping, purple in the face and too near strangled to shout, and Conan redoubled his efforts, in an endeavor to dispose of his antagonist and cut down his rivals before they could recover from the effects of the poison. The boatswain dripped blood at each step, as he was driven back before the ferocious onslaught, and he began desperately to bellow for his companions. But before Conan could deal the finishing stroke, the two chiefs, gasping but murderous, came at him with swords in their hands, croaking for their men.

The Cimmerian bounded back and leaped out onto the ledge. He felt himself a match for all three men, though each was a famed swordsman, but he did not wish to be trapped by the crews which would come charging up the path at the sound of the battle.

These were not coming with as much celerity as he expected, however. They were bewildered at the sounds and muffled shouts issuing from the cavern above them, but no man dared start up the path for fear of a sword in the back. Each band faced the other tensely, grasping their weapons but incapable of decision, and when they saw the Cimmerian bound out on the ledge, they still hesitated. While they stood with their arrows nocked he ran up the ladder of handholds niched in the rock near the cleft, and threw himself prone on the summit of the crag, out of their sight.

The captains stormed out on the ledge, raving and brandishing their swords, and their men, seeing their leaders were not at sword-strokes, ceased menacing each other, and gaped bewilderedly.

"Dog!" screamed Zarono. "You planned to poison us! Traitor!"

Conan mocked them from above.

"Well, what did you expect? You two were planning to cut my throat as soon as I got the plunder for you. If it hadn't been for that fool Galbro I'd have trapped the four of you, and explained to your men how you rushed in heedless to your doom."

"And with us both dead, you'd have taken my ship, and all the loot too!" frothed Strom.

"Aye! And the pick of each crew! I've been wanting to get back on the Main for months, and this was a good opportunity!

"It was Galbro's foot-prints I saw on the trail. I wonder how the fool learned of this cave, or how he expected to lug away the loot by himself."

"But for the sight of his body we'd have walked into that death-trap," muttered Zarono, his swarthy face still ashy. "That blue smoke was like unseen fingers crushing my throat."

"Well, what *are* you going to do?" their unseen tormentor yelled sardonically.

"What are we to do?" Zarono asked of Strom. "The treasure-cavern is filled with that poisonous mist, though for some reason it does not flow across the threshold."

"You can't get the treasure," Conan assured them with satisfaction from his aerie. "That smoke will strangle you. It nearly got me, when I stepped in there. Listen, and I'll tell you a tale the Picts tell in their huts when the fires burn low! Once, long ago, twelve strange men came out of the sea, and found a cave and heaped it with gold and jewels; but a Pictish *shaman* made magic and the earth shook, and smoke came out of the earth and strangled them where they sat at wine. The smoke, which was the smoke of hell's fire, was confined within the cavern by the magic of the wizard. The tale was told from tribe to tribe, and all the clans shun the accursed spot.

"When I crawled in there to escape the Eagle-Picts, I realized that the old legend was true, and referred to old Tranicos and his men. An earthquake cracked the rock floor of the cavern while he and his captains sat at wine, and let the mist out of the depths of the earth – doubtless out of hell, as the Picts say. Death guards old Tranicos's treasure!"

"Bring up the men!" frothed Strom. "We'll climb up and hew him down!"

"Don't be a fool," snarled Zarono. "Do you think any man on earth could climb those hand-holds in the teeth of his sword? We'll have the men up here, right enough, to feather him with shafts if he dares show himself. But we'll get those gems yet. He had some plan of obtaining the loot, or he wouldn't have brought thirty men to bear it back. If he could get it, so can we. We'll bend a cutlass-blade to make a hook, tie it to a rope and cast it about the leg of that table, then drag it to the door."

"Well thought, Zarono!" came down Conan's mocking voice. "Exactly what I had in mind. But how will you find your way back to the beach-path? It'll be dark long before you reach the beach, if you have to feel your way through the woods, and I'll follow you and kill you one by one in the dark."

"It's no empty boast," muttered Strom. "He can move and strike in the dark as subtly and silently as a ghost. If he hunts us back through the forest, few of us will live to see the beach."

"Then we'll kill him here," gritted Zarono. "Some of us will shoot at him while the rest climb the crag. If he is not struck by arrows, some of us will reach him with our swords. Listen! Why does he laugh?"

"To hear dead men making plots," came Conan's grimly amused voice.

"Heed him not," scowled Zarono, and lifting his voice, shouted for the men below to join him and Strom on the ledge.

The sailors started up the slanting trail, and one started to shout a question. Simultaneously there sounded a hum like that of an angry bee, ending in a sharp thud. The buccaneer gasped and blood gushed from his open mouth. He sank to his knees, clutching the black shaft that quivered in his breast. A yell of alarm went up from his companions.

"What's the matter?" shouted Strom.

"*Picts!*" bawled a pirate, lifting his bow and loosing blindly. At his side a man moaned and went down with an arrow through his throat.

"Take cover, you fools!" shrieked Zarono. From his vantage point he glimpsed painted figures moving in the bushes. One of the men on the winding path fell back dying. The rest scrambled hastily down among the rocks about the foot of the crag. They took cover clumsily, not used to this kind of fighting. Arrows flickered from the bushes, splintering on the boulders. The men on the ledge lay prone at full length.

"We're trapped!" Strom's face was pale. Bold enough with a deck under his feet, this silent, savage warfare shook his ruthless nerves.

"Conan said they feared this crag," said Zarono. "When night falls the men must climb up here. We'll hold the crag. The Picts won't rush us."

"Aye!" mocked Conan above them. "They won't climb the crag to get at you, that's true. They'll merely surround it and keep you here until you all die of thirst and starvation."

"He speaks truth," said Zarono helplessly. "What shall we do?"

"Make a truce with him," muttered Strom. "If any man can get us out of this jam, he can. Time enough to cut his throat later." Lifting his voice he called: "Conan, let's forget our feud for the time being. You're in this fix as much as we are. Come down and help us out of it."

"How do you figure that?" retorted the Cimmerian. "I have but to wait until dark, climb down the other side of this crag and melt into the forest. I can crawl through the line the Picts have thrown around this hill, and return to the fort to report you all slain by the savages – which will shortly be truth!"

Zarono and Strom stared at each other in pallid silence.

"But I'm not going to do that!" Conan roared. "Not because I have any love for you dogs, but because a white man doesn't leave white men, even his enemies, to be butchered by Picts."

The Cimmerian's tousled black head appeared over the crest of the crag.

"Now listen closely: that's only a small band down there. I saw them sneaking through the brush when I laughed, awhile ago. Anyway, if there had been many of them, every man at the foot of the crag would be dead already. I think that's a band of fleet-footed young men sent ahead of the main war-party to cut us off from the beach. I'm certain a big war-band is heading in our direction from somewhere.

"They've thrown a cordon around the west side of the crag, but I don't think there are any on the east side. I'm going down on that side and get in the forest and work around behind them. Meanwhile, you crawl down the path and join your men among the rocks. Tell them to sling their bows and draw their swords. When you hear me yell, rush for the trees on the west side of the clearing."

"What of the treasure?"

"To hell with the treasure! We'll be lucky if we get out of here with our heads on our shoulders."

The black-maned head vanished. They listened for sounds to indicate that Conan had crawled to the almost sheer eastern wall and was working his way down, but they heard nothing. Nor was there any sound in the forest. No more arrows broke against the rocks where the sailors were hidden. But all knew that fierce black eyes were watching with murderous patience. Gingerly Strom, Zarono and the boatswain started down the winding path. They were half way down when the black shafts began to whisper around them. The boatswain groaned and toppled limply down the slope, shot through the heart. Arrows shivered on the helmets and breastplates of the chiefs as they tumbled in frantic haste down the steep trail. They reached the foot in a scrambling rush and lay panting among the boulders, swearing breathlessly.

"Is this more of Conan's trickery?" wondered Zarono profanely.

"We can trust him in this matter," asserted Strom. "These barbarians live by their own particular code of honor, and Conan would never desert men of his own complection to be slaughtered by people of another race. He'll help us against the Picts, even though he plans to murder us himself – *hark!*"

A blood-freezing yell knifed the silence. It came from the woods to the west, and simultaneously an object arched out of the trees, struck the ground and rolled bouncingly toward the rocks – a severed human head, the hideously painted face frozen in a snarl of death.

"Conan's signal!" roared Strom, and the desperate freebooters rose like a wave from the rocks and rushed headlong toward the woods.

Arrows whirred out of the bushes, but their flight was hurried and erratic; only three men fell. Then the wild men of the sea plunged through the fringe of foliage and fell on the naked painted figures that rose out of the gloom before them. There was a murderous instant of panting, ferocious effort, hand-to-hand, cutlasses beating down war-axes, booted feet trampling naked bodies, and then bare feet were rattling through the bushes in headlong flight as the survivors of that brief carnage quit the fray, leaving seven still, painted figures stretched on the bloodstained leaves that littered the earth. Further back in the thickets sounded a thrashing and heaving, and then it ceased and Conan strode into view, his lacquered hat gone, his coat torn, his cutlass dripping in his hand.

"What now?" panted Zarono. He knew the charge had succeeded only because Conan's unexpected attack on the rear of the Picts had demoralized the painted men, and prevented them from falling back before the rush. But he exploded into curses as Conan passed his cutlass through a buccaneer who writhed on the ground with a shattered hip.

"We can't carry him with us," grunted Conan. "It wouldn't be any kindness to leave him to be taken alive by the Picts. Come on!"

They crowded close at his heels as he trotted through the trees. Alone they would have sweated and blundered among the thickets for hours before they found the beach-trail – if they had ever found it. The Cimmerian led them as unerringly as if he had been following a blazed path, and the rovers shouted with hysterical relief as they burst suddenly upon the trail that ran westward.

"Fool!" Conan clapped a hand on the shoulder of a pirate who started to break into a run, and hurled him back among his companions. "You'll burst your heart and fall within a thousand yards. We're miles from the beach. Take an easy gait. We may have to sprint the last mile. Save some of your wind for it. Come on, now."

He set off down the trail at a steady jog-trot; the seamen followed him, suiting their pace to his.

THE sun was touching the waves of the western ocean. Tina stood at the window from which Belesa had watched the storm.

"The setting sun turns the ocean to blood," she said. "The carack's sail is a white fleck on the crimson waters. The woods are already darkened with clustering shadows."

"What of the seamen on the beach?" asked Belesa languidly. She reclined on a couch, her eyes closed, her hands clasped behind her head.

"Both camps are preparing their supper," said Tina. "They gather driftwood and build fires. I can hear them shouting to one another – *what is that?*"

The sudden tenseness in the girl's tone brought Belesa upright on the couch. Tina grasped the window-sill, her face white.

"Listen! A howling, far off, like many wolves!"

"Wolves?" Belesa sprang up, fear clutching her heart. "Wolves do not hunt in packs at this time of the year –"

"Oh, look!" shrilled the girl, pointing. "Men are running out of the forest!"

In an instant Belesa was beside her, staring wide-eyed at the figures, small in the distance, streaming out of the woods.

"The sailors!" she gasped. "Empty-handed! I see Zarono – Strom –"

"Where is Conan?" whispered the girl.

Belesa shook her head.

"Listen! Oh, listen!" whimpered the child, clinging to her. "The Picts!"

All in the fort could hear it now – a vast ululation of mad exultation and blood-lust, from the depths of the dark forest.

That sound spurred on the panting men reeling toward the palisade.

"Hasten!" gasped Strom, his face a drawn mask of exhausted effort. "They are almost at our heels. My ship –"

"She is too far out for us to reach," panted Zarono. "Make for the stockade. See, the men camped on the beach have seen us!" He waved his arms in breathless pantomime, but the men on the strand understood, and they recognized the significance of that wild howling, rising to a triumphant crescendo. The sailors abandoned their fires and cooking pots and fled for the stockade gate. They were pouring through it as the fugitives from the forest rounded the south angle and reeled into the gate, a heaving, frantic mob, half-dead from exhaustion. The gate was slammed with frenzied haste, and sailors began to climb the firing-ledge, to join the men-at-arms already there.

Belesa confronted Zarono.

"Where is Conan?"

The buccaneer jerked a thumb toward the blackening woods; his chest heaved; sweat poured down his face. "Their scouts were at our heels before we gained the beach. He paused to slay a few and give us time to get away."

He staggered away to take his place on the firing-ledge, whither Strom had already mounted. Valenso stood there, a somber, cloak-wrapped figure, strangely silent and aloof. He was like a man bewitched.

"Look!" yelped a pirate, above the deafening howling of the yet unseen horde.

A man emerged from the forest and raced fleetly across the open belt.

"Conan!"

Zarono grinned wolfishly.

"We're safe in the stockade; we know where the treasure is. No reason why we shouldn't feather him with arrows now."

"Nay!" Strom caught his arm. "We'll need his sword! Look!"

Behind the fleet-footed Cimmerian a wild horde burst from the forest, howling as they ran — naked Picts, hundreds and hundreds of them. Their arrows rained about the Cimmerian. A few strides more and Conan reached the eastern wall of the stockade, bounded high, seized the points of the logs and heaved himself up and over, his cutlass in his teeth. Arrows thudded venomously into the logs where his body had just been. His resplendent coat was gone, his white silk shirt torn and blood-stained.

"Stop them!" he roared as his feet hit the ground inside. "If they get on the wall, we're done for!"

Pirates, buccaneers and men-at-arms responded instantly, and a storm of arrows and quarrels tore into the oncoming horde.

Conan saw Belesa, with Tina clinging to her hand, and his language was picturesque.

"Get into the manor," he commanded in conclusion. "Their shafts will arch over the wall — what did I tell you?" As a black shaft cut into the earth at Belesa's feet and quivered like a serpent-head, Conan caught up a longbow and leaped to the firing-ledge. "Some of you fellows prepare torches!" he roared, above the rising clamor of battle. "We can't fight them in the dark!"

The sun had sunk in a welter of blood; out in the bay the men aboard the carack had cut the anchor chain and *The Red Hand* was rapidly receding on the crimson horizon.

VII

MEN OF THE WOODS

Night had fallen, but torches streamed across the strand, casting the mad scene into lurid revealment. Naked men in paint swarmed the beach; like waves they came against the palisade, bared teeth and blazing eyes gleaming in the glare of the torches thrust over the wall. Toucan feathers waved in black manes, and the feathers of the cormorant and the sea-falcon. A few warriors, the wildest and most barbaric of them all, wore shark's teeth woven in their tangled locks. The sea-land tribes had gathered from up and down the coast in all directions to rid their country of the white-skinned invaders.

They surged against the palisade, driving a storm of arrows before them, fighting into the teeth of the shafts and bolts that tore into their masses from the stockade. Sometimes they came so close to the wall they were hewing at the gate with their war-axes and thrusting their spears through the loop-holes. But each time the tide ebbed back without flowing over the palisade, leaving its drift of dead. At this kind of fighting the freebooters of the sea were at their stoutest; their arrows and bolts tore holes in the charging horde, their cutlasses hewed the wild men from the palisades they strove to scale.

Yet again and again the men of the woods returned to the onslaught with all the stubborn ferocity that had been roused in their fierce hearts.

"They are like mad dogs!" gasped Zarono, hacking downward at the dark hands that grasped at the palisade points, the dark faces that snarled up at him.

"If we can hold the fort until dawn they'll lose heart," grunted Conan, splitting a feathered skull with professional precision. "They won't maintain a long siege. Look, they're falling back."

The charge rolled back and the men on the wall shook the sweat out of their eyes, counted their dead and took a fresh grasp on the blood-slippery hilts of their swords. Like blood-hungry wolves, grudgingly driven from a cornered prey, the Picts skulked back beyond the ring of torches. Only the bodies of the slain lay before the palisade.

"Have they gone?" Strom shook back his wet, tawny locks. The cutlass in his fist was notched and red, his brawny bare arm was splashed with blood.

"They're still out there," Conan nodded toward the outer darkness which ringed the circle of torches, made more intense by their light. He glimpsed movements in the shadows, glitter of eyes and the dull sheen of steel.

"They've drawn off for a bit, though," he said. "Put sentries on the wall, and let the rest drink and eat. It's past midnight. We've been fighting for hours without much interval."

The chiefs clambered down from the ledges, calling their men from the walls. A sentry was posted in the middle of each wall, east, west, north and south, and a clump of men-at-arms were left at the gate. The Picts, to reach the wall, would have to charge across a wide, torch-lit space, and the defenders could resume their places long before the attackers could reach the palisade.

"Where's Valenso?" demanded Conan, gnawing a huge beef-bone as he stood beside the fire the men had built in the center of the compound. Pirates, buccaneers and henchmen mingled with each other, wolfing the meat and ale the women brought them, and allowing their wounds to be bandaged.

"He disappeared an hour ago," grunted Strom. "He was fighting on the wall beside me, when suddenly he stopped short and glared out into the darkness as if he saw a ghost. 'Look!' he croaked. 'The black devil! I see him! Out there in the night!' Well, I could swear I saw a figure moving among the shadows that was too tall for a Pict. But it was just a glimpse and it was gone. But Valenso jumped down from the firing-ledge and staggered into the manor like a man with a mortal wound. I haven't seen him since."

"He probably saw a forest-devil," said Conan tranquilly. "The Picts say this coast is lousy with them. What I'm more afraid of is fire-arrows. The Picts are likely to start shooting them any time. What's that? It sounded like a cry for help."

WHEN the lull came in the fighting, Belesa and Tina had crept to their window, from which they had been driven by the danger of flying arrows. Silently they watched the men gather about the fire.

"There are not enough men on the stockade," said Tina.

In spite of her nausea at the sight of the corpses sprawled about the palisade, Belesa was forced to laugh.

"Do you think you know more about wars and sieges than the freebooters?" she chided gently.

"There should be more men on the walls," insisted the child, shivering. "Suppose the black man came back?"

Belesa shuddered at the thought.

"I am afraid," murmured Tina. "I hope Strom and Zarono are killed."

"And not Conan?" asked Belesa curiously.

"Conan would not harm us," said the child, confidently. "He lives up to his barbaric code of honor, but they are men who have lost all honor."

"You are wise beyond your years, Tina," said Belesa, with the vague uneasiness the precocity of the girl frequently roused in her.

"Look!" Tina stiffened. "The sentry is gone from the south wall! I saw him on the ledge a moment ago; now he has vanished."

From their window the palisade points of the south wall were just visible over the slanting roofs of a row of huts which paralleled that wall almost its entire length. A sort of open-topped corridor, three or four yards wide, was formed by the stockade and the back of the huts, which were built in a solid row. These huts were occupied by the serfs.

"Where could the sentry have gone?" whispered Tina uneasily.

Belesa was watching one end of the hut-row which was not far from a side door of the manor. She could have sworn she saw a shadowy figure glide from behind the huts and disappear at the door. Was that the vanished sentry? Why had he left the wall, and why should he steal so subtly into the manor? She did not believe it was the sentry she had seen and a nameless fear congealed her blood.

"Where is the Count, Tina?" she asked.

"In the great hall, my Lady. He sits alone at the table, wrapped in his cloak and drinking wine, with a face grey as death."

"Go and tell him what we have seen. I will keep watch from this window, lest the Picts steal to the unguarded wall."

Tina scampered away. Belesa heard her slippered feet pattering along the corridor, receding down the stair. Then abruptly, terribly, there rang out a scream of such poignant fear that Belesa's heart almost stopped with the shock of it. She was out of the chamber and flying down the corridor before she was aware that her limbs were in motion. She ran down the stair – and halted as if turned to stone.

She did not scream as Tina had screamed. She was incapable of sound or motion. She saw Tina, was aware of the reality of small hands grasping her frantically. But these were the only sane realities in a scene of black nightmare and lunacy and death, dominated by the monstrous, anthropomorphic shadow which spread awful arms against a lurid, hell-fire glare.

Out in the stockade Strom shook his head at Conan's question.

"I heard nothing."

"I did!" Conan's wild instincts were roused; he was tensed, his eyes blazing. "It came from the south wall, behind those huts!"

Drawing his cutlass he strode toward the palisade. From the compound the wall on the south and the sentry posted there were not visible, being hidden behind the huts. Strom followed, impressed by the Cimmerian's manner.

At the mouth of the open space between the huts and wall Conan halted, warily. The space was dimly lighted by torches flaring at either corner of the stockade. And about mid-way of that natural corridor a crumpled shape sprawled on the ground.

"Bracus!" swore Strom, running forward and dropping on one knee beside the figure. "By Mitra, his throat's been cut from ear to ear!"

Conan swept the space with a quick glance, finding it empty save for himself, Strom and the dead man. He peered through a loop-hole. No living man moved within the ring of torch-light outside the fort.

"Who could have done this?" he wondered.

"Zarono!" Strom sprang up, spitting fury like a wildcat, his hair bristling, his face convulsed. "He has set his thieves to stabbing my men in the back! He plans to wipe me out by treachery! Devils! I am leagued within and without!"

"Wait!" Conan reached a restraining hand. "I don't believe Zarono —"

But the maddened pirate jerked away and rushed around the end of the hut-row, breathing blasphemies. Conan ran after him, swearing. Strom made straight toward the fire by which Zarono's tall lean form was visible as the buccaneer chief quaffed a jack of ale.

His amazement was supreme when the jack was dashed violently from his hand, spattering his breastplate with foam, and he was jerked around to confront the passion-distorted face of the pirate captain.

"You murdering dog!" roared Strom. "Will you slay my men behind my back while they fight for your filthy hide as well as for mine?"

Conan was hurrying toward them and on all sides men ceased eating and drinking to stare in amazement.

"What do you mean?" sputtered Zarono.

"You've set your men to stabbing mine at their posts!" screamed the maddened Barachan.

"You lie!" Smoldering hate burst into sudden flame.

With an incoherent howl Strom heaved up his cutlass and cut at the buccaneer's head. Zarono caught the blow on his armored left arm and sparks flew as he staggered back, ripping out his own sword.

In an instant the captains were fighting like madmen, their blades flaming and flashing in the firelight. Their crews reacted instantly and blindly. A deep roar went up as pirates and buccaneers drew their swords and fell upon each other. The men left on the walls abandoned their posts and leaped down into the stockade, blades in hand. In an instant the compound was a battle-ground, where knotting, writhing groups of men smote and slew in a blind frenzy. Some of the men-at-arms and serfs were drawn into the melee, and the soldiers at the gate turned and stared down in amazement, forgetting the enemy which lurked outside.

It had all happened so quickly – smoldering passions exploding into sudden battle – that men were fighting all over the compound before Conan could reach the maddened chiefs. Ignoring their swords he tore them apart with such violence that they staggered backward, and Zarono tripped and fell headlong.

"You cursed fools, will you throw away all our lives?"

Strom was frothing mad and Zarono was bawling for assistance. A buccaneer ran at Conan from behind and cut at his head. The Cimmerian half turned and caught his arm, checking the stroke in mid-air.

"Look, you fools!" he roared, pointing with his sword. Something in his tone caught the attention of the battle-crazed mob; men froze in their places, with lifted swords, Zarono on one knee, and twisted their heads to stare. Conan was pointing at a soldier on the firing-ledge. The man was reeling, arms clawing the air, choking as he tried to shout. Suddenly he pitched headlong to the ground and all saw the black arrow standing up between his shoulders.

A cry of alarm rose from the compound. On the heels of the shout came a clamor of blood-freezing screams, the shattering impact of axes on the gate. Flaming arrows arched over the wall and stuck in logs, and thin wisps of blue smoke curled upward. Then from behind the huts that ranged the south wall came swift and furtive figures racing across the compound.

"The Picts are in!" roared Conan.

Bedlam followed his shout. The freebooters ceased their feud, some turned to meet the savages, some to spring to the wall. Savages were pouring from behind the huts and they streamed over the compound; their axes clashed against the cutlasses of the sailors.

Zarono was struggling to his feet when a painted savage rushed upon him from behind and brained him with a war-axe.

Conan with a clump of sailors behind him was battling with the Picts inside the stockade, and Strom, with most of his men, was climbing up on the firing-ledges, slashing at the dark figures already swarming over the wall. The Picts, who had crept up unobserved and surrounded the fort while the defenders were fighting among themselves, were attacking from all sides. Valenso's soldiers were clustered at the gate, trying to hold it against a howling swarm of exultant demons.

More and more savages streamed from behind the huts, having scaled the undefended south wall. Strom and his pirates were beaten back from the other sides of the palisade and in an instant the compound was swarming with naked warriors. They dragged down the defenders like wolves; the battle revolved into swirling whirlpools of painted figures surging about small groups of desperate white men. Picts, sailors and henchmen littered the earth, stamped underfoot by the heedless feet. Blood-smeared braves dived howling into huts and the shrieks that rose from the interiors where women and children died beneath the red axes rose above the din of the battle. The men-at-arms abandoned the gate when they heard those pitiful cries, and in an instant the Picts had burst it and were pouring into the palisade at that point also. Huts began to go up in flames.

"Make for the manor!" roared Conan, and a dozen men surged in behind him as he hewed an inexorable way through the snarling pack.

Strom was at his side, wielding his red cutlass like a flail.

"We can't hold the manor," grunted the pirate.

"Why not?" Conan was too busy with his crimson work to spare a glance.

"Because – uh!" A knife in a dark hand sank deep in the Barachan's back. "Devil eat you, bastard!" Strom turned staggeringly and split the savage's head to his teeth. The pirate reeled and fell to his knees, blood starting from his lips.

"The manor's burning!" he croaked, and slumped over in the dust.

Conan cast a swift look about him. The men who had followed him were all down in their blood. The Pict gasping out his life under the Cimmerian's feet was the last of the group which had barred his way. All about him battle was swirling and surging, but for the moment he stood alone. He was not far from the south wall. A few strides and he could leap to the ledge, swing over and be gone through the night. But he remembered the helpless girls in the manor – from which, now, smoke was rolling in billowing masses. He ran toward the manor.

A feathered chief wheeled from the door, lifting a war-axe, and behind the racing Cimmerian lines of fleet-footed braves were converging upon him. He did not check his stride. His downward sweeping cutlass met and deflected the axe and split the skull of the wielder. An instant later Conan was through the door and had slammed and bolted it against the axes that splintered into the wood.

The great hall was full of drifting wisps of smoke through which he groped half-blinded. Somewhere a woman was whimpering, little, catchy, hysterical sobs of nerve-shattering horror. He emerged from a whorl of smoke and stopped dead in his tracks, glaring down the hall.

The hall was dim and shadowy with drifting smoke; the silver candelabrum was overturned, the candles extinguished; the only illumination was a lurid glow from the great fireplace and the wall in which it was set, where the flames licked from burning floor to smoking roof-beams. And limned against that lurid glare Conan saw a human form swinging slowly at the end of a rope. The dead face turned toward him as the body swung, and it was distorted beyond recognition. But Conan knew it was Count Valenso, hanged to his own roof-beam.

But there was something else in the hall. Conan saw it through the drifting smoke – a monstrous black figure, outlined against the hell-fire glare. That outline was vaguely human; but the shadow thrown on the burning wall was not human at all.

"Crom!" muttered Conan aghast, paralyzed by the realization that he was confronted with a being against which his sword was helpless. He saw Belesa and Tina, clutched in each other's arms, crouching at the bottom of the stair.

The black monster reared up, looming gigantic against the flame, great arms spread wide; a dim face leered through the drifting smoke, semi-human, demoniac, altogether terrible – Conan glimpsed the close-set horns, the gaping mouth, the peaked ears – it was lumbering toward him through the smoke, and an old memory woke with desperation.

Near the Cimmerian stood a massive silver bench, ornately carven, once part of the splendor of Korzetta castle. Conan grasped it, heaved it high above his head.

"Silver and fire!" he roared in a voice like a clap of wind and hurled the bench with all the power of his iron muscles. Full on the great black breast it crashed, a hundred pounds of silver winged with terrific velocity. Not even the black one could stand before such a missile. He was carried off his feet – hurtled backward headlong into the open fireplace which was a roaring mouth of flame. A horrible scream shook the hall, the cry of an unearthly thing gripped suddenly by earthly death. The mantel cracked and stones fell from the great chimney; half-hiding the black writhing limbs at which the flames were eating in elemental fury. Burning beams crashed down from the roof and thundered on the stones, and the whole heap was enveloped by a roaring burst of fire.

Flames were racing down the stair when Conan reached it. He caught up the fainting child under one arm and dragged Belesa to her feet. Through the crackle and snap of the fire sounded the splintering of the door under the war-axes.

He glared about, sighted a door opposite the stair-landing, and hurried through it, carrying Tina and half-dragging Belesa who seemed dazed. As they came into the chamber beyond a reverberation behind them announced that the roof was falling in the hall. Through a strangling wall of smoke Conan saw an open, outer door on the other side of the chamber. As he lugged his charges through it, he saw it sagged on broken hinges, lock and bolt snapped and splintered as if by some terrific force.

"The black man came in by this door!" Belesa sobbed hysterically. "I saw him — but I did not know —"

They emerged into the fire-lit compound, a few feet from the hut-row that lined the south wall. A Pict was skulking toward the door, eyes red in the firelight, axe lifted. Turning the girl on his arm away from the blow, Conan drove his cutlass through the savage's breast, and then, sweeping Belesa off her feet, ran toward the south wall, carrying both girls.

The compound was full of billowing smoke clouds that hid half the red work going on there; but the fugitives had been seen. Naked figures, black against the dull glare, pranced out of the smoke, brandishing gleaming axes. They were still yards behind him when Conan ducked into the space between the huts and the wall. At the other end of the corridor he saw other howling shapes, running to cut him off. Halting short he tossed Belesa bodily to the firing-ledge and leaped after her. Swinging her over the palisade he dropped her into the sand outside, and dropped Tina after her. A thrown axe crashed into a log by his shoulder, and then he too was over the wall and gathering up his dazed and helpless charges. When the Picts reached the wall the space before the palisade was empty of all except the dead.

VIII
A PIRATE RETURNS TO THE SEA

Dawn was tinging the dim waters with an old rose hue. Far out across the tinted waters a fleck of white grew out of the mist — a sail that seemed to hang suspended in the pearly sky. On a bushy headland Conan the Cimmerian held a ragged cloak over a fire of green wood. As he manipulated the cloak, puffs of smoke rose upward, quivered against the dawn and vanished.

Belesa crouched near him, one arm about Tina.

"Do you think they'll see it and understand?"

"They'll see it, right enough," he assured her. "They've been hanging off and on this coast all night, hoping to sight some survivors. They're scared stiff. There's only half a dozen of them, and not one can navigate well enough to sail from here to the Barachan Isles. They'll understand my signals; it's the pirate code. I'm telling them that the captains are dead and all the sailors, and for them to come in shore and take us aboard. They know I can navigate, and they'll be glad to ship under me; they'll have to. I'm the only captain left."

"But suppose the Picts see the smoke?" She shuddered, glancing back over the misty sands and bushes to where, miles to the north, a column of smoke stood up in the still air.

"They're not likely to see it. After I hid you in the woods I crept back and saw them dragging barrels of wine and ale out of the storehouses. Already most of them were reeling. They'll all be lying around too drunk to move by this time. If I had a hundred men I could wipe out the whole horde. Look! There goes a rocket from *The Red Hand*! That means they're coming to take us off!"

Conan stamped out the fire, handed the cloak back to Belesa and stretched like a great lazy cat. Belesa watched him in wonder. His unperturbed manner was not assumed; the night of fire and blood and slaughter, and the flight through the black woods afterward had left his nerves untouched. He was as calm as if he had spent the night in feast and revel. Belesa did not fear him; she felt safer than she had felt since she landed on that wild coast. He was not like the freebooters, civilized men who had repudiated all standards of honor, and lived without any. Conan, on the other hand, lived according to the code of his people, which was barbaric and bloody, but at least upheld its own peculiar standards of honor.

"Do you think he is dead?" she asked, with seeming irrelevancy.

He did not ask her to whom she referred.

"I believe so. Silver and fire are both deadly to evil spirits, and he got a bellyfull of both."

Neither spoke of that subject again; Belesa's mind shrank from the task of conjuring up the scene when a black figure skulked into the great hall and a long delayed vengeance was horribly consummated.

"What will you do when you get back to Zingara?" Conan asked.

She shook her head helplessly. "I do not know. I have neither money nor friends. I am not trained to earn my living. Perhaps it would have been better had one of those arrows struck my heart."

"Do not say that, my Lady!" begged Tina. "I will work for us both!"

Conan drew a small leather bag from inside his girdle.

"I didn't get Tothmekri's jewels," he rumbled. "But here are some baubles I found in the chest where I got the clothes I'm wearing." He spilled a handful of flaming rubies into his palm. "They're worth a fortune, themselves." He dumped them back into the bag and handed it to her.

"But I can't take these —" she began.

"Of course you'll take them. I might as well leave you for the Picts to scalp as to take you back to Zingara to starve," said he. "I know what it is to be penniless in a Hyborian land. Now in my country sometimes there are famines; but people are hungry only when there's no food in the land at all. But in civilized countries I've seen people sick of gluttony while others were starving. Aye, I've seen men fall and die of hunger against the walls of shops and storehouses crammed with food.

"Sometimes I was hungry, too, but then I took what I wanted at sword's-point. But you can't do that. So you take these rubies. You can sell them and buy a castle, and slaves and fine clothes, and with them it won't be hard to get a husband, because civilized men all desire wives with these possessions."

"But what of you?"

Conan grinned and indicated *The Red Hand* drawing swiftly inshore.

"A ship and a crew are all I want. As soon as I set foot on that deck, I'll have a ship, and as soon as I can raise the Barachans I'll have a crew. The lads of the Red Brotherhood are eager to ship with me, because I always lead them to rare loot. And as soon as I've set you and the girl ashore on the Zingaran coast, I'll show the dogs some looting! Nay, nay, no thanks! What are a handful of gems to me, when all the loot of the southern seas will be mine for the grasping?"

The Man-Eaters of Zamboula

The Man-Eaters of Zamboula

I

A DRUM BEGINS

"Peril hides in the house of Aram Baksh!"

The speaker's voice quivered with earnestness and his lean, black-nailed fingers clawed at Conan's mightily-muscled arm as he croaked his warning. He was a wiry, sun-burnt man with a straggling black beard, and his ragged garments proclaimed him a nomad. He looked smaller and meaner than ever in contrast to the giant Cimmerian with his black brows, broad breast, and powerful limbs. They stood in a corner of the Sword-Makers' Bazaar, and on either side of them flowed past the many-tongued, many-colored stream of the Zamboula streets, which is exotic, hybrid, flamboyant and clamorous.

Conan pulled his eyes back from following a bold-eyed, red-lipped Ghanara, whose short slit skirt bared her brown thigh at each insolent step, and frowned down at his importunate companion.

"What do you mean by peril?" he demanded.

The desert man glanced furtively over his shoulder before replying, and lowered his voice.

"Who can say? But desert men and travellers *have* slept in the house of Aram Baksh, and never been seen or heard of again! What became of them? *He* swore they rose and went their way — and it is true that no citizen of the city has ever disappeared from his house. But no one saw the travellers again, and men say that goods and equipment recognized as theirs have been seen in the bazaars. If Aram did not sell them, after doing away with their owners, how came them there?"

"I have no goods," growled the Cimmerian, touching the shagreen-bound hilt of the broadsword that hung at his hip. "I have even sold my horse."

"But it is not always rich strangers who vanish by night from the house of Aram Baksh!" chattered the Zuagir. "Nay, poor desert men have slept there – because his score is less than that of the other taverns – and have been seen no more! Once a chief of the Zuagirs whose son had thus vanished complained to the satrap, Jungir Khan, who ordered the house searched by soldiers."

"And they found a cellar full of corpses?" asked Conan in good-humored derision.

"Nay! They found naught! And drove the chief from the city with threats and curses! But –" he drew closer to Conan and shivered, "something else was found! At the edge of the desert, beyond the houses, there is a clump of palm-trees, and within that grove there is a pit. And within that pit have been found human bones, charred and blackened! Not once but many times!"

"Which proves what?" grunted the Cimmerian.

"Aram Baksh is a demon! Nay, in this accursed city which Stygians built and which Hyrkanians rule – where white, brown and black folk mingle together to produce hybrids of all unholy hues and breeds – who can tell who is a man, and who a demon in disguise? Aram Baksh is a demon in the form of a man! At night he assumes his true guise and carries his guests off into the desert where his fellow demons from the waste meet in conclave!"

"Why does he always carry off strangers?" asked Conan skeptically.

"The people of the city would not suffer him to slay their people! But they care naught for the strangers who fall into his hands. Conan, you are of the West, and know not the secrets of this ancient land. But, since the beginning of happenings, the demons of the desert have worshipped Yog, the Lord of the Empty Abodes, with fire – fire that devours human victims!

"Be warned! Thou hast dwelt for many moons in the tents of the Zuagirs, and thou art our brother! Go not to the house of Aram Baksh!"

"Get out of sight!" Conan said suddenly. "Yonder comes a squad of the city-watch. If they see you they may remember a horse that was stolen from the satrap's stable –"

The Zuagir gasped, and moved convulsively. He ducked between a booth and a stone horse trough, pausing only long enough to chatter: "Be warned, my brother! There are demons in the house of Aram Baksh!" Then he darted down a narrow alley and was gone.

Conan shifted his broad sword-belt to his liking, and calmly returned the searching stares directed at him by the squad of watchmen as they swung past. They eyed him curiously and suspiciously, for he was a man who stood out even in such a motley throng as crowded the winding streets of Zamboula. His blue eyes and alien features distinguished him from the Eastern swarms, and the straight sword at his hip added point to the racial difference.

The watchmen did not accost him, but swung on down the street, while the crowd opened a lane for them. They were Pelishtim, squat, hook-nosed, with blue-black beards sweeping their mailed breasts – mercenaries hired for work the ruling Turanians considered beneath themselves, and no less hated by the mongrel population for that reason.

Conan glanced at the sun, just beginning to dip behind the flat-topped houses on the western side of the bazaar, and hitching once more at his belt, moved off in the direction of Aram Baksh's tavern.

With a hillman's stride he moved through the ever-shifting colors of the streets, where the ragged tunics of whining beggars brushed against the ermine-trimmed *khalats* of lordly merchants, and the pearl-sewn satin of rich courtesans. Giant black slaves slouched along, jostling blue-bearded wanderers from the Shemitish cities, ragged nomads from the surrounding deserts, traders and adventurers from all the lands of the East.

The native population was no less heterogeneous. Here, centuries ago, the armies of Stygia had come, carving an empire out of the eastern desert. Zamboula was but a small trading town then, lying amidst a ring of oases, and inhabited by descendants of nomads. The Stygians built it into a city and settled it with their own people, and with Shemite and Kushite slaves. The ceaseless caravans, threading the desert from east to west and back again, brought riches and more mingling of races. Then came the conquering Turanians, riding out of the East to thrust back the boundaries of Stygia, and now for a generation Zamboula had been Turan's western-most out-post, ruled by a Turanian satrap.

The babel of a myriad tongues smote on the Cimmerian's ears as the restless pattern of the Zamboula streets weaved about him – cleft now and then by a squad of clattering horsemen, the tall, supple warriors of Turan, with dark hawk-faces, clinking metal and curved swords. The throng scampered from under their horses' hoofs, for they were the lords of Zamboula. But tall, somber Stygians, standing back in the shadows, glowered darkly, remembering their ancient glories. The hybrid population cared little whether the king who controlled their destinies dwelt in dark Khemi or gleaming Aghrapur. Jungir Khan ruled Zamboula, and men whispered that Nafertari, the satrap's mistress, ruled Jungir Khan; but the people went their way, flaunting their myriad colors in the streets, bargaining, disputing, gambling, swilling, loving, as the people of Zamboula have done for all the centuries its towers and minarets have lifted over the sands of the Kharamun.

Bronze lanterns, carven with leering dragons, had been lighted in the streets before Conan reached the house of Aram Baksh. The tavern was the last occupied house on the street, which ran west. A wide garden, enclosed by a wall, where date palms grew thick, separated it from the houses farther east. To the west of the inn stood another grove of palms, through which the street, now become a road, wound out into the desert. Across the road from the tavern stood a row of deserted huts, shaded by straggling palm trees, and occupied only by bats and jackals. As Conan came down the road he wondered why the beggars, so plentiful in Zamboula, had not appropriated these empty houses for sleeping quarters. The lights ceased some distance behind him. Here were no lanterns, except the one hanging before the tavern gate: only the stars, the soft dust of the road underfoot, and the rustle of the palm-leaves in the desert breeze.

Aram's gate did not open upon the road, but upon the alley which ran between the tavern and the garden of the date-palms. Conan jerked lustily at the rope which depended from the bell beside the lantern, augmenting its clamor by hammering on the iron-bound teak-wood gate with the hilt of his sword. A wicket opened in the gate and a black face peered through.

"Open, blast you," requested Conan. "I'm a guest. I've paid Aram for a room, and a room I'll have, by Crom!"

The black craned his neck to stare into the starlit road behind Conan; but he opened the gate without comment, and closed it again behind the Cimmerian, locking it and bolting it. The wall was unusually high; but there were many thieves in Zamboula, and a house on the edge of the desert might have to be defended against a nocturnal nomad raid. Conan strode through a garden where great pale blossoms nodded in the starlight, and entered the tap-room, where a Stygian with the shaven head of a student sat at a table brooding over nameless mysteries, and some nondescripts wrangled over a game of dice in a corner.

Aram Baksh came forward, walking softly, a portly man, with a black beard that swept his breast, a jutting hook nose, and small black eyes which were never still.

"You wish food?" he asked. "Drink?"

"I ate a joint of beef and a loaf of bread in the *suk*," grunted Conan. "Bring me a tankard of Ghazan wine — I've got just enough left to pay for it." He tossed a copper coin on the wine-splashed board.

"You did not win at the gaming tables?"

"How could I, with only a handful of silver to begin with? I paid you for the room this morning, because I knew I'd probably lose. I wanted to be sure I had a roof over my head tonight. I notice nobody sleeps in the streets in Zamboula. The very beggars hunt a niche they can barricade before dark. The city must be full of a particularly blood-thirsty brand of thieves."

He gulped the cheap wine with relish, and then followed Aram out of the tap-room. Behind him the players halted their game to stare after him with a cryptic speculation in their eyes. They said nothing, but the Stygian laughed, a ghastly laugh of inhuman cynicism and mockery. The others lowered their eyes uneasily, avoiding each others' glance. The arts studied by a Stygian scholar are not calculated to make him share the feelings of a normal human being.

Conan followed Aram down a corridor lighted by copper lamps, and it did not please him to note his host's noiseless tread. Aram's feet were clad in soft slippers and the hall-way was carpeted with thick Turanian rugs; but there was an unpleasant suggestion of innate stealthiness about the Zamboulan. At the end of the winding corridor Aram halted at a door, across which a heavy iron bar rested in powerful metal brackets. This Aram lifted and showed the Cimmerian into a well appointed chamber, the windows of which, Conan instantly noted, were small and strongly set with twisted bars of iron, tastefully gilded. There were rugs on the floor, a couch, after the Eastern fashion, and ornately carven stools. It was a much more elaborate chamber than Conan could have procured for the price nearer the center of the city — a fact that had first attracted him, when, that morning, he discovered how slim a purse his roisterings for the past few days had left him. He had ridden into Zamboula from the desert a week before.

Aram had lighted a bronze lamp, and he now called Conan's attention to the two doors. Both were provided with heavy bolts.

"You may sleep safely tonight, Cimmerian," said Aram, blinking over his bushy beard from the inner doorway. Conan grunted and tossed his naked broadsword on the couch.

"Your bolts and bars are strong; but I always sleep with steel by my side."

Aram made no reply; he stood fingering his thick beard for a moment as he stared at the grim weapon. Then silently he withdrew, closing the door behind him. Conan shot the bolt into place, crossed the room, opened the opposite door and looked out. The room was on the side of the house that faced the road running west from the city. The door opened into a small court that was enclosed by a wall of its own. The end-walls, which shut it off from the rest of the tavern compound, were high and without entrances; but the wall that flanked the road was low, and there was no lock on the gate.

Conan stood for a moment in the door, the glow of the bronze lamp behind him, looking down the road to where it vanished among the dense palms. Their leaves rustled together in the faint breeze; beyond them lay the naked desert. Far up the street, in the other direction, lights gleamed and the noises of the city came faintly to him. Here was only starlight, the whispering of the palm-leaves, and beyond that low wall, the dust of the road and the deserted huts thrusting their flat roofs against the low stars. Somewhere beyond the palm groves a drum began.

The garbled warnings of the Zuagir returned to him, seeming somehow less fantastic than they had seemed on the crowded, sunlit streets. He wondered again at the riddle of those empty huts. Why did the beggars shun them? He turned back into the chamber, shut the door and bolted it.

The light began to flicker and he investigated, swearing when he found the palm-oil in the lamp was almost exhausted. He started to shout for Aram, then shrugged his shoulders and blew out the light. In the soft darkness he stretched himself fully clad on the couch, his sinewy hand by instinct searching for and closing on the hilt of his broadsword. Glancing idly at the stars framed in the barred windows, with the murmur of the breeze through the palms in his ears, he sank into slumber with a vague consciousness of the muttering drum, out on the desert – the low rumble and mutter of a leather-covered drum, beaten with soft, rhythmic strokes of an open black hand....................

II

THE NIGHT SKULKERS

It was the stealthy opening of a door which awakened the Cimmerian. He did not awake as civilized men do, drowsy and drugged and stupid. He awoke instantly, with a clear mind, recognizing the sound that had interrupted his sleep. Lying there tensely in the dark he saw the outer door slowly open. In a widening crack of starlit sky he saw framed a great black bulk – broad stooping shoulders and a misshapen head blocked out against the stars.

Conan felt the skin crawl between his shoulders. He had bolted that door securely. How could it be opening now, save by supernatural agency? And how could a human being possess a head like that outlined against the stars? All the tales he had heard in the Zuagir tents of devils and goblins came back to bead his flesh with clammy sweat. Now the monster slid noiselessly into the room, with a crouching posture and a shambling gait, and a familiar scent assailed the Cimmerian's nostrils, but did not reassure him, since Zuagir legendry represented demons as smelling like that.

Noiselessly Conan coiled his long legs under him; his naked sword was in his right hand, and when he struck it was as suddenly and murderously as a tiger lunging out of the dark. Not even a demon could have avoided that catapulting charge. His sword met and clove through flesh and bone, and something went heavily to the floor with a strangling cry. Conan crouched in the dark above it, sword dripping in his hand. Devil or beast or man, the thing was dead there on the floor. He sensed death as any wild thing senses it. He glared through the half-open door into the starlit court beyond. The gate stood open, but the court was empty.

Conan shut the door but did not bolt it. Groping in the darkness he found the lamp and lighted it. There was enough oil in it to burn for a minute or so. An instant later he was bending over the figure that sprawled on the floor in a pool of blood.

It was a gigantic black man, naked but for a loin cloth. One hand still grasped a knotty-headed bludgeon. The fellow's kinky wool was built up into horn-like spindles with twigs and dried mud. This barbaric coiffure had given the head its misshapen appearance in the starlight. Provided with a clue to the riddle, Conan pushed back the thick red lips, and grunted, as he stared down at teeth filed to points.

He understood now the mystery of the strangers who had disappeared from the house of Aram Baksh; the riddle of the black drum thrumming out there beyond the palm groves, and of that pit of charred bones – that pit where strange meat might be roasted under the stars, while black beasts squatted about to glut a hideous hunger. The man on the floor was a cannibal slave from Darfar.

There were many of his kind in the city. Cannibalism was not tolerated openly in Zamboula. But Conan knew now why people locked themselves in so securely at night, and why even beggars shunned the open alleys and doorless ruins. He grunted in disgust as he visualized brutish black shadows skulking up and down the nighted streets, seeking human prey – and such men as Aram Baksh to open the doors to them. The inn-keeper was not a demon, he was worse. The slaves from Darfar were notorious thieves; there was no doubt that some of their pilfered loot found its way into the hands of Aram Baksh. And in return he sold them human flesh.

Conan blew out the light, stepped to the door and opened it, and ran his hand over the ornaments on the outer side. One of them was movable and worked the bolt inside. The room was a trap to catch human prey like rabbits. But this time instead of a rabbit it had caught a saber-toothed tiger.

Conan returned to the other door, lifted the bolt and pressed against it. It was immovable and he remembered the bolt on the other side. Aram was taking no chances either with his victims or the men with whom he dealt. Buckling on his sword-belt, the Cimmerian strode out into the court, closing the door behind him. He had no intention of delaying the settlement of his reckoning with Aram Baksh. He wondered how many poor devils had been bludgeoned in their sleep and dragged out of that room and down the road that ran through the shadowed palm groves to the roasting pit.

He halted in the court. The drum was still muttering, and he caught the reflection of a leaping red glare through the groves. Cannibalism was more than a perverted appetite with the black men of Darfar; it was an integral element of their ghastly cult. The black vultures were already in conclave. But whatever flesh filled their bellies that night, it would not be his.

To reach Aram Baksh he must climb one of the walls which separated the small enclosure from the main compound. They were high, meant to keep out the man-eaters; but Conan was no swamp-bred black man; his thews had been steeled in boyhood on the sheer cliffs of his native hills. He was standing at the foot of the nearer wall when a cry re-echoed under the trees.

In an instant Conan was crouching at the gate, glaring down the road. The sound had come from the shadows of the huts across the road. He heard a frantic choking and gurgling such as might result from a desperate attempt to shriek, with a black hand fastened over the victim's mouth. A close-knit clump of figures emerged from the shadows beyond the huts, and started down the road – three huge black men carrying a slender, struggling figure between them. Conan caught the glimmer of pale limbs writhing in the starlight, even as, with a convulsive wrench, the captive slipped from the grasp of the brutal fingers and came flying up the road, a supple young woman, naked as the day she was born. Conan saw her plainly before she ran out of the road and into the shadows between the huts. The blacks were at her heels, and back in the shadows the figures merged and an intolerable scream of anguish and horror rang out.

Stirred to red rage by the ghoulishness of the episode, Conan raced across the road.

Neither victim nor abductors were aware of his presence until the soft swish of the dust about his feet brought them about, and then he was almost upon them, coming with the gusty fury of a hill wind. Two of the blacks turned to meet him, lifting their bludgeons. But they failed to properly estimate the speed at which he was coming. One of them was down, disembowelled, before he could strike, and wheeling catlike, Conan evaded the stroke of the other's cudgel, and lashed in a whistling counter-cut. The black's head flew into the air; the headless body took three staggering steps, spurting blood and clawing horribly at the air with groping hands, and then slumped to the dust.

The remaining cannibal gave back with a strangled yell, hurling his captive from him. She tripped and rolled in the dust, and the black fled in blind panic, toward the direction of the city. Conan was at his heels. Fear winged the black feet, but before they reached the eastern-most hut, he sensed death at his back, and bellowed like an oxen in the slaughter-yards.

"Black dog of hell!" Conan drove his sword between the dusky shoulders with such vengeful fury that the broad blade stood out half its length from the black breast. With a choking cry the black stumbled headlong, and Conan braced his feet and dragged out his sword as his victim fell.

Only the breeze disturbed the leaves. Conan shook his head as a lion shakes its mane and growled his unsatiated blood-lust. But no more shapes slunk from the shadows, and before the huts the starlit road stretched empty. He whirled at the quick patter of feet behind him, but it was only the girl, rushing to throw herself on him and clasp his neck in a desperate grasp, frantic from terror of the abominable fate she had just escaped.

"Easy, girl," he grunted. "You're all right. How did they catch you?"

She sobbed something unintelligible. He forgot all about Aram Baksh as he scrutinized her by the light of the stars. She was white, though a very definite brunet, obviously one of Zamboula's many mixed breeds. She was tall, with a slender, supple form as he was in a good position to observe. Admiration burned in his fierce eyes as he looked down on her splendid bosom and her lithe limbs which still quivered from fright and exertion. He passed an arm about her flexible waist and said, reassuringly: "Stop shaking, wench; you're safe enough."

His touch seemed to restore her shaken sanity. She tossed back her thick, glossy locks and cast a fearful glance over her shoulder, while she pressed closer to the Cimmerian as if seeking security in the contact.

"They caught me in the streets," she muttered, shuddering. "Lying in wait, beneath a dark arch – black men, like great, hulking apes! Set have mercy on me! I shall dream of it!"

"What were you doing out on the streets this time of night?" he inquired, fascinated by the satiny feel of her sleek skin under his questing fingers.

She raked back her hair and stared blankly up into his face. She did not seem aware of his caresses.

"My lover," she said. "My lover drove me into the streets. He went mad and tried to kill me. As I fled from him I was seized by those beasts."

"Beauty like yours might drive a man mad," quoth Conan, running his fingers experimentally through her glossy tresses.

She shook her head, like one emerging from a daze. She no longer trembled, and her voice was steady.

"It was the spite of a priest – of Totrasmek, the high priest of Hanuman, who desires me for himself – the dog!"

"No need to curse him for that," grinned Conan. "The old hyena has better taste than I thought."

She ignored the bluff compliment. She was regaining her poise swiftly.

"My lover is a – a young Turanian soldier. To spite me, Totrasmek gave him a drug that drove him mad. Tonight he snatched up a sword and came at me to slay me in his madness, but I fled from him into the streets. The negroes seized me and brought me to this – *what was that?*"

Conan had already moved. Soundlessly as a shadow he drew her behind the nearest hut, beneath the straggling palms. They stood in tense stillness, while the low mutterings both had heard grew louder until voices were distinguishable. A group of negroes, some nine or ten, were coming along the road from the direction of the city. The girl clutched Conan's arm and he felt the terrified quivering of her supple body against his.

Now they could understand the gutturals of the black men.

"Our brothers are already assembled at the pit," said one. "We have had no luck. I hope they have enough for us."

"Aram promised us a man," muttered another, and Conan mentally promised Aram something.

"Aram keeps his word," grunted yet another. "Many a man we have taken from his tavern. But we pay him well. I myself have given him ten bales of silk I stole from my master. It was good silk, by Set!"

The blacks shuffled past, bare splay feet scuffing up the dust, and their voices dwindled down the road.

"Well for us those corpses are lying behind these huts," muttered Conan. "If they look in Aram's death-room they'll find another. Let's begone."

"Yes, let us hasten!" begged the girl, almost hysterical again. "My lover is wandering somewhere in the streets alone. The negroes may take him."

"A devil of a custom, this is," growled Conan, as he led the way toward the city, paralleling the road, but keeping behind the huts and straggling trees. "Why don't the citizens clean out these black dogs?"

"They are valuable slaves," murmured the girl. "There are so many of them they might revolt if they were denied the flesh for which they lust. The people of Zamboula know they skulk the streets at night, and all are careful to remain within locked doors, except when something unforeseen happens, as it did to me. The blacks prey on anything they catch, but they seldom catch anybody but strangers. The people of Zamboula are not concerned with the strangers that pass through the city.

"Such men as Aram Baksh sell these strangers to the blacks. He would not dare attempt such a thing with a citizen."

Conan spat in disgust, and a moment later led his companion out into the road which was becoming a street, with still, unlighted houses on each side. Slinking in the shadows was not congenial to his nature.

"Where do you want to go?" he asked. The girl did not seem to object to his arm about her waist.

"To my house, to rouse my servants," she answered. "To bid them search for my lover. I do not wish the city – the priests – anyone – to know of his madness. He – he is a young officer with a promising future. Perhaps we can drive this madness from him if we can find him."

"If *we* find him?" rumbled Conan. "What makes you think I want to spend the night scouring the streets for a lunatic?"

She cast a quick glance into his face, and properly interpreted the gleam in his blue eyes. Any woman could have known that he would follow her wherever she led – for awhile, at least. But being a woman she concealed her knowledge of that fact.

"Please –" she began with a hint of tears in her voice. "I have no one else to ask for help – you have been kind –"

"All right," he grunted. "All right! What's the young reprobate's name?"

"Why – Alafdhal. I am Zabibi, a dancing girl. I have danced often before the satrap, Jungir Khan, and his mistress Nafertari, and before all the lords and royal ladies of Zamboula. Totrasmek desired me, and because I repulsed him, he made me the innocent tool of his vengeance against Alafdhal. I asked a love potion of Totrasmek, not suspecting the depth of his guile and hate. He gave me a drug to mix with my lover's wine, and he swore that when Alafdhal drank it, he would love me even more madly than ever, and grant my every wish. I mixed the drug secretly with my lover's wine. But having drunk, my lover went raving mad and things came about as I have told you. Curse Totrasmek, the hybrid snake – ahhh!"

She caught his arm convulsively and both stopped short. They had come into a district of shops and stalls, all deserted and unlighted, for the hour was late. They were passing an alley, and in its mouth a man was standing, motionless and silent. His head was lowered, but Conan caught the weird gleam of eery eyes regarding them unblinkingly. His skin crawled, not with fear of the sword in the man's hand, but because of the uncanny suggestion of his posture and silence. They suggested madness. Conan pushed the girl aside and drew his sword.

"Don't kill him!" she begged. "In the name of Set, do not slay him! You are strong – overpower him!"

"We'll see," he muttered, grasping his sword in his right hand and clenching his left into a mallet-like fist.

He took a wary step toward the alley – and with a horrible moaning laugh the Turanian charged. As he came he swung his sword, rising on his toes as he put all the power of his body behind the blows. Sparks flashed blue as Conan parried the blade, and the next instant the madman was stretched senseless in the dust from a thundering buffet of Conan's left fist.

The girl ran forward.

"Oh, he is not – he is not –"

Conan bent swiftly, turned the man on his side and ran quick fingers over him.

"He's not hurt much," he grunted. "Bleeding at the nose, but anybody's likely to do that, after a clout on the jaw. He'll come to after a bit, and maybe his mind will be right. In the meantime I'll tie his wrists with his sword-belt – so. Now where do you want me to take him?"

"Wait!" She knelt beside the senseless figure, seized the bound hands and scanned them avidly. Then, shaking her head as if in baffled disappointment, she rose. She came close to the giant Cimmerian, and laid her slender hands on his arching breast. Her dark eyes, like wet black jewels in the starlight, gazed up into his.

"You are a man! Help me! Totrasmek must die! Slay him for me!"

"And put my neck into a Turanian noose?" he grunted.

"Nay!" The slender arms, strong as pliant steel, were around his corded neck.

Her supple body throbbed against his. "The Hyrkanians have no love for Totrasmek. The priests of Set fear him. He is a mongrel, who rules men by fear and superstition. I worship Set, and the Turanians bow to Erlik, but Totrasmek sacrifices to Hanuman the accursed! The Turanian lords fear his black arts and his power over the hybrid population, and they hate him. Even Jungir Khan and his mistress Nafertari fear and hate him. If he were slain in his temple at night, they would not seek his slayer very closely."

"And what of his magic?" rumbled the Cimmerian.

"You are a fighting man," she answered. "To risk your life is part of your profession."

"For a price," he admitted.

"There will be a price!" she breathed, rising on tip-toes, to gaze into his eyes. The nearness of her vibrant body drove a flame through his veins. The perfume of her breath mounted to his brain. But as his arms closed about her supple figure she avoided them with a lithe movement, saying: "Wait! First serve me in this matter."

"Name your price." He spoke with some difficulty.

"Pick up my lover," she directed, and the Cimmerian stooped and swung the tall form easily to his broad shoulder. At the moment he felt as if he could have toppled over Jungir Khan's palace with equal ease. The girl murmured an endearment to the unconscious man, and there was no hypocrisy in her attitude. She obviously loved Alafdhal sincerely. Whatever business arrangement she made with Conan would have no bearing on her relationship with Alafdhal. Women are more practical about these things than men. What Alafdhal never knew would not hurt him.

"Follow me!" She hurried along the street, while the Cimmerian strode easily after her, in no way discomforted by his limp burden. He kept a wary eye out for black shadows skulking under arches, but saw nothing suspicious. Doubtless the men of Darfar were all gathered at the roasting pit. The girl turned down a narrow side street, and presently knocked cautiously at an arched door.

Almost instantly a wicket opened in the upper panel, and a black face glanced out. She bent close to the opening, whispering swiftly. Bolts creaked in their sockets, and the door opened. A giant black man stood framed against the soft glow of a copper lamp. A quick glance showed Conan the man was not from Darfar. His teeth were unfiled and his kinky hair was cropped close to his skull. He was from the Wadai.

At a word from Zabibi Conan gave the limp body into the black's arms, and saw the young officer laid on a velvet divan. He showed no signs of returning consciousness. The blow that had rendered him senseless might have felled an ox. Zabibi bent over him for an instant, her fingers nervously twining and twisting. Then she straightened and beckoned the Cimmerian.

The door closed softly, the locks clicked behind them, and the closing wicket shut off the glow of the lamps. In the starlight of the street Zabibi took Conan's hand. Her own hand trembled a little.

"You will not fail me?"

He shook his maned head, massive against the stars.

"Then follow me to Hanuman's shrine, and the gods have mercy on our souls!"

Along the silent streets they moved like phantoms of antiquity. They went in silence. Perhaps the girl was thinking of her lover lying senseless on the divan under the copper lamps; or was shrinking with fear of what lay ahead of them in the demon-haunted shrine of Hanuman. The barbarian was thinking only of the woman moving so supply beside him. The perfume of her scented hair was in his nostrils, the sensuous aura of her presence filled his brain and left room for no other thoughts.

Once they heard the clank of brazen-shod feet, and drew into the shadows of a gloomy arch while a squad of Pelishtim watchmen swung past. There were fifteen of them; they marched in close formation, pikes at the ready, and the rearmost men had their broad brass shields slung on their backs, to protect them from a knife-stroke from behind. The skulking menace of the black man-eaters was a threat even to armed men.

As soon as the clang of their sandals had receded up the street, Conan and the girl emerged from their hiding place and hurried on. A few moments later they saw the squat, flat-topped edifice they sought looming ahead of them.

The temple of Hanuman stood alone in the midst of a broad square, which lay silent and deserted beneath the stars. A marble wall surrounded the shrine, with a broad opening directly before the portico. This opening had no gate or any sort of barrier.

"Why don't the blacks seek their prey here?" muttered Conan. "There's nothing to keep them out of the temple."

He could feel the trembling of Zabibi's body as she pressed close to him.

"They fear Totrasmek, as all in Zamboula fear him, even Jungir Khan and Nafertari. Come! Come quickly, before my courage flows from me like water!"

The girl's fear was evident, but she did not falter. Conan drew his sword and strode ahead of her as they advanced through the open gateway. He knew the hideous habits of the priests of the East, and was aware that an invader of Hanuman's shrine might expect to encounter almost any sort of nightmare horror. He knew there was a good chance that neither he nor the girl would ever leave the shrine alive, but he had risked his life too many times before to devote much thought to that consideration.

They entered a court paved with marble which gleamed whitely in the starlight. A short flight of broad marble steps led up to the pillared portico. The great bronze doors stood wide open as they had stood for centuries. But no worshippers burnt incense within. In the day men and women might come timidly into the shrine and place offerings to the ape-god on the black altar. At night the people shunned the temple of Hanuman as hares shun the lair of the serpent.

Burning censers bathed the interior in a soft weird glow that created an illusion of unreality. Near the rear wall, behind the black stone altar, sat the god with his gaze fixed for ever on the open door, through which for centuries his victims had come, dragged by chains of roses. A faint groove ran from the sill to the altar, and when Conan's foot felt it, he stepped away as quickly as if he had trodden upon a snake. That groove had been worn by the faltering feet of the multitude of those who had died screaming on that grim altar.

Bestial in the uncertain light Hanuman leered with his carven mask. He sat, not as an ape would crouch, but cross-legged as a man would sit, but his aspect was no less simian for that reason. He was carved from black marble, but his eyes were rubies, which glowed red and lustful as the coals of hell's deepest pits. His great hands lay upon his lap, palms upward, taloned fingers spread and grasping. In the gross emphasis of his attributes, in the leer of his satyr-countenance, was reflected the abominable cynicism of the degenerate cult which deified him.

The girl moved around the image, making toward the back wall, and when her sleek flank brushed against a carven knee, she shrank aside and shuddered as if a reptile had touched her. There was a space of several feet between the broad back of the idol and the marble wall with its frieze of gold leaves. On either hand, flanking the idol, an ivory door under a gold arch was set in the wall.

"Those doors open into each end of a hair-pin shaped corridor," she said hurriedly. "Once I was in the interior of the shrine – once!" She shivered and twitched her slim shoulders at a memory both terrifying and obscene. "The corridor is bent like a horseshoe, with each horn opening into this room. Totrasmek's chambers are enclosed within the curve of the corridor and open into it. But there is a secret door in this wall which opens directly into an inner chamber –"

She began to run her hands over the smooth surface, where no crack or crevice showed. Conan stood beside her, sword in hand, glancing warily about him. The silence, the emptiness of the shrine, with imagination picturing what might lie behind that wall, made him feel like a wild beast nosing a trap.

"Ah!" The girl had found a hidden spring at last; a square opening gaped blackly in the wall. Then: *"Set!"* she screamed, and even as Conan leaped toward her, he saw that a great misshapen hand had fastened itself in her hair. She was snatched off her feet and jerked headfirst through the opening. Conan, grabbing ineffectually at her, felt his fingers slip from a naked limb, and in an instant she had vanished and the wall showed blank as before. Only from beyond it came briefly the muffled sounds of a struggle, a scream, faintly heard, and a low laugh that made Conan's blood congeal in his veins.

III
BLACK HANDS GRIPPING

With an oath the Cimmerian smote the wall a terrific blow with the pommel of his sword, and the marble cracked and chipped. But the hidden door did not give way, and reason told him that doubtless it had been bolted on the other side of the wall. Turning, he sprang across the chamber to one of the ivory doors.

He lifted his sword to shatter the panels, but on a venture tried the door first with his left hand. It swung open easily, and he glared into a long corridor that curved into dimness under the weird light of censers similar to those in the shrine. A heavy gold bolt showed on the jamb of the door, and he touched it lightly with his finger tips. The faint warmness of the metal could have been detected only by a man whose faculties were akin to those of a wolf. That bolt had been touched – and therefore drawn – within the last few seconds. The affair was taking on more and more of the aspect of a baited trap. He might have known Totrasmek would know when anyone entered the temple.

To enter the corridor would undoubtedly be to walk into whatever trap the priest had set for him. But Conan did not hesitate. Somewhere in that dim-lit interior Zabibi was a captive, and, from what he knew of the characteristics of Hanuman's priests, he was sure that she needed help badly. Conan stalked into the corridor with a pantherish tread, poised to strike right or left.

On his left ivory, arched doors opened into the corridor, and he tried each in turn. All were locked. He had gone perhaps seventy-five feet when the corridor bent sharply to the left, describing the curve the girl had mentioned. A door opened into this curve, and it gave under his hand.

He was looking into a broad square chamber, somewhat more clearly lighted than the corridor. Its walls were of white marble, the floor of ivory, the ceiling of fretted silver. He saw divans of rich satin, gold-worked footstools of ivory, a disk-shaped table of some massive, metal-like substance. On one of the divans a man was reclining, looking toward the door. He laughed as he met the Cimmerian's startled glare.

This man was naked except for a loin cloth and high-strapped sandals. He was brown-skinned, with close-cropped black hair and restless black eyes that set off a broad arrogant face. In girth and breadth he was enormous, with huge limbs on which the great muscles swelled and rippled at each slightest movement. His hands were the largest Conan had ever seen. The assurance of gigantic physical strength colored his every action and inflection.

"Why not enter, barbarian?" he called mockingly, with an exaggerated gesture of invitation. Conan's eyes began to smolder ominously, but he trod warily into the chamber, his sword ready.

"Who the devil are you?" he growled.

"I am Baal-pteor," the man answered. "Once, long ago and in another land, I had another name. But this is a good name, and why Totrasmek gave it to me, any temple-wench can tell you."

"So you're his dog," grunted Conan. "Well, curse your brown hide, Baal-pteor, where's the wench you jerked through the wall?"

"My master entertains her!" laughed Baal-pteor. "Listen!"

From beyond a door opposite the one by which Conan had entered there sounded a woman's scream, faint and muffled in the distance.

"Blast your soul!" Conan took a stride toward the door, then wheeled with his skin tingling. Baal-pteor was laughing at him, and that laugh was edged with menace that made the hackles rise on Conan's neck and sent an answering red wave of murder-lust driving across his vision.

He started toward Baal-pteor, the knuckles on his sword-hand showing white. With a swift motion the brown man threw something at him — a shining crystal sphere that glistened in the weird light.

Conan dodged instinctively, but, miraculously, the globe stopped short in mid-air, a few feet from his face. It did not fall to the floor. It hung suspended, as if by invisible filaments, some five feet above the floor. And as he glared in amazement, it began to rotate with growing speed. And as it revolved it grew, it expanded, it became nebulous. It filled the chamber. It enveloped him. It blotted out furniture, walls, the smiling countenance of Baal-pteor. He was lost in the midst of a blinding bluish blur of whirling speed. Terrific winds screamed past Conan, tugging, tearing at him, striving to wrench him from his feet, to drag him into the vortex that spun madly before him.

With a choking cry Conan lurched backward, reeled, felt the solid wall against his back. At the contact the illusion ceased to be. The whirling, titanic sphere vanished like a bursting bubble. Conan reeled upright in the silver-ceilinged room, with a grey mist coiling about his feet, and saw Baal-pteor lolling on the divan, shaking with silent laughter.

"Son of a slut!" Conan lunged at him. But the mist swirled up from the floor, blotting out that giant brown form. Groping in a rolling cloud that blinded him, Conan felt a rending sensation of dislocation – and then room and mist and brown man were gone together. He was standing alone among the high reeds of a marshy fen, and a buffalo was lunging at him, head down. He leaped aside from the ripping scimitar-curved horns, and drove his sword in behind the foreleg, through ribs and heart. And then it was not a buffalo dying there in the mud, but the brown-skinned Baal-pteor. With a curse Conan struck off his head, and the head soared from the ground and snapped beast-like tusks into his throat. For all his mighty strength he could not tear it loose – he was choking – strangling – then there was a rush and roar through space, the dislocating shock of an immeasurable impact, and he was back in the chamber with Baal-pteor, his head once more set firmly on his shoulders, laughing silently at him from the divan.

"Mesmerism!" muttered Conan, crouching and digging his toes hard against the marble. His eyes blazed. This brown dog was playing with him, making sport of him! But this mummery, this child's play of mists and shadows of thought, it could not harm him. He had but to leap and strike and the brown acolyte would be a mangled corpse under his heel. This time he would not be fooled by shadows of illusion – but he was.

A blood-curdling snarl behind him, and he wheeled and struck in a flash at the panther crouching to spring on him from the metal-colored table. Even as he struck the apparition vanished and his blade clashed deafeningly on the adamantine surface. Instantly he sensed something abnormal. The blade stuck to the table! He wrenched at it savagely. It did not give. This was no mesmeristic trick. The table was a giant magnet. He gripped the hilt with both hands, when a voice at his shoulder brought him about, to face the brown man who had at last risen from the divan.

Slightly taller than Conan, and much heavier, Baal-pteor loomed before him, a daunting image of muscular development. His mighty arms were unnaturally long, and his great hands opened and closed, twitching convulsively. Conan released the hilt of his imprisoned sword and fell silent, watching his enemy through slitted lids.

"Your head, Cimmerian!" taunted Baal-pteor. "I shall take, with my bare hands, twisting it from your shoulders as the head of a fowl is twisted! Thus the sons of Kosala offer sacrifice to Yajur! Barbarian, you looked upon a Strangler of

Yota-pong! I was chosen by the priests of Yajur in my infancy, and throughout childhood, boyhood and youth, I was trained in the art of slaying with the naked hands – for only thus are the sacrifices enacted. Yajur loves blood, and we waste not a drop from the victim's veins! When I was a child they gave me infants to throttle; when I was a boy I strangled young girls; as a youth, women, old men and young boys. Not until I reached my full manhood was I given a strong man to slay on the altar of Yota-pong.

"For years I offered the sacrifices to Yajur. Hundreds of necks have snapped between these fingers –" he worked them before the Cimmerian's angry eyes. "Why I fled from Yota-pong to become Totrasmek's servant is no concern of yours. In a moment you will be beyond curiosity. The priests of Kosala, the Stranglers of Yajur, are strong beyond the belief of men. And I was stronger than any. With my hands, barbarian, I shall break your neck!"

And like the stroke of twin cobras, the great hands closed on Conan's throat. The Cimmerian made no attempt to dodge or fend them away, but his own hands darted to the Kosalan's bull-neck. Baal-pteor's black eyes widened as he felt the thick cords of muscles that protected the barbarian's throat. With a snarl he exerted his inhuman strength, and knots and lumps and ropes of thews rose along his massive arms. And then a choking gasp burst from him as Conan's fingers locked on his throat. For an instant they stood there like statues, their faces masks of effort, veins beginning to stand out purply on their temples. Conan's thin lips drew back from his teeth in a grinning snarl. Baal's eyes were distended; in them grew an awful surprize and the glimmer of fear. They stood motionless as images, except for the expanding of their muscles on rigid arms and braced legs, but strength beyond common conception was warring there – strength that might have uprooted trees and crushed the skulls of bullocks.

The wind whistled suddenly from between Baal-pteor's parted teeth. His face was growing purple. Fear flooded his eyes. His thews seemed ready to burst from his arms and shoulders, yet the muscles of the Cimmerian's thick neck did not give, they felt like masses of woven iron cords under his desperate fingers. But his own flesh was giving way under the iron fingers of the Cimmerian which ground deeper and deeper into the yielding throat-muscles, crushing them in upon jugular and wind-pipe.

The statuesque immobility of the group gave way to sudden, frenzied motion, as the Kosalan began to wrench and heave, seeking to throw himself backward. He let go of Conan's throat and grasped his wrists, trying to tear away those inexorable fingers.

With a sudden lunge Conan bore him backward until the small of his back crashed against the table. And still farther over its edge Conan bent him, back and back, until his spine was ready to snap.

Conan's low laugh was merciless as the ring of steel.

"You fool!" he all but whispered. "I think you never saw a man from the West before. Did you deem yourself strong, because you were able to twist the heads off civilized folk, poor weaklings with muscles like rotten string? Hell! Break the neck of a wild Cimmerian bull before you call yourself strong. I did that, before I was a full-grown man – like this!"

And with a savage wrench he twisted Baal-pteor's head around until the ghastly face leered over the left shoulder, and the vertebrae snapped like a rotten branch.

Conan hurled the flopping corpse to the floor, turned to the sword again and gripped the hilt with both hands, bracing his feet against the floor. Blood trickled down his broad breast from the wounds Baal-pteor's finger nails had torn in the skin of his neck. His black hair was damp, sweat ran down his face, and his chest heaved. For all his vocal scorn of Baal-pteor's strength, he had almost met his match in the inhuman Kosalan. But without pausing to catch his breath, he exerted all his strength in a mighty wrench that tore the sword from the magnet where it clung. Another instant and he had pushed open the door from behind which the scream had sounded, and was looking down a long straight corridor, lined with ivory doors. The other end was masked by a rich velvet curtain, and from beyond that curtain came the devilish strains of such music as Conan had never heard, not even in nightmares. It made the short hairs bristle on the back of his neck. Mingled with it was the panting, hysterical sobbing of a woman. Grasping his sword firmly, he glided down the corridor.

IV
A Sword-Thrust Through the Curtain

When Zabibi was jerked headfirst through the aperture which opened in the wall behind the idol, her first, dizzy, disconnected thought was that her time had come. She instinctively shut her eyes and waited for the blow to fall. But instead she felt herself dumped unceremoniously onto the smooth marble floor which bruised her knees and hip. Opening her eyes she stared fearfully around her, just as a muffled impact sounded from beyond the wall. She saw a brown-skinned giant in a loin-cloth standing over her, and, across the chamber into which she had come, a man sat on a divan, with his back to a rich black velvet curtain, a broad, fleshy man, with fat white hands and snaky eyes. And her flesh crawled, for this man was Totrasmek, the priest of Hanuman, who for years had spun his slimy webs of power throughout the city of Zamboula.

"The barbarian seeks to batter his way through the wall," said Totrasmek sardonically, "but the bolt will hold."

The girl saw that a heavy golden bolt had been shot across the hidden door, which was plainly discernible from this side of the wall. The bolt and its sockets would have resisted the charge of an elephant.

"Go open one of the doors for him, Baal-pteor," ordered Totrasmek. "Slay him in the square chamber at the other end of the corridor."

The Kosalan salaamed and departed by the way of a door in the side wall of the chamber. Zabibi rose, staring fearfully at the priest, whose eyes ran avidly over her splendid figure. To this she was indifferent. A dancer of Zamboula was accustomed to nakedness. But the cruelty in his eyes started her limbs to quivering.

"Again you come to me in my retreat, beautiful one," he purred with cynical hypocrisy. "It is an unexpected honor. You seemed to enjoy your former visit so little, that I dared not hope for you to repeat it. Yet I did all in my power to provide you with an interesting experience."

For a Zamboula dancer to blush would be an impossibility, but a smolder of anger mingled with the fear in Zabibi's dilated eyes.

"Fat pig! You know I did not come here for love of you."

"No," laughed Totrasmek, "you came like a fool, creeping through the night with a stupid barbarian to cut my throat! Why should you seek my life?"

"You know why!" she cried, knowing the futility of trying to dissemble.

"You are thinking of your lover," he laughed. "The fact that you are here seeking my life shows that he quaffed the drug I gave you. Well, did you not ask for it? And did I not send what you asked for, out of the love I bear you?"

"I asked you for a drug that would make him slumber harmlessly for a few hours," she said bitterly. "And you – you sent your servant with a drug that drove him mad! I was a fool ever to trust you. I might have known your protestations of friendship were lies, to disguise your hate and spite."

"Why did you wish your lover to sleep?" he retorted. "So you could steal from him the only thing he would never give you – the ring with the jewel men call the Star of Khorala – the star stolen from the queen of Ophir, who would pay a roomful of gold for its return. He would not give it to you willingly, because he knew that it holds a magic which, when properly controlled, will enslave the hearts of any of the opposite sex. You wished to steal it from him fearing that his magicians would discover the key to that magic, and he would forget you in his conquests of the queens of the world. You would sell it back to the queen of Ophir, who understands its power and would use it to enslave men, as she did before it was stolen."

"And why did you want it?" she demanded sulkily.

"I understand its powers. It would increase the power of my arts."

"Well," she snapped, "you have it now!"

"*I* have the Star of Khorala? Nay, you err."

"Why bother to lie?" she retorted bitterly. "He had it on his finger when he drove me into the streets. He did not have it when I found him again. Your servant must have been watching the house, and have taken it from him, after I escaped him. To the devil with it! I want my lover back sane and whole. You have the ring; you have punished us both. Why do you not restore his mind to him? Can you?"

"I could," he assured her, in evident enjoyment of her distress. He drew a phial from among his robes. "This contains the juice of the golden lotus. If your lover drank it he would be sane again. Yes, I will be merciful. You have both thwarted and flouted me, not once but many times; he has constantly opposed my wishes. But I will be merciful. Come and take the phial from my hand."

She stared at Totrasmek, trembling with eagerness to seize it, but fearing it was but some cruel jest. She advanced timidly, with a hand extended, and he laughed heartlessly and drew back out of her reach. Even as her lips parted to curse him, some instinct snatched her eyes upward. From the gilded ceiling four jade-hued vessels were falling. She dodged, but they did not strike her. They crashed to the floor about her, forming the four corners of a square. And she screamed, and screamed again. For out of each ruin reared the hooded head of a cobra, and one struck at her bare leg. Her convulsive movement to evade it brought her within reach of the one on the other side and again she had to shift like lightning to avoid the flash of its hideous head.

She was caught in a frightful trap. All four serpents were swaying and striking at foot, ankle, calf, knee, thigh, hip, whatever portion of her voluptuous body chanced to be nearest to them, and she could not spring over them or pass between them to safety. She could only whirl and spring aside and twist her body to avoid the strokes, and each time she moved to dodge one snake, the motion brought her within range of another, so that she had to keep shifting with the speed of light. She could move only a short space in any direction, and the fearful hooded crests were menacing her every second. Only a dancer of Zamboula could have lived in that grisly square.

She became, herself, a blur of bewildering motion. The heads missed her by hair's breadths, but they missed, as she pitted her twinkling feet, flickering limbs, and perfect eye against the blinding speed of the scaly monsters her enemy had conjured out of thin air.

Somewhere a thin whining music struck up, mingling with the hissing of the serpents, like an evil nightwind blowing through the empty sockets of a skull. Even in the flying speed of her urgent haste she realized that the darting of the serpents was no longer at random. They obeyed the grisly piping of the eery music. They struck with a horrible rhythm, and perforce her swaying, writhing, spinning body attuned itself to their rhythm. Her frantic motions melted into the measures of a dance compared to which the most obscene tarantella of Zamora would have seemed sane and restrained. Sick with shame and terror Zabibi heard the hateful mirth of her merciless tormentor.

"The Dance of the Cobras, my lovely one!" laughed Totrasmek. "So maidens danced in the sacrifice to Hanuman centuries ago – but never with such beauty and suppleness. Dance, girl, dance! How long can you avoid the fangs of the Poison People? Minutes? Hours? You will weary at last. Your swift, sure feet will stumble, your legs falter, your hips slow in their rotations. Then the fangs will begin to sink deep into your ivory flesh –"

Behind him the curtain shook as if struck by a gust of wind, and Totrasmek screamed. His eyes dilated and his hands caught convulsively at the length of bright steel which jutted suddenly from his breast.

The music broke off short. The girl swayed dizzily in her dance, crying out in dreadful anticipation of the flickering fangs — and then only four wisps of harmless blue smoke curled up from the floor about her, as Totrasmek sprawled headlong from the divan.

Conan came from behind the curtain, wiping his broad blade. Looking through the hangings he had seen the girl dancing desperately between four swaying spirals of smoke, but he had guessed that their appearance was very different to her. He knew he had killed Totrasmek.

Zabibi sank down on the floor, panting, but even as Conan started toward her, she staggered up again, though her legs trembled with exhaustion.

"The phial!" she gasped. "The phial!"

Totrasmek still grasped it in his stiffening hand. Ruthlessly she tore it from his locked fingers, and then began frantically to ransack his garments.

"What the devil are you looking for?" Conan demanded.

"A ring — he stole it from Alafdhal. He must have, while my lover walked in madness through the streets. Set's devils!"

She had convinced herself that it was not on the person of Totrasmek. She began to cast about the chamber, tearing up divan covers and hangings, and upsetting vessels.

She paused and raked a damp lock of hair out of her eyes.

"I forgot Baal-pteor!"

"He's in hell with his neck broken," Conan assured her.

She expressed vindictive gratification at the news, but an instant later swore expressively.

"We can't stay here. It's not many hours until dawn. Lesser priests are likely to visit the temple at any hour of the night, and if we're discovered here with his corpse, the people will tear us to pieces. The Turanians could not save us."

She lifted the bolt on the secret door, and a few moments later they were in the streets and hurrying away from the silent square where brooded the age-old shrine of Hanuman.

In a winding street a short distance away Conan halted and checked his companion with a heavy hand on her naked shoulder.

"Don't forget there was a price —"

"I have not forgotten!" She twisted free. "But we must go to — to Alafdhal first!"

A few minutes later the black slave let them through the wicket door. The young Turanian lay upon the divan, his arms and legs bound with heavy velvet ropes. His eyes were open, but they were like those of a mad dog, and foam was thick on his lips. Zabibi shuddered.

"Force his jaws open!" she commanded, and Conan's iron fingers accomplished the task. Zabibi emptied the phial down the maniac's gullet. The effect was like magic. Instantly he became quiet. The glare faded from his eyes; he stared up at the girl in a puzzled way, but with recognition and intelligence. Then he fell into a normal slumber.

"When he awakes he will be quite sane," she whispered, motioning to the silent slave. With a deep bow he gave into her hands a small leathern bag, and drew about her shoulders a silken cloak. Her manner had subtly changed when she beckoned Conan to follow her out of the chamber.

In an arch that opened on the street, she turned to him, drawing herself up with a new regality.

"I must now tell you the truth," she said. "I am not Zabibi. I am Nafertari. And *he* is not Alafdhal, a poor captain of the guardsmen. He is Jungir Khan, satrap of Zamboula."

Conan made no comment; his scarred dark countenance was immobile.

"I lied to you because I dared not divulge the truth to anyone," she said. "We were alone when Jungir Khan went mad. None knew of it but myself. Had it been known that the satrap of Zamboula was a madman, there would have been instant revolt and rioting, even as Totrasmek planned, who plotted our destruction.

"You see now how impossible is the reward for which you hoped. The satrap's mistress is not – can not be for you. But you shall not go unrewarded. Here is a sack of gold." She gave him the bag she had received from the slave.

"Go, now, and when the sun is up come to the palace. I will have Jungir Khan make you captain of his guard. But you will take your orders from me, secretly. Your first duty will be to march a squad to the shrine of Hanuman, ostensibly to search for clues of the priest's slayer; in reality to search for the Star of Khorala. It must be hidden there somewhere. When you find it, bring it to me. You have my leave to go now."

He nodded, still silent, and strode away. The girl, watching the swing of his broad shoulders, was piqued to note that there was nothing in his bearing to show that he was in any way chagrined or abashed.

When he had rounded a corner, he glanced back, and then changed his direction and quickened his pace. A few moments later he was in the quarter of the city containing the Horse Market. There he smote on a door until from the window above a bearded head was thrust to demand the reason for the disturbance.

"A horse," demanded Conan. "The swiftest steed you have."

"I open no gates at this time of night," grumbled the horse trader.

Conan rattled his coins.

"Dog's son knave! Don't you see I'm white, and alone? Come down, before I smash your door!"

Presently, on a bay stallion, Conan was riding toward the house of Aram Baksh.

He turned off the road into the alley that lay between the tavern compound and the date-palm garden, but he did not pause at the gate. He rode on to the northeast corner of the wall, then turned and rode along the north wall to halt within a few paces of the northwest angle. No trees grew near the wall, but there were some low bushes. To one of these he tied his horse, and was about to climb into the saddle again, when he heard a low muttering of voices beyond the corner of the wall.

Drawing his foot from the stirrup he stole to the angle and peered around it. Three men were moving down the road toward the palm-groves, and from their slouching gait he knew they were negroes. They halted at his low call, bunching themselves together as he strode toward them, his sword in his hand. Their eyes gleamed whitely in the starlight. Their brutish lust shone in their ebony faces, but they knew their three cudgels could not prevail against his sword, just as he knew it.

"Where are you going?" he challenged.

"To bid our brothers put out the fire in the pit beyond the groves," was the sullen, guttural reply. "Aram Baksh promised us a man, but he lied. We found one of our brothers dead in the trap-chamber. We go hungry this night."

"I think not," smiled Conan. "Aram Baksh will give you a man. Do you see that door?"

He pointed to a small, iron-bound portal set in the midst of the western wall.

"Wait there. Aram Baksh will give you a man."

Backing warily away until he was out of reach of a sudden bludgeon blow, he turned and melted around the northwest angle of the wall. Reaching his horse he paused to ascertain that the blacks were not sneaking after him, and then he climbed into the saddle and stood upright on it, quieting the uneasy steed with a low word. He reached up, grasped the coping of the wall and drew himself up and over. There he studied the grounds for an instant. The tavern was built in the southwest corner of the enclosure, the remaining space of which was occupied by groves and gardens. He saw no one in the grounds. The tavern was dark and silent, and he knew all the doors and windows were barred and bolted.

Conan knew that Aram Baksh slept in a chamber that opened into a cypress-bordered path that led to the door in the western wall. Like a shadow he glided among the trees and a few moments later he rapped lightly on the chamber door.

"What is it?" asked a rumbling voice within.

"Aram Baksh!" hissed Conan. "The blacks are stealing over the wall!"

Almost instantly the door opened, framing the tavern-keeper, naked but for his shirt, with a dagger in his hand.

He craned his neck to stare into the Cimmerian's face.

"What tale is this – *you!*"

Conan's vengeful fingers strangled the yell in his throat. They went to the floor together and Conan wrenched the dagger from his enemy's hand. The blade glinted in the starlight, and blood spurted. Aram Baksh made hideous noises, gasping and gagging on a mouthful of blood. Conan dragged him to his feet and again the dagger slashed, and most of the curly beard fell to the floor.

Still gripping his captive's throat – for a man can scream incoherently even with his tongue slit —Conan dragged him out of the dark chamber and down the cypress-shadowed path, to the iron-bound door in the outer wall. With one hand he lifted the bolt and threw the door open, disclosing the three shadowy figures which waited like black vultures outside. Into their eager arms Conan thrust the inn-keeper.

A horrible, blood-choked scream rose from the Zamboulan's throat, but there was no response from the silent tavern. The people there were used to screams outside the wall. Aram Baksh fought like a wild man, his distended eyes turned frantically on the Cimmerian's face. He found no mercy there. Conan was thinking of the scores of wretches who owed their bloody doom to this man's vile greed.

In glee the negroes dragged him down the road, mocking his frenzied gibberings. How could they recognize Aram Baksh in this half-naked, blood-stained figure, with the grotesquely shorn beard and unintelligible babblings? The sounds of the struggle came back to Conan, standing beside the gate, even after the clump of figures had vanished among the palms.

Closing the door behind him, Conan returned to his horse, mounted and turned westward, toward the open desert, swinging wide to skirt the sinister belt of palm-groves. As he rode he drew from his belt a ring in which gleamed a jewel that snared the starlight in a shimmering iridescence. He held it up to admire it, turning it this way and that. The compact bag of gold pieces clinked gently at his saddle bow, like a promise of the greater riches to come.

"I wonder what she'd say if she knew I recognized her as Nafertari and him as Jungir Khan the instant I saw them," he mused. "I knew the Star of Khorala, too. There'll be a fine scene if she ever guesses that I slipped it off his finger while I was tying him with his sword-belt. But they'll never catch me with the start I'm getting."

He glanced back at the shadowy palm groves, among which a red glare was mounting. A chanting rose to the night, vibrating with savage exultation. And another sound mingled with it, a mad, incoherent screaming, a frenzied gibbering in which no words could be distinguished. The noise followed Conan as he rode westward beneath the paling stars.

Red Nails

Red Nails

I

THE SKULL ON THE CRAG

THE woman on the horse reined in her weary steed. It stood with its legs wide-braced, its head drooping, as if it found even the weight of the gold-tassled, red-leather bridle too heavy. The woman drew a booted foot out of the silver stirrup and swung down from the gilt-worked saddle. She made the reins fast to the fork of a sapling, and turned about, hands on her hips, to survey her surroundings.

They were not inviting. Giant trees hemmed in the small pool where her horse had just drunk. Clumps of undergrowth limited the vision that quested under the somber twilight of the lofty arches formed by intertwining branches. The woman shivered with a twitch of her magnificent shoulders, and then cursed.

She was tall, full-bosomed and large-limbed, with compact shoulders. Her whole figure reflected an unusual strength, without detracting from the femininity of her appearance. She was all woman, in spite of her bearing and her garments. The latter were incongruous, in view of her present environs. Instead of a skirt she wore short, wide-legged silk breeches, which ceased a hand's breadth short of her knees, and were upheld by a wide silken sash worn as a girdle. Flaring-topped boots of soft leather came almost to her knees, and a low-necked, wide-collared, wide-sleeved silk shirt completed her costume. On one shapely hip she wore a straight double-edged sword, and on the other a long dirk. Her unruly golden hair, cut square at her shoulders, was confined by a band of crimson satin.

Against the background of somber, primitive forest she posed with an unconscious picturesqueness, bizarre and out of place. She should have been posed against a background of sea-clouds, painted masts and wheeling gulls. There was the color of the sea in her wide eyes. And that was as it should have been, because this was Valeria of the Red Brotherhood, whose deeds are celebrated in song and ballad wherever seafarers gather.

She strove to pierce the sullen green roof of the arched branches and see the sky which presumably lay about it, but presently gave it up with a muttered oath.

Leaving her horse tied she strode off toward the east, glancing back toward the pool from time to time in order to fix her route in her mind. The silence of the forest depressed her. No birds sang in the lofty boughs, nor did any rustling in the bushes indicate the presence of any small animals. For leagues she had traveled in a realm of brooding stillness, broken only by the sounds of her own flight.

She had slaked her thirst at the pool, but she felt the gnawings of hunger and began looking about for some of the fruit on which she had sustained herself since exhausting the food she had brought in her saddle-bags.

Ahead of her, presently, she saw an outcropping of dark, flint-like rock that sloped upward into what looked like a rugged crag rising among the trees. Its summit was lost to view amidst a cloud of encircling leaves. Perhaps its peak rose above the tree-tops, and from it she could see what lay beyond – if, indeed, anything lay beyond but more of this apparently illimitable forest through which she had ridden for so many days.

A narrow ridge formed a natural ramp that led up the steep face of the crag. After she had ascended some fifty feet she came to the belt of leaves that surrounded the rock. The trunks of the trees did not crowd close to the crag, but the ends of their lower branches extended about it, veiling it with their foliage. She groped on in leafy obscurity, not able to see either above or below her; but presently she glimpsed blue sky, and a moment later came out in the clear, hot sunlight and saw the forest roof stretching away under her feet.

She was standing on a broad shelf which was about even with the tree-tops, and from it rose a spire-like jut that was the ultimate peak of the crag she had climbed. But something else caught her attention at the moment. Her foot had struck something in the litter of blown dead leaves which carpeted the shelf. She kicked them aside and looked down on the skeleton of a man. She ran an experienced eye over the bleached frame, but saw no broken bones nor any sign of violence. The man must have died a natural death; though why he should have climbed a tall crag to die she could not imagine.

SHE scrambled up to the summit of the spire and looked toward the horizons. The forest roof – which looked like a floor from her vantage-point – was just as impenetrable as from below. She could not even see the pool by which she had left her horse. She glanced northward, in the direction from which she had come. She saw only the rolling green ocean stretching away and away, with only a vague blue line in the distance to hint of the hill-range she had crossed days before, to plunge into this leafy waste.

West and east the view was the same; though the blue hill-line was lacking in those directions. But when she turned her eyes southward she stiffened and caught her breath. A mile away in that direction the forest thinned out and ceased abruptly, giving way to a cactus-dotted plain. And in the midst of that plain rose the walls and towers of a city. Valeria swore in amazement. This passed belief. She would not have been surprised to sight human habitations of another sort – the beehive-shaped huts of the black people, or the cliff-dwellings of the mysterious brown race which legends declared inhabited some country of this unexplored region. But it was a startling experience to come upon a walled city here so many long weeks' march from the nearest outposts of any sort of civilization.

Her hands tiring from clinging to the spire-like pinnacle, she let herself down on the shelf, frowning in indecision. She had come far – from the camp of the mercenaries by the border town of Sukhmet amidst the level grasslands, where desperate adventurers of many races guard the Stygian frontier against the raids that come up like a red wave from Darfar. Her flight had been blind, into a country of which she was wholly ignorant. And now she wavered between an urge to ride directly to that city in the plain, and the instinct of caution which prompted her to skirt it widely and continue her solitary flight.

Her thoughts were scattered by the rustling of the leaves below her. She wheeled cat-like, snatched at her sword; and then she froze motionless, staring wide-eyed at the man before her.

He was almost a giant in stature, muscles rippling smoothly under his skin which the sun had burned brown. His garb was similar to hers, except that he wore a broad leather belt instead of a girdle. Broadsword and poniard hung from this belt.

"Conan, the Cimmerian!" ejaculated the woman. "What are *you* doing on my trail?"

He grinned hardly, and his fierce blue eyes burned with a light any woman could understand as they ran over her magnificent figure, lingering on the swell of her splendid breasts beneath the light shirt, and the clear white flesh displayed between breeches and boot-tops.

"Don't you know?" he laughed. "Haven't I made my admiration for you plain ever since I first saw you?"

"A stallion could have made it no plainer," she answered disdainfully. "But I never expected to encounter you so far from the ale-barrels and meat-pots of Sukhmet. Did you really follow me from Zarallo's camp, or were you whipped forth for a rogue?"

He laughed at her insolence and flexed his mighty biceps.

"You know Zarallo didn't have enough knaves to whip me out of camp," he grinned. "Of course I followed you. Lucky thing for you, too, wench! When you knifed that Stygian officer, you forfeited Zarallo's favor and protection, and you outlawed yourself with the Stygians."

"I know it," she replied sullenly. "But what else could I do? You know what my provocation was."

"Sure," he agreed. "If I'd been there, I'd have knifed him myself. But if a woman must live in the war-camps of men, she can expect such things."

Valeria stamped her booted foot and swore.

"Why won't men let me live a man's life?"

"That's obvious!" Again his eager eyes devoured her. "But you were wise to run away. The Stygians would have had you skinned. That officer's brother followed you; faster than you thought, I don't doubt. He wasn't far behind you when I caught up with him. His horse was better than yours. He'd have caught you and cut your throat within a few more miles."

"Well?" she demanded.

"Well what?" He seemed puzzled.

"What of the Stygian?"

"Why, what do you suppose?" he returned impatiently. "I killed him, of course, and left his carcass for the vultures. That delayed me, though, and I almost lost your trail when you crossed the rocky spurs of the hills. Otherwise I'd have caught up with you long ago."

"And now you think you'll drag me back to Zarallo's camp?" she sneered.

"Don't talk like a fool," he grunted. "Come, girl, don't be such a spitfire. I'm not like that Stygian you knifed, and you know it."

"A penniless vagabond," she taunted.

He laughed at her.

"What do you call yourself? You haven't enough money to buy a new seat for your breeches. Your disdain doesn't deceive me. You know I've commanded bigger ships and more men than you ever did in your life. As for being penniless – what rover isn't, most of the time? I've squandered enough gold in the sea-ports of the world to fill a galleon. You know that, too."

"Where are the fine ships and the bold lads you commanded, now?" she sneered.

"At the bottom of the sea, mostly," he replied cheerfully. "The Zingarans sank my last ship off the Shemite shore – that's why I joined Zarallo's Free Companions. But I saw I'd been stung when we marched to the Darfar border. The pay was poor and the wine was sour, and I don't like black women. And that's the only kind that came to our camp at Sukhmet – rings in their noses and their teeth filed – bah! Why did you join Zarallo? Sukhmet's a long way from salt water."

"Red Ortho wanted to make me his mistress," she answered sullenly. "I jumped overboard one night and swam ashore when we were anchored off the Kushite coast. Off Zabhela, it was. There a Shemite trader told me that Zarallo had brought his Free Companies south to guard the Darfar border. No better employment offered. I joined an east-bound caravan and eventually came to Sukhmet."

"IT WAS madness to plunge southward as you did," commented Conan, "but it was wise, too, for Zarallo's patrols never thought to look for you in this direction. Only the brother of the man you killed happened to strike your trail."

"And now what do you intend doing?" she demanded.

"Turn west," he answered. "I've been this far south, but not this far east. Many days' traveling to the west will bring us to the open savannas, where the black tribes graze their cattle. I have friends among them. We'll get to the coast and find a ship. I'm sick of the jungle."

"Then be on your way," she advised. "I have other plans."

"Don't be a fool!" He showed irritation for the first time. "You can't keep on wandering through this forest."

"I can if I choose."

"But what do you intend doing?"

"That's none of your affair," she snapped.

"Yes, it is," he answered calmly. "Do you think I've followed you this far, to turn around and ride off empty-handed? Be sensible, wench. I'm not going to harm you."

He stepped toward her, and she sprang back, whipping out her sword.

"Keep back, you barbarian dog! I'll spit you like a roast pig!"

He halted, reluctantly, and demanded: "Do you want me to take that toy away from you and spank you with it?"

"Words! Nothing but words!" she mocked, lights like the gleam of the sun on blue water dancing in her reckless eyes.

He knew it was the truth. No living man could disarm Valeria of the Brotherhood with his bare hands. He scowled, his sensations a tangle of conflicting emotions. He was angry, yet he was amused and filled with admiration for her spirit. He burned with eagerness to seize that splendid figure and crush it in his iron arms, yet he greatly desired not to hurt the girl. He was torn between a desire to shake her soundly, and a desire to caress her. He knew if he came any nearer her sword would be sheathed in his heart. He had seen Valeria kill too many men in border forays and tavern brawls to have any illusions about her. He knew she was as quick and ferocious as a tigress. He could draw his broadsword and disarm her, beat the blade out of her hand, but the thought of drawing a sword on a woman, even without intent of injury, was extremely repugnant to him.

215

"Blast your soul, you hussy!" he exclaimed in exasperation. "I'm going to take off your —"

He started toward her, his angry passion making him reckless, and she poised herself for a deadly thrust. Then came a startling interruption to a scene at once ludicrous and perilous.

"What's that?"

It was Valeria who exclaimed, but they both started violently, and Conan wheeled like a cat, his great sword flashing into his hand. Back in the forest had burst forth an appalling medley of screams — the screams of horses in terror and agony. Mingled with their screams there came the snap of splintering bones.

"Lions are slaying the horses!" cried Valeria.

"Lions, nothing!" snorted Conan, his eyes blazing. "Did you hear a lion roar? Neither did I! Listen at those bones snap — not even a lion could make that much noise killing a horse."

HE HURRIED down the natural ramp and she followed, their personal feud forgotten in the adventurers' instinct to unite against common peril. The screams had ceased when they worked their way downward through the green veil of leaves that brushed the rock.

"I found your horse tied by the pool back there," he muttered, treading so noiselessly that she no longer wondered how he had surprized her on the crag. "I tied mine beside it and followed the tracks of your boots. Watch, now!"

They had emerged from the belt of leaves, and stared down into the lower reaches of the forest. Above them the green roof spread its dusky canopy. Below them the sunlight filtered in just enough to make a jade-tinted twilight. The giant trunks of trees less than a hundred yards away looked dim and ghostly.

"The horses should be beyond that thicket, over there," whispered Conan, and his voice might have been a breeze moving through the branches. "Listen!"

Valeria had already heard, and a chill crept through her veins; so she unconsciously laid her white hand on her companion's muscular brown arm. From beyond the thicket came the noisy crunching of bones and the loud rending of flesh, together with the grinding, slobbering sounds of a horrible feast.

"Lions wouldn't make that noise," whispered Conan. "Something's eating our horses, but it's not a lion – Crom!"

The noise stopped suddenly, and Conan swore softly. A suddenly risen breeze was blowing from them directly toward the spot where the unseen slayer was hidden.

"Here it comes!" muttered Conan, half lifting his sword.

The thicket was violently agitated, and Valeria clutched Conan's arm hard. Ignorant of jungle-lore, she yet knew that no animal she had ever seen could have shaken the tall brush like that.

"It must be as big as an elephant," muttered Conan, echoing her thought. "What the devil —" His voice trailed away in stunned silence.

Through the thicket was thrust a head of nightmare and lunacy. Grinning jaws bared rows of dripping yellow tusks; above the yawning mouth wrinkled a saurian-like snout. Huge eyes, like those of a python a thousand times magnified, stared unwinkingly at the petrified humans clinging to the rock above it. Blood smeared the scaly, flabby lips and dripped from the huge mouth.

The head, bigger than that of a crocodile, was further extended on a long scaled neck on which stood up rows of serrated spikes, and after it, crushing down the briars and saplings, waddled the body of a titan, a gigantic, barrel-bellied torso on absurdly short legs. The whitish belly almost raked the ground, while the serrated back-bone rose higher than Conan could have reached on tiptoe. A long spiked tail, like that of a gargantuan scorpion, trailed out behind.

"Back up the crag, quick!" snapped Conan, thrusting the girl behind him. "I don't think he can climb, but he can stand on his hind-legs and reach us —"

With a snapping and rending of bushes and saplings the monster came hurtling through the thickets, and they fled up the rock before him like leaves blown before a wind. As Valeria plunged into the leafy screen a backward glance showed her the titan rearing up fearsomely on his massive hinder legs, even as Conan had predicted. The sight sent panic racing through her. As he reared, the beast seemed more gigantic than ever; his snouted head towered among the trees. Then Conan's iron hand closed on her wrist and she was jerked headlong into the blinding welter of the leaves, and out again into the hot sunshine above, just as the monster fell forward with his front feet on the crag with an impact that made the rock vibrate.

BEHIND the fugitives the huge head crashed through the twigs, and they looked down for a horrifying instant at the nightmare visage framed among the green leaves, eyes flaming, jaws gaping. Then the giant tusks clashed together futilely, and after that the head was withdrawn, vanishing from their sight as if it had sunk in a pool.

Peering down through broken branches that scraped the rock, they saw it squatting on its haunches at the foot of the crag, staring unblinkingly up at them.

Valeria shuddered.

"How long do you suppose he'll crouch there?"

Conan kicked the skull on the leaf-strewn shelf.

"That fellow must have climbed up here to escape him, or one like him. He must have died of starvation. There are no bones broken. That thing must be a dragon, such as the black people speak of in their legends. If so, it won't leave here until we're both dead."

Valeria looked at him blankly, her resentment forgotten. She fought down a surging of panic. She had proved her reckless courage a thousand times in wild battles on sea and land, on the blood-slippery decks of burning war-ships, in the storming of walled cities, and on the trampled sandy beaches where the desperate men of the Red Brotherhood bathed their knives in one another's blood in their fights for leadership. But the prospect now confronting her congealed her blood. A cutlas stroke in the heat of battle was nothing; but to sit idle and helpless on a bare rock until she perished of starvation, besieged by a monstrous survival of an elder age – the thought sent panic throbbing through her brain.

"He must leave to eat and drink," she said helplessly.

"He won't have to go far to do either," Conan pointed out. "He's just gorged on horse-meat, and like a real snake, he can go for a long time without eating or drinking again. But he doesn't sleep after eating, like a real snake, it seems. Anyway, he can't climb this crag."

Conan spoke imperturbably. He was a barbarian, and the terrible patience of the wilderness and its children was as much a part of him as his lusts and rages. He could endure a situation like this with a coolness impossible to a civilized person.

"Can't we get into the trees and get away, traveling like apes through the branches?" she asked desperately.

He shook his head. "I thought of that. The branches that touch the crag down there are too light. They'd break with our weight. Besides, I have an idea that devil could tear up any tree around here by its roots."

"Well, are we going to sit here on our rumps until we starve, like that?" she cried furiously, kicking the skull clattering across the ledge. "I won't do it! I'll go down there and cut his damned head off –"

Conan had seated himself on a rocky projection at the foot of the spire. He looked up with a glint of admiration at her blazing eyes and tense, quivering figure, but, realizing that she was in just the mood for any madness, he let none of his admiration sound in his voice.

"Sit down," he grunted, catching her by her wrist and pulling her down on his knee. She was too surprised to resist as he took her sword from her hand and shoved it back in its sheath. "Sit still and calm down. You'd only break your steel on his scales. He'd gobble you up at one gulp, or smash you like an egg with that spiked tail of his. We'll get out of this jam some way, but we shan't do it by getting chewed up and swallowed."

She made no reply, nor did she seek to repulse his arm from about her waist. She was frightened, and the sensation was new to Valeria of the Red Brotherhood. So she sat on her companion's – or captor's – knee with a docility that would have amazed Zarallo, who had anathematized her as a she-devil out of hell's seraglio.

Conan played idly with her curly yellow locks, seemingly intent only upon his conquest. Neither the skeleton at his feet nor the monster crouching below disturbed his mind or dulled the edge of his interest.

The girl's restless eyes, roving the leaves below them, discovered splashes of color among the green. It was fruit, large, darkly crimson globes suspended from the boughs of a tree whose broad leaves were a peculiarly rich and vivid green. She became aware of both thirst and hunger, though thirst had not assailed her until she knew she could not descend from the crag to find food and water.

"We need not starve," she said. "There is fruit we can reach."

Conan glanced where she pointed.

"If we ate that we wouldn't need the bite of a dragon," he grunted. "That's what the black people of Kush call the Apples of Derketa. Derketa is the Queen of the Dead. Drink a little of the juice, or spill it on your flesh, and you'd be dead before you could tumble to the foot of this crag."

"Oh!"

She lapsed into dismayed silence. There seemed no way out of their predicament, she reflected gloomily. She saw no way of escape, and Conan seemed to be concerned only with her supple waist and curly tresses. If he was trying to formulate a plan of escape he did not show it.

"If you'll take your hands off me long enough to climb up on that peak," she said presently, "you'll see something that will surprise you."

He cast her a questioning glance, then obeyed with a shrug of his massive shoulders. Clinging to the spire-like pinnacle, he stared out over the forest roof.

HE STOOD a long moment in silence, posed like a bronze statue on the rock.

"It's a walled city, right enough," he muttered presently. "Was that where you were going, when you tried to send me off alone to the coast?"

"I saw it before you came. I knew nothing of it when I left Sukhmet."

"Who'd have thought to find a city here? I don't believe the Stygians ever penetrated this far. Could black people build a city like that? I see no herds on the plain, no signs of cultivation, or people moving about."

"How could you hope to see all that, at this distance?" she demanded.

He shrugged his shoulders and dropped down on the shelf.

"Well, the folk of the city can't help us just now. And they might not, if they could. The people of the Black Countries are generally hostile to strangers. Probably stick us full of spears —"

He stopped short and stood silent, as if he had forgotten what he was saying, frowning down at the crimson spheres gleaming among the leaves.

"Spears!" he muttered. "What a blasted fool I am not to have thought of that before! That shows what a pretty woman does to a man's mind."

"What are you talking about?" she inquired.

Without answering her question, he descended to the belt of leaves and looked down through them. The great brute squatted below, watching the crag with the frightful patience of the reptile folk. So might one of his breed have glared up at their troglodyte ancestors, treed on a high-flung rock, in the dim dawn ages. Conan cursed him without heat, and began cutting branches, reaching out and severing them as far from the end as he could reach. The agitation of the leaves made the monster restless. He rose from his haunches and lashed his hideous tail, snapping off saplings as if they had been toothpicks. Conan watched him warily from the corner of his eye, and just as Valeria believed the dragon was about to hurl himself up the crag again, the Cimmerian drew back and climbed up to the ledge with the branches he had cut. There were three of these, slender shafts about seven feet long, but not larger than his thumb. He had also cut several strands of tough, thin vine.

"Branches too light for spear-hafts, and creepers no thicker than cords," he remarked, indicating the foliage about the crag. "It won't hold our weight – but there's strength in union. That's what the Aquilonian renegades used to tell us Cimmerians when they came into the hills to raise an army to invade their own country. But we always fight by clans and tribes."

"What the devil has that got to do with those sticks?" she demanded.

"You wait and see."

Gathering the sticks in a compact bundle, he wedged his poniard hilt between them at one end. Then with the vines he bound them together, and when he had completed his task, he had a spear of no small strength, with a sturdy shaft seven feet in length.

"What good will that do?" she demanded. "You told me that a blade couldn't pierce his scales –"

"He hasn't got scales all over him," answered Conan. "There's more than one way of skinning a panther."

Moving down to the edge of the leaves, he reached the spear up and carefully thrust the blade through one of the Apples of Derketa, drawing aside to avoid the darkly purple drops that dripped from the pierced fruit. Presently he withdrew the blade and showed her the blue steel stained a dull purplish crimson.

"I don't know whether it will do the job or not," quoth he. "There's enough poison there to kill an elephant, but – well, we'll see."

VALERIA was close behind him as he let himself down among the leaves. Cautiously holding the poisoned pike away from him, he thrust his head through the branches and addressed the monster.

"What are you waiting down there for, you misbegotten offspring of questionable parents?" was one of his more printable queries. "Stick your ugly head up here again, you long-necked brute – or do you want me to come down there and kick you loose from your illegitimate spine?"

There was more of it – some of it couched in eloquence that made Valeria stare, in spite of her profane education among the seafarers. And it had its effect on the monster. Just as the incessant yapping of a dog worries and enrages more constitutionally silent animals, so the clamorous voice of a man rouses fear in some bestial bosoms and insane rage in others. Suddenly and with appalling quickness, the mastodonic brute reared up on its mighty hind legs and elongated its neck and body in a furious effort to reach this vociferous pigmy whose clamor was disturbing the primeval silence of its ancient realm.

But Conan had judged his distance with precision. Some five feet below him the mighty head crashed terribly but futilely through the leaves. And as the monstrous mouth gaped like that of a great snake, Conan drove his spear into the red angle of the jaw-bone hinge. He struck downward with all the strength of both arms, driving the long poniard blade to the hilt in flesh, sinew and bone.

Instantly the jaws clashed convulsively together, severing the triple-pieced shaft and almost precipitating Conan from his perch. He would have fallen but for the girl behind him, who caught his sword-belt in a desperate grasp. He clutched at a rocky projection, and grinned his thanks back at her.

Down on the ground the monster was wallowing like a dog with pepper in its eyes. He shook his head from side to side, pawed at it, and opened his mouth repeatedly to its widest extent. Presently he got a huge front foot on the stump of the shaft and managed to tear the blade out. Then he threw up his head, jaws wide and spouting blood, and glared up at the crag with such concentrated and intelligent fury that Valeria trembled and drew her sword. The scales along his back and flanks turned from rusty brown to a dull lurid red. Most horribly the monster's silence was broken. The sounds that issued from his blood-streaming jaws did not sound like anything that could have been produced by an earthly creation.

With harsh, grating roars, the dragon hurled himself at the crag that was the citadel of his enemies. Again and again his mighty head crashed upward through the branches, snapping vainly on empty air. He hurled his full ponderous weight against the rock until it vibrated from base to crest. And rearing upright he gripped it with his front legs like a man and tried to tear it up by the roots, as if it had been a tree.

This exhibition of primordial fury chilled the blood in Valeria's veins, but Conan was too close to the primitive himself to feel anything but a comprehending interest. To the barbarian, no such gulf existed between himself and other men, and the animals, as existed in the conception of Valeria. The monster below them, to Conan, was merely a form of life differing from himself mainly in physical shape. He attributed to it characteristics similar to his own, and saw in its wrath a counterpart of his rages, in its roars and bellowings merely reptilian equivalents to the curses he had bestowed upon it. Feeling a kinship with all wild things, even dragons, it was impossible for him to experience the sick horror which assailed Valeria at the sight of the brute's ferocity.

He sat watching it tranquilly, and pointed out the various changes that were taking place in its voice and actions.

"The poison's taking hold," he said with conviction.

"I don't believe it." To Valeria it seemed preposterous to suppose that anything, however lethal, could have any effect on that mountain of muscle and fury.

"There's pain in his voice," declared Conan. "First he was merely angry because of the stinging in his jaw. Now he feels the bite of the poison. Look! He's staggering. He'll be blind in a few more minutes. What did I tell you?"

For suddenly the dragon had lurched about and went crashing off through the bushes.

"Is he running away?" inquired Valeria uneasily.

"He's making for the pool!" Conan sprang up, galvanized into swift activity. "The poison makes him thirsty. Come on! He'll be blind in a few moments, but he can smell his way back to the foot of the crag, and if our scent's here still, he'll sit there until he dies. And others of his kind may come at his cries. Let's go!"

"Down there?" Valeria was aghast.

"Sure! We'll make for the city! They may cut our heads off there, but it's our only chance. We may run into a thousand more dragons on the way, but it's sure death to stay here. If we wait until he dies, we may have a dozen more to deal with. After me, in a hurry!"

He went down the ramp as swiftly as an ape, pausing only to aid his less agile companion, who, until she saw the Cimmerian climb, had fancied herself the equal of any man in the rigging of a ship or on the sheer face of a cliff.

THEY descended into the gloom below the branches and slid to the ground silently, though Valeria felt as if the pounding of her heart must surely be heard from far away. A noisy gurgling and lapping beyond the dense thicket indicated that the dragon was drinking at the pool.

"As soon as his belly is full he'll be back," muttered Conan. "It may take hours for the poison to kill him – if it does at all."

Somewhere beyond the forest the sun was sinking to the horizon. The forest was a misty twilight place of black shadows and dim vistas. Conan gripped Valeria's wrist and glided away from the foot of the crag. He made less noise than a breeze blowing among the tree-trunks, but Valeria felt as if her soft boots were betraying their flight to all the forest.

"I don't think he can follow a trail," muttered Conan. "But if a wind blew our body-scent to him, he could smell us out."

"Mitra grant that the wind blow not!" Valeria breathed.

Her face was a pallid oval in the gloom. She gripped her sword in her free hand, but the feel of the shagreen-bound hilt inspired only a feeling of helplessness in her.

They were still some distance from the edge of the forest when they heard a snapping and crashing behind them. Valeria bit her lip to check a cry.

"He's on our trail!" she whispered fiercely.

Conan shook his head.

"He didn't smell us at the rock, and he's blundering about through the forest trying to pick up our scent. Come on! It's the city or nothing now! He could tear down any tree we'd climb. If only the wind stays down —"

They stole on until the trees began to thin out ahead of them. Behind them the forest was a black impenetrable ocean of shadows. The ominous crackling still sounded behind them, as the dragon blundered in his erratic course.

"There's the plain ahead," breathed Valeria. "A little more and we'll —"

"Crom!" swore Conan.

"Mitra!" whispered Valeria.

Out of the south a wind had sprung up.

It blew over them directly into the black forest behind them. Instantly a horrible roar shook the woods. The aimless snapping and crackling of the bushes changed to a sustained crashing as the dragon came like a hurricane straight toward the spot from which the scent of his enemies was wafted.

"Run!" snarled Conan, his eyes blazing like those of a trapped wolf. "It's all we can do!"

Sailors' boots are not made for sprinting, and the life of a pirate does not train one for a runner. Within a hundred yards Valeria was panting and reeling in her gait, and behind them the crashing gave way to a rolling thunder as the monster broke out of the thickets and into the more open ground.

Conan's iron arm about the woman's waist half lifted her; her feet scarcely touched the earth as she was borne along at a speed she could never have attained herself. If he could keep out of the beast's way for a bit, perhaps that betraying wind would shift — but the wind held, and a quick glance over his shoulder showed Conan that the monster was almost upon them, coming like a war-galley in front of a hurricane. He thrust Valeria from him with a force that sent her reeling a dozen feet to fall in a crumpled heap at the foot of the nearest tree, and the Cimmerian wheeled in the path of the thundering titan.

Convinced that his death was upon him, the Cimmerian acted according to his instinct, and hurled himself full at the awful face that was bearing down on him. He leaped, slashing like a wildcat, felt his sword cut deep into the scales that sheathed the mighty snout — and then a terrific impact knocked him rolling and tumbling for fifty feet with all the wind and half the life battered out of him.

How the stunned Cimmerian regained his feet, not even he could have ever told. But the only thought that filled his brain was of the woman lying dazed and helpless almost in the path of the hurtling fiend, and before the breath came whistling back into his gullet he was standing over her with his sword in his hand.

She lay where he had thrown her, but she was struggling to a sitting posture. Neither tearing tusks nor trampling feet had touched her. It had been a shoulder or front leg that struck Conan, and the blind monster rushed on, forgetting the victims whose scent it had been following, in the sudden agony of its death throes. Headlong on its course it thundered until its low-hung head crashed into a gigantic tree in its path. The impact tore the tree up by the roots and must have dashed the brains from the misshapen skull. Tree and monster fell together, and the dazed humans saw the branches and leaves shaken by the convulsions of the creature they covered – and then grow quiet.

Conan lifted Valeria to her feet and together they started away at a reeling run. A few moments later they emerged into the still twilight of the treeless plain.

CONAN paused an instant and glanced back at the ebon fastness behind them. Not a leaf stirred, nor a bird chirped. It stood as silent as it must have stood before Man was created.

"Come on," muttered Conan, taking his companion's hand. "It's touch and go now. If more dragons come out of the woods after us –"

He did not have to finish the sentence.

The city looked very far away across the plain, farther than it had looked from the crag. Valeria's heart hammered until she felt as if it would strangle her. At every step she expected to hear the crashing of the bushes and see another colossal nightmare bearing down upon them. But nothing disturbed the silence of the thickets.

With the first mile between them and the woods, Valeria breathed more easily. Her buoyant self-confidence began to thaw out again. The sun had set and darkness was gathering over the plain, lightened a little by the stars that made stunted ghosts out of the cactus growths.

"No cattle, no plowed fields," muttered Conan. "How do these people live?"

"Perhaps the cattle are in pens for the night," suggested Valeria, "and the fields and grazing-pastures are on the other side of the city."

"Maybe," he grunted. "I didn't see any from the crag, though."

The moon came up behind the city, etching walls and towers blackly in the yellow glow. Valeria shivered. Black against the moon the strange city had a somber, sinister look.

Perhaps something of the same feeling occurred to Conan, for he stopped, glanced about him, and grunted: "We stop here. No use coming to their gates in the night. They probably wouldn't let us in. Besides, we need rest, and we don't know how they'll receive us. A few hours' sleep will put us in better shape to fight or run."

He led the way to a bed of cactus which grew in a circle – a phenomenon common to the southern desert. With his sword he chopped an opening, and motioned Valeria to enter.

"We'll be safe from snakes here, anyhow."

She glanced fearfully back toward the black line that indicated the forest some six miles away.

"Suppose a dragon comes out of the woods?"

"We'll keep watch," he answered, though he made no suggestion as to what they would do in such an event. He was staring at the city, a few miles away. Not a light shone from spire or tower. A great black mass of mystery, it reared cryptically against the moonlit sky.

"Lie down and sleep. I'll keep the first watch."

She hesitated, glancing at him uncertainly, but he sat down cross-legged in the opening, facing toward the plain, his sword across his knees, his back to her. Without further comment she lay down on the sand inside the spiky circle.

"Wake me when the moon is at its zenith," she directed.

He did not reply nor look toward her. Her last impression, as she sank into slumber, was of his muscular figure, immobile as a statue hewn out of bronze, outlined against the low-hanging stars.

II

BY THE BLAZE OF THE FIRE JEWELS

VALERIA awoke with a start, to the realization that a gray dawn was stealing over the plain.

She sat up, rubbing her eyes. Conan squatted beside the cactus, cutting off the thick pears and dexterously twitching out the spikes.

"You didn't awake me," she accused. "You let me sleep all night!"

"You were tired," he answered. "Your posterior must have been sore, too, after that long ride. You pirates aren't used to horseback."

"What about yourself?" she retorted.

"I was a *kozak* before I was a pirate," he answered. "They live in the saddle. I snatch naps like a panther watching beside the trail for a deer to come by. My ears keep watch while my eyes sleep."

And indeed the giant barbarian seemed as much refreshed as if he had slept the whole night on a golden bed. Having removed the thorns, and peeled off the tough skin, he handed the girl a thick, juicy cactus leaf.

"Skin your teeth in that pear. It's food and drink to a desert man. I was a chief of the Zuagirs once – desert men who live by plundering the caravans."

"Is there anything you haven't been?" inquired the girl, half in derision and half in fascination.

"I've never been king of an Hyborian kingdom," he grinned, taking an enormous mouthful of cactus. "But I've dreamed of being even that. I may be too, some day. Why shouldn't I?"

She shook her head in wonder at his calm audacity, and fell to devouring her pear. She found it not unpleasing to the palate, and full of cool and thirst-satisfying juice. Finishing his meal, Conan wiped his hands in the sand, rose, ran his fingers through his thick black mane, hitched at his sword-belt and said:

"Well, let's go. If the people in that city are going to cut our throats they may as well do it now, before the heat of the day begins."

His grim humor was unconscious, but Valeria reflected that it might be prophetic. She too hitched her sword-belt as she rose. Her terrors of the night were past. The roaring dragons of the distant forest were like a dim dream. There was a swagger in her stride as she moved off beside the Cimmerian. Whatever perils lay ahead of them, their foes would be men. And Valeria of the Red Brotherhood had never seen the face of the man she feared.

Conan glanced down at her as she strode along beside him with her swinging stride that matched his own.

"You walk more like a hillman than a sailor," he said. "You must be an Aquilonian. The suns of Darfar never burnt your white skin brown. Many a princess would envy you."

"I am from Aquilonia," she replied. His compliments no longer irritated her. His evident admiration pleased her. For another man to have kept her watch while she slept would have angered her; she had always fiercely resented any man's attempting to shield or protect her because of her sex. But she found a secret pleasure in the fact that this man had done so. And he had not taken advantage of her fright and the weakness resulting from it. After all, she reflected, her companion was no common man.

THE sun rose behind the city, turning the towers to a sinister crimson.

"Black last night against the moon," grunted Conan, his eyes clouding with the abysmal superstition of the barbarian. "Blood-red as a threat of blood against the sun this dawn. I do not like this city."

But they went on, and as they went Conan pointed out the fact that no road ran to the city from the north.

"No cattle have trampled the plain on this side of the city," said he. "No plowshare has touched the earth for years, maybe centuries. But look: once this plain was cultivated."

Valeria saw the ancient irrigation ditches he indicated, half filled in places, and overgrown with cactus. She frowned with perplexity as her eyes swept over the plain that stretched on all sides of the city to the forest edge, which marched in a vast, dim ring. Vision did not extend beyond that ring.

She looked uneasily at the city. No helmets or spear-heads gleamed on battlements, no trumpets sounded, no challenge rang from the towers. A silence as absolute as that of the forest brooded over the walls and minarets.

The sun was high above the eastern horizon when they stood before the great gate in the northern wall, in the shadow of the lofty rampart. Rust flecked the iron bracings of the mighty bronze portal. Spiderwebs glistened thickly on hinge and sill and bolted panel.

"It hasn't been opened for years!" exclaimed Valeria.

"A dead city," grunted Conan. "That's why the ditches were broken and the plain untouched."

"But who built it? Who dwelt here? Where did they go? Why did they abandon it?"

"Who can say? Maybe an exiled clan of Stygians built it. Maybe not. It doesn't look like Stygian architecture. Maybe the people were wiped out by enemies, or a plague exterminated them."

"In that case their treasures may still be gathering dust and cobwebs in there," suggested Valeria, the acquisitive instincts of her profession waking in her; prodded, too, by feminine curiosity. "Can we open the gate? Let's go in and explore a bit."

Conan eyed the heavy portal dubiously, but placed his massive shoulder against it and thrust with all the power of his muscular calves and thighs. With a rasping screech of rusty hinges the gate moved ponderously inward, and Conan straightened and drew his sword. Valeria stared over his shoulder, and made a sound indicative of surprize.

They were not looking into an open street or court as one would have expected. The opened gate, or door, gave directly into a long, broad hall which ran away and away until its vista grew indistinct in the distance. It was of heroic proportions, and the floor of a curious red stone, cut in square tiles, that seemed to smolder as if with the reflection of flames. The walls were of a shiny green material.

"Jade, or I'm a Shemite!" swore Conan.

"Not in such quantity!" protested Valeria.

"I've looted enough from the Khitan caravans to know what I'm talking about," he asserted. "That's jade!"

The vaulted ceiling was of lapis lazuli, adorned with clusters of great green stones that gleamed with a poisonous radiance.

"Green fire-stones," growled Conan. "That's what the people of Punt call them. They're supposed to be the petrified eyes of those prehistoric snakes the ancients called Golden Serpents. They glow like a cat's eyes in the dark. At night this hall would be lighted by them, but it would be a hellishly weird illumination. Let's look around. We might find a cache of jewels."

"Shut the door," advised Valeria. "I'd hate to have to outrun a dragon down this hall."

Conan grinned, and replied: "I don't believe the dragons ever leave the forest."

But he complied, and pointed out the broken bolt on the inner side.

"I thought I heard something snap when I shoved against it. That bolt's freshly broken. Rust has eaten nearly through it. If the people ran away, why should it have been bolted on the inside?"

"They undoubtedly left by another door," suggested Valeria.

She wondered how many centuries had passed since the light of outer day had filtered into that great hall through the open door. Sunlight was finding its way somehow into the hall, and they quickly saw the source. High up in the vaulted ceiling skylights were set in slot-like openings – translucent sheets of some crystalline substance. In the splotches of shadow between them, the green jewels winked like the eyes of angry cats. Beneath their feet the dully lurid floor smoldered with changing hues and colors of flame. It was like treading the floors of hell with evil stars blinking overhead.

Three balustraded galleries ran along on each side of the hall, one above the other.

"A four-storied house," grunted Conan, "and this hall extends to the roof. It's long as a street. I seem to see a door at the other end."

Valeria shrugged her white shoulders.

"Your eyes are better than mine, then, though I'm accounted sharp-eyed among the sea-rovers."

THEY turned into an open door at random, and traversed a series of empty chambers, floored like the hall, and with walls of the same green jade, or of marble or ivory or chalcedony, adorned with friezes of bronze, gold or silver. In the ceilings the green fire-gems were set, and their light was as ghostly and illusive as Conan had predicted. Under the witch-fire glow the intruders moved like specters.

Some of the chambers lacked this illumination, and their doorways showed black as the mouth of the Pit. These Conan and Valeria avoided, keeping always to the lighted chambers.

Cobwebs hung in the corners, but there was no perceptible accumulation of dust on the floor, or on the tables and seats of marble, jade or carnelian which occupied the chambers. Here and there were rugs of that silk known as Khitan which is practically indestructible. Nowhere did they find any windows, or doors opening into streets or courts. Each door merely opened into another chamber or hall.

"Why don't we come to a street?" grumbled Valeria. "This place or whatever we're in must be as big as the king of Turan's seraglio."

"They must not have perished of plague," said Conan, meditating upon the mystery of the empty city. "Otherwise we'd find skeletons. Maybe it became haunted, and everybody got up and left. Maybe –"

"Maybe, hell!" broke in Valeria rudely. "We'll never know. Look at these friezes. They portray men. What race do they belong to?"

Conan scanned them and shook his head.

"I never saw people exactly like them. But there's the smack of the East about them – Vendhya, maybe, or Kosala."

"Were you a king in Kosala?" she asked, masking her keen curiosity with derision.

"No. But I was a war-chief of the Afghulis who live in the Himelian mountains above the borders of Vendhya. These people favor the Kosalans. But why should Kosalans be building a city this far to west?"

The figures portrayed were those of slender, olive-skinned men and women, with finely chiseled, exotic features. They wore filmy robes and many delicate jeweled ornaments, and were depicted mostly in attitudes of feasting, dancing or love-making.

"Easterners, all right," grunted Conan, "but from where I don't know. They must have lived a disgustingly peaceful life, though, or they'd have scenes of wars and fights. Let's go up that stair."

It was an ivory spiral that wound up from the chamber in which they were standing. They mounted three flights and came into a broad chamber on the fourth floor, which seemed to be the highest tier in the building. Skylights in the ceiling illuminated the room, in which light the fire-gems winked pallidly. Glancing through the doors they saw, except on one side, a series of similarly lighted chambers. This other door opened upon a balustraded gallery that overhung a hall much smaller than the one they had recently explored on the lower floor.

"Hell!" Valeria sat down disgustedly on a jade bench. "The people who deserted this city must have taken all their treasures with them. I'm tired of wandering through these bare rooms at random."

"All these upper chambers seem to be lighted," said Conan. "I wish we could find a window that overlooked the city. Let's have a look through that door over there."

"You have a look," advised Valeria. "I'm going to sit here and rest my feet."

CONAN disappeared through the door opposite that one opening upon the gallery, and Valeria leaned back with her hands clasped behind her head, and thrust her booted legs out in front of her. These silent rooms and halls with their gleaming green clusters of ornaments and burning crimson floors were beginning to depress her. She wished they could find their way out of the maze into which they had wandered and emerge into a street. She wondered idly what furtive, dark feet had glided over those flaming floors in past centuries, how many deeds of cruelty and mystery those winking ceiling-gems had blazed down upon.

It was a faint noise that brought her out of her reflections. She was on her feet with her sword in her hand before she realized what had disturbed her. Conan had not returned, and she knew it was not he that she had heard.

The sound had come from somewhere beyond the door that opened on to the gallery. Soundlessly in her soft leather boots she glided through it, crept across the balcony and peered down between the heavy balustrades.

A man was stealing along the hall.

The sight of a human being in this supposedly deserted city was a startling shock. Crouching down behind the stone balusters, with every nerve tingling, Valeria glared down at the stealthy figure.

The man in no way resembled the figures depicted on the friezes. He was slightly above middle height, very dark, though not negroid. He was naked but for a scanty silk clout that only partly covered his muscular hips, and a leather girdle, a hand's breadth broad, about his lean waist. His long black hair hung in lank strands about his shoulders, giving him a wild appearance. He was gaunt, but knots and cords of muscles stood out on his arms and legs, without that fleshy padding that presents a pleasing symmetry of contour. He was built with an economy that was almost repellent.

Yet it was not so much his physical appearance as his attitude that impressed the woman who watched him. He slunk along, stooped in a semi-crouch, his head turning from side to side. He grasped a wide-tipped blade in his right hand, and she saw it shake with the intensity of the emotion that gripped him. He was afraid, trembling in the grip of some dire terror. When he turned his head she caught the blaze of wild eyes among the lank strands of black hair.

He did not see her. On tiptoe he glided across the hall and vanished through an open door. A moment later she heard a choking cry, and then silence fell again.

Consumed with curiosity, Valeria glided along the gallery until she came to a door above the one through which the man had passed. It opened into another, smaller gallery that encircled a large chamber.

This chamber was on the third floor, and its ceiling was not so high as that of the hall. It was lighted only by the fire-stones, and their weird green glow left the spaces under the balcony in shadows.

Valeria's eyes widened. The man she had seen was still in the chamber.

He lay face down on a dark crimson carpet in the middle of the room. His body was limp, his arms spread wide. His curved sword lay near him.

She wondered why he should lie there so motionless. Then her eyes narrowed as she stared down at the rug on which he lay. Beneath and about him the fabric showed a slightly different color, a deeper, brighter crimson.

Shivering slightly, she crouched down closer behind the balustrade, intently scanning the shadows under the overhanging gallery. They gave up no secret.

Suddenly another figure entered the grim drama. He was a man similar to the first, and he came in by a door opposite that which gave upon the hall.

His eyes glared at the sight of the man on the floor, and he spoke something in a staccato voice that sounded like "Chicmec!" The other did not move.

The man stepped quickly across the floor, bent, gripped the fallen man's shoulder and turned him over. A choking cry escaped him as the head fell back limply, disclosing a throat that had been severed from ear to ear.

The man let the corpse fall back upon the blood-stained carpet, and sprang to his feet, shaking like a wind-blown leaf. His face was an ashy mask of fear. But with one knee flexed for flight, he froze suddenly, became as immobile as an image, staring across the chamber with dilated eyes.

In the shadows beneath the balcony a ghostly light began to glow and grow, a light that was not part of the fire-stone gleam. Valeria felt her hair stir as she watched it; for, dimly visible in the throbbing radiance, there floated a human skull, and it was from this skull – human yet appallingly misshapen – that the spectral light seemed to emanate. It hung there like a disembodied head, conjured out of night and the shadows, growing more and more distinct; human, and yet not human as she knew humanity.

The man stood motionless, an embodiment of paralyzed horror, staring fixedly at the apparition. The thing moved out from the wall and a grotesque shadow moved with it. Slowly the shadow became visible as a man-like figure whose naked torso and limbs shone whitely, with the hue of bleached bones. The bare skull on its shoulders grinned eyelessly, in the midst of its unholy nimbus, and the man confronting it seemed unable to take his eyes from it. He stood still, his sword dangling from nerveless fingers, on his face the expression of a man bound by the spells of a mesmerist.

VALERIA realized that it was not fear alone that paralyzed him. Some hellish quality of that throbbing glow had robbed him of his power to think and act. She herself, safely above the scene, felt the subtle impact of a nameless emanation that was a threat to sanity.

The horror swept toward its victim and he moved at last, but only to drop his sword and sink to his knees, covering his eyes with his hands. Dumbly he awaited the stroke of the blade that now gleamed in the apparition's hand as it reared above him like Death triumphant over mankind.

Valeria acted according to the first impulse of her wayward nature. With one tigerish movement she was over the balustrade and dropping to the floor behind the awful shape. It wheeled at the thud of her soft boots on the floor, but even as it turned, her keen blade lashed down, and a fierce exultation swept her as she felt the edge cleave solid flesh and mortal bone.

The apparition cried out gurglingly and went down, severed through shoulder, breast-bone and spine, and as it fell the burning skull rolled clear, revealing a lank mop of black hair and a dark face twisted in the convulsions of death. Beneath the horrific masquerade there was a human being, a man similar to the one kneeling supinely on the floor.

The latter looked up at the sound of the blow and the cry, and now he glared in wild-eyed amazement at the white-skinned woman who stood over the corpse with a dripping sword in her hand.

He staggered up, yammering as if the sight had almost unseated his reason. She was amazed to realize that she understood him. He was gibbering in the Stygian tongue, though in a dialect unfamiliar to her.

"Who are you? Whence come you? What do you in Xuchotl?" Then rushing on, without waiting for her to reply: "But you are a friend – goddess or devil, it makes no difference! You have slain the Burning Skull! It was but a man beneath it, after all! We deemed it a demon *they* conjured up out of the catacombs! *Listen!*"

He stopped short in his ravings and stiffened, straining his ears with painful intensity. The girl heard nothing.

"We must hasten!" he whispered. "*They* are west of the Great Hall! They may be all around us here! They may be creeping upon us even now!"

He seized her wrist in a convulsive grasp she found hard to break.

"Whom do you mean by 'they'?" she demanded.

He stared at her uncomprehendingly for an instant, as if he found her ignorance hard to understand.

"They?" he stammered vaguely. "Why – why, the people of Xotalanc! The clan of the man you slew. They who dwell by the eastern gate."

"You mean to say this city is inhabited?" she exclaimed.

"Aye! Aye!" He was writhing in the impatience of apprehension. "Come away! Come quick! We must return to Tecuhltli!"

"Where is that?" she demanded.

"The quarter by the western gate!" He had her wrist again and was pulling her toward the door through which he had first come. Great beads of perspiration dripped from his dark forehead, and his eyes blazed with terror.

"Wait a minute!" she growled, flinging off his hand. "Keep your hands off me, or I'll split your skull. What's all this about? Who are you? Where would you take me?"

He took a firm grip on himself, casting glances to all sides, and began speaking so fast his words tripped over each other.

"My name is Techotl. I am of Tecuhltli. I and this man who lies with his throat cut came into the Halls of Silence to try and ambush some of the Xotalancas. But we became separated and I returned here to find him with his gullet slit. The Burning Skull did it, I know, just as he would have slain me had you not killed him. But perhaps he was not alone. Others may be stealing from Xotalanc! The gods themselves blench at the fate of those they take alive!"

At the thought he shook as with an ague and his dark skin grew ashy. Valeria frowned puzzledly at him. She sensed intelligence behind this rigmarole, but it was meaningless to her.

She turned toward the skull, which still glowed and pulsed on the floor, and was reaching a booted toe tentatively toward it, when the man who called himself Techotl sprang forward with a cry.

"Do not touch it! Do not even look at it! Madness and death lurk in it. The wizards of Xotalanc understand its secret — they found it in the catacombs, where lie the bones of terrible kings who ruled in Xuchotl in the black centuries of the past. To gaze upon it freezes the blood and withers the brain of a man who understands not its mystery. To touch it causes madness and destruction."

She scowled at him uncertainly. He was not a reassuring figure, with his lean, muscle-knotted frame, and snaky locks. In his eyes, behind the glow of terror, lurked a weird light she had never seen in the eyes of a man wholly sane. Yet he seemed sincere in his protestations.

"Come!" he begged, reaching for her hand, and then recoiling as he remembered her warning. "You are a stranger. How you came here I do not know, but if you were a goddess or a demon, come to aid Tecuhltli, you would know all the things you have asked me. You must be from beyond the great forest, whence our ancestors came. But you are our friend, or you would not have slain my enemy. Come quickly, before the Xotalancas find us and slay us!"

From his repellent, impassioned face she glanced to the sinister skull, smoldering and glowing on the floor near the dead man. It was like a skull seen in a dream, undeniably human, yet with disturbing distortions and malformations of contour and outline. In life the wearer of that skull must have presented an alien and monstrous aspect. Life? It seemed to possess some sort of life of its own. Its jaws yawned at her and snapped together. Its radiance grew brighter, more vivid, yet the impression of nightmare grew too; it was a dream; all life was a dream — it was Techotl's urgent voice which snapped Valeria back from the dim gulfs whither she was drifting.

"Do not look at the skull! Do not look at the skull!" It was a far cry from across unreckoned voids.

Valeria shook herself like a lion shaking his mane. Her vision cleared. Techotl was chattering: "In life it housed the awful brain of a king of magicians! It holds still the life and fire of magic drawn from outer spaces!"

WITH a curse Valeria leaped, lithe as a panther, and the skull crashed to flaming bits under her swinging sword. Somewhere in the room, or in the void, or in the dim reaches of her consciousness, an inhuman voice cried out in pain and rage.

Techotl's hand was plucking at her arm and he was gibbering: "You have broken it! You have destroyed it! Not all the black arts of Xotalanc can rebuild it! Come away! Come away quickly, now!"

"But I can't go," she protested. "I have a friend somewhere near by —"

The flare of his eyes cut her short as he stared past her with an expression grown ghastly. She wheeled just as four men rushed through as many doors, converging on the pair in the center of the chamber.

They were like the others she had seen, the same knotted muscles bulging on otherwise gaunt limbs, the same lank blue-black hair, the same mad glare in their wide eyes. They were armed and clad like Techotl, but on the breast of each was painted a white skull.

There were no challenges or war-cries. Like blood-mad tigers the men of Xotalanc sprang at the throats of their enemies. Techotl met them with the fury of desperation, ducked the swipe of a wide-headed blade, and grappled with the wielder, and bore him to the floor where they rolled and wrestled in murderous silence.

The other three swarmed on Valeria, their weird eyes red as the eyes of mad dogs.

SHE killed the first who came within reach before he could strike a blow, her long straight blade splitting his skull even as his own sword lifted for a stroke. She sidestepped a thrust, even as she parried a slash. Her eyes danced and her lips smiled without mercy. Again she was Valeria of the Red Brotherhood, and the hum of her steel was like a bridal song in her ears.

Her sword darted past a blade that sought to parry, and sheathed six inches of its point in a leather-guarded midriff. The man gasped agonizedly and went to his knees, but his tall mate lunged in, in ferocious silence, raining blow on blow so furiously that Valeria had no opportunity to counter. She stepped back coolly, parrying the strokes and watching for her chance to thrust home. He could not long keep up that flailing whirlwind. His arm would tire, his wind would fail; he would weaken, falter, and then her blade would slide smoothly into his heart. A sidelong glance showed her Techotl kneeling on the breast of his antagonist and striving to break the other's hold on his wrist and to drive home a dagger.

Sweat beaded the forehead of the man facing her, and his eyes were like burning coals. Smite as he would, he could not break past nor beat down her guard. His breath came in gusty gulps, his blows began to fall erratically. She stepped back to draw him out — and felt her thighs locked in an iron grip. She had forgotten the wounded man on the floor.

Crouching on his knees, he held her with both arms locked about her legs, and his mate croaked in triumph and began working his way around to come at her from the left side. Valeria wrenched and tore savagely, but in vain. She could free herself of this clinging menace with a downward flick of her sword, but in that instant the curved blade of the tall warrior would crash through her skull. The wounded man began to worry at her bare thigh with his teeth like a wild beast.

She reached down with her left hand and gripped his long hair, forcing his head back so that his white teeth and rolling eyes gleamed up at her. The tall Xotalanc cried out fiercely and leaped in, smiting with all the fury of his arm. Awkwardly she parried the stroke, and it beat the flat of her blade down on her head so that she saw sparks flash before her eyes, and staggered. Up went the sword again, with a low, beast-like cry of triumph – and then a giant form loomed behind the Xotalanc and steel flashed like a jet of blue lightning. The cry of the warrior broke short and he went down like an ox beneath the pole-ax, his brains gushing from his skull that had been split to the throat.

"Conan!" gasped Valeria. In a gust of passion she turned on the Xotalanc whose long hair she still gripped in her left hand. "Dog of hell!" Her blade swished as it cut the air in an upswinging arc with a blur in the middle, and the headless body slumped down, spurting blood. She hurled the severed head across the room.

"What the devil's going on here?" Conan bestrode the corpse of the man he had killed, broadsword in hand, glaring about him in amazement.

Techotl was rising from the twitching figure of the last Xotalanc, shaking red drops from his dagger. He was bleeding from the stab deep in the thigh. He stared at Conan with dilated eyes.

"What is all this?" Conan demanded again, not yet recovered from the stunning surprize of finding Valeria engaged in a savage battle with these fantastic figures in a city he had thought empty and uninhabited. Returning from an aimless exploration of the upper chambers to find Valeria missing from the room where he had left her, he had followed the sounds of strife that burst on his dumfounded ears.

"Five dead dogs!" exclaimed Techotl, his flaming eyes reflecting a ghastly exultation. "Five slain! Five crimson nails for the black pillar! The gods of blood be thanked!"

He lifted quivering hands on high, and then, with the face of a fiend, he spat on the corpses and stamped on their faces, dancing in his ghoulish glee. His recent allies eyed him in amazement, and Conan asked, in the Aquilonian tongue: "Who is this madman?"

Valeria shrugged her shoulders.

"He says his name's Techotl. From his babblings I gather that his people live at one end of this crazy city, and these others at the other end. Maybe we'd better go with him. He seems friendly, and it's easy to see that the other clan isn't."

TECHOTL had ceased his dancing and was listening again, his head tilted sidewise, dog-like, triumph struggling with fear in his repellent countenance.

"Come away, now!" he whispered. "We have done enough! Five dead dogs! My people will welcome you! They will honor you! But come! It is far to Tecuhltli. At any moment the Xotalancas may come on us in numbers too great even for your swords."

"Lead the way," grunted Conan.

Techotl instantly mounted a stair leading up to the gallery, beckoning them to follow him, which they did, moving rapidly to keep on his heels. Having reached the gallery, he plunged into a door that opened toward the west, and hurried through chamber after chamber, each lighted by skylights or green fire-jewels.

"What sort of a place can this be?" muttered Valeria under her breath.

"Crom knows!" answered Conan. "I've seen *his* kind before, though. They live on the shores of Lake Zuad, near the border of Kush. They're a sort of mongrel Stygians, mixed with another race that wandered into Stygia from the east some centuries ago and were absorbed by them. They're called Tlazitlans. I'm willing to bet it wasn't they who built this city, though."

Techotl's fear did not seem to diminish as they drew away from the chamber where the dead men lay. He kept twisting his head on his shoulder to listen for sounds of pursuit, and stared with burning intensity into every doorway they passed.

Valeria shivered in spite of herself. She feared no man. But the weird floor beneath her feet, the uncanny jewels over her head, dividing the lurking shadows among them, the stealth and terror of their guide, impressed her with a nameless apprehension, a sensation of lurking, inhuman peril.

"They may be between us and Tecuhltli!" he whispered once. "We must beware lest they be lying in wait!"

"Why don't we get out of this infernal palace, and take to the streets?" demanded Valeria.

"There are no streets in Xuchotl," he answered. "No squares nor open courts. The whole city is built like one giant palace under one great roof. The nearest approach to a street is the Great Hall which traverses the city from the north gate to the south gate. The only doors opening into the outer world are the city gates, through which no living man has passed for fifty years."

"How long have you dwelt here?" asked Conan.

"I was born in the castle of Tecuhltli thirty-five years ago. I have never set foot outside the city. For the love of the gods, let us go silently! These halls may be full of lurking devils. Olmec shall tell you all when we reach Tecuhltli."

So in silence they glided on with the green fire-stones blinking overhead and the flaming floors smoldering under their feet, and it seemed to Valeria as if they fled through hell, guided by a dark-faced, lank-haired goblin.

Yet it was Conan who halted them as they were crossing an unusually wide chamber. His wilderness-bred ears were keener even than the ears of Techotl, whetted though these were by a lifetime of warfare in those silent corridors.

"You think some of your enemies may be ahead of us, lying in ambush?"

"They prowl through these rooms at all hours," answered Techotl, "as do we. The halls and chambers between Tecuhltli and Xotalanc are a disputed region, owned by no man. We call it the Halls of Silence. Why do you ask?"

"Because men are in the chambers ahead of us," answered Conan. "I heard steel clink against stone."

Again a shaking seized Techotl, and he clenched his teeth to keep them from chattering.

"Perhaps they are your friends," suggested Valeria.

"We dare not chance it," he panted, and moved with frenzied activity. He turned aside and glided through a doorway on the left which led into a chamber from which an ivory staircase wound down into darkness.

"This leads to an unlighted corridor below us!" he hissed, great beads of perspiration standing out on his brow. "They may be lurking there, too. It may all be a trick to draw us into it. But we must take the chance that they have laid their ambush in the rooms above. Come swiftly, now!"

SOFTLY as phantoms they descended the stair and came to the mouth of a corridor black as night. They crouched there for a moment, listening, and then melted into it. As they moved along, Valeria's flesh crawled between her shoulders in momentary expectation of a sword-thrust in the dark. But for Conan's iron fingers gripping her arm she had no physical cognizance of her companions. Neither made as much noise as a cat would have made. The darkness was absolute. One hand, outstretched, touched a wall, and occasionally she felt a door under her fingers. The hallway seemed interminable.

Suddenly they were galvanized by a sound behind them. Valeria's flesh crawled anew, for she recognized it as the soft opening of a door. Men had come into the corridor behind them. Even with the thought she stumbled over something that felt like a human skull. It rolled across the floor with an appalling clatter.

"Run!" yelped Techotl, a note of hysteria in his voice, and was away down the corridor like a flying ghost.

Again Valeria felt Conan's hand bearing her up and sweeping her along as they raced after their guide. Conan could see in the dark no better than she, but he possessed a sort of instinct that made his course unerring. Without his support and guidance she would have fallen or stumbled against the wall. Down the corridor they sped, while the swift patter of flying feet drew closer and closer, and then suddenly Techotl panted: "Here is the stair! After me, quick! Oh, quick!"

His hand came out of the dark and caught Valeria's wrist as she stumbled blindly on the steps. She felt herself half dragged, half lifted up the winding stair, while Conan released her and turned on the steps, his ears and instincts telling him their foes were hard at their backs. *And the sounds were not all those of human feet.*

Something came writhing up the steps, something that slithered and rustled and brought a chill in the air with it. Conan lashed down with his great sword and felt the blade shear through something that might have been flesh and bone, and cut deep into the stair beneath. Something touched his foot that chilled like the touch of frost, and then the darkness beneath him was disturbed by a frightful thrashing and lashing, and a man cried out in agony.

The next moment Conan was racing up the winding staircase, and through a door that stood open at the head.

Valeria and Techotl were already through, and Techotl slammed the door and shot a bolt across it – the first Conan had seen since they left the outer gate.

Then he turned and ran across the well-lighted chamber into which they had come, and as they passed through the farther door, Conan glanced back and saw the door groaning and straining under heavy pressure violently applied from the other side.

Though Techotl did not abate either his speed or his caution, he seemed more confident now. He had the air of a man who has come into familiar territory, within call of friends.

But Conan renewed his terror by asking: "What was that thing that I fought on the stair?"

"The men of Xotalanc," answered Techotl, without looking back. "I told you the halls were full of them."

"This wasn't a man," grunted Conan. "It was something that crawled, and it was as cold as ice to the touch. I think I cut it asunder. It fell back on the men who were following us, and must have killed one of them in its death throes."

Techotl's head jerked back, his face ashy again. Convulsively he quickened his pace.

"It was the Crawler! A monster *they* have brought out of the catacombs to aid them! What it is, we do not know, but we have found our people hideously slain by it. In Set's name, hasten! If they put it on our trail, it will follow us to the very doors of Tecuhltli!"

"I doubt it," grunted Conan. "That was a shrewd cut I dealt it on the stair."

"Hasten! Hasten!" groaned Techotl.

They ran through a series of green-lit chambers, traversed a broad hall, and halted before a giant bronze door.

Techotl said: "This is Tecuhltli!"

III

The People of the Feud

TECHOTL smote on the bronze door with his clenched hand, and then turned sidewise, so that he could watch back along the hall.

"Men have been smitten down before this door, when they thought they were safe," he said.

"Why don't they open the door?" asked Conan.

"They are looking at us through the Eye," answered Techotl. "They are puzzled at the sight of you." He lifted his voice and called: "Open the door, Xecelan! It is I, Techotl, with friends from the great world beyond the forest! — They will open," he assured his allies.

"They'd better do it in a hurry, then," said Conan grimly. "I hear something crawling along the floor beyond the hall."

Techotl went ashy again and attacked the door with his fists, screaming: "Open, you fools, open! The Crawler is at our heels!"

Even as he beat and shouted, the great bronze door swung noiselessly back, revealing a heavy chain across the entrance, over which spearheads bristled and fierce countenances regarded them intently for an instant. Then the chain was

241

dropped and Techotl grasped the arms of his friends in a nervous frenzy and fairly dragged them over the threshold. A glance over his shoulder just as the door was closing showed Conan the long dim vista of the hall, and dimly framed at the other end an ophidian shape that writhed slowly and painfully into view, flowing in a dull-hued length from a chamber door, its hideous blood-stained head wagging drunkenly. Then the closing door shut off the view.

Inside the square chamber into which they had come heavy bolts were drawn across the door, and the chain locked into place. The door was made to stand the battering of a siege. Four men stood on guard, of the same lank-haired, dark-skinned breed as Techotl, with spears in their hands and swords at their hips. In the wall near the door there was a complicated contrivance of mirrors which Conan guessed was the Eye Techotl had mentioned, so arranged that a narrow, crystal-paned slot in the wall could be looked through from within without being discernible from without. The four guardsmen stared at the strangers with wonder, but asked no question, nor did Techotl vouchsafe any information. He moved with easy confidence now, as if he had shed his cloak of indecision and fear the instant he crossed the threshold.

"Come!" he urged his new-found friends, but Conan glanced toward the door.

"What about those fellows who were following us? Won't they try to storm that door?"

Techotl shook his head.

"They know they cannot break down the Door of the Eagle. They will flee back to Xotalanc, with their crawling fiend. Come! I will take you to the rulers of Tecuhltli."

ONE of the four guards opened the door opposite the one by which they had entered, and they passed through into a hallway which, like most of the rooms on that level, was lighted by both the slot-like skylights and the clusters of winking fire-gems. But unlike the other rooms they had traversed, this hall showed evidences of occupation. Velvet tapestries adorned the glossy jade walls, rich rugs were on the crimson floors, and the ivory seats, benches and divans were littered with satin cushions.

The hall ended in an ornate door, before which stood no guard. Without ceremony Techotl thrust the door open and ushered his friends into a broad chamber, where some thirty dark-skinned men and women lounging on satin-covered couches sprang up with exclamations of amazement.

The men, all except one, were of the same type as Techotl, and the women were equally dark and strange-eyed, though not unbeautiful in a weird dark way. They wore sandals, golden breast-plates, and scanty silk skirts supported by gem-crusted girdles, and their black manes, cut square at their naked shoulders, were bound with silver circlets.

On a wide ivory seat on a jade dais sat a man and a woman who differed subtly from the others. He was a giant, with an enormous sweep of breast and the shoulders of a bull. Unlike the others, he was bearded, with a thick, blue-black beard which fell almost to his broad girdle. He wore a robe of purple silk which reflected changing sheens of color with his every movement, and one wide sleeve, drawn back to his elbow, revealed a forearm massive with corded muscles. The band which confined his blue-black locks was set with glittering jewels.

The woman beside him sprang to her feet with a startled exclamation as the strangers entered, and her eyes, passing over Conan, fixed themselves with burning intensity on Valeria. She was tall and lithe, by far the most beautiful woman in the room. She was clad more scantily even than the others; for instead of a skirt she wore merely a broad strip of gilt-worked purple cloth fastened to the middle of her girdle which fell below her knees. Another strip at the back of her girdle completed that part of her costume, which she wore with a cynical indifference. Her breast-plates and the circlet about her temples were adorned with gems. In her eyes alone of all the dark-skinned people there lurked no brooding gleam of madness. She spoke no word after her first exclamation; she stood tensely, her hands clenched, staring at Valeria.

The man on the ivory seat had not risen.

"Prince Olmec," spoke Techotl, bowing low, with arms outspread and the palms of his hands turned upward, "I bring allies from the world beyond the forest. In the Chamber of Tezcoti the Burning Skull slew Chicmec, my companion —"

"The Burning Skull!" It was a shuddering whisper of fear from the people of Tecuhltli.

"Aye! Then came I, and found Chicmec lying with his throat cut. Before I could flee, the Burning Skull came upon me, and when I looked upon it my blood became as ice and the marrow of my bones melted. I could neither fight nor run. I could only await the stroke. Then came this white-skinned woman and struck him down with her sword; and lo, it was only a dog of Xotalanc with white paint upon his skin and the living skull of an ancient wizard upon his head! Now that skull lies in many pieces, and the dog who wore it is a dead man!"

An indescribably fierce exultation edged the last sentence, and was echoed in the low, savage exclamations from the crowding listeners.

"But wait!" exclaimed Techotl. "There is more! While I talked with the woman, four Xotalancas came upon us! One I slew — there is the stab in my thigh to prove how desperate was the fight. Two the woman killed. But we were hard pressed when this man came into the fray and split the skull of the fourth! Aye! Five crimson nails there are to be driven into the pillar of vengeance!"

He pointed at a black column of ebony which stood behind the dais. Hundreds of red dots scarred its polished surface — the bright scarlet heads of heavy copper nails driven into the black wood.

"Five red nails for five Xotalanca lives!" exulted Techotl, and the horrible exultation in the faces of the listeners made them inhuman.

"Who are these people?" asked Olmec, and his voice was like the low, deep rumble of a distant bull. None of the people of Xuchotl spoke loudly. It was as if they had absorbed into their souls the silence of the empty halls and deserted chambers.

"I am Conan, a Cimmerian," answered the barbarian briefly. "This woman is Valeria of the Red Brotherhood, an Aquilonian pirate. We are deserters from an army on the Darfar border, far to the north, and are trying to reach the coast."

The woman on the dais spoke loudly, her words tripping in her haste.

"You can never reach the coast! There is no escape from Xuchotl! You will spend the rest of your lives in this city!"

"What do you mean?" growled Conan, clapping his hand to his hilt and stepping about so as to face both the dais and the rest of the room. "Are you telling us we're prisoners?"

"She did not mean that," interposed Olmec. "We are your friends. We would not restrain you against your will. But I fear other circumstances will make it impossible for you to leave Xuchotl."

His eyes flickered to Valeria, and he lowered them quickly.

"This woman is Tascela," he said. "She is a princess of Tecuhltli. But let food and drink be brought our guests. Doubtless they are hungry, and weary from their long travels."

He indicated an ivory table, and after an exchange of glances, the adventurers seated themselves. The Cimmerian was suspicious. His fierce blue eyes roved about the chamber, and he kept his sword close to his hand. But an invitation to eat and drink never found him backward. His eyes kept wandering to Tascela, but the princess had eyes only for his white-skinned companion.

TECHOTL, who had bound a strip of silk about his wounded thigh, placed himself at the table to attend to the wants of his friends, seeming to consider it a privilege and honor to see after their needs. He inspected the food and drink the others brought in gold vessels and dishes, and tasted each before he placed it before his guests. While they ate, Olmec sat in silence on his ivory seat, watching them from under his broad black brows. Tascela sat beside him, chin cupped in her hands and her elbows resting on her knees. Her dark, enigmatic eyes, burning with a mysterious light, never left Valeria's supple figure. Behind her seat a sullen handsome girl waved an ostrich-plume fan with a slow rhythm.

The food was fruit of an exotic kind unfamiliar to the wanderers, but very palatable, and the drink was a light crimson wine that carried a heady tang.

"You have come from afar," said Olmec at last. "I have read the books of our fathers. Aquilonia lies beyond the lands of the Stygians and the Shemites, beyond Argos and Zingara; and Cimmeria lies beyond Aquilonia."

"We have each a roving foot," answered Conan carelessly.

"How you won through the forest is a wonder to me," quoth Olmec. "In by-gone days a thousand fighting-men scarcely were able to carve a road through its perils."

"We encountered a bench-legged monstrosity about the size of a mastodon," said Conan casually, holding out his wine goblet which Techotl filled with evident pleasure. "But when we'd killed it we had no further trouble."

The wine vessel slipped from Techotl's hand to crash on the floor. His dusky skin went ashy. Olmec started to his feet, an image of stunned amazement, and a low gasp of awe or terror breathed up from the others. Some slipped to their knees as if their legs would not support them. Only Tascela seemed not to have heard. Conan glared about him bewilderedly.

"What's the matter? What are you gaping about?"

"You – you slew the dragon-god?"

"God? I killed a dragon. Why not? It was trying to gobble us up."

"But dragons are immortal!" exclaimed Olmec. "They slay each other, but no man ever killed a dragon! The thousand fighting-men of our ancestors who fought their way to Xuchotl could not prevail against them! Their swords broke like twigs against their scales!"

"If your ancestors had thought to dip their spears in the poisonous juice of Derketa's Apples," quoth Conan, with his mouth full, "and jab them in the eyes or mouth or somewhere like that, they'd have seen that dragons are not more immortal than any other chunk of beef. The carcass lies at the edge of the trees, just within the forest. If you don't believe me, go and look for yourself."

Olmec shook his head, not in disbelief but in wonder.

"It was because of the dragons that our ancestors took refuge in Xuchotl," said he. "They dared not pass through the plain and plunge into the forest beyond. Scores of them were seized and devoured by the monsters before they could reach the city."

"Then your ancestors didn't build Xuchotl?" asked Valeria.

"It was ancient when they first came into the land. How long it had stood here, not even its degenerate inhabitants knew."

"Your people came from Lake Zuad?" questioned Conan.

"Aye. More than half a century ago a tribe of the Tlazitlans rebelled against the Stygian king, and, being defeated in battle, fled southward. For many weeks they wandered over grasslands, desert and hills, and at last they came into the great forest, a thousand fighting-men with their women and children.

"It was in the forest that the dragons fell upon them, and tore many to pieces; so the people fled in a frenzy of fear before them, and at last came into the plain and saw the city of Xuchotl in the midst of it.

"They camped before the city, not daring to leave the plain, for the night was made hideous with the noise of the battling monsters throughout the forest. They made war incessantly upon one another. Yet they came not into the plain.

"The people of the city shut their gates and shot arrows at our people from the walls. The Tlazitlans were imprisoned on the plain, as if the ring of the forest had been a great wall; for to venture into the woods would have been madness.

"That night there came secretly to their camp a slave from the city, one of their own blood, who with a band of exploring soldiers had wandered into the forest long before, when he was a young man. The dragons had devoured all his companions, but he had been taken into the city to dwell in servitude. His name was Tolkemec." A flame lighted the dark eyes at mention of the name, and some of the people muttered obscenely and spat. "He promised to open the gates to the warriors. He asked only that all captives taken be delivered into his hands.

"At dawn he opened the gates. The warriors swarmed in and the halls of Xuchotl ran red. Only a few hundred folk dwelt there, decaying remnants of a once great race. Tolkemec said they came from the east, long ago, from Old Kosala, when the ancestors of those who now dwell in Kosala came up from the south and drove forth the original inhabitants of the land. They wandered far westward and finally found this forest-girdled plain, inhabited then by a tribe of black people.

"These they enslaved and set to building a city. From the hills to the east they brought jade and marble and lapis lazuli, and gold, silver and copper. Herds of elephants provided them with ivory. When their city was completed, they slew all the black slaves. And their magicians made a terrible magic to guard the city; for by their necromantic arts they re-created the dragons which had once dwelt in this lost land, and whose monstrous bones they found in the forest. Those bones they clothed in flesh and life, and the living beasts walked the earth as they walked it when Time was young. But the wizards wove a spell that kept them in the forest and they came not into the plain.

"SO FOR many centuries the people of Xuchotl dwelt in their city, cultivating the fertile plain, until their wise men learned how to grow fruit within the city – fruit which is not planted in soil, but obtains its nourishment out of the air – and then they let the irrigation ditches run dry, and dwelt more and more in luxurious sloth, until decay seized them. They were a dying race when our ancestors broke through the forest and came into the plain. Their wizards had died, and the people had forgot their ancient necromancy. They could fight neither by sorcery nor the sword.

"Well, our fathers slew the people of Xuchotl, all except a hundred which were given living into the hands of Tolkemec, who had been their slave; and for many days and nights the halls re-echoed to their screams under the agony of his tortures.

"So the Tlazitlans dwelt here, for a while in peace, ruled by the brothers Tecuhltli and Xotalanc, and by Tolkemec. Tolkemec took a girl of the tribe to wife, and because he had opened the gates, and because he knew many of the arts of the Xuchotlans, he shared the rule of the tribe with the brothers who had led the rebellion and the flight.

"For a few years, then, they dwelt at peace within the city, doing little but eating, drinking and making love, and raising children. There was no necessity to till the plain, for Tolkemec taught them how to cultivate the air-devouring fruits. Besides, the slaying of the Xuchotlans broke the spell that held the dragons in the forest, and they came nightly and bellowed about the gates of the city. The plain ran red with the blood of their eternal warfare, and it was then that –" He bit his tongue in the midst of the sentence, then presently continued, but Valeria and Conan felt that he had checked an admission he had considered unwise.

"Five years they dwelt in peace. Then" – Olmec's eyes rested briefly on the silent woman at his side – "Xotalanc took a woman to wife, a woman whom both Tecuhltli and old Tolkemec desired. In his madness, Tecuhltli stole her from her husband. Aye, she went willingly enough. Tolkemec, to spite Xotalanc, aided Tecuhltli. Xotalanc demanded that she be given back to him, and the council of the tribe decided that the matter should be left to the woman. She chose to remain with Tecuhltli. In wrath Xotalanc sought to take her back by force, and the retainers of the brothers came to blows in the Great Hall.

"There was much bitterness. Blood was shed on both sides. The quarrel became a feud, the feud an open war. From the welter three factions emerged – Tecuhltli, Xotalanc, and Tolkemec. Already, in the days of peace, they had divided the city between them. Tecuhltli dwelt in the western quarter of the city, Xotalanc in the eastern, and Tolkemec with his family by the southern gate.

"Anger and resentment and jealousy blossomed into bloodshed and rape and murder. Once the sword was drawn there was no turning back; for blood called for blood, and vengeance followed swift on the heels of atrocity. Tecuhltli fought with Xotalanc, and Tolkemec aided first one and then the other, betraying each faction as it fitted his purposes. Tecuhltli and his people withdrew into the quarter of the western gate, where we now sit. Xuchotl is built in the shape of an oval. Tecuhltli, which took its name from its prince, occupies the western end of the oval. The people blocked up all doors connecting the quarter with the rest of the city, except one on each floor, which could be defended easily. They went into the pits below the city and built a wall cutting off the western end of the catacombs, where lie the bodies of the ancient Xuchotlans, and of those Tlazitlans slain in the feud. They dwelt as in a besieged castle, making sorties and forays on their enemies.

"The people of Xotalanc likewise fortified the eastern quarter of the city, and Tolkemec did likewise with the quarter by the southern gate. The central part of the city was left bare and uninhabited. Those empty halls and chambers became a battle-ground, and a region of brooding terror.

"Tolkemec warred on both clans. He was a fiend in the form of a human, worse than Xotalanc. He knew many secrets of the city he never told the others. From the crypts of the catacombs he plundered the dead of their grisly secrets — secrets of ancient kings and wizards, long forgotten by the degenerate Xuchotlans our ancestors slew. But all his magic did not aid him the night we of Tecuhltli stormed his castle and butchered all his people. Tolkemec we tortured for many days."

His voice sank to a caressing slur, and a far-away look grew in his eyes, as if he looked back over the years to a scene which caused him intense pleasure.

"Aye, we kept the life in him until he screamed for death as for a bride. At last we took him living from the torture chamber and cast him into a dungeon for the rats to gnaw as he died. From that dungeon, somehow, he managed to escape, and dragged himself into the catacombs. There without doubt he died, for the only way out of the catacombs beneath Tecuhltli is through Tecuhltli, and he never emerged by that way. His bones were never found, and the superstitious among our people swear that his ghost haunts the crypts to this day, wailing among the bones of the dead. Twelve years ago we butchered the people of Tolkemec, but the feud raged on between Tecuhltli and Xotalanc, as it will rage until the last man, the last woman is dead.

"It was fifty years ago that Tecuhltli stole the wife of Xotalanc. Half a century the feud has endured. I was born in it. All in this chamber, except Tascela, were born in it. We expect to die in it.

"We are a dying race, even as those Xuchotlans our ancestors slew. When the feud began there were hundreds in each faction. Now we of Tecuhltli number only these you see before you, and the men who guard the four doors: forty in all. How many Xotalancas there are we do not know, but I doubt if they are much more numerous than we. For fifteen years no children have been born to us, and we have seen none among the Xotalancas.

"We are dying, but before we die we will slay as many of the men of Xotalanc as the gods permit."

And with his weird eyes blazing, Olmec spoke long of that grisly feud, fought out in silent chambers and dim halls under the blaze of the green fire-jewels, on floors smoldering with the flames of hell and splashed with deeper crimson from severed veins. In that long butchery a whole generation had perished. Xotalanc was dead, long ago, slain in a grim battle on an ivory stair. Tecuhltli was dead, flayed alive by the maddened Xotalancas who had captured him.

Without emotion Olmec told of hideous battles fought in black corridors, of ambushes on twisting stairs, and red butcheries. With a redder, more abysmal gleam in his deep dark eyes he told of men and women flayed alive, mutilated and dismembered, of captives howling under tortures so ghastly that even the barbarous

Cimmerian grunted. No wonder Techotl had trembled with the terror of capture. Yet he had gone forth to slay if he could, driven by hate that was stronger than his fear. Olmec spoke further, of dark and mysterious matters, of black magic and wizardry conjured out of the black night of the catacombs, of weird creatures invoked out of darkness for horrible allies. In these things the Xotalancas had the advantage, for it was in the eastern catacombs where lay the bones of the greatest wizards of the ancient Xuchotlans, with their immemorial secrets.

VALERIA listened with morbid fascination. The feud had become a terrible elemental power driving the people of Xuchotl inexorably on to doom and extinction. It filled their whole lives. They were born in it, and they expected to die in it. They never left their barricaded castle except to steal forth into the Halls of Silence that lay between the opposing fortresses, to slay and be slain. Sometimes the raiders returned with frantic captives, or with grim tokens of victory in fight. Sometimes they did not return at all, or returned only as severed limbs cast down before the bolted bronze doors. It was a ghastly, unreal nightmare existence these people lived, shut off from the rest of the world, caught together like rabid rats in the same trap, butchering one another through the years, crouching and creeping through the sunless corridors to maim and torture and murder.

While Olmec talked, Valeria felt the blazing eyes of Tascela fixed upon her. The princess seemed not to hear what Olmec was saying. Her expression, as he narrated victories or defeats, did not mirror the wild rage or fiendish exultation that alternated on the faces of the other Tecuhltli. The feud that was an obsession to her clansmen seemed meaningless to her. Valeria found her indifferent callousness more repugnant than Olmec's naked ferocity.

"And we can never leave the city," said Olmec. "For fifty years no one has left it except those —" Again he checked himself.

"Even without the peril of the dragons," he continued, "we who were born and raised in the city would not dare leave it. We have never set foot outside the walls. We are not accustomed to the open sky and the naked sun. No; we were born in Xuchotl, and in Xuchotl we shall die."

"Well," said Conan, "with your leave we'll take our chances with the dragons. This feud is none of our business. If you'll show us to the west gate we'll be on our way."

Tascela's hands clenched, and she started to speak, but Olmec interrupted her: "It is nearly nightfall. If you wander forth into the plain by night, you will certainly fall prey to the dragons."

"We crossed it last night, and slept in the open without seeing any," returned Conan.

Tascela smiled mirthlessly. "You dare not leave Xuchotl!"

Conan glared at her with instinctive antagonism; she was not looking at him, but at the woman opposite him.

"I think they dare," retorted Olmec. "But look you, Conan and Valeria, the gods must have sent you to us, to cast victory into the laps of the Tecuhltli! You are professional fighters – why not fight for us? We have wealth in abundance – precious jewels are as common in Xuchotl as cobblestones are in the cities of the world. Some the Xuchotlans brought with them from Kosala. Some, like the firestones, they found in the hills to the east. Aid us to wipe out the Xotalancas, and we will give you all the jewels you can carry."

"And will you help us destroy the dragons?" asked Valeria. "With bows and poisoned arrows thirty men could slay all the dragons in the forest."

"Aye!" replied Olmec promptly. "We have forgotten the use of the bow, in years of hand-to-hand fighting, but we can learn again."

"What do you say?" Valeria inquired of Conan.

"We're both penniless vagabonds," he grinned hardily. "I'd as soon kill Xotalancas as anybody."

"Then you agree?" exclaimed Olmec, while Techotl fairly hugged himself with delight.

"Aye. And now suppose you show us chambers where we can sleep, so we can be fresh tomorrow for the beginning of the slaying."

Olmec nodded, and waved a hand, and Techotl and a woman led the adventurers into a corridor which led through a door off to the left of the jade dais. A glance back showed Valeria Olmec sitting on his throne, chin on knotted fist, staring after them. His eyes burned with a weird flame. Tascela leaned back in her seat, whispering to the sullen-faced maid, Yasala, who leaned over her shoulder, her ear to the princess' moving lips.

THE hallway was not so broad as most they had traversed, but it was long. Presently the woman halted, opened a door, and drew aside for Valeria to enter.

"Wait a minute," growled Conan. "Where do I sleep?"

Techotl pointed to a chamber across the hallway, but one door farther down. Conan hesitated, and seemed inclined to raise an objection, but Valeria smiled spitefully at him and shut the door in his face. He muttered something uncomplimentary about women in general, and strode off down the corridor after Techotl.

In the ornate chamber where he was to sleep, he glanced up at the slot-like skylights. Some were wide enough to admit the body of a slender man, supposing the glass were broken.

"Why don't the Xotalancas come over the roofs and shatter those skylights?" he asked.

"They cannot be broken," answered Techotl. "Besides, the roofs would be hard to clamber over. They are mostly spires and domes and steep ridges."

He volunteered more information about the "castle" of Tecuhltli. Like the rest of the city it contained four stories, or tiers of chambers, with towers jutting up from the roof. Each tier was named; indeed, the people of Xuchotl had a name for each chamber, hall and stair in the city, as people of more normal cities designate streets and quarters. In Tecuhltli the floors were named The Eagle's Tier, The Ape's Tier, The Tiger's Tier and The Serpent's Tier, in the order as enumerated, The Eagle's Tier being the highest, or fourth, floor.

"Who is Tascela?" asked Conan. "Olmec's wife?"

Techotl shuddered and glanced furtively about him before answering.

"No. She is – Tascela! She was the wife of Xotalanc – the woman Tecuhltli stole, to start the feud."

"What are you talking about?" demanded Conan. "That woman is beautiful and young. Are you trying to tell me that she was a wife fifty years ago?"

"Aye! I swear it! She was a full-grown woman when the Tlazitlans journeyed from Lake Zuad. It was because the king of Stygia desired her for a concubine that Xotalanc and his brother rebelled and fled into the wilderness. She is a witch, who possesses the secret of perpetual youth."

"What's that?" asked Conan.

Techotl shuddered again.

"Ask me not! I dare not speak. It is too grisly, even for Xuchotl!"

And touching his finger to his lips, he glided from the chamber.

IV
Scent of Black Lotus

VALERIA unbuckled her sword-belt and laid it with the sheathed weapon on the couch where she meant to sleep. She noted that the doors were supplied with bolts, and asked where they led.

"Those lead into adjoining chambers," answered the woman, indicating the doors on right and left. "That one" – pointing to a copper-bound door opposite that which opened into the corridor – "leads to a corridor which runs to a stair that descends into the catacombs. Do not fear; naught can harm you here."

"Who spoke of fear?" snapped Valeria. "I just like to know what sort of harbor I'm dropping anchor in. No, I don't want you to sleep at the foot of my couch. I'm not accustomed to being waited on – not by women, anyway. You have my leave to go."

Alone in the room, the pirate shot the bolts on all the doors, kicked off her boots and stretched luxuriously out on the couch. She imagined Conan similarly situated across the corridor, but her feminine vanity prompted her to visualize him as scowling and muttering with chagrin as he cast himself on his solitary couch, and she grinned with gleeful malice as she prepared herself for slumber.

Outside, night had fallen. In the halls of Xuchotl the green fire-jewels blazed like the eyes of prehistoric cats. Somewhere among the dark towers a night wind moaned like a restless spirit. Through the dim passages stealthy figures began stealing, like disembodied shadows.

Valeria awoke suddenly on her couch. In the dusky emerald glow of the fire-gems she saw a shadowy figure bending over her. For a bemused instant the apparition seemed part of the dream she had been dreaming. She had seemed to lie on the couch in the chamber as she was actually lying, while over her pulsed and throbbed a gigantic black blossom so enormous that it hid the ceiling. Its exotic perfume pervaded her being, inducing a delicious, sensuous languor that was something more and less than sleep. She was sinking into scented billows of insensible bliss, when something touched her face. So supersensitive were her drugged senses, that the light touch was like a dislocating impact, jolting her rudely into full wakefulness. Then it was that she saw, not a gargantuan blossom, but a dark-skinned woman standing above her.

With the realization came anger and instant action. The woman turned lithely, but before she could run Valeria was on her feet and had caught her arm. She fought like a wildcat for an instant, and then subsided as she felt herself crushed by the superior strength of her captor. The pirate wrenched the woman around to face her, caught her chin with her free hand and forced her captive to meet her gaze. It was the sullen Yasala, Tascela's maid.

"What the devil were you doing bending over me? What's that in your hand?"

The woman made no reply, but sought to cast away the object. Valeria twisted her arm around in front of her, and the thing fell to the floor – a great black exotic blossom on a jade-green stem, large as a woman's head, to be sure, but tiny beside the exaggerated vision she had seen.

"The black lotus!" said Valeria between her teeth. "The blossom whose scent brings deep sleep. You were trying to drug me! If you hadn't accidentally touched my face with the petals, you'd have – why did you do it? What's your game?"

Yasala maintained a sulky silence, and with an oath Valeria whirled her around, forced her to her knees and twisted her arm up behind her back.

"Tell me, or I'll tear your arm out of its socket!"

Yasala squirmed in anguish as her arm was forced excruciatingly up between her shoulder-blades, but a violent shaking of her head was the only answer she made.

"Slut!" Valeria cast her from her to sprawl on the floor. The pirate glared at the prostrate figure with blazing eyes. Fear and the memory of Tascela's burning eyes stirred in her, rousing all her tigerish instincts of self-preservation. These people were decadent; any sort of perversity might be expected to be encountered among them. But Valeria sensed here something that moved behind the scenes, some secret terror fouler than common degeneracy. Fear and revulsion of this weird city swept her. These people were neither sane nor normal; she began to doubt if they were even human. Madness smoldered in the eyes of them all – all except the cruel, cryptic eyes of Tascela, which held secrets and mysteries more abysmal than madness.

She lifted her head and listened intently. The halls of Xuchotl were as silent as if it were in reality a dead city. The green jewels bathed the chamber in a nightmare glow, in which the eyes of the woman on the floor glittered eerily up at her. A thrill of panic throbbed through Valeria, driving the last vestige of mercy from her fierce soul.

"Why did you try to drug me?" she muttered, grasping the woman's black hair, and forcing her head back to glare into her sullen, long-lashed eyes. "Did Tascela send you?"

No answer. Valeria cursed venomously and slapped the woman first on one cheek and then the other. The blows resounded through the room, but Yasala made no outcry.

"Why don't you scream?" demanded Valeria savagely. "Do you fear someone will hear you? Whom do you fear? Tascela? Olmec? Conan?"

YASALA made no reply. She crouched, watching her captor with eyes baleful as those of a basilisk. Stubborn silence always fans anger. Valeria turned and tore a handful of cords from a nearby hanging.

"You sulky slut!" she said between her teeth. "I'm going to strip you stark naked and tie you across that couch and whip you until you tell me what you were doing here, and who sent you!"

Yasala made no verbal protest, nor did she offer any resistance, as Valeria carried out the first part of her threat with a fury that her captive's obstinacy only sharpened. Then for a space there was no sound in the chamber except the whistle and crackle of hard-woven silken cords on naked flesh. Yasala could not move her fast-bound hands or feet. Her body writhed and quivered under the chastisement, her head swayed from side to side in rhythm with the blows. Her teeth were sunk into her lower lip and a trickle of blood began as the punishment continued. But she did not cry out.

The pliant cords made no great sound as they encountered the quivering body of the captive; only a sharp crackling snap, but each cord left a red streak across Yasala's dark flesh. Valeria inflicted the punishment with all the strength of her war-hardened arm, with all the mercilessness acquired during a life where pain and torment were daily happenings, and with all the cynical ingenuity which only a woman displays toward a woman. Yasala suffered more, physically and mentally, than she would have suffered under a lash wielded by a man, however strong.

It was the application of this feminine cynicism which at last tamed Yasala.

A low whimper escaped from her lips, and Valeria paused, arm lifted, and raked back a damp yellow lock. "Well, are you going to talk?" she demanded. "I can keep this up all night, if necessary!"

"Mercy!" whispered the woman. "I will tell."

Valeria cut the cords from her wrists and ankles, and pulled her to her feet. Yasala sank down on the couch, half reclining on one bare hip, supporting herself on her arm, and writhing at the contact of her smarting flesh with the couch. She was trembling in every limb.

"Wine!" she begged, dry-lipped, indicating with a quivering hand a gold vessel on an ivory table. "Let me drink. I am weak with pain. Then I will tell you all."

Valeria picked up the vessel, and Yasala rose unsteadily to receive it. She took it, raised it toward her lips — then dashed the contents full into the Aquilonian's face. Valeria reeled backward, shaking and clawing the stinging liquid out of her eyes. Through a smarting mist she saw Yasala dart across the room, fling back a bolt, throw open the copper-bound door and run down the hall. The pirate was after her instantly, sword out and murder in her heart.

But Yasala had the start, and she ran with the nervous agility of a woman who has just been whipped to the point of hysterical frenzy. She rounded a corner in the corridor, yards ahead of Valeria, and when the pirate turned it, she saw only an empty hall, and at the other end a door that gaped blackly. A damp moldy scent reeked up from it, and Valeria shivered. That must be the door that led to the catacombs. Yasala had taken refuge among the dead.

Valeria advanced to the door and looked down a flight of stone steps that vanished quickly into utter blackness. Evidently it was a shaft that led straight to the pits below the city, without opening upon any of the lower floors. She shivered slightly at the thought of the thousands of corpses lying in their stone crypts down there, wrapped in their moldering cloths. She had no intention of groping her way down those stone steps. Yasala doubtless knew every turn and twist of the subterranean tunnels.

She was turning back, baffled and furious, when a sobbing cry welled up from the blackness. It seemed to come from a great depth, but human words were faintly distinguishable, and the voice was that of a woman. "Oh, help! Help, in Set's name! Ahhh!" It trailed away, and Valeria thought she caught the echo of a ghostly tittering.

Valeria felt her skin crawl. What had happened to Yasala down there in the thick blackness? There was no doubt that it had been she who had cried out. But what peril could have befallen her? Was a Xotalanca lurking down there? Olmec had assured them that the catacombs below Tecuhltli were walled off from the rest, too securely for their enemies to break through. Besides, that tittering had not sounded like a human being at all.

Valeria hurried back down the corridor, not stopping to close the door that opened on the stair. Regaining her chamber, she closed the door and shot the bolt behind her. She pulled on her boots and buckled her sword-belt about her. She was determined to make her way to Conan's room and urge him, if he still lived, to join her in an attempt to fight their way out of that city of devils.

But even as she reached the door that opened into the corridor, a long-drawn scream of agony rang through the halls, followed by the stamp of running feet and the loud clangor of swords.

V

Twenty Red Nails

TWO warriors lounged in the guardroom on the floor known as the Tier of the Eagle. Their attitude was casual, though habitually alert. An attack on the great bronze door from without was always a possibility, but for many years no such assault had been attempted on either side.

"The strangers are strong allies," said one. "Olmec will move against the enemy tomorrow, I believe."

He spoke as a soldier in a war might have spoken. In the miniature world of Xuchotl each handful of feudists was an army, and the empty halls between the castles was the country over which they campaigned.

The other meditated for a space.

"Suppose with their aid we destroy Xotalanc," he said. "What then, Xatmec?"

"Why," returned Xatmec, "we will drive red nails for them all. The captives we will burn and flay and quarter."

"But afterward?" pursued the other. "After we have slain them all? Will it not seem strange, to have no foes to fight? All my life I have fought and hated the Xotalancas. With the feud ended, what is left?"

Xatmec shrugged his shoulders. His thoughts had never gone beyond the destruction of their foes. They could not go beyond that.

Suddenly both men stiffened at a noise outside the door.

256

"To the door, Xatmec!" hissed the last speaker. "I shall look through the Eye —"

Xatmec, sword in hand, leaned against the bronze door, straining his ear to hear through the metal. His mate looked into the mirror. He started convulsively. Men were clustered thickly outside the door; grim, dark-faced men with swords gripped in their teeth – *and their fingers thrust into their ears.* One who wore a feathered head-dress had a set of pipes which he set to his lips, and even as the Tecuhltli started to shout a warning, the pipes began to skirl.

The cry died in the guard's throat as the thin, weird piping penetrated the metal door and smote on his ears. Xatmec leaned frozen against the door, as if paralyzed in that position. His face was that of a wooden image, his expression one of horrified listening. The other guard, farther removed from the source of the sound, yet sensed the horror of what was taking place, the grisly threat that lay in that demoniac fifing. He felt the weird strains plucking like unseen fingers at the tissues of his brain, filling him with alien emotions and impulses of madness. But with a soul-tearing effort he broke the spell, and shrieked a warning in a voice he did not recognize as his own.

But even as he cried out, the music changed to an unbearable shrilling that was like a knife in the ear-drums. Xatmec screamed in sudden agony, and all the sanity went out of his face like a flame blown out in a wind. Like a madman he ripped loose the chain, tore open the door and rushed out into the hall, sword lifted before his mate could stop him. A dozen blades struck him down, and over his mangled body the Xotalancas surged into the guardroom, with a long-drawn, blood-mad yell that sent the unwonted echoes reverberating.

His brain reeling from the shock of it all, the remaining guard leaped to meet them with goring spear. The horror of the sorcery he had just witnessed was submerged in the stunning realization that the enemy were in Tecuhltli. And as his spearhead ripped through a dark-skinned belly he knew no more, for a swinging sword crushed his skull, even as wild-eyed warriors came pouring in from the chambers behind the guardroom.

It was the yelling of men and the clanging of steel that brought Conan bounding from his couch, wide awake and broadsword in hand. In an instant he had reached the door and flung it open, and was glaring out into the corridor just as Techotl rushed up it, eyes blazing madly.

"The Xotalancas!" he screamed, in a voice hardly human. *"They are within the door!"*

Conan ran down the corridor, even as Valeria emerged from her chamber.

"What the devil is it?" she called.

"Techotl says the Xotalancas are in," he answered hurriedly. "That racket sounds like it."

WITH the Tecuhltli on their heels they burst into the throneroom and were confronted by a scene beyond the most frantic dream of blood and fury. Twenty men and women, their black hair streaming, and the white skulls gleaming on their breasts, were locked in combat with the people of Tecuhltli. The women on both sides fought as madly as the men, and already the room and the hall beyond were strewn with corpses.

Olmec, naked but for a breech-clout, was fighting before his throne, and as the adventurers entered, Tascela ran from an inner chamber with a sword in her hand.

Xatmec and his mate were dead, so there was none to tell the Tecuhltli how their foes had found their way into their citadel. Nor was there any to say what had prompted that mad attempt. But the losses of the Xotalancas had been greater, their position more desperate, than the Tecuhltli had known. The maiming of their scaly ally, the destruction of the Burning Skull, and the news, gasped by a dying man, that mysterious white-skin allies had joined their enemies, had driven them to the frenzy of desperation and the wild determination to die dealing death to their ancient foes.

The Tecuhltli, recovering from the first stunning shock of the surprize that had swept them back into the throneroom and littered the floor with their corpses, fought back with an equally desperate fury, while the door-guards from the lower floors came racing to hurl themselves into the fray. It was the death-fight of rabid wolves, blind, panting, merciless. Back and forth it surged, from door to dais, blades whickering and striking into flesh, blood spurting, feet stamping the crimson floor where redder pools were forming. Ivory tables crashed over, seats were splintered, velvet hangings torn down were stained red. It was the bloody climax of a bloody half-century, and every man there sensed it.

But the conclusion was inevitable. The Tecuhltli outnumbered the invaders almost two to one, and they were heartened by that fact and by the entrance into the mêlée of their light-skinned allies.

These crashed into the fray with the devastating effect of a hurricane plowing through a grove of saplings. In sheer strength no three Tlazitlans were a match for Conan, and in spite of his weight he was quicker on his feet than any of them. He moved through the whirling, eddying mass with the surety and destructiveness of a gray wolf amidst a pack of alley curs, and he strode over a wake of crumpled figures.

Valeria fought beside him, her lips smiling and her eyes blazing. She was stronger than the average man, and far quicker and more ferocious. Her sword was like a living thing in her hand. Where Conan beat down opposition by the sheer weight and power of his blows, breaking spears, splitting skulls and cleaving bosoms to the breastbone, Valeria brought into action a finesse of sword-play that dazzled and bewildered her antagonists before it slew them. Again and again a warrior, heaving high his heavy blade, found her point in his jugular before he could strike.

258

Conan, towering above the field, strode through the welter smiting right and left, but Valeria moved like an illusive phantom, constantly shifting, and thrusting and slashing as she shifted. Swords missed her again and again as the wielders flailed the empty air and died with her point in their hearts or throats, and her mocking laughter in their ears.

Neither sex nor condition was considered by the maddened combatants. The five women of the Xotalancas were down with their throats cut before Conan and Valeria entered the fray, and when a man or woman went down under the stamping feet, there was always a knife ready for the helpless throat, or a sandaled foot eager to crush the prostrate skull.

From wall to wall, from door to door rolled the waves of combat, spilling over into adjoining chambers. And presently only Tecuhltli and their white-skinned allies stood upright in the great throne-room. The survivors stared bleakly and blankly at each other, like survivors after Judgment Day or the destruction of the world. On legs wide-braced, hands gripping notched and dripping swords, blood trickling down their arms, they stared at one another across the mangled corpses of friends and foes. They had no breath left to shout, but a bestial mad howling rose from their lips. It was not a human cry of triumph. It was the howling of a rabid wolf-pack stalking among the bodies of its victims.

Conan caught Valeria's arm and turned her about.

"You've got a stab in the calf of your leg," he growled.

She glanced down, for the first time aware of a stinging in the muscles of her leg. Some dying man on the floor had fleshed his dagger with his last effort.

"You look like a butcher yourself," she laughed.

He shook a red shower from his hands.

"Not mine. Oh, a scratch here and there. Nothing to bother about. But that calf ought to be bandaged."

OLMEC came through the litter, looking like a ghoul with his naked massive shoulders splashed with blood, and his black beard dabbled in crimson. His eyes were red, like the reflection of flame on black water.

"We have won!" he croaked dazedly. "The feud is ended! The dogs of Xotalanc lie dead! Oh, for a captive to flay alive! Yet it is good to look upon their dead faces. Twenty dead dogs! Twenty red nails for the black column!"

"You'd best see to your wounded," grunted Conan, turning away from him. "Here, girl, let me see that leg."

"Wait a minute!" she shook him off impatiently. The fire of fighting still burned brightly in her soul. "How do we know these are all of them? These might have come on a raid of their own."

"They would not split the clan on a foray like this," said Olmec, shaking his head, and regaining some of his ordinary intelligence. Without his purple robe the man seemed less like a prince than some repellent beast of prey. "I will stake my head upon it that we have slain them all. There were less of them than I dreamed, and they must have been desperate. But how came they in Tecuhltli?"

Tascela came forward, wiping her sword on her naked thigh, and holding in her other hand an object she had taken from the body of the feathered leader of the Xotalancas.

"The pipes of madness," she said. "A warrior tells me that Xatmec opened the door to the Xotalancas and was cut down as they stormed into the guardroom. This warrior came to the guardroom from the inner hall just in time to see it happen and to hear the last of a weird strain of music which froze his very soul. Tolkemec used to talk of these pipes, which the Xuchotlans swore were hidden somewhere in the catacombs with the bones of the ancient wizard who used them in his lifetime. Somehow the dogs of Xotalanc found them and learned their secret."

"Somebody ought to go to Xotalanc and see if any remain alive," said Conan. "I'll go if somebody will guide me."

Olmec glanced at the remnants of his people. There were only twenty left alive, and of these several lay groaning on the floor. Tascela was the only one of the Tecuhltli who had escaped without a wound. The princess was untouched, though she had fought as savagely as any.

"Who will go with Conan to Xotalanc?" asked Olmec.

Techotl limped forward. The wound in his thigh had started bleeding afresh, and he had another gash across his ribs.

"I will go!"

"No, you won't," vetoed Conan. "And you're not going either, Valeria. In a little while that leg will be getting stiff."

"I will go," volunteered a warrior, who was knotting a bandage about a slashed forearm.

"Very well, Yanath. Go with the Cimmerian. And you, too, Topal." Olmec indicated another man whose injuries were slight. "But first aid us to lift the badly wounded on these couches where we may bandage their hurts."

This was done quickly. As they stooped to pick up a woman who had been stunned by a war-club, Olmec's beard brushed Topal's ear. Conan thought the prince muttered something to the warrior, but he could not be sure. A few moments later he was leading his companions down the hall.

Conan glanced back as he went out the door, at that shambles where the dead lay on the smoldering floor, blood-stained dark limbs knotted in attitudes of fierce muscular effort, dark faces frozen in masks of hate, glassy eyes glaring up at the green fire-jewels which bathed the ghastly scene in a dusky emerald witch-light. Among the dead the living moved aimlessly, like people moving in a trance. Conan heard Olmec call a woman and direct her to bandage Valeria's leg. The pirate followed the woman into an adjoining chamber, already beginning to limp slightly.

WARILY the two Tecuhltli led Conan along the hall beyond the bronze door, and through chamber after chamber shimmering in the green fire. They saw no one, heard no sound. After they crossed the Great Hall which bisected the city from north to south, their caution was increased by the realization of their nearness to enemy territory. But chambers and halls lay empty to their wary gaze, and they came at last along a broad dim hallway and halted before a bronze door similar to the Eagle Door of Tecuhltli. Gingerly they tried it, and it opened silently under their fingers. Awed, they stared into the green-lit chambers beyond. For fifty years no Tecuhltli had entered those halls save as a prisoner going to a hideous doom. To go to Xotalanc had been the ultimate horror that could befall a man of the western castle. The terror of it had stalked through their dreams since earliest childhood. To Yanath and Topal that bronze door was like the portal of hell.

They cringed back, unreasoning horror in their eyes, and Conan pushed past them and strode into Xotalanc.

Timidly they followed him. As each man set foot over the threshold he stared and glared wildly about him. But only their quick, hurried breathing disturbed the silence.

They had come into a square guardroom, like that behind the Eagle Door of Tecuhltli, and, similarly, a hall ran away from it to a broad chamber that was a counterpart of Olmec's throneroom.

Conan glanced down the hall with its rugs and divans and hangings, and stood listening intently. He heard no noise, and the rooms had an empty feel. He did not believe there were any Xotalancas left alive in Xuchotl.

"Come on," he muttered, and started down the hall.

He had not gone far when he was aware that only Yanath was following him. He wheeled back to see Topal standing in an attitude of horror, one arm out as if to fend off some threatening peril, his distended eyes fixed with hypnotic intensity on something protruding from behind a divan.

"What the devil?" Then Conan saw what Topal was staring at, and he felt a faint twitching of the skin between his giant shoulders. A monstrous head protruded from behind the divan, a reptilian head, broad as the head of a crocodile, with down-curving fangs that projected over the lower jaw. But there was an unnatural limpness about the thing, and the hideous eyes were glazed.

Conan peered behind the couch. It was a great serpent which lay there limp in death, but such a serpent as he had never seen in his wanderings. The reek and chill of the deep black earth were about it, and its color was an indeterminable hue which changed with each new angle from which he surveyed it. A great wound in the neck showed what had caused its death.

"It is the Crawler!" whispered Yanath.

"It's the thing I slashed on the stair," grunted Conan. "After it trailed us to the Eagle Door, it dragged itself here to die. How could the Xotalancas control such a brute?"

The Tecuhltli shivered and shook their heads.

"They brought it up from the black tunnels *below* the catacombs. They discovered secrets unknown to Tecuhltli."

"Well, it's dead, and if they'd had any more of them, they'd have brought them along when they came to Tecuhltli. Come on."

They crowded close at his heels as he strode down the hall and thrust on the silver-worked door at the other end.

"If we don't find anybody on this floor," he said, "we'll descend into the lower floors. We'll explore Xotalanc from the roof to the catacombs. If Xotalanc is like Tecuhltli, all the rooms and halls in this tier will be lighted – what the devil!"

They had come into the broad throne-chamber, so similar to that one in Tecuhltli. There were the same jade dais and ivory seat, the same divans, rugs and hangings on the walls. No black, red-scarred column stood behind the throne-dais, but evidences of the grim feud were not lacking.

Ranged along the wall behind the dais were rows of glass-covered shelves. And on those shelves hundreds of human heads, perfectly preserved, stared at the startled watchers with emotionless eyes, as they had stared for only the gods knew how many months and years.

TOPAL muttered a curse, but Yanath stood silent, the mad light growing in his wide eyes. Conan frowned, knowing that Tlazitlan sanity was hung on a hair-trigger.

Suddenly Yanath pointed to the ghastly relics with a twitching finger.

"There is my brother's head!" he murmured. "And there is my father's younger brother! And there beyond them is my sister's eldest son!"

Suddenly he began to weep, dry-eyed, with harsh, loud sobs that shook his frame. He did not take his eyes from the heads. His sobs grew shriller, changed to frightful, high-pitched laughter, and that in turn became an unbearable screaming. Yanath was stark mad.

Conan laid a hand on his shoulder, and as if the touch had released all the frenzy in his soul, Yanath screamed and whirled, striking at the Cimmerian with his sword. Conan parried the blow, and Topal tried to catch Yanath's arm. But the madman avoided him and with froth flying from his lips, he drove his sword deep into Topal's body. Topal sank down with a groan, and Yanath whirled for an instant like a crazy dervish; then he ran at the shelves and began hacking at the glass with his sword, screeching blasphemously.

Conan sprang at him from behind, trying to catch him unaware and disarm him, but the madman wheeled and lunged at him, screaming like a lost soul. Realizing that the warrior was hopelessly insane, the Cimmerian side-stepped, and as the maniac went past, he swung a cut that severed the shoulder-bone and breast, and dropped the man dead beside his dying victim.

Conan bent over Topal, seeing that the man was at his last gasp. It was useless to seek to stanch the blood gushing from the horrible wound.

"You're done for, Topal," grunted Conan. "Any word you want to send to your people?"

"Bend closer," gasped Topal, and Conan complied – and an instant later caught the man's wrist as Topal struck at his breast with a dagger.

"Crom!" swore Conan. "Are you mad, too?"

"Olmec ordered it!" gasped the dying man. "I know not why. As we lifted the wounded upon the couches he whispered to me, bidding me to slay you as we returned to Tecuhltli –" And with the name of his clan on his lips, Topal died.

Conan scowled down at him in puzzlement. This whole affair had an aspect of lunacy. Was Olmec mad, too? Were all the Tecuhltli madder than he had realized? With a shrug of his shoulders he strode down the hall and out of the bronze door, leaving the dead Tecuhltli lying before the staring dead eyes of their kinsmen's heads.

Conan needed no guide back through the labyrinth they had traversed. His primitive instinct of direction led him unerringly along the route they had come. He traversed it as warily as he had before, his sword in his hand, and his eyes fiercely searching each shadowed nook and corner; for it was his former allies he feared now, not the ghosts of the slain Xotalancas.

He had crossed the Great Hall and entered the chambers beyond when he heard something moving ahead of him – something which gasped and panted, and moved with a strange, floundering, scrambling noise. A moment later Conan saw a man crawling over the flaming floor toward him – a man whose progress left a broad bloody smear on the smoldering surface. It was Techotl and his eyes were already glazing; from a deep gash in his breast blood gushed steadily between the fingers of his clutching hand. With the other he clawed and hitched himself along.

"Conan," he cried chokingly, "Conan! Olmec has taken the yellow-haired woman!"

"So that's why he told Topal to kill me!" murmured Conan, dropping to his knee beside the man, who his experienced eye told him was dying. "Olmec isn't so mad as I thought."

Techotl's groping fingers plucked at Conan's arm. In the cold, loveless and altogether hideous life of the Tecuhltli his admiration and affection for the invaders from the outer world formed a warm, human oasis, constituted a tie that connected him with a more natural humanity that was totally lacking in his fellows, whose only emotions were hate, lust and the urge of sadistic cruelty.

"I sought to oppose him," gurgled Techotl, blood bubbling frothily to his lips. "But he struck me down. He thought he had slain me, but I crawled away. Ah, Set, how far I have crawled in my own blood! Beware, Conan! Olmec may have set an ambush for your return! Slay Olmec! He is a beast. Take Valeria and flee! Fear not to traverse the forest. Olmec and Tascela lied about the dragons. They slew each other years ago, all save the strongest. For a dozen years there has been only one dragon. If you have slain him, there is naught in the forest to harm you. He was the god Olmec worshipped; and Olmec fed human sacrifices to him, the very old and the very young, bound and hurled from the wall. Hasten! Olmec has taken Valeria to the Chamber of the —"

His head slumped down and he was dead before it came to rest on the floor.

CONAN sprang up, his eyes like live coals. So that was Olmec's game, having first used the strangers to destroy his foes! He should have known that something of the sort would be going on in that black-bearded degenerate's mind.

The Cimmerian started toward Tecuhltli with reckless speed. Rapidly he reckoned the numbers of his former allies. Only twenty-one, counting Olmec, had survived that fiendish battle in the throneroom. Three had died since, which left seventeen enemies with which to reckon. In his rage Conan felt capable of accounting for the whole clan single-handed.

But the innate craft of the wilderness rose to guide his berserk rage. He remembered Techotl's warning of an ambush. It was quite probable that the prince would make such provisions, on the chance that Topal might have failed to carry out his order. Olmec would be expecting him to return by the same route he had followed in going to Xotalanc.

Conan glanced up at a skylight under which he was passing and caught the blurred glimmer of stars. They had not yet begun to pale for dawn. The events of the night had been crowded into a comparatively short space of time.

He turned aside from his direct course and descended a winding staircase to the floor below. He did not know where the door was to be found that let into the castle on that level, but he knew he could find it. How he was to force the locks he did not know; he believed that the doors of Tecuhltli would all be locked and bolted, if for no other reason than the habits of half a century. But there was nothing else but to attempt it.

Sword in hand, he hurried noiselessly on through a maze of green-lit or shadowy rooms and halls. He knew he must be near Tecuhltli, when a sound brought him up short. He recognized it for what it was — a human being trying to cry out through a stifling gag. It came from somewhere ahead of him, and to the left. In those deathly-still chambers a small sound carried a long way.

Conan turned aside and went seeking after the sound, which continued to be repeated. Presently he was glaring through a doorway upon a weird scene. In the room into which he was looking a low rack-like frame of iron lay on the floor, and a giant figure was bound prostrate upon it. His head rested on a bed of iron spikes, which were already crimson-pointed with blood where they had pierced his scalp. A peculiar harness-like contrivance was fastened about his head, though in such a manner that the leather band did not protect his scalp from the spikes. This harness was connected by a slender chain to the mechanism that upheld a huge iron ball which was suspended above the captive's hairy breast. As long as the man could force himself to remain motionless the iron ball hung in its place. But when the pain of the iron points caused him to lift his head, the ball lurched downward a few inches. Presently his aching neck muscles would no longer support his head in its unnatural position and it would fall back on the spikes again. It was obvious that eventually the ball would crush him to a pulp, slowly and inexorably. The victim was gagged, and above the gag his great black ox-eyes rolled wildly toward the man in the doorway, who stood in silent amazement. The man on the rack was Olmec, prince of Tecuhltli.

VI

THE EYES OF TASCELA

"WHY did you bring me into this chamber to bandage my legs?" demanded Valeria. "Couldn't you have done it just as well in the throneroom?"

She sat on a couch with her wounded leg extended upon it, and the Tecuhltli woman had just bound it with silk bandages. Valeria's red-stained sword lay on the couch beside her.

She frowned as she spoke. The woman had done her task silently and efficiently, but Valeria liked neither the lingering, caressing touch of her slim fingers nor the expression in her eyes.

"They have taken the rest of the wounded into the other chambers," answered the woman in the soft speech of the Tecuhltli women, which somehow did not suggest either softness or gentleness in the speakers. A little while before, Valeria had seen this same woman stab a Xotalanca woman through the breast and stamp the eyeballs out of a wounded Xotalanca man.

"They will be carrying the corpses of the dead down into the catacombs," she added, "lest the ghosts escape into the chambers and dwell there."

"Do you believe in ghosts?" asked Valeria.

"I know the ghost of Tolkemec dwells in the catacombs," she answered with a shiver. "Once I saw it, as I crouched in a crypt among the bones of a dead queen. It passed by in the form of an ancient man with flowing white beard and locks, and luminous eyes that blazed in the darkness. It was Tolkemec; I saw him living when I was a child and he was being tortured."

Her voice sank to a fearful whisper: "Olmec laughs, but I *know* Tolkemec's ghost dwells in the catacombs! They say it is rats which gnaw the flesh from the bones of the newly dead – but ghosts eat flesh. Who knows but that –"

She glanced up quickly as a shadow fell across the couch. Valeria looked up to see Olmec gazing down at her. The prince had cleansed his hands, torso and beard of the blood that had splashed them; but he had not donned his robe, and his great dark-skinned hairless body and limbs renewed the impression of strength bestial in its nature. His deep black eyes burned with a more elemental light, and there was the suggestion of a twitching in the fingers that tugged at his thick blue-black beard.

He stared fixedly at the woman, and she rose and glided from the chamber. As she passed through the door she cast a look over her shoulder at Valeria, a glance full of cynical derision and obscene mockery.

"She has done a clumsy job," criticized the prince, coming to the divan and bending over the bandage. "Let me see –"

With a quickness amazing in one of his bulk he snatched her sword and threw it across the chamber. His next move was to catch her in his giant arms.

Quick and unexpected as the move was, she almost matched it; for even as he grabbed her, her dirk was in her hand and she stabbed murderously at his throat. More by luck than skill he caught her wrist, and then began a savage wrestling-match. She fought him with fists, feet, knees, teeth and nails, with all the strength of her magnificent body and all the knowledge of hand-to-hand fighting she had acquired in her years of roving and fighting on sea and land. It availed her nothing against his brute strength. She lost her dirk in the first moment of contact, and thereafter found herself powerless to inflict any appreciable pain on her giant attacker.

The blaze in his weird black eyes did not alter, and their expression filled her with fury, fanned by the sardonic smile that seemed carved upon his bearded lips. Those eyes and that smile contained all the cruel cynicism that seethes below the surface of a sophisticated and degenerate race, and for the first time in her life Valeria experienced fear of a man. It was like struggling against some huge elemental force; his iron arms thwarted her efforts with an ease that sent panic racing through her limbs. He seemed impervious to any pain she could inflict. Only once, when she sank her white teeth savagely into his wrist so that the blood started, did he react. And that was to buffet her brutally upon the side of the head with his open hand, so that stars flashed before her eyes and her head rolled on her shoulders.

Her shirt had been torn open in the struggle, and with cynical cruelty he rasped his thick beard across her bare breasts, bringing the blood to suffuse the fair skin, and fetching a cry of pain and outraged fury from her. Her convulsive resistance was useless; she was crushed down on a couch, disarmed and panting, her eyes blazing up at him like the eyes of a trapped tigress.

A moment later he was hurrying from the chamber, carrying her in his arms. She made no resistance, but the smoldering of her eyes showed that she was unconquered in spirit, at least. She had not cried out. She knew that Conan was not within call, and it did not occur to her that any in Tecuhltli would oppose their prince. But she noticed that Olmec went stealthily, with his head on one side as if listening for sounds of pursuit, and he did not return to the throne chamber. He carried her through a door that stood opposite that through which he had entered, crossed another room and began stealing down a hall. As she became convinced that he feared some opposition to the abduction, she threw back her head and screamed at the top of her lusty voice.

She was rewarded by a slap that half stunned her, and Olmec quickened his pace to a shambling run.

But her cry had been echoed, and twisting her head about, Valeria, through the tears and stars that partly blinded her, saw Techotl limping after them.

Olmec turned with a snarl, shifting the woman to an uncomfortable and certainly undignified position under one huge arm, where he held her writhing and kicking vainly, like a child.

"Olmec!" protested Techotl. "You cannot be such a dog as to do this thing! She is Conan's woman! She helped us slay the Xotalancas, and –"

WITHOUT a word Olmec balled his free hand into a huge fist and stretched the wounded warrior senseless at his feet. Stooping, and hindered not at all by the struggles and imprecations of his captive, he drew Techotl's sword from its sheath and stabbed the warrior in the breast. Then casting aside the weapon he fled on along the corridor. He did not see a woman's dark face peer cautiously after him from behind a hanging. It vanished, and presently Techotl groaned and stirred, rose dazedly and staggered drunkenly away, calling Conan's name.

Olmec hurried on down the corridor, and descended a winding ivory staircase. He crossed several corridors and halted at last in a broad chamber whose doors were veiled with heavy tapestries, with one exception – a heavy bronze door similar to the Door of the Eagle on the upper floor.

He was moved to rumble, pointing to it: "That is one of the outer doors of Tecuhltli. For the first time in fifty years it is unguarded. We need not guard it now, for Xotalanc is no more."

"Thanks to Conan and me, you bloody rogue!" sneered Valeria, trembling with fury and the shame of physical coercion. "You treacherous dog! Conan will cut your throat for this!"

Olmec did not bother to voice his belief that Conan's own gullet had already been severed according to his whispered command. He was too utterly cynical to be at all interested in her thoughts or opinions. His flame-lit eyes devoured her, dwelling burningly on the generous expanses of clear white flesh exposed where her shirt and breeches had been torn in the struggle.

"Forget Conan," he said thickly. "Olmec is lord of Xuchotl. Xotalanc is no more. There will be no more fighting. We shall spend our lives in drinking and love-making. First let us drink!"

He seated himself on an ivory table and pulled her down on his knees, like a dark-skinned satyr with a white nymph in his arms. Ignoring her un-nymphlike profanity, he held her helpless with one great arm about her waist while the other reached across the table and secured a vessel of wine.

"Drink!" he commanded, forcing it to her lips, as she writhed her head away.

The liquor slopped over, stinging her lips, splashing down on her naked breasts.

"Your guest does not like your wine, Olmec," spoke a cool, sardonic voice.

Olmec stiffened; fear grew in his flaming eyes. Slowly he swung his great head about and stared at Tascela who posed negligently in the curtained doorway, one hand on her smooth hip. Valeria twisted herself about in his iron grip, and when she met the burning eyes of Tascela, a chill tingled along her supple spine. New experiences were flooding Valeria's proud soul that night. Recently she had learned to fear a man; now she knew what it was to fear a woman.

Olmec sat motionless, a gray pallor growing under his swarthy skin. Tascela brought her other hand from behind her and displayed a small gold vessel.

"I feared she would not like your wine, Olmec," purred the princess, "so I brought some of mine, some I brought with me long ago from the shores of Lake Zuad – do you understand, Olmec?"

Beads of sweat stood out suddenly on Olmec's brow. His muscles relaxed, and Valeria broke away and put the table between them. But though reason told her to dart from the room, some fascination she could not understand held her rigid, watching the scene.

Tascela came toward the seated prince with a swaying, undulating walk that was mockery in itself. Her voice was soft, slurringly caressing, but her eyes gleamed. Her slim fingers stroked his beard lightly.

"You are selfish, Olmec," she crooned, smiling. "You would keep our handsome guest to yourself, though you knew I wished to entertain her. You are much at fault, Olmec!"

The mask dropped for an instant; her eyes flashed, her face was contorted and with an appalling show of strength her hand locked convulsively in his beard and tore out a great handful. This evidence of unnatural strength was no more terrifying than the momentary baring of the hellish fury that raged under her bland exterior.

Olmec lurched up with a roar, and stood swaying like a bear, his mighty hands clenching and unclenching.

"Slut!" His booming voice filled the room. "Witch! She-devil! Tecuhltli should have slain you fifty years ago! Begone! I have endured too much from you! This white-skinned wench is mine! Get hence before I slay you!"

The princess laughed and dashed the blood-stained strands into his face. Her laughter was less merciful than the ring of flint on steel.

"Once you spoke otherwise, Olmec," she taunted. "Once, in your youth, you spoke words of love. Aye, you were my lover once, years ago, and because you loved me, you slept in my arms beneath the enchanted lotus – and thereby put into my hands the chains that enslaved you. You know you cannot withstand me. You know I have but to gaze into your eyes, with the mystic power a priest of Stygia taught me, long ago, and you are powerless. You remember the night beneath the black lotus that waved above us, stirred by no worldly breeze; you scent again the unearthly perfumes that stole and rose like a cloud about you to enslave you. You cannot fight against me. You are my slave as you were that night – as you shall be so long as you shall live, Olmec of Xuchotl!"

HER voice had sunk to a murmur like the rippling of a stream running through starlit darkness. She leaned close to the prince and spread her long tapering fingers upon his giant breast. His eyes glazed, his great hands fell limply to his sides.

With a smile of cruel malice, Tascela lifted the vessel and placed it to his lips. "Drink!"

Mechanically the prince obeyed. And instantly the glaze passed from his eyes and they were flooded with fury, comprehension and an awful fear. His mouth gaped, but no sound issued. For an instant he reeled on buckling knees, and then fell in a sodden heap on the floor.

His fall jolted Valeria out of her paralysis. She turned and sprang toward the door, but with a movement that would have shamed a leaping panther, Tascela was before her. Valeria struck at her with her clenched fist, and all the power of her supple body behind the blow. It would have stretched a man senseless on the floor. But with a lithe twist of her torso, Tascela avoided the blow and caught the pirate's wrist. The next instant Valeria's left hand was imprisoned, and holding her wrists together with one hand, Tascela calmly bound them with a cord she drew from her girdle. Valeria thought she had tasted the ultimate in humiliation already that night, but her shame at being manhandled by Olmec was nothing to the sensations that now shook her supple frame. Valeria had always been inclined to despise the other members of her sex; and it was overwhelming to encounter another woman who could handle her like a child. She scarcely resisted at all when Tascela forced her into a chair and drawing her bound wrists down between her knees, fastened them to the chair.

Casually stepping over Olmec, Tascela walked to the bronze door and shot the bolt and threw it open, revealing a hallway without.

"Opening upon this hall," she remarked, speaking to her feminine captive for the first time, "there is a chamber which in old times was used as a torture room. When we retired into Tecuhltli, we brought most of the apparatus with us, but there was one piece too heavy to move. It is still in working order. I think it will be quite convenient now."

An understanding flame of terror rose in Olmec's eyes. Tascela strode back to him, bent and gripped him by the hair.

"He is only paralyzed temporarily," she remarked conversationally. "He can hear, think, and feel – aye, he can feel very well indeed!"

With which sinister observation she started toward the door, dragging the giant bulk with an ease that made the pirate's eyes dilate. She passed into the hall and moved down it without hesitation, presently disappearing with her captive into a chamber that opened into it, and whence shortly thereafter issued the clank of iron.

Valeria swore softly and tugged vainly, with her legs braced against the chair. The cords that confined her were apparently unbreakable.

Tascela presently returned alone; behind her a muffled groaning issued from the chamber. She closed the door but did not bolt it. Tascela was beyond the grip of habit, as she was beyond the touch of other human instincts and emotions.

Valeria sat dumbly, watching the woman in whose slim hands, the pirate realized, her destiny now rested.

Tascela grasped her yellow locks and forced back her head, looking impersonally down into her face. But the glitter in her dark eyes was not impersonal.

"I have chosen you for a great honor," she said. "You shall restore the youth of Tascela. Oh, you stare at that! My appearance is that of youth, but through my veins creeps the sluggish chill of approaching age, as I have felt it a thousand times before. I am old, so old I do not remember my childhood. But I was a girl once, and a priest of Stygia loved me, and gave me the secret of immortality and youth everlasting. He died, then – some said by poison. But I dwelt in my palace by the shores of Lake Zuad and the passing years touched me not. So at last a king of Stygia desired me, and my people rebelled and brought me to this land. Olmec called me a princess. I am not of royal blood. I am greater than a princess. I am Tascela, whose youth your own glorious youth shall restore."

Valeria's tongue clove to the roof of her mouth. She sensed here a mystery darker than the degeneracy she had anticipated.

The taller woman unbound the Aquilonian's wrists and pulled her to her feet. It was not fear of the dominant strength that lurked in the princess' limbs that made Valeria a helpless, quivering captive in her hands. It was the burning, hypnotic, terrible eyes of Tascela.

VII

HE COMES FROM THE DARK

"WELL, I'm a Kushite!"

Conan glared down at the man on the iron rack.

"What the devil are *you* doing on that thing?"

Incoherent sounds issued from behind the gag and Conan bent and tore it away, evoking a bellow of fear from the captive; for his action caused the iron ball to lurch down until it nearly touched the broad breast.

"Be careful, for Set's sake!" begged Olmec.

"What for?" demanded Conan. "Do you think I care what happens to you? I only wish I had time to stay here and watch that chunk of iron grind your guts out. But I'm in a hurry. Where's Valeria?"

"Loose me!" urged Olmec. "I will tell you all!"

"Tell me first."

"Never!" The prince's heavy jaws set stubbornly.

"All right." Conan seated himself on a near-by bench. "I'll find her myself, after you've been reduced to a jelly. I believe I can speed up that process by twisting my sword-point around in your ear," he added, extending the weapon experimentally.

"Wait!" Words came in a rush from the captive's ashy lips. "Tascela took her from me. I've never been anything but a puppet in Tascela's hands."

"Tascela?" snorted Conan, and spat. "Why, the filthy –"

"No, no!" panted Olmec. "It's worse than you think. Tascela is old – centuries old. She renews her life and her youth by the sacrifice of beautiful young women. That's one thing that has reduced the clan to its present state. She will draw the essence of Valeria's life into her own body, and bloom with fresh vigor and beauty."

"Are the doors locked?" asked Conan, thumbing his sword edge.

"Aye! But I know a way to get into Tecuhltli. Only Tascela and I know, and she thinks me helpless and you slain. Free me and I swear I will help you rescue Valeria. Without my help you cannot win into Tecuhltli; for even if you tortured me into revealing the secret, you couldn't work it. Let me go, and we will steal on Tascela and kill her before she can work magic – before she can fix her eyes on us. A knife thrown from behind will do the work. I should have killed her thus long ago, but I feared that without her to aid us the Xotalancas would overcome us. She needed my help, too; that's the only reason she let me live this long. Now neither needs the other, and one must die. I swear that when we have slain the witch, you and Valeria shall go free without harm. My people will obey me when Tascela is dead."

Conan stooped and cut the ropes that held the prince, and Olmec slid cautiously from under the great ball and rose, shaking his head like a bull and muttering imprecations as he fingered his lacerated scalp. Standing shoulder to shoulder the two men presented a formidable picture of primitive power. Olmec was as tall as Conan, and heavier; but there was something repellent about the Tlazitlan, something abysmal and monstrous that contrasted unfavorably with the clean-cut, compact hardness of the Cimmerian. Conan had discarded the remnants of his tattered, blood-soaked shirt, and stood with his remarkable muscular development impressively revealed. His great shoulders were as broad as those of Olmec, and more cleanly outlined, and his huge breast arched with a more impressive sweep to a hard waist that lacked the paunchy thickness of Olmec's midsection. He might have been an image of primal strength cut out of bronze. Olmec was darker, but not from the burning of the sun. If Conan was a figure out of the dawn of Time, Olmec was a shambling, somber shape from the darkness of Time's pre-dawn.

"Lead on," demanded Conan. "And keep ahead of me. I don't trust you any farther than I can throw a bull by the tail."

Olmec turned and stalked on ahead of him, one hand twitching slightly as it plucked at his matted beard.

OLMEC did not lead Conan back to the bronze door, which the prince naturally supposed Tascela had locked, but to a certain chamber on the border of Tecuhltli.

"This secret has been guarded for half a century," he said. "Not even our own clan knew of it, and the Xotalancas never learned. Tecuhltli himself built this secret entrance, afterward slaying the slaves who did the work; for he feared that he might find himself locked out of his own kingdom some day because of the spite of Tascela, whose passion for him soon changed to hate. But she discovered the secret, and barred the hidden door against him one day as he fled back from an unsuccessful raid, and the Xotalancas took him and flayed him. But once, spying upon her, I saw her enter Tecuhltli by this route, and so learned the secret."

He pressed upon a gold ornament in the wall, and a panel swung inward, disclosing an ivory stair leading upward.

"This stair is built within the wall," said Olmec. "It leads up to a tower upon the roof, and thence other stairs wind down to the various chambers. Hasten!"

"After you, comrade!" retorted Conan satirically, swaying his broadsword as he spoke, and Olmec shrugged his shoulders and stepped onto the staircase. Conan instantly followed him, and the door shut behind them. Far above a cluster of fire-jewels made the staircase a well of dusky dragon-light.

They mounted until Conan estimated that they were above the level of the fourth floor, and then came out into a cylindrical tower, in the domed roof of which was set the bunch of fire-jewels that lighted the stair. Through gold-barred windows, set with unbreakable crystal panes, the first windows he had seen in Xuchotl, Conan got a glimpse of high ridges, domes and more towers, looming darkly against the stars. He was looking across the roofs of Xuchotl.

Olmec did not look through the windows. He hurried down one of the several stairs that wound down from the tower, and when they had descended a few feet, this stair changed into a narrow corridor that wound tortuously on for some distance. It ceased at a steep flight of steps leading downward. There Olmec paused.

Up from below, muffled, but unmistakable, welled a woman's scream, edged with fright, fury and shame. And Conan recognized Valeria's voice.

In the swift rage roused by that cry, and the amazement of wondering what peril could wring such a shriek from Valeria's reckless lips, Conan forgot Olmec. He pushed past the prince and started down the stair. Awakening instinct brought him about again, just as Olmec struck with his great mallet-like fist. The blow, fierce and silent, was aimed at the base of Conan's brain. But the Cimmerian wheeled in time to receive the buffet on the side of his neck instead. The impact would have snapped the vertebræ of a lesser man. As it was, Conan swayed backward, but even as he reeled he dropped his sword, useless at such close quarters, and grasped Olmec's extended arm, dragging the prince with him as he fell. Headlong they went down the steps together, in a revolving whirl of limbs and heads and bodies. And as they went Conan's iron fingers found and locked in Olmec's bull-throat.

The barbarian's neck and shoulder felt numb from the sledge-like impact of Olmec's huge fist, which had carried all the strength of the massive forearm, thick triceps and great shoulder. But this did not affect his ferocity to any appreciable extent. Like a bulldog he hung on grimly, shaken and battered and beaten against the steps as they rolled, until at last they struck an ivory panel-door at the bottom with such an impact that they splintered it its full length and crashed through its ruins. But Olmec was already dead, for those iron fingers had crushed out his life and broken his neck as they fell.

CONAN rose, shaking the splinters from his great shoulder, blinking blood and dust out of his eyes.

He was in the great throneroom. There were fifteen people in that room besides himself. The first person he saw was Valeria. A curious black altar stood before the throne-dais. Ranged about it, seven black candles in golden candle-sticks sent up oozing spirals of thick green smoke, disturbingly scented. These spirals united in a cloud near the ceiling, forming a smoky arch above the altar. On that altar lay Valeria, stark naked, her white flesh gleaming in shocking contrast to the glistening ebon stone. She was not bound. She lay at full length, her arms stretched out above her head to their fullest extent. At the head of the altar knelt a young man, holding her wrists firmly. A young woman knelt at the other end of the altar, grasping her ankles. Between them she could neither rise nor move.

Eleven men and women of Tecuhltli knelt dumbly in a semicircle, watching the scene with hot, lustful eyes.

On the ivory throne-seat Tascela lolled. Bronze bowls of incense rolled their spirals about her; the wisps of smoke curled about her naked limbs like caressing fingers. She could not sit still; she squirmed and shifted about with sensuous abandon, as if finding pleasure in the contact of the smooth ivory with her sleek flesh.

The crash of the door as it broke beneath the impact of the hurtling bodies caused no change in the scene. The kneeling men and women merely glanced incuriously at the corpse of their prince and at the man who rose from the ruins of the door, then swung their eyes greedily back to the writhing white shape on the black altar. Tascela looked insolently at him, and sprawled back on her seat, laughing mockingly.

"Slut!" Conan saw red. His hands clenched into iron hammers as he started for her. With his first step something clanged loudly and steel bit savagely into his leg. He stumbled and almost fell, checked in his headlong stride. The jaws of an iron trap had closed on his leg, with teeth that sank deep and held. Only the ridged muscles of his calf saved the bone from being splintered. The accursed thing had sprung out of the smoldering floor without warning. He saw the slots now, in the floor where the jaws had lain, perfectly camouflaged.

"Fool!" laughed Tascela. "Did you think I would not guard against your possible return? Every door in this chamber is guarded by such traps. Stand there and watch now, while I fulfill the destiny of your handsome friend! Then I will decide your own."

Conan's hand instinctively sought his belt, only to encounter an empty scabbard. His sword was on the stair behind him. His poniard was lying back in the forest, where the dragon had torn it from his jaw. The steel teeth in his leg were like burning coals, but the pain was not as savage as the fury that seethed in his soul. He was trapped, like a wolf. If he had had his sword he would have hewn off his leg and crawled across the floor to slay Tascela. Valeria's eyes rolled toward him with mute appeal, and his own helplessness sent red waves of madness surging through his brain.

Dropping on the knee of his free leg, he strove to get his fingers between the jaws of the trap, to tear them apart by sheer strength. Blood started from beneath his finger nails, but the jaws fitted close about his leg in a circle whose segments jointed perfectly, contracted until there was no space between his mangled flesh and the fanged iron. The sight of Valeria's naked body added flame to the fire of his rage.

Tascela ignored him. Rising languidly from her seat she swept the ranks of her subjects with a searching glance, and asked: "Where are Xamec, Zlanath and Tachic?"

"They did not return from the catacombs, princess," answered a man. "Like the rest of us, they bore the bodies of the slain into the crypts, but they have not returned. Perhaps the ghost of Tolkemec took them."

"Be silent, fool!" she ordered harshly. "The ghost is a myth."

She came down from her dais, playing with a thin gold-hilted dagger. Her eyes burned like nothing on the hither side of hell. She paused beside the altar and spoke in the tense stillness.

"Your life shall make me young, white woman!" she said. "I shall lean upon your bosom and place my lips over yours, and slowly – ah, slowly! – sink this blade through your heart, so that your life, fleeing your stiffening body, shall enter mine, making me bloom again with youth and with life everlasting!"

Slowly, like a serpent arching toward its victim, she bent down through the writhing smoke, closer and closer over the now motionless woman who stared up into her glowing dark eyes – eyes that grew larger and deeper, blazing like black moons in the swirling smoke.

The kneeling people gripped their hands and held their breath, tense for the bloody climax, and the only sound was Conan's fierce panting as he strove to tear his leg from the trap.

All eyes were glued on the altar and the white figure there; the crash of a thunderbolt could hardly have broken the spell, yet it was only a low cry that shattered the fixity of the scene and brought all whirling about – a low cry, yet one to make the hair stand up stiffly on the scalp. They looked, and they saw.

Framed in the door to the left of the dais stood a nightmare figure. It was a man, with a tangle of white hair and a matted white beard that fell over his breast. Rags only partly covered his gaunt frame, revealing half-naked limbs strangely unnatural in appearance. The skin was not like that of a normal human. There was a suggestion of *scaliness* about it, as if the owner had dwelt long under conditions almost antithetical to those conditions under which human life ordinarily thrives. And there was nothing at all human about the eyes that blazed from the tangle of white hair. They were great gleaming disks that stared unwinkingly, luminous, whitish, and without a hint of normal emotion or sanity. The mouth gaped, but no coherent words issued – only a high-pitched tittering.

"TOLKEMEC!" whispered Tascela, livid, while the others crouched in speechless horror. "No myth, then, no ghost! Set! You have dwelt for twelve years in darkness! Twelve years among the bones of the dead! What grisly food did you find? What mad travesty of life did you live, in the stark blackness of that eternal night? I see now why Xamec and Zlanath and Tachic did not return from the catacombs – and never will return. But why have you waited so long to strike? Were you seeking something, in the pits? Some secret weapon you knew was hidden there? And have you found it at last?"

That hideous tittering was Tolkemec's only reply, as he bounded into the room with a long leap that carried him over the secret trap before the door – by chance, or by some faint recollection of the ways of Xuchotl. He was not mad, as a man is mad. He had dwelt apart from humanity so long that he was no longer human. Only an unbroken thread of memory embodied in hate and the urge for vengeance had connected him with the humanity from which he had been cut off, and held him lurking near the people he hated. Only that thin string had kept him from racing and prancing off for ever into the black corridors and realms of the subterranean world he had discovered, long ago.

"You sought something hidden!" whispered Tascela, cringing back. "And you have found it! You remember the feud! After all these years of blackness, you remember!"

For in the lean hand of Tolkemec now waved a curious jade-hued wand, on the end of which glowed a knob of crimson shaped like a pomegranate. She sprang aside as he thrust it out like a spear, and a beam of crimson fire lanced from the pomegranate. It missed Tascela, but the woman holding Valeria's ankles was in the way. It smote between her shoulders. There was a sharp crackling sound and the ray of fire flashed from her bosom and struck the black altar, with a snapping of blue sparks. The woman toppled sidewise, shriveling and withering like a mummy even as she fell.

Valeria rolled from the altar on the other side, and started for the opposite wall on all fours. For hell had burst loose in the throneroom of dead Olmec.

The man who had held Valeria's hands was the next to die. He turned to run, but before he had taken half a dozen steps, Tolkemec, with an agility appalling in such a frame, bounded around to a position that placed the man between him and the altar. Again the red fire-beam flashed and the Tecuhltli rolled lifeless to the floor, as the beam completed its course with a burst of blue sparks against the altar.

Then began slaughter. Screaming insanely the people rushed about the chamber, caroming from one another, stumbling and falling. And among them Tolkemec capered and pranced, dealing death. They could not escape by the doors; for apparently the metal of the portals served like the metal-veined stone altar to complete the circuit for whatever hellish power flashed like thunderbolts from the witch-wand the ancient waved in his hand. When he caught a man or a woman between him and a door or the altar, that one died instantly. He chose no special victim. He took them as they came, with his rags flapping about his wildly gyrating limbs, and the gusty echoes of his tittering sweeping the room above the screams. And bodies fell like falling leaves about the altar and at the doors. One warrior in desperation rushed at him, lifting a dagger, only to fall before he could strike. But the rest were like crazed cattle, with no thought for resistance, and no chance of escape.

The last Tecuhltli except Tascela had fallen when the princess reached the Cimmerian and the girl who had taken refuge beside him. Tascela bent and touched the floor, pressing a design upon it. Instantly the iron jaws released the bleeding limb and sank back into the floor.

"Slay him if you can!" she panted, and pressed a heavy knife into his hand. "I have no magic to withstand him!"

With a grunt he sprang before the women, not heeding his lacerated leg in the heat of the fighting-lust. Tolkemec was coming toward him, his weird eyes ablaze, but he hesitated at the gleam of the knife in Conan's hand. Then began a grim game, as Tolkemec sought to circle about Conan and get the barbarian between him and the altar or a metal door, while Conan sought to avoid this and drive home his knife. The women watched tensely, holding their breath.

There was no sound except the rustle and scrape of quick-shifting feet. Tolkemec pranced and capered no more. He realized that grimmer game confronted him than the people who had died screaming and fleeing. In the elemental blaze of the barbarian's eyes he read an intent deadly as his own. Back and forth they weaved, and when one moved the other moved as if invisible threads bound them together. But all the time Conan was getting closer and closer to his enemy. Already the coiled

muscles of his thighs were beginning to flex for a spring, when Valeria cried out. For a fleeting instant a bronze door was in line with Conan's moving body. The red line leaped, searing Conan's flank as he twisted aside, and even as he shifted he hurled the knife. Old Tolkemec went down, truly slain at last, the hilt vibrating on his breast.

TASCELA sprang – not toward Conan, but toward the wand where it shimmered like a live thing on the floor. But as she leaped, so did Valeria, with a dagger snatched from a dead man, and the blade, driven with all the power of the pirate's muscles, impaled the princess of Tecuhltli so that the point stood out between her breasts. Tascela screamed once and fell dead, and Valeria spurned the body with her heel as it fell.

"I had to do that much, for my own self-respect!" panted Valeria, facing Conan across the limp corpse.

"Well, this cleans up the feud," he grunted. "It's been a hell of a night! Where did these people keep their food? I'm hungry."

"You need a bandage on that leg." Valeria ripped a length of silk from a hanging and knotted it about her waist, then tore off some smaller strips which she bound efficiently about the barbarian's lacerated limb.

"I can walk on it," he assured her. "Let's begone. It's dawn, outside this infernal city. I've had enough of Xuchotl. It's well the breed exterminated itself. I don't want any of their accursed jewels. They might be haunted."

"There is enough clean loot in the world for you and me," she said, straightening to stand tall and splendid before him.

The old blaze came back in his eyes, and this time she did not resist as he caught her fiercely in his arms.

"It's a long way to the coast," she said presently, withdrawing her lips from his.

"What matter?" he laughed. "There's nothing we can't conquer. We'll have our feet on a ship's deck before the Stygians open their ports for the trading season. And then we'll show the world what plundering means!"

Miscellanea

Untitled Notes

The Westermarck: located between the Bossonian marches and the Pictish wilderness. Provinces: Thandara, Conawaga, Oriskonie, Schohira. Political situation: Oriskonie, Conawaga, and Schohira were ruled by royal patent. Each was under the jurisdiction of a baron of the western marches, which lie just east of the Bossonian marches. These barons were accountable only to the king of Aquilonia. Theoretically they owned the land, and received a certain percentage of the gain. In return they supplied troops to protect the frontier against the Picts, built fortresses and towns, and appointed judges and other officials. Actually their power was not nearly so absolute as it seemed. There was a sort of supreme court located in the largest town of Conawaga, Scanaga, presided over by a judge appointed directly by the king of Aquilonia, and it was a defendent's privilege, under certain circumstances, to appeal to this court. Thandara was the southernmost province, Oriskonie the northernmost, and the most thinly settled. Conawaga lay south of Oriskonie, and south of Conawaga lay lay Schohira, the smallest of the provinces. Conawaga was the largest, richest and most thickly settled, and the only one in which landed patricians had settled to any extent. Thandara was the most purely pioneer province. Originally it had only been a fortress by that name, on Warhorse River, built by direct order of the king of Aquilonia, and commanded by royal troops. After the conquest of the province of Conajohara by the Picts, the settlers from that province moved southward and settled the country in the vicinity of the fortress. They held their land by force of arms, and neither received nor needed any patent. They acknowledged no baron as overlord. Their governor was merely a military commander, elected from among themselves, their choice being always submitted to and approved by the king of Aquilonia as a matter of form. No troops were ever sent to Thandara. They built forts, or rather block-houses, and manned them themselves, and formed companies of military bodies called Rangers. They were incessantly at warfare with the Picts. When the word came that Aquilonia was being torn by civil war, and that the Cimmerian Conan was striking for the crown, Thandara instantly declared for Conan, renounced their allegiance to King Namedes and sent word asking Conan to endorse their elected governor, which the Cimmerian instantly did. This enraged the commander of a fort in the Bossonian marches, and he marched with his host to ravage Thandara. But the frontiersmen met him at their borders and gave him a savage defeat, after which there was no attempt to meddle with Thandara. But the province was isolated, separated from Schohira by a stretched of uninhabited wilderness, and behind them lay the Bossonian country, where most of the people were loyalists. The baron of Schohira declared for Conan, and marched to join his army, but asked no levies of Schohira where indeed every man was needed to guard the frontier. But in Conawaga were many loyalists, and the baron of Conawaga rode in person into Scandaga and demanded that the people supply him with a force to ride and aid king Namedes. There was civil war in Conawaga, and the baron planned to crush all other provinces and make himself governor of them all. Meantime, in Oriskonie, the people had driven out the governor appointed by their baron and were savagely fighting such loyalists as skulked among them.

Wolves Beyond the Border
Draft A

CHAPTER 1

It was the mutter of a drum that awakened me. I lay still amongst the brush where I had taken refuge, straining my ears to locate it, for such sounds are illusive in the deep forest. In the dense woods about me there was no sound. Above me the tangled vines and brambles bent close to form a massed roof, and above them there loomed the higher, gloomier arch of the branches of the great trees. Not a star shone through that leafy vault. Low-hanging clouds seemed to press down upon the very tree-tops. There was no moon. The night was dark as a witch's hate.

The better for me. If I could not see my enemies, neither could they see me. But the whisper of that ominous drum stole through the night: thrum! thrum! thrum!: a steady monotone that seemed to hint at grisly secrets. I could not mistake the sound. Only one drum in the world makes just that deep, menacing, sullen thunder: the war-drum of the Picts, those wild painted savages who haunt the Wilderness beyond the borders of the Westermarck.

And I was beyond that border, alone, and concealed in a brambly covert in the midst of the great forest where those naked fiends have reigned since Time's earliest dawns.

Now I located the sound; the drum was beating southwestward of my position, and I believed at no great distance. Quickly I girt my belt closer, settled war-axe and knife in their beaded sheaths, strung my heavy bow and saw that my buckskin quiver of arrows was in place at my left hip – groping with my fingers in the utter darkness – and then I crawled from the thicket and went warily in the direction of the drum.

That it personally concerned me I did not believe. If the forest-men had discovered me, their discovery would have been announced by a sudden knife in my throat, not by a drum beating in the distance. But the throb of a war-drum had a significance no forest-runner could ignore. Its sullen pulsing was a warning and a threat, a promise of doom for those white-skinned invaders whose lonely cabins and axe-marked clearings menaced the immemorial solitude of the wilderness. It meant fire and death and torture, flaming arrows dropping like falling stars through the midnight sky, and the dripping axe crunching through skulls of men and women and children.

So through the blackness of the nighted forest I went, feeling my way delicately among the mighty boles, sometimes creeping on hands and knees, and now and then my heart in my throat when a creeper brushed across my face or groping hand. For there are huge serpents in that forest which sometimes hang by their tails from branches high above and so snare their prey. But the beings I sought were more terrible than any serpent, and as the drum grew louder I went as cautiously as if I treaded on naked swords. And presently I glimpsed a red gleam among the trees, and heard a mutter of fierce voices mingling with the snarl of the drum.

Whatever weird ceremony might be taking place yonder under the black trees, it was likely that they had outposts scattered about the place, and I knew how silent and motionless a Pict could stand, merging with the natural forest-growth even in dim light, and unsuspected until his blade was through his victim's heart. My flesh crawled at the thought of colliding with one such grim sentry in the darkness, and I drew my knife and held it extended before me. But I knew that not even a Pict could see me in that blackness of tangled forest-roof and cloud-massed sky.

The light danced and flickered and revealed itself as a fire before which silhouettes crossed and re-crossed, like black devils against the red fires of hell. And presently I crouched close in a dense thicket of alders and brambles and looked into a black-walled glade and the figures that moved therein.

There were forty or fifty Picts, naked but for loin-cloths, and hideously painted, who squatted in a wide semi-circle, facing the fire, with their backs to me. By the hawk feathers in their thick black manes, I knew them to be of the Hawk Clan, or Skondaga. In the midst of the glade there was a crude altar made of rough stones heaped togather, and at the sight of this I shuddered. For I had seen these Pictish altars before, all charred with fire and stained with blood, in empty and deserted glades, but none knew exactly for what they were used, not even the oldest frontiersmen. But now I instinctively knew that I was about to witness confirmation of the horrible tales told about them and the feathered shamans who used them.

One of these devils was dancing between the fire and the altar – a slow, shuffling dance that caused his plumes to swing and sway about him, but I could tell nothing of his features, in the uncertain light of the flames.

Between him and the ring of squatting warriors stood a man who differed from the others so much that it was evident he was not a Pict. For he was tall as I, and they are a squat race, and his skin was light in the play of the fire. But he was clad in doe-skin loin-clout and moccasins, and there was a hawk-feather in his hair, so I knew he must be a Socandaga, one of those white savages who dwell in small clans in the great forest, generally at war with the Picts, but sometimes at peace. The Picts are a white race too, in that they are not black nor brown nor yellow, but they are black-eyed and black-haired and dark of skin, and neither they nor the Socandagas are spoken of as "white" by the people of Westermarck, who only designate thus a man of Hyborian blood.

Now as I watched, I saw three Picts drag a man into the ring of firelight – another Pict, naked and blood-stained, whom they cast down upon the altar, bound hand and foot.

Then the shaman began dancing again, weaving intricate patterns about the altar and the man upon it, and the warrior who beat the drum wrought himself into a frenzy, and presently, down from a branch overhanging the glade dropped one of those great serpents of which I spoke. The firelight glistened on its scales as it writhed toward the altar, its beady eyes glittered and its forked tongue darted in and out, but the warriors showed no fear, though it passed within a few feet of some of them. And that was strange, for ordinarily these serpents are the only things a Pict fears.

The monster reared its head up on arched neck above the altar and it and the shaman faced one another across the trembling body of the prisoner. The shaman danced with a writhing of body and arms, scarcely moving his feet, and as he danced, the great serpent danced, weaving and swaying, as though mesmerized. And presently it reared higher and began looping itself about the altar and the man upon it, upon his body was hidden by its shimmering folds, and only his head was visible, and the great head of the serpent swaying close above it.

Then the shaman cried out shrilly and cast something upon the fire and a great green cloud of smoke billowed up and rolled about the altar, so that it hid the pair upon it. But in the midst of that cloud I saw a hideous writhing and *altering* and for a moment I could not tell which was the serpent and which the man, and a shuddering sigh swept over the assembled Picts like a wind moaning through nighted branches.

Then the smoke cleared and man and snake lay limply on the altar, and I thought both were dead. But the shaman dragged them from the stones and let them fall limply on the earth, and he cut the raw-hide thongs that bound the man, and began to dance and chant above them.

And presently the man moved. But he did not rise. His head swayed from side to side, and I saw his tongue dart out and in again. And, Mitra, he began to *wriggle* away from the fire, as a great snake crawls, on his belly!

And the serpent was suddenly shaken with convulsions and arched its neck and reared up almost its full length and then fell back and tried again and again, horribly like a man trying to rise and stand and walk upright, after being deprived of his limbs.

And the wild howling of the Picts shook the night. I was sick where I crouched among the bushes, and fought an urge to retch. I had heard tales of this ghastly ceremony. The shaman had transferred the soul of a captured enemy into a serpent, so that his foe should dwell in the body of a serpent throughout his next reincarnation.

And so they writhed and agonized side by side, the man and the serpent, until a sword flashed in the hand of the shaman and boths heads fell together – and gods, it was the serpent's trunk which but quivered and jerked and then lay still, and the man's body which rolled and knotted and thrashed like a beheaded snake.

Then the shaman sprang up and faced the ring of warriors and threw up his head and howled like a wolf, and the firelight fell full on his face and I recognized him. And at that recognition all thought of my personal peril was swept away, and with it recollection of my mission. For that shaman was old Garogh of the Hawks, he who burnt alive my friend Jon Galter's son.

In the lust of my hate I acted almost instinctively – whipped up my bow, notched an arrow and loosed, all in an instant. The firelight was uncertain, but the range was not great, and we of the Westermarck live by twang of bow. But he moved just as I loosed. Old Garogh yowled like a cat and reeled back and his warriors howled with amazement to see a shaft quivering suddenly in his shoulder. The tall light-skinned warrior wheeled, and Mitra, he was a white man!

The horrid shock of that surprise held me paralyzed for a moment, and had almost undone me. For the Picts instantly sprang up and rushed into the forest like panthers, knowing the general direction from which the shaft had come, if not the actual spot. Then I jerked out of the spell of my amazement and horror, sprang up and raced away, ducking and dodging among trees which I avoided more by instinct than anything else, for it was dark as ever. But I knew the Picts could not strike my trail in the dark but must hunt as blindly as I fled.

I headed southward, and behind me presently I heard a hideous howling, whose blood-mad fury was enough to freeze the blood, even, of a forest-runner. And I believed that they had plucked my arrow from the shaman's shoulder and discovered it to be a white man's shaft.

But I fled on, my heart pounding from fear and excitement, and the horror of the nightmare I had witnessed. And that a white man, a Hyborian, should have stood there as a welcome and evidently honored guest was so monstrous I wondered if after all, the whole thing were a nightmare. For never before had a white man observed a Pictish ceremony save as a prisoner, or a spy, as I had. And what monstrous thing it portended I knew not, but I was shaken with foreboding and horror at the thought.

And because of my horror I went more carelessly than is my wont, seeking haste at the expense of stealth, and occasionally blundering into a tree I ciuld have avoided had I taken more care. And I doubt it was the noise of this blundering which brought the Pict upon my trail, for he could not have seen me or my footprints in that blackness.

But once he had crept to within a score of feet of me he located me by the faint noises I made, and came like a devil of the black night. I knew of him first by the swift faint pad of his naked feet across the ground and wheeled and could not even make out the dim bulk of him, but knew that he must have seen me, for they see like cats in the dark. But he could not have seen me very well, for he impaled himself on the knife I thrust out blindly, and his death-yell rang like a note of doom under the forest-roof as he went down. And was answered by a score of wild shouts behind me. And I turned and ran for it, abandoning stealth for speed, and trusting to luck that I would not dash out my brains against a tree-stem in the darkness.

But I had come to a place where there was little underbrush and something almost like light filtered in through the branches, for the clouds were clearing a little. And through this forest I fled like a damned soul pursued by demons, until the yells grew fainter and fell away behind me, for in a straight-away race no Pict can match the long legs of a white forest-runner. And presently as I advanced, I saw a glimmer through the trees far ahead of me and knew it was the light of the first outpost of Schohira.

CHAPTER 2

Perhaps, before continuing with this chronicle of the bloody years, it might be well were I to give an account of myself, and the reason for which I traversed the Pictish Wilderness, by night and alone.

My name is Gault Hagar's son. I was born in the province of Conajohara But when I was five years of age, the Picts broke over Black River and stormed Fort Tuscelan and slew all within save one man, and drove all the settlers of the province east of Thunder River. Conajohara was never reconquered, but became again part of the Wilderness, inhabited only by wild beasts and wild men. The people of Conajohara scattered throughout the Westermarck, in Schohira, Conawaga, or Oriskonie, but many of them went southward and settled near Fort Thandara, an isolated outpost on the Warhorse River, my family among them. There they were later joined by other settlers for whom the older provinces were too thickly inhabited, and presently there grew up the province of Thandara. It was known as the Free Province of Thandara, because it was not ruled by grant or patent of any lord, as were the other provinces, since its people had cut it out of the wilderness without aid of the nobility. We paid no taxes to any baron beyond the Bossonian marches who claimed the land by right of royal grant. Our governor was not appointed by any lord, but we elected him ourselves, from our own number, and he was responsible only to the king. We manned the forts with our own men, and sustained ourselves in war as in peace. And Mitra knows war was a constant state of affairs, for our neighbors were the wild Panther, Alligator and Otter tribes of Picts, and there was never peace between us.

But we throve, and seldom questioned what went on east of the marches in the kingdom whence our grandsires had come. But at last an event in Aquilonia did touch upon us in the wilderness. Word came of civil war, and a fighting man risen to wrest the throne from the ancient dynasty. And sparks from that conflagration set the frontier ablaze, and turned neighbor against neighbor and brother against brother. And so I was hastening alone through the stretch of wilderness that separated Thandara from Schohira, with news that might well change the destiny of all the Westermarck.

I crossed Sword River in the early dawn, wading through the shallows, and was challenged by an outpost on the other bank. When he knew I was from Thandara: "By Mitra!" quoth he. "your business must be urgent, that you cross the Hawk Country, instead of coming by the longer road.

For Thandara was separated from the other provinces by the Little Wilderness east of us, but no Picts dwelt there, and there was a road through it into the Bossonian marches and thence ran road to the other provinces.

Then he desired me to tell him the state of affairs in Thandara, for he swore they in Schohira knew naught definite, but I told him that I knew little, having been on a long scout into Pictish country, and desired to be told if Hakon Strom's son was in the fort. For I knew not how events were shaping in Schohira and wished to be acquainted with the situation before I spoke.

He told me he was not in the fort, but was at the town of Schondara, which lay a few miles east of the fort.

"I hope Thandara declares for Conan," said he with an oath, "for I tell you plainly it is our political complection. Even now our army lies beyond Schondara, waiting the onslaught of Baron Brocas of Torh, and but for the necessity of watching the cursed Picts we would all be there."

I said naught, but was surprized, for Brocas was lord of Conawaga, and not Schohira, whose patroon was Lord Thespius of Kormon. Thespius, I knew, was away in Aquilonia fighting in the civil war raging there, and I wondered that Brocas was not so employed.

I borrowed a horse from the fort went on to Schondara, a handsome town for a frontier village, with neat houses of squared logs, some painted, but not so much as a ditch or palisade about it, which was strange to me. For we of Thandara build our dwelling places for defense, and there is not so much as a village in all our province.

At the tavern I was told that Hakon Strom's son had ridden to Orklay Creek where the militia-army of Schohira lay encamped, but would return shortly. So being hungry and weary, I ate a meal in the tap-room, and then lay down in a corner and slept. And was so slumbering when Hakon Strom's son returned, close to sunset.

He was a tall man, rangy and broad-shouldered, like most Westlanders, and clad in buckskin hunting shirt and fringed leggins and moccasins like myself.

When I named myself and told him that I had word for him, he looked at me closely, and bade me sit with him at a table in the corner where mine host brought us leathern jacks of ale.

"What is the word you bring me?" he asked.

"Has no word come through of the state of affairs in Thandara?"

"No sure word; only rumors."

"Very well. This is the word I bring you from Brant Drago's son, governor of Thandara, and the council of captains: Thandara has declared for Conan, and stands ready to aid his friends and defy his allies."

At that he smiled and sighed as if in relief, and grasped my brown hand warmly with his own rugged fingers.

"Good!" he exclaimed. "A doubt has gone from my mind. We knew that which ever way Thandara went, that province would not go quietly. We have enemies on all sides, and dreaded a raid from the south, over the Hawk Country, in case Thandara held fast to Namedides."

"What man of Thandara could forget Conan?" said I. "Nay, I was but a child in Conajohara, but I remember him when he was a forest-runner and a scout there. When his rider came into Thandara telling us that Conan had struck for the throne, and asking our support – he asked no volunteers, saying he knew all our men were needed to guard our frontier – we sent him one phrase: "Tell Conan we have not forgotten Conajohara." Later came the Baron Attalius over the marches to crush us, but we ambushed him in the Little Wilderness and cut his host to pieces. The longbows of his Bossonians were useless; we harried them from behind trees and bushes, and then, working into close quarters, fell on them with war-axe and knife and cut them to pieces. We drove the remnants beyond the border, and I do not think any will dare attack Thandara again."

"I would I could say as much for Schohira," he said grimly. "Baron Thespius sent us word that we could do as we chose – he has declared for Conan and joined the rebel army. But he did not ask for any western levies.

"He removed the troops from the fort, however, and we manned it with our own foresters. Then Brocas moved against us. At least nine-tenths of us in Schohira are for Conan, and the loyalists either keep silent or have fled into Conawaga, swearing they would return and cut our throats. In Conawaga Brocas and the land-owners are for Namedides and the people who are for Conan are afraid to speak."

I nodded. I had been in Conawaga before the revolt, and was aware of conditions there. It was the largest, richest and most thickly settled provinces in all the Westermarck, and only there was there an extensive, comparatively, class of titled land-holders.

"Having crushed revolt among his own people," said Hakon, "Brocas thinks to subdue Schhiro. I think the black-jowled fool plans to rule all the Westermarck as Namedides' viceroy. He has brought his army of Aquilonian men-at-arms, Bossonian archers, and Conawaga loyalists across the broder and now they lie at Coyaga, ten miles beyond Orklaga Creek. We know what when he will move against us. Ventrium, where our army lies, is full of refugees from the eastern country he has devastated.

"We do not fear him. He must cross Orklaga Creek to strike us, and we have fortified the west bank and blocked the road his cavalry must follow. We are outnumbered, but we will give him his needings."

"That touches upon my mission," I said. "I am authorized by the governor of Thandara to offer the services of a hundred and fifty Thandaran Rangers. We look for no attack from Aquilonia, and we can spare that many men from our war with the Panther Picts."

"Good!" quoth he. "When the commandant of the fort hears of this —"

"What?" quoth I. "Are *you* not the commandant?"

"Nay," said he, "it is my brother Dirk Strom's son."

"Had I known I would have given my message to him," I said. "But Brant Drago's son thought you were the commandant. However, it is as well."

"Another jack of ale," quoth Hakon, "and we'll start for the fort so that Dirk shall hear your word first-hand."

And I saw that Hakon was indeed not the man to command an outpost, for he was a brave man, and strong, but too reckless and having a merry devil in his heart.

"What of your landed gentry?" I asked, for though they are fewer in Schohira than in Conawaga, yet there are a few.

"Gone over the border and joined Brocas," he answered. "All except lord Valerian. His estate lies adjacent to this town. The other lords lie to the east. He has remained, and has disbanded his retainers and his Gundermen guardsmen and promised to dwell quietly in Valerian Hall, taking no part one way or the other. He is alone at the Hall, which stands south of the town, except for a few servants. Where his fighting men have gone, none knows. But he has sent them off. We were relieved when he declared his neutrality, for he is one of the few white men to whom the wild Picts will listen. If it had entered his head to stir them up against our borders we might be hard put to it to defend ourselves against them on one side and Brocas on the other.

"Our nearest neighbors, the Hawks, look on Valerian with great friendship; and the Wildcats and Turtles are not hostile to them. Behind them all it is even said that he can visit the Wolf Picts and come away alive."

If true that were strange indeed, for all men knew the ferocity of the great confederacy of allied clans known as the Wolf tribe which dwelt in the west beyond the hunting grounds of the three lesser tribes he had named. Mostly they held aloof from the frontier, but the threat of their invasion was ever a menace along the borders of Schohira.

Hakon looked up as a tall man in trunk-hose, boots and scarlet cloak entered the taproom.

"There is Lord Valerian now," he said.

I stared, and was on my feet.

"That man?" I ejaculated. "I saw that man last night beyond the border, in a camp of the Hawks, witnessing the sacrifice of a war-victim!"

He turned pale and: "Damn you!" he ripped out fiercely. "You lie!"

And whipping aside his cloak he caught at the hilt of his sword. But before he could draw it I closed with him and bore him to the floor, where he snarled and snapped like a beast at my throat and failing there, caught at my throat with both hands. Then there was a stamp of feet, and men were dragging us apart, grasping my lord firmly, who stood white and panting with fury, still grasping my neckcloth in his fingers.

"If this be true –" began Hakon.

"It is true!" I exclaimed. "Look there! He has not had time to erase the paint from his bosom!"

His doublet and shirt had been torn open in the scuffle, and there, dim on his breast, showed the symbol of the skull which the Picts paint only when they mean war against the whites. He had sought to wash it off his skin, but Pictish paint stains strongly.

"Take him to the gaol," said Hakon, white to the lips.

"Give me back my neckcloth," quoth I, but his lordship spat at me and thrust the cloth inside his shirt.

"When it is returned to you it shall be knotted in a hangman's noose about your rebel neck," he snarled, and then the men grasped him and took him away.

CHAPTER 3

At the fort we found a man who said he would take word back to Thandara, where he had kin, so I said I would remain in Schohira. Scouts gave news that Brocas still lay encamped at Coyaga, and showed no signs of moving against us, which made me believe that he was waiting for Valerian to lead his Picts against the border and so catch the free men of Schohira between two fires. Valerian had been placed in the gaol – a small building of hewn logs – and only one other prisoner there, a man in the cell next to him who had been placed there for drunkeness and fighting in the streets. Valerian said nothing, but sat in a corner and gnawed his nails, with his eyes like those of a jungle-cat.

I slept in the tavern that night, and had a room upstairs. During the night I was awakened by the forcing of my window and sat up in bed, demandin to know who it was. The next instant something rushed at me from the darkness and then there was a piece of cloth around my neck, being twisted and strangling me. I groped for my hatchet and smote one blow, and the creature fell. When I had struck a light, I saw a misshapen ape-like creature lying on the floor, and knew it for a *Chakan*, one of those semi-human beings who dwell deep in the forests, and smell out trails like bloodhounds. It still held my neck-cloth in its misshapen hands, and by that I knew that it had been set upon my trail by Lord Valerian.

Hakon and I hurried to the gaol and there found the guard lying before the door with his throat cut, and my lord gone. The drunkard in the next cell was nigh dead with fright, but he told us that a dark woman, naked but for a loin cloth, had come up to the sentry and looked into his eyes and the man had become like one in a trance. So the woman took his knife from its sheath and cut his throat with it, and released Lord Valerian. And there was a horrible monstrosity which accompanied her but which lurked in the background. So we knew the woman was his Pictish half-breed mistress by whom he had his power over the Picts; some said old Goragh's daughter. The drunkard had pretended slumber, so they let him live. But he overheard them say that they would go to a certain hut by Lynx Creek, a few miles from the town, and there meet the retainers and Gundermen guards who had been hiding there, and then cross the border and bring back the Hawks and the Wildcats and the Turtles to cut our throats.

But the woman told him these tribes dared not fight without first consulting the wizard who dwelt in Ghost Swamp, and he said he would see that the wizard told them to fight.

So they fled away. Then Hakon roused a dozen men and we followed, and cornered the Gundermen in the cabin on Lynx Creek and slew most of them, but several of our men likewise were slain, and Lord Valerian and a dozen others got clean away.

We followed, and in fights and skirmishes slew several others, and presently all our men were slain except Hakon and I. We trailed Valerian across the border and into a camp of the war-tribes near Ghost Swamp, where the chiefs were going to consult the wizard, a pre-Pictish shaman.

We trailed Valerian into the swamp, he going secretly to give the shamans instructions, and Hakon waited on the trail to slay Valerian while I stole into the camp to slay the wizard. But both of us were captured by the wizard, who gave his consent to the war and gave them a ghastly magic to use against the white men, and the tribes went howling toward the border. But Hakon and I escaped and slew the wizard and followed, in time to turn their magic against them, and rout them.

Wolves Beyond the Border
Draft B

CHAPTER 1

It was the mutter of a drum that awakened me. I lay still amidst the bushes where I had taken refuge, straining my ears to locate it, for such sounds are illusive in the deep forest. In the dense woods about me there was no sound. Above me the tangled vines and brambles bent close to form a massed roof, and above them there loomed the higher, gloomier arch of the branches of the great trees. Not a star shone through that leafy vault. Low-hanging clouds seemed to press down upon the very tree-tops. There was no moon. The night was dark as a witch's hate.

The better for me. If I could not see my enemies, neither could they see me. But the whisper of that ominous drum stole through the night: thrum! thrum! thrum! a steady monotone that grunted and growled of nameless secrets. I could not mistake the sound. Only one drum in the world makes just that deep, menacing, sullen thunder: a Pictish war-drum, in the hands of those wild painted savages who haunted the Wilderness beyond the border of the Westermarck.

And I was beyond that border, alone, and concealed in a brambly covert in the midst of the great forest where those naked fiends have reigned since Time's earliest dawns.

Now I located the sound; the drum was beating westward of my position and I believed at no great distance. Quickly I girt my belt more firmly, settled war-axe and knife in their beaded sheaths, strung my heavy bow and made sure that my quivers was in place at my left hip – groping with my fingers in the utter darkness – and then I crawled from the thicket and went warily toward the sound of the drum.

That it personally concerned me I did not believe. If the forest-men had discovered me, their discovery would have been announced by a sudden knife in my throat, not by a drum beating in the distance. But the throb of the war-drum had a significance no forest-runner could ignore. It was a warning and a threat, a promise of doom for those white-skinned invaders whose lonely cabins and axe-marked clearings menaced the immemorial solitude of the wilderness. It meant fire and torture, flaming arrows dropping like falling stars through the darkness, and the red axe crunching through skulls of men and women and children.

So through the blackness of the nighted forest I went, feeling my way delicately among the mighty boles, sometimes creeping on hands and knees, and now and then my heart in my throat when a creeper brushed across my face or groping hand. For there are huge serpents in that forest which sometimes hang by their tails from branches and so snare their prey. But the creatures I sought were more terrible than any serpent, and as the drum grew louder I went as cautiously as if I trod on naked swords. And presently I glimpsed a red gleam among the trees, and heard a mutter of barbaric voices mingling with the snarl of the drum.

Whatever weird ceremony might be taking place yonder under the black trees, it was likely that they had outposts scattered about the place, and I knew how silent and motionless a Pict could stand, merging with the natural forest growth even in dim light, and unsuspected until his blade was through his victim's heart. My flesh crawled at the thought of colliding with one such grim sentry in the darkness, and I drew my knife and held it extended before me. But I knew not even a Pict could see me in that blackness of tangled forest-roof and cloud-massed sky.

The light revealed itself as a fire before which black silhouettes moved like black devils against the red fires of hell, and presently I crouched close among the dense tamarack and looked into a black-walled glade and the figures that moved therein.

There were forty or fifty Picts, naked but for loin-cloths, and hideously painted, who squatted in a wide semi-circle, facing the fire, with their backs to me. By the hawk feathers in their thick black manes, I knew them to be of the Hawk Clan, or Onayaga. In the midst of the glade there was a crude altar made of rough stones heaped together, and at the sight of this my flesh crawled anew. For I had seen these Pictish altars before, all charred with fire and stained with blood, in empty forest glades, and though I had never witnessed the rituals wherein these things were used, I had heard the tales told about them by men who had been captives among the Picts, or spied upon them even as I was spying.

A feathered shaman was dancing between the fire and the altar, a slow, shuffling dance indescribably grotesque, which caused his plumes to swing and sway about him, and his features were hidden by a grinning scarlet mask that looked like a forest-devil's face.

In the midst of the semi-circle of warriors squatted one with the great drum between his knees and as he smote it with his clenched fist it gave forth that low, growling rumble which is like the mutter of distant thunder.

Between the warriors and the dancing shaman stood one who was no Pict. For he was tall as I, and his skin was light in the play of the fire. But he was clad only in doe-skin loin-clout and moccasins, and his body was painted, and there was a hawk-feather in his hair, so I knew he must be a Ligurean, one of those light-skinned savages who dwell in small clans in the great forest, generally at war with the Picts, but sometimes at peace and allied with them. Their skins are white as an Aquilonian's. The Picts are a white race too, in that they are not black nor brown nor yellow, but they are black-eyed and black-haired and dark of skin, and neither they nor the Ligureans are spoken of as "white" by the people of Westermarck, who only designate thus a man of Hyborian blood.

Now as I watched I saw three warriors drag a man into the ring of the firelight – another Pict, naked and blood-stained, who still wore in his tangled mane a feather that identified him as a member of the Raven Clan, with whom the Hawkmen were ever at war. His captors cast him down upon the altar, bound hand and foot, and I saw his muscles swell and writhe in the firelight as he sought in vain to break the rawhide thongs which prisoned him.

Then the shaman began dancing again, weaving intricate patterns about the altar, and the man upon it, and he who beat the drum wrought himself into a fine frenzy, thundering away like one possessed of a devil. And suddenly, dowm from an overhanging branch dropped one of those great serpents of which I have spoken. The firelight glistened on its scales as it writhed toward the altar, its beady eyes glittered, and its forked tongue darted in and out, but the warriors showed no fear, though it passed within a few feet of some of them. And that was strange, for ordinarily these serpents are the only living creatures a Pict fears.

The monster reared its head up on arched neck above the altar, and it and the shaman faced one another across the prone body of the prisoner. The shaman danced with a writhing of body and arms, scarcely moving his feet, and as he danced, the great serpent danced with him, weaving and swaying as though mesmerized, and from the mask of the shaman rose a weird wailing that shuddered like the wind through the dry reeds along the sea-marshes. And slowly the great reptile reared higher and higher, and began looping itself about the altar and the man upon it, until his body was hidden by its shimmering folds, and only his head was visible, with that other terrible head swaying close above it.

The shrilling of the shaman rose to a crescendo of infernal triumph, and he cast something into the fire. A great green cloud of smoke billowed up and rolled about the altar, so that it almost hid the pair upon it, making their outlines indistinct and illusive. But in the midst of that cloud I saw a hideous writhing and *changing* – those outlines melted and flowed together horribly, and for a moment I could not tell which was the serpent and which the man. A shuddering sigh swept over the assembled Picts like a wind moaning through nighted branches.

Then the smoke cleared and man and snake lay limply on the altar, and I thought both were dead. But the shaman seized the neck of the serpent and unlooped the limp trunk from about the altar and let the great reptile ooze to the ground, and he tumbled the body of the man from the stones to fall beside the monster, and cut the rawhide thongs that bound wrist and ankle.

Then he began a weaving dance about them, chanting as he danced and swaying his arms in mad gestures. And presently the man moved. But he did not rise. His head swayed from side to side, and I saw his tongue dart out and in again. And Mitra, he began to *wriggle* away from the fire, squirming along on his belly, as a snake crawls!

And the serpent was suddenly shaken with convulsions and arched its neck and reared up almost its full length, and then fell back loop on loop, and reared up again vainly, horribly like a man trying to rise and stand and walk upright, after being deprived of his limbs.

The wild howling of the Picts shook the night, and I was sick where I crouched among the bushes, and fought an urge to retch. I understood the meaning of this ghastly ceremony now. I had heard tales of it. By black, primordial sorcery that spawned and throve in the depths of this black primal forest, that painted shaman had trnasferred the soul of a captured enemy into the foul body of a serpent. It was the revenge of a fiend. And the screaming of the blood-mad Picts was like the yelling of all hell's demons.

And the victims writhed and agonized side by side, the man and the serpent, until a sword flashed in the hand of the shaman and both heads fell together — and gods, it was the serpent's trunk which but quivered and jerked a little and then lay still, and the man's body which rolled and knotted and thrashed like a beheaded snake. A deathly faintness and weakness took hold of me, for what white man could watch such black diabolism unmoved? And these painted savages, smeared with war-paint, howling and posturing and triumphing over the ghastly doom of a foe, seemed not humans at all to me, but foul fiends of the black world whom it was a duty and an obligation to slay.

The shaman sprang up and faced the ring of warriors, and ripping off his mask, threw up his head and howled like a wolf. And as the firelight fell full on his face, I recognized him, and with that recognition all horror and revulsion gave place to red rage, and all thought of personal peril and the recollection of my mission, which was my first obligation, was swept away. For that shaman was old Teyanoga of the South Hawks, he who burnt alive my friend Jon Galter's son.

In the lust of my hate I acted almost instinctively — whipped up my bow, nothced an arrow and loosed, all in an instant. The firelight was uncertain, but the range was no great, and we of the Westermarck live by twang of bow. Old Teyanoga yowled like a cat and reeled back and his warriors howled with amaze to see a shaft quivering suddenly in his breast. The tall, light-skinned warrior wheeled, and for the first time I saw his face — and Mitra, he was a white man!

The horrid shock of that surprise held me paralyzed for a moment and had almost undone me. For the Picts instantly sprang up and rushed into the forest like panthers, seeking the foe who fired that arrow. They had reached the first fringe of bushes when I jerked out of my spell of amaze and horror, and sprang up and raced away in the darkness, ducking and dodging among trees which I avoided more by instinct than otherwise, for it was dark as ever. But I knew the Picts could not strike my trail, but must hunt as blindly as I fled.

And presently, as I ran northward, behind me I heard a hideous howling whose blood-mad fury was enough to freeze the blood even of a forest-runner. And I believed that they had plucked my arrow from the shaman's breast and discovered it to be a white man's shaft. That would bring them after me with fiercer blood-lust than ever.

I fled on, my heart pounding from fear and excitement, and the horror of the nightmare I had witnessed. And that a white man, a Hyborian, should have stood there as a welcome and evidently honored guest – for he was armed – I had seen knife and hatchet at his belt – was so monstrous I wondered if, after all, the whole thing were a nightmare. For never before had a white man observed The Dance of the Changing Serpent save as a prisoner, or a spy, as I had. And what monstrous thing it portended I knew not, but I was shaken with foreboding and horror at the thought.

And because of my horror I went more carelessly than is my wont, seeking haste at the expense of stealth, and occasionally blundering into a tree I could have avoided had I taken more care. And I doubt not it was the noise of this blundering progress which brought the Pict upon me, for he could not have seen me in that pitch-darkness.

Behind me sounded no more yells, but I knew that the Picts were ranging like fire-eyed wolves through the forest, spreading in a vast semi-circle and combing it as they ran. That they had not picked up my trail was evidenced by their silence, for they never yell except when they believe only a short dash is ahead of them, and feel sure of their prey.

The warrior who heard the sounds of my flight could not have been one of that party, for he was too far ahead of them. He must have been a scout ranging the forest to guard against his comrades being surprized from the north.

At any rate he heard me running close to him, and came like a devil of the black night. I knew of him first only by the swift faint pad of his naked feet, and when I wheeled I could not even make out the dim bulk of him, but only heard the soft thudding of those inexorable feet coming at me unseen in the darkness.

They see like cats in the dark, and I know he saw well enough to locate me, though doubtless I was only a dim blur in the darkness. But my blindly upswung hatchet met his falling knife and he impaled himself on my knife as he lunged in, his death-yell ringing like a peal of doom under the forest-roof. And it was answered by a ferocious clamor to the south, only a few hundred yards away, and then they were racing through the bushes giving tongue like wolves, certain of their quarry.

I ran for it in good earnest now, abandoning stealth entirely for the sake of speed, and trusting to luck that I would not dash out my brains against a tree-stem in the darkness.

But here the forest opened up somewhat; there was no underbrush, and something almost like light filtered in through the branches, for the clouds were clearing a little. And through this forest I fled like a damned soul pursued by demons, hearing the yells at first rising higher and higher in blood-thirsty triumph, then edged with anger and rage as they grew fainter and fell away behind me, for in a straight-away race no Pict can match the long legs of a white forest-runner. The desperate risk was that there were other scouts or war-parties ahead of me who could easily cut me off, hearing my flight; but it was a risk I had to take. But no painted figures started up like phantoms out of the shadows ahead of me, and presently, through the thickening growth that betokened the nearness of a creek, I saw a glimmer through the trees far ahead of me and knew it was the light of Fort Kwanyara, the southern-most outpost of Schohira.

CHAPTER 2

Perhaps, before continuing with this chronicle of the bloody years, it might be well were I to give an account of myself, and the reason why I traversed the Pictish Wilderness, by night and alone.

My name is Gault Hagar's son. I was born in the province of Conajohara. But when I was ten years of age, the Picts broke over Black River and stormed Fort Tuscelan and slew all within save one man, and drove all the settlers of the province east of Thunder River. Conajohara became again part of the Wilderness, haunted only by wild beasts and wild men. The people of Conajohara scattered throughout the Westermarck, in Schohira, Conawaga, or Oriskawny, but many of them went southward and settled near Fort Thandara, an isolated outpost on the Warhorse River, my family among them. There they were later joined by other settlers for whom the older provinces were too thickly inhabited, and presently there grew up the district known as the Free Province of Thandara, because it was not like the other provinces, royal grants to great lords east of the marches and settled by them, but cut out of the wilderness by the pioneers themselves without aid of the Aquilonian nobility. We paid no taxes to any baron. Our governor was not appointed by any lord, but we elected him ourselves, from our own people, and he was responsible only to the king. We manned and built our forts ourselves, and sustained ourselves in war as in peace. And Mitra knows war was a constant state of affairs, for there was never peace between us and our savage neighbors, the wild Panther, Alligator and Otter tribes of Picts.

But we throve, and seldom questioned what went on east of the marches in the kingdom whence our grandsires had come. But at last events in Aquilonia did touch upon us in the wilderness. Word came of civil war, and a fighting man risen to wrest the throne from the ancient dynasty. And sparks from that conflagration set the frontier ablaze, and turned neighbor against neighbor and brother against brother. And it was because knights in their gleaming steel were fighting and slaying on the plains of Aquilonia that I was hastening alone through the stretch of wilderness that separated Thandara from Schohira, with news that might well change the destiny of all the Westermarck.

Fort Kwanyara was a small outpost, a square fortress of hewn logs with a palisade; on the bank of Knife Creek. I saw its banner streaming against the pale rose of the morning sky, and noted that only the ensign of the province floated there. The royal standard that should have risen above it, flaunting the golden serpent, was not in evidence. That might mean much, or nothing. We of the frontier are careless about the delicate punctillios of custom and etiquet which mean so much to the knights beyond the marches.

I crossed Knife Creek in the early dawn, wading through the shallows, and was challenged by a picket on the other bank, a tall man in the buckskins of a ranger. When he knew I was from Thandara: "By Mitra!" quoth he, "your business must be urgent, that you cross the wilderness instead of taking the longer road."

For Thandara was separated from the other provinces, as I have said, and the Little Wilderness lay between it and the Bossonian marches; but a safe road ran through it into the marches and thence to the other provinces but it was a long and tedius road.

Then he asked for news from Thandara, but I told him I knew little of the latest events, having just returned from a long scout into the country of the Ottermen; which was a lie, but I had no way of knowing Schohira's political color, and was not inclined to betray my own until I knew. Then I asked him if Hakon Strom's son was in Fort Kwanyara, and he told me that the man I sought was not in the fort, but was at the town of Schondara, which lay a few miles east of the fort.

"I hope Thandara declares for Conan," said he with an oath, "for I tell you plainly it is our political complection. And it is my cursed luck which keeps me here with the handful of rangers who watch the border for raiding Picts. I would give my bow and hunting shirt to be with our army which lies even now at Thenitea on Ogaha Creek waiting the onslaught of Brocas of Torh with his damned renegades."

I said naught but was astounded. This was news indeed. For the Baron of Torh was lord of Conawaga, not Schohira, whose patroon was Lord Thasperas of Kormon.

"Where is Thasperas?" I asked, and the ranger answered, a thought shortly: "Away in Aquilonia, fighting for Conan." And he looked at me narrowly as if he had begun to wonder if I were a spy.

"Is there a man in Schohira," I began, "who has such connections with the Picts that he dwells, naked and painted among them, and attends their ceremonies of blood-feast and —"

I checked myself at the fury that contorted the Schohiran's features.

"Damn you," says he, choking with passion, "what is your purpose in coming here to insult us thus?"

And indeed, to call a man a renegade was the direst insult that could be offered along the Westermarck, though I had not meant it in that way. But I saw the man was ignorant of any knowledge concerning the renegade I had seen, and not wishing to give out information, I merely told him that he misunderstood my meaning.

"I understand it well enough," said he, shaking with passion. "But for your dark skin and southern accent I would deem you a spy from Conawaga. But spy or no, you can not insult the men of Schohira in such manner. Were I not on military duty I would lay down my weapon-belt and show you what manner of men we breed in Schohira."

"I want no quarrel," said I. "But I am going to Schondara, where it will not be hard for you to find me, if you so desire."

"I will be there anon," quoth he grimly. "I am Storm Grom's son and they know me in Schohira."

I left him striding his post along the bank, and fingering his knife hilt and hatchet as if he itched to try their edge on my head, and I swung wide of the small fort to avoid other scouts or pickets. For in these troublous times suspicion might fall on me as a spy very easily. Nay, this Storm Grom's son was beginning to turn such thoughts in his thick noddle when they were swept away by his personal resentment at what he mistook for a slur. And having quarreled with me, his sense of personal honor would not allow him to arrest me on suspicion of being a spy – even had he thought of it. In ordinary times none would think of halting or questioning a white man crossing the border – but everything was in a mad whirl now – it must be, if the patroon of Conawaga was invading the domain of his neighbors.

The forest had been cleared about the fort for a few hundred yards in each direction, forming a solid green wall. I kept within this wall as I skirted the clearing, and met no one, even when I crossed several paths leading from the fort. I avoided clearings and farms. I headed eastward and the sun was not high in the heavens when I sighted the roofs of Schondara.

The forest ran to within less than half a mile of the town, which was a handsome one for a frontier village, with neat houses mostly of squared logs, some painted, but also some fine frame buildings which is something we have not in Thandara. But there was not so much as a ditch or a palisade about the village, which was strange to me. For we of Thandara build our dwelling places for defense as much as shelter, and while there is not a village in the width and breadth of the province, yet every cabin is like a tiny fort.

Off to the right of the village stood a fort, in the midst of a meadow, with palisade and ditch, somewhat larger than Fort Kwanyara, but I saw few heads moving above the parapet, either helmeted or capped. And only the spreading winged hawk of Schohira flapped on the standard. And I wondered why, if Schohira were for Conan, they did not fly the banner he had chosen – the golden lion on a black field, the standard of the regiment he commanded as a mercenary general of Aquilonia.

Away to the left, at the edge of the forest I saw a large house of stone set amidst gardens and orchards, and knew it for the estate of Lord Valerian, the richest land-owner in western Schohira. I had never seen the man, but knew he was wealthy and powerful. But now the Hall, as it was called, seemed deserted.

The town seemed curiously deserted, likewise; at least of men, though there were women and children in plenty, and it seemed to me that the men had assembled their families here for safety. I saw few able-bodied men. As I went up the street many eyes followed me suspiciously, but none spoke except to reply briefly to my questions.

At the tavern only a few old men and cripples huddled about the ale-stained tables and conversed in low tones, all conversation ceasing as I loomed in the doorway in my worn buckskins, and all turned to stare at me silently.

More significant silence when I asked for Hakon Strom's son, and the host told me that Hakon was ridden to Thenitea shortly after sun-up, where the militia-army lay encamped, but would return shortly. So being hungry and weary, I ate a meal in the tap-room, aware of those questioning eyes fixed upon me, and then lay down in a corner on a bear skin the host fetched for me, and slept. And was so slumbering when Hakon Strom's son returned, close upon sun-set.

He was a tall man, rangy and broad-shouldered, like most Westlanders, and clad in buckskin hunting shirt and fringed leggins and moccasins like myself. Half a dozen rangers were with him, and they sat them down at a board close to the door and watched him and me over the rims of their ale jacks.

When I named myself and told him I had word for him, he looked at me closely, and bade me sit with him at a table in the corner where mine host brought us ale foaming in leathern jacks.

"Has no word come through of the state of affairs in Thandara?" I asked.

"No sure word; only rumors."

"Very well," said I. "I bring you word from Brant Drago's son, governor of Thandara, and the council of captains, and by this sign you shall know me for a true man." And so saying I dipped my finger in the foamy ale and with it drew a symbol on the table, and instantly erased it. He nodded, his eyes blazing with interest.

"This is the word I bring you," quoth I: "Thandara has declared for Conan and stands ready to aid his friends and defy his enemies."

At that he smiled joyfully and grasped my brown hand warmly with his own rugged fingers.

"Good!" he exclaimed. "But it is no more than I expected."

"What man of Thandara could forget Conan?" said I. "Nay, I was but a child in Conajohara, but I remember him when he was a forest-runner and a scout there. When his rider came into Thandara telling us that Poitain was in revolt, with Conan striking for the throne, and asking our support – he asked no volunteers for his army, merely our loyalty – we sent him one word: 'We have not forgotten Conajohara.' Then came the Baron Attelius over the marches against us, but we ambushed him in the Little Wilderness and cut his army to pieces. And now I think we need fear no invasion in Thandara."

"I would I could say as much for Schohira," he said grimly. "Baron Thasperas sent us word that we could do as we chose – he has declared for Conan and joined the rebel army. But he did not demand western levies. Nay, both he and Conan know the Westermarck needs every man it has to guard the border.

"He removed his troops from the forts, however, and we manned them with our own foresters. There was some little skirmishing among ourselves, especially in the towns like Coyaga, where dwell the land-holders, for some of them held to Namedides – well, these loyalists either fled away to Conawaga with their retainers, or else surrendered and gave their pledge to remain neutral in their castles, like Lord Valerian of Schondara. The loyalists which fled swore to return and cut all our throats. And presently Lord Brocas marched over the border.

"In Conawaga the land-owners and Brocas are for Namedides, and we have heard pitiful tales of their treatment of the common people who favor Conan."

I nodded, not surprised. Conawaga was the largest, richest and most thickly settled province in all the Westermarck, and it had a comparatively large, and very powerful class of titled land-holders – which we have not in Thandara, and by the favor of Mitra, never shall.

"It is an open invasion for conquest," said Hakon. "Brocas commanded us to swear loyalty to Namedides – the dog. I think the black-jowled fool plots to subdue all the Westermarck and rule it as Namedides' viceroy. With an army of Aquilonian men-at-arms, Bossonian archers, Conawaga loyalists, and Schohira renegades, he lies at Coyaga, ten miles beyond Ogaha Creek. Thenitea is full of refugees from the eastern country he has devastated.

"We do not fear him, though we are outnumbered. He must cross Ogaha Creek to strike us, and we have fortified the west bank and blocked the road against his cavalry."

"That touches upon my mission," I said. "I am authorized to offer the services of a hundred and fifty Thandaran rangers. We are all of one mind in Thandara and fight no internal wars; and we can spare that many men from our war with the Panther Picts."

"That will be good news for the commandant of Fort Kwanyara!"

"What?" quoth I. "Are *you* not the commandant?"

"Nay," said he, "it is my brother Dirk Strom's son."

"Had I known that I would have given my message to him," I said. "Brant Drago's son thought you commanded Kwanyara. However, it does not matter."

"Another jack of ale," quoth Hakon, "and we'll start for the fort so that Dirk shall hear your news first-hand. A plague on commanding a fort. A party of scouts is good enough for me."

And in truth Hakon was not the man to command an outpost or any large body of men, for he was too reckless and hasty, though a brave man and a gay rogue.

"You have but a skeleton force left to watch the border, "I said. "What of the Picts?"

"They keep the peace to which they swore," answered he. "For some months there has been peace along the border, except for the usual skirmishing between individuals of both races."

"Valerian Hall seemed deserted."

"Lord Valerian dwells there alone except for a few servants. Where his fighting men have gone, none knows. But he has sent them off. If he had not given his pledge we would have felt it necessary to place him under guard, for he is one of the few white men to whom the Picts give heed. If it had entered his head to stir them up against our borders we might be hard put to it to defend ourselves against them on one side and Brocas on the other.

"The Hawks, Wildcats and Turtles listen when Valerian speaks, and he has even visited the towns of the Wolf Picts and come away alive."

If that were true that were strange indeed, for all men knew the ferocity of the great confederacy of allied clans known as the Wolf tribe which dwelt in the west beyond the hunting grounds of the three lesser tribes he had named. Mostly they held aloof from the frontier, but the threat of their hatred was ever a menace along the borders of Schohira.

Hakon looked up as a tall man in trunk-hose, boots and scarlet cloak entered the taproom.

"There is Lord Valerian now," he said.

I stared, started and was on my feet instantly.

"That man?" I ejaculated. "I saw that man last night beyond the border, in a camp of the Hawks, watching the Dance of the Changing Snake!"

Valerian heard me and he whirled, going pale. His eyes blazed like those of a panther.

Hakon sprang up too.

"What are you saying?" he cried. "Lord Valerian gave his pledge –"

"I care not!" I exclaimed fiercely, striding forward to confront the tall noble. "I saw him where I lay hidden among the tamarack. I could not mistake that hawk-like face. I tell you he was there, naked and painted like a Pict –"

"You lie, damn you!" cried Valerian, and whipping aside his cloak he caught at the hilt of his sword. But before he could draw it I closed with him and bore him to the floor, where he caught at my throat with both hands, blaspheming like a madman. Then there was a swift stamp of feet, and men were dragging us apart, grasping my lord firmly, who stood white and panting with fury, still clutching my neckcloth which had been torn away from my throat in the struggle.

"Loose me, you dogs!" he raved. "Take your peasant hands from me! I'll cleave this liar to the chin —"

"Here is no lie," I said more calmly. "I lay in the tamarack last night and watched while old Teyanoga dragged a Raven chief's soul from his body and forced it into that of a tree-serpent. It was my arrow which struck down the shaman. And I saw you there — you, a white man, naked and painted, accepted as one of the clan."

"If this be true —" began Hakon.

"It is true, and there is your proof!" I exclaimed. "Look there! On his bosom!"

His doublet and shirt had been torn open in the scuffle, and there, dim on his naked breast, showed the outline of the white skull which the Picts paint only when they mean war against the whites. He had sought to wash it off his skin, but Pictish paint stains strongly.

"Disarm him," said Hakon, white to the lips.

"Give me my neckcloth," I demanded, but his lordship spat at me, and thrust the cloth inside his shirt.

"When it is returned to you it shall be knotted in a hangman's noose about your rebel neck," he snarled.

Hakon seemed undecided.

"Let us take him to the fort," I said. "Give him in custody of the commander. It was for no good purpose he took part in the Dance of the Snake. Those Picts were painted for battle. That symbol on his breast means he intended to take part in the war for which they danced."

"But great Mitra, this is incredible!" exclaimed Hakon. "A white man, loosing those painted devils on his friends and neighbors?"

My lord said naught. He stood there between the men who grasped his arms, livid, his thin lips drawn back in a snarl that bared his teeth, but all hell burned like yellow fire in his eyes where I seemed to sense lights of madness.

But Hakon was uncertain. He dared not release Valerian, and he feared what the effect might be on the people if they saw the lord being led a captive to the fort.

"They will demand the reason," he argued, "and when they learn he has been dealing with the Picts in their war-paint, a panic might well ensue. Let us lock him into the gaol until we can bring Dirk here to question him."

"It is dangerous to compromise with a situation like this," I answered bluntly. "But it is for you to decide. You are in command here."

So we took his lordship out the back door, secretly, and it being dusk by that time, reached the gaol without being noticed by the people, who indeed stayed indoors mostly. The gaol was a small affair of logs, somewhat apart from the town. with four cells, and one only occupied, that by a fat rogue who had been imprisoned overnight for drunkenness and fighting in the street. He stared to see our prisoner. Not a word said Lord Valerian as Hakon locked the grilled door upon him, and detailed one of the men to stand guard. But a demon fire burned in his dark eyes as if behind the mask of his pale face he were laughing at us with fiendish triumph.

"You place only one man on guard?" I asked Hakon.

"Why more?" said he. "Valerian can not break out, and there is no one to rescue him."

It seemed to me that Hakon was prone to take too much for granted, but after all, it was none of my affair, so I said no more.

Then Hakon and I went to the fort, and there I talked with Dirk Strom's son, the commander, who was in command of the town, in the absence of Jon Storm's son, the governor appointed by Lord Thasperas, who was now in command of the militia-army which lay at Thenitea. He looked sober indeed when he heard my tale, and said he come to the gaol and question Lord Valerian as soon as his duties permitted, though he had little belief that my lord would talk, for he came of a stubborn and haughty breed. He was glad to hear of the men Thandara offered him, and told me that he could find a man to return to Thandara accepting the offer, if I wished to remain in Schohira awhile, which I did. Then I returned to the tavern with Hakon, for it was our purpose to sleep there that night, and set out for Thenitea in the morning. Scouts kept the Schohirans posted on the movements of Brocas, and Hakon, who had been in their camp that day, said Brocas showed no signs of moving against us, which made me believe that he was waiting for Valerian to lead his Picts against the border. But Hakon still doubted, in spite of all I had told him, believing Valerian had but visited the Picts through friendliness as he often did. But I pointed out that no white man, however friendly to the Picts, was ever allowed to witness such a ceremony as the Dance of the Snake; he would have to be a blood-member of the clan.

CHAPTER 3

I awakened suddenly and sat up in bed. My window was open, both shutters and pane, for coolness, for it was an upstairs room, and there was no tree near by which a thief might gain access. But some noise had awakened me, and now as I stared at the window, I saw the star-lit sky blotted out by a bulky, misshapen figure. I swung my legs around off the bed, demanding to know who it was, and groping for my hatchet, but the thing was on me with frightful speed and before I could even rise something was around my neck, choking and strangling me. Thrust almost against my face there was a dim frightful visage, but all I could make out in the darkness was a pair of flaming red eyes, and a peaked head. My nostrils were filled with a bestial reek.

I caught one of the thing's wrists and it was hairy as an ape's, and thick with iron muscles. But then I had found the haft of my hatchet and I lifted it and split that misshapen skull with one blow. It fell clear of me and I sprang up, gagging and gasping, and quivering in every limb. I found flint, steel and tinder, and struck a light and lit a candle, and glared wildly at the creature lying on the floor.

In form it was like a man, gnarled and misshapen, covered with thick hair. Its nails were long and black, like the talons of a beast, and its chinnless, low-browed head was like that of an ape. The thing was a *Chakan*, one of those semi-human beings which dwell deep in the forests.

There came a knocking on my door and Hakon's voice called to know what the trouble was, so I bade him enter. He rushed in, axe in hand, his eyes widened at the sight of the thing on the floor.

"A *Chakan!*" he whispered. "I have seen them, far to the west, smelling out trails through the forests – the damned bloodhounds! What is that in his fingers?"

A chill of horror crept along my spine as I saw the creature still clutched a neck cloth in his fingers – the cloth which he had tried to knot like a hangman's noose about my neck.

"I have heard that Pictish shaman catch these creatures and tame them and use them to smell out their enemies," he said slowly. "But how could Lord Valerian so use one?"

"I know not," I answered. "But that neck cloth was given to the beast, and according to its nature it smelled my trail out and sought to break my neck. Let us go to the gaol, and quickly."

Hakon roused his rangers and we hurried there; and found the guard lying before the open door of Valerian's empty cell with his throat cut. Hakon stood like one turned to stone, and then a faint call made us turn and we saw the white face of the drunkard peering at us from the next cell.

"He's gone," quoth he; "Lord Valerian's gone. Hark' ee: an hour agone while I lay on my bunk, I was awakened by a sound outside, and saw a strange dark woman come out of the shadows and walk up to the guard. He lifted his bow and bade her halt, but she laughed at him, staring into his eyes and he became as one in a trance. He stood staring stupidly – and Mitra, she took his own knife from his girdle and cut his throat, and he fell down and died. Then she took the keys from his belt and opened the door, and Valerian came out, and laughed like a devil out of hell, and kissed the wench, and she laughed with him. And she was not alone, for *something* lurked in the shadows behind her – some vague, monstrous being that never came into the light of the lanthorn hanging over the door.

"I heard her say best to kill the fat drunkard in the next cell, and by Mitra I was so nigh dead of fright I knew not if I were even alive. But Valerian said I was dead drunk, and I could have kissed him for that word. So they went away and as they went he said he would send her companion on a mission, and then they would go to a cabin on Lynx Creek, and there meet his retainers who had been hiding in the forest ever since he sent them from Valerian Hall. He said that Teyanoga would come to them there and they would cross the border and go among the Picts, and bring them back to cut all our throats."

Hakon looked livid in the lanthorn light.

"Who is this woman?" I asked curiously.

"His half-breed Pictish mistress," he said. "Half Hawk-Pict and half-Ligurean. I have heard of her. They call her the witch of Skandaga. I have never seen her, never before credited the tales whispered of her and Lord Valerian. But it is the truth."

"I thought I had slain old Teyanoga," I muttered. "The old fiend must bear a charmed life – I saw my shaft quivering in his breast. What now?"

"We must go to the hut on Lynx Creek and slay them all," said Hakon. "If they loose the Picts on the border hell will be to pay. We can spare no men from the fort or the town. We are enough. I know not how many men there will be on Lynx Creek, and I do not care. We will take them by surprize."

We set out at once through the starlight. The land lay silent, lights twinkling dimly in the houses. To the westward loomed the black forest, silent, primordial, a brooding threat to the people who dared it.

We went in single file, bows strung and held in our left hands, hatchets swinging in our right hands. Our moccasins made no sound in the dew-wet grass. We melted into the woods and struck a trail that wound among oaks and alders. Here we strung out with some fifteen feet between each man, Hakon leading, and presently we dipped down into a grassy hollow and saw light streaming faintly from the cracks of shutters that covered a cabin's windows.

Hakon halted us and whispered for the men to wait, while we crept forward and spied upon them. We stole forward and surprized the sentry – a Schohiran renegade, who must have heard our stealthy approach but for the wine which staled his breath. I shall never forget the fierce hiss of satisfaction that breathed between Hakon's clenched teeth as he drove his knife into the villian's heart. We left the body hidden in the tall rank grass and stole up to the very wall of the cabin and dared to peer in at a crack. There was Valerian, with his fierce eyes blazing, and a dark, wildly beautiful girl in doe-skin loin-clout and beaded moccasins, and her blackly burnished hair bound back by a gold band, curiously wrought. And there were half a dozen Schohiran renegades, sullen rogues in the woollen breeches and jerkins of farmers, with cutlasses at their belts, three forest-runners in buckskins, wild-looking men, and half a dozen Gundermen guards, compactly-built men with yellow hair cut square and confined under steel caps, corselets of chain mail, and polished leg-pieces. They were girt with swords and daggers – yellow-haired men with fair complections and steely eyes and an accent differing greatly from the natives of the Westermarck. They were sturdy fighters, ruthless and well-disciplined, and very popular as guardsmen among the land-owners of the frontier.

Listening there we heard them all laughing and conversing, Valerian boastful of his escape and swearing that he had sent a visitor to that cursed Thandaran that should do his proper business for him; the renegades sullen and full of oaths and curses for their former friends; the forest-runners silent and attentive; the Gundermen careless and jovial, which joviality thinly masked their utterly ruthless natures. And the half-breed girl, whom they called Kwarada, laughed, and plagued Valerian, who seemed grimly amused. And Hakon trembled with fury as we listened to him boasting how he meant to rouse the Picts and lead them across the border to smite the Schohirans in the back while Brocas attacked from Coyaga.

Then we heard a light patter of feet and hugged the wall close, and saw the door open, and seven painted Picts entered, horrific figures in paint and feathers. They were led by old Teyanoga, whose breast-muscles were bandaged, whereby I knew my shaft had but fleshed itself in those heavy muscles. And wondered if the old demon were really a were-wolf which could not be killed by mortal weapons as he boasted and many believed.

We lay close there, Hakon and I, and heard of Teyanoga say that the Hawks, Wildcats and Turtles dared not strike across the border unless an alliance with the powerful Wolfmen could be struck up, for they feared that the Wolves might ravage their country while they fought the Schohirans. Teyonoga said that the three lesser tribes met the Wolves on the edge of Ghost Swamp for a council; and that the Wolves would abide by the counsel of the Wizard of the Swamp.

So Valerian said they would go to the Ghost Swamp and see if they could not persuade the Wizard to induce the Wolves to join the others. At that Hakon told me to crawl back and get the others, and I saw it was in his mind that we should attack, outnumbered as we were, but so fired was I by the infamous plot to which we had listened that I was as eager as he. I stole back and brought the others, and as soon as he heard us coming, he sprang up and ran at the door to beat it in with his war-axe.

At the same instant others of us burst in the shutters and poured arrows into the room, striking down some, and set the cabin on fire.

They were thrown into confusion, and made no attempt to hold the cabin. The candles were upset and went out, but the fire lent a dim glow. They rushed the door and some were slain then, and others as we grappled with them. But presently all fled into the woods except those we slew, Gundermen, renegades and painted Picts, but Valerian and the girl were still in the cabin. Then they came forth and she laughed and hurled something on the ground that burst and blinded us with a foul smoke, through which they escaped.

All but four of our men had been slain in the desperate fighting, but we started instantly in pursuit, sending back one of the wounded men to warn the town.

The trail led into the wilderness.

The Black Stranger
Synopsis A

Conan the Cimmerian, vengefully following a Pictish war-party which had raided and killed among the Aquilonian settlements on Black River, was captured by Picts, and carried by them to their far western home-land. The ferocious Cimmerian killed the chief and escaped, fleeing toward the west, pursued by the enraged Picts. Throwing them off the trail, he discovered a path that wound up a cliff and following it, discovered a cave where stood a great ebony table about which sat dead men. He stepped into the cave and was instantly fighting for his life.

On a wide stretch of beach, backed against a deep forest, stood the settlement of a Zingara nobleman who had fled with his servant and his neice and taken refuge there. His retainers had built log houses and surrounded them with a stockade. None ventured far into the forest because they feared the ferocious Picts. But the neice was seated on the sand south of the promontory which rose beyond the bay, when her companion, a flaxen-haired Ophirean waif she had picked up, came running across the sand, naked and dripping from a plunge into the ocean, and cried that a ship was coming. The Zingara girl saw as she went up the gentle slope, and with the younger girl hurried to the fort, as they called it. The nobleman instantly called in his retainers from the fishing boats and the tiny fields along the forest edge, and ran up the banner of Zingara. The ship sailed into the bay and broke out the flag of the Barachan pirates, and a Zingaran recognized the ship as that of a noted pirate. The pirates came ashore and attacked the fortress, and had almost swarmed over the stockade, when another ship hove in sight, and broke out the colors of Zingara. But the pirate had already recognized it as the craft of a Zingaran buccaneer, and fearing to be trapped between two foes, he took his men aboard and sailed away up the coast.

The Zingaran anchored and came ashore with most of his men, but the nobleman distrusted him and refused to allow him to bring his men in the stockade. They camped on the beach, the Zingaran sent them out wine, and the buccaneer came into the nobleman's hall. He told the buccaneer that his ship had been wrecked in a storm, and that the increasing menace of the Picts made it imperative that he take his band away. The buccaneer offered to take them all off in return for a treasure which he said was hidden in the vicinity – and for the hand of the neice. The nobleman refused that angrily, and denied all knowledge of the treasure. The buccaneer than told of a treasure hidden by a pirate centuries before, or a century, at least. He offered to have his men aid the nobleman's men in finding the treasure. Then they would sail away to some foreign port, where he would marry the neice and give up his wild ways. While they were arguing, the neice stole away to find the little Ophirean girl had slipped out and returned to the beach to find a prized bracelet. She brought her into the banquet hall, and the girl informed the nobleman that she had seen a black man land on the beach in a queer craft. The nobleman instantly seemed seized with madness, and had the girl cruelly whipped, until he saw she was telling the truth. Then he agreed to the terms set forth by the buccaneer. The neice took the child and retired in horror to her room; she and the younger girl were about to flee in desperation to the woods, when they heard stealthy footsteps outside the door which terrified them. The child said it was the black man she had seen come ashore. Before dawn a terrible storm arose which wrecked the buccaneer's ship on the rocky shore.

At dawn, just as the storm was clearing away, far up the coast a pirate met a stranger on the beach and was killed by him; the stranger took a map from his girdle.

The nobleman swore it was the black stranger who had raised the storm, a curse on his house, and the buccaneer said his men would build a ship. But just then the pirate sailed into the bay and demanded a parley. Protected by a point of land, he had ridden out the storm. He thought a Zingaran had killed his mate and stolen the map; he offered a trade; if they would give him the map, he would take off as many as he could and set them ashore some safe place. But while they argued Conan entered, and told them he had killed the man and stolen and map, and destroyed it. He did not need it, because he had found the treasure. He offered the plan: he and the captains would go after the treasure, leaving their men on the beach. They would divide it equally. The pirate was short of supplies. The nobleman would give them supplies; the pirate would take him off in the ship. The nobleman and the buccaneer would be left to build their own ship. After much wrangling, Conan and the sea-rovers made through the woods to the cave he had discovered where he hoped to trap them in the poison gas that filled it; but one of the nobleman's men had hurried before them and was found dead in it, and the pirate accused Conan of trying to get he and the buccaneer out of the way to seize his ship and crew. In the fight that followed, the Picts attacked them, infuriated by the black stranger having murdered a Pict and stuck a gold chain stolen by the black man that night in the fort from the nobleman.

Conan joined forces with the others and they fought their way back to the fort, where they were besieged by hundreds of howling Picts. The black man got among them and killed a buccaneer, whereupon buccaneers and pirates fell to fighting and the Picts swarmed over the wall. Conan, running into the hall to rescue the girls, saw the nobleman hanging from a beam, and the black man gloating over him. He hurled a chair and knocked the thing down, then seized the girls and took shelter in a corner of the stockade. The pirate and buccaneer were killed in the red massacre; and Conan, with the girls, got away and fled in the pirate ship anchored in a bay on the coast.

The Black Stranger
Synopsis B

Conan the Cimmerian, pursued by savages in the forests near the western coast of the Pictish Wilderness, takes refuge in a cavern which contains the bodies of Tranicos, a pirate admiral, and his eleven captains, and the treasure hidden by them a hundred years before.

On the coast, not far from the cavern, stands a small settlement founded by Count Valenso Korzetta, a Zingaran nobleman who has fled to this naked land to escape a mysterious enemy. The destruction of his galleon by a storm has marooned the whole party at that spot.

Strom, a Barachan pirate, searching for the treasure of Tranicos, arrives in the bay, and believing Valenso to be in possession of the treasure, attacks the fort. While the fight is in progress another ship sails into the bay, commanded by Black Zarono, a buccaneer, also hunting the treasure. Fearing to be caught between two enemies Strom sails away and takes refuge in a cove several miles distant.

Zarono strikes a truce with Valenso, and makes him a proposal that night in the fort, having learned that Valenso knows nothing about the treasure of Tranicos, which Strom and Zarono both know is hidden somewhere near the bay. Zarono proposes that he and the Count join forces, secure the treasure and then sail to some civilized country in Zarono's ship. In return Zarono demands the hand of Valenso's neice, Belesa. The Count refuses, furiously, when he is thrown into a state of panic by Tina, Belesa's young protege, who tells him of a strange black man who has come out of the sea, and taken refuge in the forest. Valenso almost goes mad with fear, and agrees to Zarono's proposal, despite his neice's horrified protests.

Later in the night Belesa sees the black man stealing through the corridors of the fort, and realizes that he is no natural human being.

A storm, raised by the black man's sorcery, destroy's Zarono's ship.

The Man-Eaters of Zamboula
Synopsis

Conan, who had been living with a wandering tribe of Zuagirs, Shemitish nomads, wandered into Zamboula, a strange, hybrid city in the desert on the disputed border of Stygia and the Hyrkanian domains. Zamboula was inhabited by Stygians, Shemites, and many mixed breeds, and ruled over by the Hyrkanians. A satrap ruled there, one Jungir Khan, with Hyrkanian soldiers. The city contained and was adjacent too many oases with palm groves. Conan, intending to spend the night at the tavern of one Aram Baksh, was warned by a Shemite tribesman that other desert men and travellers had spent the night at Aram's house, and never been seen again. He said that no bodies had ever been found on the place, but beyond the city's outskirts – the city was not wall – there was a hollow with a pit in it where charred human bones had been found. The Shemite believed Aram was was a devil in disguise who had traffic with demons of the desert. Conan gave no heed to the warning, and went to Aram's house, which was on the outskirts of the city. Aram gave him a room opening onto a street which ran directly into the desert between groves of palms. During the night Conan was awakened by the stealthy opening of the one door, and sprang up to cut down a huge black slave who had stolen into his room. He was a cannibal slave from Darfar, far to the south, and Conan realized that Aram was selling his guests to these beasts. Go into the street, intending to enter the tavern by another door and cut Aram down, he saw three blacks skulking along the street with a captive girl. He attacked them and cut them down, and hid with the girl while a large band of them stole past, headed for the cooking-pit beyond the outskirts. The girl told him she was a dancing girl in the temple of Hanuman, that she loved a young Hyrkanian soldier, and was desired by the priest of Hanuman, a Stygian, Totrasmek. She said the priest by his magic had driven the young soldier, and he had tried to slay her. Fleeing from him she had been seized by the black who skulked about the streets at night, seizing and devouring all they could. As she ceased to talk the mad soldier came upon them and Conan knocked him senseless and bound him. Then lifting him, he followed her to a place in the city where a negro slave – not a cannibal – took charge of the senseless soldier, whom she had first searched for a ring and a great jewel – the only thing he would not give her. She had given him the drug given her by the priest to make him sleep, to steal this jewel. But it had driven him mad. She persuaded Conan to help her kill the priest. They went to the temple of Hanuman and entering, she tried to open the secret door behind the idol, but a hand seized her hair and dragged her through. A monstrous dwarf dragged her before Totrasmek who made her dance naked between four cobras conjured out of smoke. Conan, trying to reach the hidden chamber by another route, killed a giant executioner, and leaning through curtains, slew

Totrasmek. She search him after Conan had killed the dwarf, but did not find the jewel. Then she told Conan that she was a famous courtesan of the city, and the young soldier was in reality Jungir Khan, the satrap. They returned and found him dazed but sane, and she told Conan to return to the palace the next morning for his reward. He returned to the house of Aram and gave the tavern-keeper in the hands of the negroes, first slitting his tongue so he could not talk. Then he took to the desert, for he had known the girl and the soldier all along, and had himself stolen the jewel she sought.

Red Nails
Draft

The woman on the horse reined in her weary steed. It stood with its legs wide-braced, its head drooping, as if it found even the weight of the gold-tasseled, red leather bridle too heavy. The woman drew a booted foot out of the silver stirrup and swung down from the gold-worked saddle. She made the reins fast to a tree fork, and turned, hands on her hips, to survey her surroundings.

They were not inviting. Giant trees hemmed in the small pool where her horse had just drunk. Clumps of undergrowth limited the vision that quested under the sombre twilight of the lofty arches formed by intertwining branches. The woman shivered with a twitch of her magnificent shoulders, and then cursed.

She was tall, full-bosomed and large-limbed, with compact shoulders that denoted an unusual strength without detracting anything from the femininity of her appearance. In spite of her garb and bearing, she was all woman. Her garments were incongruous, in view of her present environs. Instead of a skirt she wore short, wide-legged silk breeches, which stopped a hand's breadth short of her knees and were upheld by a wide sash worn as a girdle. Flaring topped boots of soft leather came almost to her knees. A low-necked, wide-collared, wide-sleeved silk shirt completed her costume. On one shapely hip she wore a straight double-edged sword, and on the other a long dirk. Her unruly golden hair, cut even with her shoulders, was confined by a cloth-of-gold band.

Against the background of sombre, primitive forest she posed with unconscious picturesqueness, bizarre and out of place. She should have had a background of sea-clouds, masts, and wheeling gulls. There was the color of the sea in her wide eyes. And there should have been, because this was Valeria of the Red Brotherhood, whose deeds are retold in song and ballad wherever sea-farers gather.

She strove to pierce the sullen green roof of the arched branches and see the sky which presumably lay above, but presently gave it up with a muttered oath.

Leaving her horse where he stood she strode off in an eastward direction, glancing back toward the pool from time to time in order to fix her route in her mind. The silence of the forest depressed her. No birds sang in the lofty boughs, nor did any rustling in the underbrush indicate the presence of any small animals. She remembered that this silence had endured for many miles. For nearly a whole day she had travelled in a realm of absolute silence, broken only by the sounds of her own flight.

Ahead of her she saw an outcropping of dark, flint-like rock that sloped upward into what looked like a rugged crag rising among the trees. Its summit was lost to view amidst a cloud of encircling leaves. Perhaps its peak rose above the trees, and from it she could see what lay beyond – if indeed, anything lay beyond but this apparently illimitable forest through which she had ridden for so many days.

A narrow ridge formed a natural ramp that led upward. After she had ascended some fifty feet she could no longer see the ground because of the intervening leaves. The trunks of the trees did not crowd close to the crag, but their smaller branches extended about it, veiling it with their foliage. She climbed on awhile in leafy obscurity, neither able to see above or below her, but presently the leaves thinned, and she came out on a flat shelf-like summit and saw the forest roof stretching away under her feet. That roof – which looked like a floor from her vantage-point – was as impenetrable from above as from below. She glanced westward, in the direction from which she had come. She saw only the rolling green ocean stretching away and away, with only a vague blue line in the distance to hint of the hill-range she had crossed days before, to plunge into this leafy waste.

North and south the view was the same, though the blue hill-line was lacking in those direction. She looked eastward, and stiffened suddenly, as her foot struck something in the litter of fallen leaves which carpeted the low shelf. She kicked some of the leaves aside and looked down on the skeleton of a man. She ran an experienced eye over the bleached frame, but saw no broken bones or any sign of violence. The man seemed to have died a natural death, though why he should have climbed to this difficult pinnacle to die, she could not imagine.

She mounted to the peak and looked eastward. She stiffened. Off to the east, within a few miles, the forest thinned out and ceased abruptly, giving way to a bare plain, where only a few stunted trees grew. And in the midst of that plain rose the walls and towers of a man-made city. The girl swore in amazement. This passed belief. She would not have been surprized to have sighted human habitations of another sort – the beehive-shaped huts of the black people, or the cliff-dwellings of the mysterious brown race which legend declared inhabited some country of this unexplored region. But it was a startling surprize to see a walled city here so many long weeks marches from the nearest outposts of any sort of civilization.

Her thoughts were scattered by the rustling of the leaves below her. She wheeled like a cat, catching at her hilt; and then she froze motionless, staring wide-eyed at the man before her.

He was a tall, powerfully-built man, almost a giant in size. His garb was similar to hers, except that he wore a broad leather belt instead of a girdle. Broadsword and poniard hung from this belt.

"Conan, the Cimmerian!" ejaculated the woman. "What are *you* doing on my trail?"

He grinned hardly, and his fierce blue eyes burned with a light any woman could understand as they ran over her magnificent figure, lingering on the swell of

322

her splendid breasts beneath the light shirt, and the clear white flesh displayed between breeches and boot-tops.

"Why, hell, girl," he laughed, "don't you know? Haven't I made my admiration for you clear ever since I first saw you?"

"A stallion could have made it no clearer," she answered disdainfully. "But I never expected to encounter you so far from the ale-barrels and meat pots. Did you really follow me from Zarallo's camp, or were you whipped forth?"

He laughed at her scorn and flexed his mighty biceps.

"You know Zarallo didn't have enough knaves to whip me out of camp," he grinned. "Of course I followed you. Lucky thing for you, too, wench! When you knifed that fellow, you lost Zarallo's friendship, and you earned his brother's hatred."

"I know it," she replied sullenly. "But what else could I do? You know what my provocation was."

"Sure," he agreed. "If I'd been there, I'd have knifed him myself. But if a woman must live a man's life, she must expect such things."

Valeria stamped her booted foot and swore.

"Why will not men let me live a man's life?"

Again Conan's eager eyes roved her.

"Hell, girl, that's obvious! But you were wise to flee the camp. Zarallo would have had you skinned. The fellow's brother followed you; faster than you thought. He was not far behind you when I caught up with him. His horse was better than yours. He'd have caught you and cut your throat within a few more miles."

"Well?" she demanded.

"Well what?" he seemed puzzled.

"What of him?"

"Why, what do you suppose?" he demanded. "I killed him, of course, and left his carcass for the vultures. That delayed me, though, and I almost lost your trail when you crossed the rocky spurs of the hills. Otherwise I'd have caught up with you long ago."

"And now you think you'll drag me back to Zarallo's camp?" she sneered.

"You know better than that," he retorted. "Come, girl, don't be such a spitfire. I'm not like that fellow you knifed, and you know it."

"A penniless vagabond," she taunted.

He laughed at her.

"What are you? You haven't enough money to buy a new seat for your breeches. You're not fooling me with your disdain. You know my reputation. You know I've commanded bigger ships and more men than you ever did. As for being penniless – hell, what rover isn't at times? I've been rich a thousand times in my life, and I'll roll in plunder again. I've squandered enough gold in the sea-ports of the world to fill a galleon. You know that, too."

"Where are the fine ships and the bold lads you commanded, now?" she sneered.

"At the bottom of the sea, and in hell, mostly," he replied cheerfully. "The Zingaran royal squadron sank my last ship off Toragis – I burned the town of Valadelad, but they caught me before I could reach the Barachas. I was the only man on board who escaped with his life. That's why I joined Zarallo's Free Companions. But the gold is scanty and the wine is poor – and I don't like black women. And that's all who came to our camp on the Darfar border – rings in their ears and their teeth filed – bah!

"Why did you join Zarallo?"

"Red Ortho killed the captain I was sailing with, and took our ship," she answered sullenly. "The dog wanted me for his mistress. I jumped overboard one night and swam ashore when we were anchored off the Kushite coast. Off Zabhela it was. There I met a Shemite trader who was also a recruiting agent for Zarallo. He told me that Zarallo had brought his Free Companies south to guard the Darfar border for the Stygians. I joined an east-bound caravan and eventually came to the camp."

"And now we've both left Zarallo to shift for himself," commented Conan. "It was madness to plunge into the south as you did – but wise, too, for Zarallo's patrols never thought to look for you in this direction. Only the brother of the man you killed came this way, and struck your trail."

"And now what do you intend doing?" she demanded.

"Turn west through the forest," he answered. "I've been this far south, but not this far east. Many days' travelling to the west will bring us to the open savannahs, where the black tribes live. I have friends among them. We'll get to the coast and find a ship. I'm sick of the jungle myself."

"Then be on your way," she advised. "I have other plans."

"Don't be a fool," he answered, showing irritation for the first time. "You can't survive in this forest."

"I *have* – for more than a week."

"But what do you intend doing?"

"That's none of your affair," she snapped.

"Yes, it is," he answered calmly. "I've followed you this far, do you think I'll turn around and ride back empty handed? Be sensible, wench; I'm not going to harm you."

He stepped toward her, and she sprang back, whipping out her sword.

"Keep back, you barbarian dog! I'll spit you like a roast pig!"

He halted, reluctantly.

"Do you want me to take that toy away from you and spank you with it?" he demanded.

"Words!" she mocked, lights like the sun on blue water dancing in her reckless eyes, and he knew it was the truth. No living man could disarm Valeria of the Brotherhood with his bare hands. He scowled; his feelings were a chaotic mixture of conflicting emotions. He was angry, yet he was amused and full of admiration. He was itching with eagerness to seize that splendid figure and crush it in his iron arms, yet he greatly desired not to hurt the girl. He was torn between a desire to shake her, and a desire to caress her. He knew if he came nearer her sword would be sheathed in his heart. He had seen Valeria kill too many men to have any illusions about her. He knew she was as quick and ferocious in attack as a she-tiger. He could draw his broadsword and disarm her, beat the blade out of her hand, but the thought of drawing a sword on a woman, even without intent of injury, was extremely repugnant to him.

"Blast your soul, you hussy," he exclaimed in exasperation. "I'm going to take your —" He started toward her, his anger making him reckless, and she poised herself for a thrust when a startling interruption came.

"What's that?"

Both of them started, and Conan wheeled like a cat, his great sword flashing into his hand. Valeria recoiled, even as she poised for her thrust. Back in the forest had risen a hideous medley of screams — the screams of terrified or agonized horses. Mingled plainly with their screams came the snap of breaking bones.

"Lions are slaying the horses!" cried Valeria.

"Lions, hell!" snorted Conan, his eyes blazing. "Did you hear a lion roar? Neither did I! Listen at those bones snap — not even a lion could make that much noise killing a horse. Follow me — but keep behind me."

He hurried down the natural ramp and she followed, their personal feud forgotten in the code of the adventurers, the instinct to unite against common peril.

They descended into the screen of leaves and worked their way downward through the green veil. Silence had fallen again over the forest.

"I found your horse tied by the pool back there," he muttered, treading so noiselessly that she no longer wondered how he had surprized her on the crag. "I tied mine beside it and followed the tracks of your boots. Watch, now!"

They had emerged from the belt of leaves and stared down into the lower reaches of the forest. Above them the green roof spread its dusky canopy. Below them the sunlight filtered in just enough to make a grey twilight. The giant trunks of trees less than a hundred yards away looked dim and ghostly.

"The horses should be beyond that thicket," whispered Conan, making no more sound than a breeze moving through the branches. *"Listen!"*

Valeria had already heard, and a chill crept through her veins so she unconsciously laid her white hand on her companion's muscular brown arm. From beyond that thicket came the noisy crunching of bones and the loud rending of flesh.

"Lions wouldn't make that noise," whispered Conan. "Something's eating our horses, but it's not a lion – look there!"

The noise stopped suddenly, and Conan swore softly. A suddenly risen breeze was blowing from them directly toward the spot where the unknown monster was hidden.

The thicket was suddenly agitated and Valeria clutched Conan's arm hard. Ignorant of jungle-lore, she yet knew that no animal she had ever seen could have shaken the thicket like that.

"An elephant wouldn't make that much disturbance," muttered Conan, echoing her thought. "What the devil –" his voice trailed away in the stunned silence of incredulous amazement.

Through the thicket was thrust the head of nightmare and horror. Grinning jaws bared rows of dripping yellow tusks; above the yawning mouth wrinkled a saurian-like snout. Huge eyes, like those of a cobra a thousand times magnified, stared unwinkingly at the petrified humans clinging to the rock. Blood smeared the scaly, flabby lips and dripped from the huge mouth. The head was farther extended, on a long, scaled neck, and after it, crushing down the briars and saplings, waddled a titan's body, a gigantic reptilian torso on absurdly short legs. The whitish belly almost raked the ground, while the serrated back-bone rose higher than Conan could have reached on tip-toe. A dragon-like tail trailed out behind the monstrosity.

"Back up the crag, quick!" snapped Conan, thrusting the girl behind him. "That devil can't climb, I hope, but he can stand on his hind-legs and reach us –"

With a snapping and crashing of underbrush and small trees the dragon charging and even as Conan predicted, reared up fearsomely on his short, massive hinder legs to fall with his front feet on the crag with a violence that made the rock vibrate. Hardly had the fugitives passed through the leafy screen than the huge head was darted through, and the mighty jaws snapped with a resounding clash of giant fangs. But they were out of its reach, and they stared down at the nightmare visage framed among the green leaves. Then the head was withdrawn, and a moment later, peering down through the branches that scraped against the rock, they saw it squatting on its haunches, staring unblinkingly up at them.

Valeria shuddered, unnerved.

"How long do you suppose he'll squat there?"

Conan kicked the skull on the leaf-strewn shelf.

"This fellow must have climbed up here to escape him, or one like him. He died here of starvation. That thing never will leave here until we're both dead. I've heard legends of these things from the black people, but I never believed them before."

Valeria looked at him blankly, her resentment forgotten. She fought down a surge of panic. She had proved her reckless courage a thousand times in wild battles on sea and land, on the blood-slippery decks of war-ships, in the storming of walled cities, and on the trampled sandy beaches where the desperate men of the Red Brotherhood bathed their knives in each other's blood in their struggles for supremacy. She had not faltered in her long flight southward from the camp on the Darfar border, over the rolling grasslands and through the hostile forests. But the prospect now confronting her congealed her blood. A cutlass stroke in the heat of battle was nothing; but to sit idle and helpless on a bare rock until starvation slew her, besieged by a monstrous survival of an elder age — the thought sent panic throbbing through her brain.

"He must leave to eat and drink," she said helplessly.

"He won't have to go far to do either," Conan pointed out. "He can run like a deer; besides, he's just gorged on our horses, and like a real snake, he can go for a long time without eating or drinking. But he doesn't sleep like a real snake."

Conan spoke imperturbably. He was a barbarian and the terrible patience of the wilderness and its children was a part of his soul. He could endure a situation like this as no civilized person could endure it.

"Can't we get into the trees and get away, travelling through the branches?" she asked desperately.

He shook his head. "I thought of that. The branches scrape the crag down there, but they're too light. Branches too light for spear handles and vines no thicker than cords. They'd break with our weight. Besides, I've got an idea that devil could tear up any tree around here by its roots."

"Well, are we to sit here on our rumps until we starve?" she cried furiously. "I won't do it! I'll go down there and cut his damned head off —"

Conan had seated himself tranquilly on a rocky projection. He looked up admiringly at her blazing eyes and tense, quivering figure, but realizing that she was in just the mood for any madness, he let none of his admiration sound in his voice.

"Sit down," he grunted, catching her by her wrist and pulling her down on his knee. Without meeting any resistance he took her sword away from her and shoved it back in its sheath. "Sit still and calm down. You'd only break your steel on his scales. We'll get out of this jam some way. But we won't do it by getting chewed up and swallowed."

She made no reply, nor did she offer any resistance to his arm about her waist. She was frightened, and the sensation was new to Valeria of the Red Brotherhood. So she sat on her companion — or captor's — knee with a docility that would have amazed Count Zarallo who had atrophised her as a she-devil out of hell's seraglio.

Conan played idly with her curly yellow locks, seemingly intent only upon his conquest. Neither the skeleton at his feet nor the monster crouching below him disturbed his mind in the slightest.

The girl's restless eyes, roving the leaves below them, rested on the darkly crimson fruit she had noticed when she first climbed the crag. They were similar to fruit she had found in the forest and eaten during her flight from Zarallo's camp. She was aware of both thirst and hunger, though neither had bothered her until she knew she could not descend from the crag to find food and water.

"We need not starve," she said. "There is fruit."

Conan glanced where she pointed.

"If we ate that we wouldn't need the bite of a dragon," he grunted. "That's what the black people of Kush call The Apples of Derketa. Derketa is the Queen of the Dead. Drink a little of the juice, or spill it on your flesh, and you'd be dead before you could climb to the foot of this crag."

"Oh!" She lapsed into dismayed silence. There seemed no way out of their predicament. She thought of something and called Conan's attention to the view eastward. He stood on the pinnacle and stared out over the forest roof.

"That's a city, right enough," he muttered. "Was that where you were going, when you tried to send me off alone to the coast?"

She nodded.

"Well, who'd have thought to find a city here? So far as I know the Stygians never penetrated this far. Could it be black people? I see no herds on the plain, no sign of cultivation, or people moving about."

"How could you hope to see all that, at that distance?" she demanded.

He shrugged his shoulders and stepped down from the pinnacle. Suddenly he swore. "Why in Crom's name didn't I think of it before?"

Without answering her question, he descended to the belt of leaves and stared down through them. The great brute squatted below, watching the the crag with the frightful patience of the reptile folk. Conan spat a curse at him, and then began cutting branches. Presently he had three long slender shafts, about seven feet long, but each no larger than his thumb.

"Branches too light for spear handles, and creepers no thicker than cords," he repeated a previous statement. "But there's strength in union – that's what the Aquilonian renegades used to tell us Cimmerians when they came into the hills to raise an army to invade their own country. But we fight by clans and tribes."

"What the devil has that got to do with those sticks?" she demanded.

"You wait and see." Cutting lengths of vines he placed the sticks together, and drawing his poniard, wedged the hilt between them at one end. Then with the vines he bound them into a compact bundle, and when he had completed, he had a spear of no small strength, with a sturdy haft seven in length.

"What good will that do?" she demanded. "You told me that a blade couldn't pierce his scales –"

"He doesn't have scales all over him," answered Conan. "There's more than one way of skinning a panther."

Moving down to the edge of the leafy belt he reached the spear up and carefully thrust it through one of the Apples of Derketa, drawing carefully aside to avoid the darkly purple drops that dripped from the pierced fruit. Presently he withdrew the blade and showed her the blue steel stained a dull purplish crimson.

"I don't know whether it will do the job or not," quoth he. "There's enough poison there to kill an elephant almost instantly but – well, we'll see."

Valeria was close behind him as he let himself down among the leaves. Cautiously holding the poisoned pike away from him, he thrust his head through the leaves and addressed the monster.

"What are you waiting down there for, you misbegotten offspring of a parent of questionable morals?" was one of his more printable inquiries. "Stick your ugly head up here again, you long-necked bastard – or do you want me to come down there and kick you loose from your illegitimate spine?"

There was more of it – some of it couched in eloquence that made Valeria stare, in spite of her profane education among the sea-farers. And it had its effect on the monster. Just as the incessant yapping of a dog worries and enrages more constitutionally silent animals, so the clamorous voice of a man rouses fear in some bestial bosoms and insane rage in others. Suddenly, and with appalling quickness the mastodonic brute reared itself on its mighty hind legs and elongated its neck and body in an effort to reach this vociferous pigmy whose clamor was disturbing the primeval silence of its horrible realm.

But Conan had judged his distance precisely. Some five feet below Conan the mighty head crashed terribly but futiley through the leaves. And as the monstrous mouth gaped like that of a great snake, Conan drove his spear into the red angle of the hinge of the jawbone. He struck down ward with all the strength of both arms, driving the long poniard blade deep into flesh bone and muscle.

Instantly the jaws clashed together, severing the triple-woven shaft and almost precipitating Conan from his perch. In fact he would have fallen but for the girl behind him, who caught his sword-belt in a desperate grasp. He clutched at a rocky projection and grinned his thanks back at her.

Down on the ground the monster was wallowing like a dog with pepper in its eyes. He shook his head from side to side, pawed at it, and opened his mouth to its fullest extent, again and again. Presently he got a huge front foot on the stump of the shaft, and managed to tear the blade out. Realizing who was the author of his annoyance, he threw up his head, jaws wide and spouting blood and glared up at the crag with such concentrated and intelligent fury that Valeria trembled and drew her sword.

With harsh grating roars, the monster hurled himself at the crag that was the citadel of his enemies. Again and again his mighty head crashed upward through the leaves, snapping vainly on empty air. He hurled his full weight again and again against the rock, until it vibrated from base to crest. And rearing upright he gripped it with his front legs like a man and tried the impossible feat of tearing it from the ground bodily.

This exhibition of primordial fury chilled the blood in Valeria's veins, but Conan was too close to the primitive himself to feel anything but a fascinated interest. To the barbarian, no such gulf existed between himself and other men, and the animals, as existed in the conception of Valeria. The monster below them, to Conan, was merely a form of life differing from himself mainly in shape. He attributed to it characteristics similar to his own, and believed its roars and bellowings were merely counterparts of the curses he had bestowed upon it. Feeling a kinship with all wild things, even dragons, it was impossible for him to experience the sick horror that assailed Valeria at the sight of the monster's wrath.

He watched it tranquilly and pointed out the various changes that were taking place in its voice and its actions.

"The poison's taking hold," he said with conviction.

"I don't believe it." To Valeria it seemed preposterous to suppose that any lethal thing could have any effect on that mountain of muscle and ferocity.

"There's pain in his voice," declared Conan. "First he was merely angry because of the stinging in his jaw. Now he feels the bite of the poison. Look! He's staggering! He'll be blind in a few more minutes. What did I tell you?"

For suddenly the dragon had lurched about and went crashing off through the underbrush.

"Is he running away?" inquired Valeria uneasily.

"He's making for the pool. The poison makes him thirsty. Come on! He'll be blind when he gets back, if he does get back. But if he can make his way back to the foot of the crag, and smell us, he'll sit there until he dies, and others of his kind may come at his cries. Let's go!"

"Down there?" Valeria was aghast.

"Sure! We'll make for the city! We may run into a thousand of the brutes, but it's sure death to stay here. Down with you, in a hurry! Follow me!"

He went down swiftly, like an ape, pausing only to aid his slower companion, who, until she saw the Cimmerian climb, had fancied herself the equal of any man in the rigging of a ship, or on the sheer of a cliff.

They slid silently to the ground, though Valeria felt as if the beating of her heart must surely be heard for miles. No sound came from the forest, except the gurgling and lapping that indicated that the dragon was drinking at the spring.

"As soon as his belly is full he'll be back," muttered Conan. "It may take hours for the poison to work."

Somewhere beyond the forest the sun was sinking to the horizon. The forest was a misty twilight place of black shadows and dim vistas. Conan gripped Valeria's wrist and glided away from the crag's foot. He made less noise than a breeze blowing among the tree-trunks, but Valeria felt as if her soft boots spoke of their flight to all the forest.

"I don't think he can follow a trail," muttered Conan. "No wind blowing. He could get our body-scent if it blew toward him."

"Mitra grant that the wind blow not," she breathed. She gripped her sword in her free hand, but the feel of the shagreen-bound hilt inspired only a feeling of helplessnes in her.

It was little over a mile to the edge of the forest. They had covered most of the distance when they heard a snapping and crashing behind them. Valeria bit her lip to check a cry.

"He's on our trail!" she whispered fiercely, galvanized.

Conan shook his head.

"He didn't smell us at the rock, and he's blundering about through the forest, trying to pick up our scent. Come on! There's no safety for us in this forest. He could tear down any tree we'd climb. Make for the plain! If he doesn't catch our scent, we'll make it! The city is our only chance!"

They stole on until the trees began to thin out. Behind them the forest was a black impenetrable ocean of shadows. The ominous crackling still sounded behind them, as the dragon blundered in his erratic course.

"There's the plain ahead," breathed Valeria. "A little more and we'll –"

"Crom!" swore Conan.

"Mitra!" whispered Valeria.

Out of the east a wind had sprung up. It blew over them directly into the black forest behind them. Instantly a horrible roar shook the woods. The aimless snapping and crackling of the bushes changed to a purposeful crashing as the dragon came like a hurricane straight toward the spot from which the scent wafted.

"Run!" snarled Conan, his eyes blazing like those of a trapped wolf. "It's all we can do!"

Sailors' boots are not made for sprinting, and the life of a pirate does not train one for a runner. Within fifty yards Valeria was panting and reeling in her gait and behind them the crashing gave way to a rolling thunder as the monster broke out of the thickets and into the clearer country.

Conan's iron arm about the woman's waist half lifted her; her feet scarcely touched the earth as she was borne along at a speed she could have attained herself. A quick glance over his shoulder showed Conan that the monster was almost upon them, coming a war-galley in front of a hurricane. He thrust Valeria from him with a force that sent her staggering a dozen feet to fall in a crumpled heap at the foot of the nearest tree, and wheeled in the path of the thundering titan.

Convinced that his death was upon him, the Cimmerian acted according to his instinct, and hurled himself full at the awful face that was bearing down on him. He leaped, striking and slashing like a wildcat, felt his sword cut deep into the scales that sheathed the mighty snout – and then a terrific impact knocked him rolling and tumbling for fifty feet with all the wind and half the life battered out of him.

How the stunned Cimmerian regained his feet, not even he could ever have told. But he thought only for the girl lying dazed almost within the path of the hurtling fiend, and before the breath came whistling back into his gullet he was standing over her with his sword in his hand.

She lay where he had thrown her, but she was struggling to a sitting posture. The dragon had not touched her, neither with tearing tusks or trampling feet. It had been a shoulder or front leg that struck Conan; and the blind monster rushed on, forgetting the victims it had scented in the sudden agony of its death throes. Headlong on its course it thundered until its low-hung head crashed into a gigantic tree in its path. The impact tore the tree up by the roots and must have dashed the brains from the misshapen skull. Tree and monster fell together, and the dazed humans saw the branches and leaves contorted and shaken by the convulsions of the creature they hid – and then grow quiet.

Conan lifted Valeria to her feet and together they started eastward at a reeling run. A few moments later they emerged into the still twilight of the treeless plain.

Conan paused an instant, and glanced back at the black forest behind him. Not a leaf stirred, not a bird chirped. It stood as silent as it must have stood before animal life was created.

"Come on," muttered Conan, taking his companion's hand. "The woods may be full of those devils. We'll try that city out there on the plain."

With every step they took away from the black woods Valeria drew a breath of relief. Each moment she expected to hear the crashing of the bushes and see another giant nightmare bearing down upon them. But nothing disturbed the silence of the forest.

With the first mile between them and the woods, Valeria breathed easy. The sun had set and darkness was gathering over the plain, lightened a little by the stars that made stunted ghosts out of the mimosa shrubs.

"No cattle, no ploughed fields," muttered Conan. "How do these people live?"

"Perhaps the fields and grazing lands are on the other side of the city," suggested Valeria.

"Maybe," he grunted. "I didn't see any from the crag, though."

The moon came up behind the city, etching walls and towers blackly in the yellow glow. Valeria shivered. Black against the moon the strange city had a sombre, sinister look.

Perhaps something of the same feeling occurred to Conan, for he stopped, glanced about him, and grunted: "We stop here. No use arriving at their gates in the night. They probably wouldn't let us in. Besides, we're tired, and we don't know how they'll receive us. A few hours rest will put us in better shape to fight or run."

He led the way to a bed of cactus which grew in a circle – a phenomenon common to the southern desert. With his sword he chopped an opening, and motioned Valeria to enter.

"We'll be safe from snakes here, anyhow."

She glanced fearfully back toward the black line that indicated the forest, some six miles away.

"Suppose a dragon comes out of the woods?"

"We'll keep watch," he answered, though he made no suggestion as to what they would do in such an event. "Lie down and sleep. I'll keep the first watch."

She hesitated, but he sat down cross-legged in the opening, facing toward the plain, his sword across his knees, his back to her. Without further comment she lay down on the sand inside the spiky circle.

"Wake me when the moon is at its zenith," she directed. He did not reply nor look toward her. Her last impression, as she sank into slumber was of his motionless figure, immobile as a statue hewn out of bronze, outlined against the low-hanging stars.

CHAPTER

Valeria awoke with a start, to the realization that a grey dawn was stealing over the desert.

She sat up, rubbing her eyes. Conan was squatting beside the cactus, cutting off the thick pears and dexterously twitching out the spikes.

"You didn't awake me," she accused. "You let me sleep all night!"

"You were tired," he answered. "Your posterior must have been sore, after that long ride. You pirates aren't used to horseback."

"What about yourself?" she retorted.

"I was a *kozak* before I was a pirate," he answered. "They live in the saddle. I snatch naps like a panther watching beside the trail for a deer to come by. My ears stay awake while my eyes sleep."

And indeed the giant Cimmerian seemed as much refreshed as if he had slept the whole night on a gold bed. Having removed the thorns, and peeled off the tough skin, Conan handed the girl a thick, juicy cactus leaf.

"Eat that pear. It's food and drink to a desert man. I was a chief of the Zuagirs once – desert men who live by plundering the caravans."

"Is there anything you haven't been?" inquired the girl, half in derision, half in fascination.

"I've never been king of an Hyborian kingdom," he grinned, taking an enormous mouthful of cactus. "But I've dreamed of being even that. I may be too, some day. Why shouldn't I?"

She shook her head in wonder and fell to devouring her pear. She found it not unpleasing to the palate, and full of a cool and thirst-satisfying juice. Finishing his meal, Conan wiped his hands in the sand, rose, ran his fingers through his thick black mane, hitched at his sword-belt and said: "Well, let's go. If the people in that city are going to cut our throats they may as well do it now, before the heat of the day begins."

His grim humor was unconscious, but Valeria reflected that it might be prophetic. She touched her sword-hilt as she rose. Her terrors of the night were past. The roaring dragons of the distant forest were like a dim dream. There was a swagger in her bearing as she moved off beside her companion. Whatever perils lay ahead of them, their foes would be men. And Valeria of the Red Brethren had never seen the face of the man she feared.

Conan glanced down at her as she strode along beside him with her easy swinging stride that matched his own.

"You walk more like a hillman than a sailor," he said. "You must be an Aquilonian. The suns of Darfar never burnt your white skin brown."

"I am from Aquilonia," she replied. His compliments no longer antagonized her. His evident admiration pleased her. After all, the desire of Conan the Cimmerian was an honor to any woman, even to Valeria of the Red Brotherhood.

The sun rose behind the city, turning the towers to a sinister crimson.

"Black last night against the moon," grunted Conan, his eyes clouding with the abysmal superstition of the barbarian. "Blood-red against the sun this dawn. I like not that city."

But they went on, and as they went Conan pointed out the fact that no road ran to the city from the west.

"No cattle have trampled the plain on this side of the village," said he. "No plough has touched the earth for years – maybe centuries. No track shows in the dust. But look – once this plain was cultivated."

Valeria saw the ancient irrigation ditches and the long dried stream-bed. On each side of the city the plain stretched to the forest edge that marched in a vast, dim ring. Vision did not extend beyond that ring.

The sun was high in the eastern sky when they stood before the great gate in the western wall, in the shadow of the lofty rampart. The city lay silent as the forest they had escaped. Rust flecked the iron bracings of the heavy bronze gate. Spider webs glistened thickly on hinge and sill and bolted panel.

"It has not been opened for years," exclaimed Valeria, awed by the brooding silence of the place.

"A dead city," grunted Conan. "That's why the ditches were broken and the plain untouched."

"But who built it? Who dwelt here? Where did they go? Why did they abandon it?"

"Who can say? There are deserted, mysterious cities scattered about in desert spots of the world. Maybe a roving tribe of Stygians built it long ago. Maybe not. It doesn't look like Stygian architecture much. Maybe they were wiped out by enemies, or a plague exterminated them."

"In that case their treasures may still be gathering dust and cobwebs there," suggested Valeria, the acquisitive instincts of her profession waking her, prodded too by feminine curiosity. "Can we open that gate? Let's go in and explore a bit."

Conan eyed the heavy portal dubiously, but placed his massive shoulder against it and thrust with all the power of his muscular calves and thighs. With a rasping screech of rusty hinges the gate moved inward and Conan instinctively drew his sword and peered in. Valeria crowded him to stare over his shoulder. They both expressed surprize.

They were not looking into an open street or court as one would have expected. The opened gate gave directly into a long, broad hall that ran away and away until its vista was rendered indistinct by distance. It must have been a hundred and fifty feet broad, and from floor to ceiling it was a greater distance. The floor was of a curious dull red stone that seemed to smolder as if with the reflection of flames. The walls were of a curious semi-translucent green substance.

"Jade, or I'm a Shemite!" swore Conan.

"Not in such quantities!" protested Valeria.

"I've looted enough from the Khitan caravans to know what I'm talking about," he asserted.

The ceiling was vaulted and of some substance like lapis lazuli, adorned with great green stones that shone with a poisonous radiance.

"Green fire stones," growled Conan. "That's what the people of Punt call them. They're supposed to be the petrified eyes of the Golden Serpents. They glow like a cat's eyes in the dark. This hall would be lighted by them at night, but it would be a devilish ghostly illumination. Let's look about. We may find a cache of jewels."

They entered, leaving the door ajar. Valeria wondered how many centuries had passed since the light of outer day had filtered into that great hall.

But light was coming in somewhere, and she saw its source. It came through some of the doors along the side walls which stood open. In the splotches of shadow between, the green jewels winked like the eyes of angry cats. Beneath their feet the lurid floor smoldered with changing hues and colors of flame. It was like treading the floors of hell with evil stars blinking overhead.

"I believe this hallway goes clean through the city to the eastern gate," grunted Conan. "I seem to glimpse a gate at the other end."

Valeria shrugged her white shoulders.

"Your eyes are better than mine, though I'm accounted sharp-eyed among the sea-rovers."

They turned into an open door at random, and traversed a series of empty chambers, floored like the hall, with the same green jade walls or walls of marble or ivory. Bronze or gold or silver freize-work adorned the walls. In some of the ceilings the green-fire stones were set; in some they were lacking. Tables and seats of marble, jade or lapis lazuli were plentiful throughout the chambers, but nowhere did they find any windows, or doors that opened into streets or courts. Each door merely opened into another chamber or hall. Some of the chambers were lighter than others, through a system of skylights in the ceilings – opaque but translucent sheets of some crystalline substance.

"Why don't we come to a street?" grumbled Valeria. "This palace or whatever we're in must be as big as the palace of the king of Turan."

"They must not have perished of plague," said Conan, meditating upon the mystery of the empty city. "Otherwise we'd find skeletons. Maybe the city became haunted and everybody got up and left. Maybe –"

"Maybe, hell!" broke in Valeria. "We'll never know. Look at these freizes. They portray men."

Conan scanned them and shook his head.

"I never saw people like them. But there's the smack of the East about them – Vendhya, maybe, or Kosala."

"Were you a king in Kosala?" she asked, masking her keen interest in derision.

"No. But I was a war-chief of the Afghulis who dwell in the Himelian mountains above the borders of Vendhya. These people might have been Kosalans. But why the hell should Kosalans be building a city this far to the West?"

The freizes portrayed slender, dark-skinned men and women, with finely-chiseled features. They wore long robes and many jeweled ornaments. Their complection, cleverly reproduced, was olive.

"Easterners, all right," grunted Conan. "But from where I don't know. Let's climb that stair."

The stair he mentioned was an ivory spiral that wound up from the chamber they were traversing. They mounted and came into a larger chamber, which also was without windows. A greenish skylight let in a vague radiance.

"Hell!" Valeria sat down disgustedly on a jade bench. "The people who lived in this city must have taken all their treasures with them. I'm getting tired of wandering around here at random."

"Let's have a look through that door over there," suggested Conan.

"You have a look," advised Valeria. "I'm going to sit here and rest my feet."

Conan disappeared through the door, and Valeria leaned back with her hands clasped behind her head, and thrust her booted legs out in front of her. These rooms and silent halls with their gleaming green clusters of ornaments and smoldering crimson floors were beginning to depress her. She wished they could find their way out of the maze into which they had wandered and emerge into a street. She idly wondered how many furtive, dark feet had rustled over those flaming floors in past centuries, how many deeds of cruelty and mystery those flaming ceiling-gems had looked down upon.

It was a faint noise that brought her out of her reflections. She was on her feet with her sword in her hand before she realized what it was that had disturbed her. Conan had not returned, and she knew it was not him she had heard.

The sound had come from somewhere beyond a door that stood opposite from the one by which the Cimmerian gone. Soundlessly on her soft leather footgear she glided to the door and looked through. It opened on a gallery that ran along a wall above a hall. She crept to the heavy balustrades and peered between them.

A man was stealing along the hall.

The unexpected shock of seeing a stranger in a deserted city almost brought a startled oath to Valeria's lips. Crouching down behind the stone balustrades, with every nerve tingling, she glared at the stealthy figure.

The man in no way resembled the figures depicted on the freize. He was slightly above middle height, very dark skinned, though not negroid. He was naked but for a scanty loin-cloth that only partially covered his muscular hips, and a broad leather girdle about his lean waist. His long black hair hung in lank strands about his shoulders. He was gaunt, but knots and cords of muscles stood out on his arms and legs. There was no symmetry of contour; he was built with an economy that was almost repellant.

Yet it was not so much his physical appearance that impressed the woman who watched him, as his attitude. He slunk along the hall in a semi-crouch, darting glances to right and left. She saw the cruel curved blade in his right hand shake with the intensity of whatever emotion it was that made him tremble as he stole along. He was afraid – was shaking in the grip of some frightful terror. That he feared some imminent peril was evident. When he turned his head she caught the blaze of wild eyes among the lank hair. On his tiptoes he glided across the hall and vanished through an open door, first halting and casting a fiercely questioning look about him. A moment she heard a choking cry and then silence again.

Who was the fellow? What did he fear in this empty city? Plagued by these and similar questions, Valeria acted on impulse. She glided along the gallery until she came to a door which she believed opened into a room over the one in which the dark-skinned stranger had vanished. To her pleasure she came upon a gallery similar to the one she had just quitted, and a stair led down into the chamber.

This chamber was not as well lighted as some of the others. A trick of the skylight above caused a corner of the chamber to remain in shadow. Valeria's eyes widened. The man she had seen was still in the chamber.

He lay face down on a dark crimson carpet on the floor. His body was limp, his arms spread wide. His wide-tipped sword lay near his hand.

She wondered why he should lie there so motionless. Then her eyes narrowed as she stared down at the rug on which he lay. Beneath and about him the carpet showed a slightly different color – a deeper, brighter crimson –

Shivering slightly she crouched down closer behind the balustrade. Suddenly another figure entered the silent play. He was a man similar to the first, and he came in by a door opposite that through which the other had entered. His eyes widened at the sight of the man on the floor, and he spoke something in a staccato voice. The other did not move.

The man stepped quickly across the floor, gripped the shoulder of the prostrate figure and turned him over. A choking cry escaped him as the head fell back limply, disclosing a throat that had been severed from ear to ear.

The man let the corpse fall back into the puddle of blood on the carpet, and sprang to his feet, shaking like a leaf. His face was a mask of fear. But before he could move, he halted, frozen.

Over in the shadowy corner a ghostly light began to glow and grow. Valeria felt her hair stir as she watched it. For dimly visible in its glow there floated a human skull – a skull with blazing green eyes. It hung there like a disembodied head, growing more and more distinct.

The man stood like an image, staring fixedly at the apparition. The thing moved out from the wall and as it emerged from the shadows it became visible as a man-like figure whose torso and limbs, stark naked, shone whitely, like the hue of bleached skulls. The bare skull on its shoulders still glowed with the lurid light, and the man confronting it seemed unable to take his eyes from it. He stood motionless, his sword dangling from his fingers, on his face an expression like that on the face of a man in a mesmeristic trance.

The horror moved toward him, and suddenly he dropped his sword and fell on his knees, covering his eyes with his hands, dumbly awaiting the stroke of the blade that now gleamed in the apparition's hand, as it reared above him like Death triumphant over mankind.

Valeria acted according to her wayward impulse. With one lithe movement she was over the balustrade and dropped to the floor behind the figure. It wheeled like a cat at the pad of her soft boot on the floor, and even as it turned her keen blade lashed down, severing shoulder and breast bone. The apparition cried out gurglingly and went down, and as it fell, the phosphorescent skull rolled clear revealing a lank-haired head and a dark face now contorted in the convulsion of death. Beneath the horrific masquerade there was a human being, a man similar to the one kneeling supinely on the floor.

The latter looked up at the sound of the blow and cry, and now he glared in wild-eyed amazement at the white-skinned woman who stood over the corpse with a dripping sword in her hand.

He staggered up, yammering as if the surprize had almost unseated his reason. She was amazed to realize that she understood him. He was gibbering in the Stygian tongue, though in a dialect unfamiliar to her.

"Who are you? Whence do you come? What do you in Xuchotl?" Then rushing on, without waiting for her to reply. "But you are a friend — a friend or a goddess! Goddess or devil, it makes no difference! You have slain the Living Skull! It was but a man after all! We thought it was a demon *they* conjured out of the catacombs below the city! Listen!"

He stiffened again, straining his ears with painful intensity; the girl heard nothing.

"We must hasten," he whispered. "They are all around us here. Perhaps even now we may be surrounded by them. They may be creeping upon us even now!"

He seized her wrist in a convulsive grasp she found it hard to break.

"Who do you mean by 'they'?" she demanded.

He stared at her uncomprehendingly for a moment, as a man stares when confronted in a stranger by ignorance of something common-place to himself.

"They?" he repeated vaguely. "Why, the people of Xecalanc! The folk of the man you killed! They who dwell by the northern gate."

"You mean to say men live in this city?" she exclaimed, dumfounded.

"Aye! Aye!" he was writhing in the impatience of apprehension. "Come! Come quick! We must return to Tecuhltli!"

"Where the hell is that?" she demanded bewilderedly.

"The region by the south gate!" He had her wrist again and was urging her to follow him. Great beads of perspiration dripped from his dark forehead. His eyes blazed with pure terror.

"Wait a minute," she growled, flinging off his hands. "Keep your fingers off me, or I'll split your skull! What's all this about? Who are you are? Where would you take me?"

He shuddered, casting glances to all sides, and speaking so fast and in such fear that his words were jerky and all but incoherent.

"My name is Techotl. I am of the Tecuhltli. This man who lies with his throat cut and I came into the Disputed Region to try and ambush some of the Xecalanc. But we became separated and I returned here to find him with his gullet slit. The dog who wore the skull must have done it. But perhaps he was not alone. Others may be stealing from Xecalanc! The gods themselves shudder when they hear what these demons have done to captives!"

He shook as with an ague, and his dark skin grew ashy at the thought. Valeria stared at him with a frown of bewilderment. She sensed intelligence behind this rigamarole, but it was meaningless to her.

"Come!" he begged, reaching for her hand and then recoiling as he remembered her warning. "You are a stranger. How you came here I do not know, but if you were a goddess come to aid us of Tecuhltli you would know all that transpires in Xuchotl. You must be from beyond the great forest. But you are our friend, or you would not have slain the dog who wore the glowing skull. Come quickly, before the Xecalanc fall on us and slay us!"

"But I can't go," she answered. "I have a friend somewhere nearby —"

The flaring of his eyes cut her short as he stared past her with a ghastly expression. She wheeled just as four men rushed through the doors of the chamber, converging on the pair in the center of the room.

They were like the others she had seen — the same knotted muscles standing out on otherwise gaunt limbs, the same lank blue black hair, the same mad glare in the staring eyes. They were armed and clad like the man who called himself Techotl, but on the breast of each was painted a white skull.

There were no challenges or war-cries. Like blood-mad tigers the men of Xecalanc sprang at the throats of their enemies. Techotl met them with the fury of desperation, parried the stroke of a curved blade and grappling with the wielder, bore him to the floor where they rolled and wrestled in murderous silence.

The other three swarmed on Valeria, their weird eyes red with the murder-lust.

She killed the first who came in reach, her long straight blade beating down his curved sword and splitting his skull. She stepped aside to avoid the stroke of another, even as she turned the blade of the third with her sword. Her eyes danced and her lips smiled without mercy. Again she was Valeria of the Red Brotherhood and the hum of her steel was like a bridal song in her ears.

Her sword darted past a blade that sought to parry and sheathed six inches of its point in a leather-guarded midriff. The man gasped and went to his knees. His mate lunged in in ferocious silence, his eyes like a mad dog's. He rained blow on blow in a whirlwind of steel, so furiously Valeria had no opportunity to strike back. She fell back coolly, parrying the wild blows, and watching her opportunity. He could not long keep up that whirlwind of flailing strokes. He would tire, would weaken and hesitate — and then her blade would slide smoothly into his heart. A side-long glance showed her Techotl crouching on the breast of his prostrate enemy, and striving to break the other's hold on his wrist and drive home a dagger.

Sweat beaded the forehead of the man facing her and his eyes were red as coals. Smite as he would he could not break past or beat down her guard. She stepped back to draw him out — and felt her thighs locked in an iron grip. She had forgotten the wounded man on the floor.

Crouching on his knees he held her in an unbreakable grasp and his mate croaked in triumph and began working his way around to come at her from the left side. Valeria wrenched and tore savagely, but in vain. She could free herself of this clinging menace with a downward flick of her sword, but in that instant the curved blade of the taller man would crash through her skull. The wounded man hung on and began to worry at her thigh with his teeth like a beast.

She reached down with her left hand and gripped his long hair, forcing his head back so his white teeth and rolling eyes gleamed up at her. The tall Xecalanc cried out fiercely and leaped in, smiting hard. Awkwardly she parried the stroke, and it beat the flat of her blade down on her head so she saw sparks flash before her eyes, and staggered. Up went the sword again, with a low, beast-like cry of triumph – and then a giant form loomed behind the Xecalanc and steel flashed like an arc of blue lightning. The cry of the Xecalanc broke short and he went down like an ox beneath the pole-axe, his brains gushing from his skull that had been split to the throat.

"Conan!" gasped Valeria. In a gust of passion she turned on the Xecalanc who still grasped her, and whose long hair she still held in her left hand. "Dog of hell!" Her blade swished as it cut the air, and completed the upswinging arc with only a blur in the middle. The body slumped, spurting blood and she hurled the severed head across the room.

"What the devil's going on here?" Conan bestrode the corpse of the man he had killed, broadsword in hand, glaring about him in amazement. Techotl was rising from the still figure of the last Xecalanc, shaking red drops from his dagger. The Tecuhltli was bleeding from a stab deep in the thigh.

He stared wildly at Conan, his eyes dilated.

"What is all this?" Conan demanded again. He had not yet recovered from his surprise at finding a savage battle going on in the midst of a city he had thought empty and uninhabited. Returning from an aimless exploration of the upper chambers, he had found Valeria gone, and had followed the unexpected sounds of strife. Coming into the room he had been astounded to see the girl engaging in a furious tussle with these strange and alien figures.

"Five dead Xecalanc!" exclaimed Techotl, his dilated eyes reflecting a ghastly joy. "Five dead! The gods be thanked!" He lifted quivering hands on high and then, with a fiendish convulsing of his dark features he spat on the corpses and kicked them, dancing in his ghoulish glee. His recent allies eyed him in amazement, and Conan asked, in Aquilonian: "Who is this madman?"

Valeria shrugged her shoulders.

"He says his name's Techotl. From his babblings I gather that his people live at one end of this crazy city, and these others at the other end. Maybe we'd better go with him. He seems friendly."

Techotl had ceased his dancing and he turned to them, triumph struggling with fear in his repellant countenance.

"Come away, now!" he chattered. "Come on! Come with me! My people will welcome you! Five dead dogs! Not in years have we slain so many of the devils at one time, without losing a man – nay, one man we lost, but we slew five! My people will honor you! But come! It is far to Techulthli. At any moment the Xecalancs may come on us in numbers too great even for your swords!"

"All right," grunted Conan. "Lead the way."

Techotl turned instantly and made off across the chamber, beckoning them to follow, which they did, having to move swiftly to keep on his heels.

"What sort of a place can this be?" muttered Valeria under her breath.

"Crom knows," answered Conan. "I've seen *his* kind before, though. There's a tribe of them living on the shores of Lake Zuad, near the Kushite border. They're a sort of mongrel Stygians, mixed with another race that wandered into Stygia from the east some centuries ago, and were absorbed by them. They're called Tlazetlans. I'm willing to bet they didn't build this city, though."

They were traversing a series of chambers and halls and Techotl's fear did not seem to diminish. He kept twisting his head on his shoulder to stare back fearfully and strain his ears for sounds of pursuit.

"They may have prepared an ambush for us!" he whispered.

"Why don't we get out of this infernal palace, and take to the streets?" demanded Valeria.

"There are no streets in Xuchotl," he answered. "No squares or open courts. All the buildings are connected; rather, all are under one great roof. The only doors opening into the outer world are the city-gates through which no one has passed for fifty years."

"How long have you dwelt here?" asked Conan.

"I was born in Tecuhltli, and I am thirty-five years old. For the love of the gods, let us be silent! These halls may be full of lurking devils. Olmec shall tell you all when we reach Tecuhltli."

They moved on with the green fire stones blinking overhead and the flaming floors crackling under their feet, and it seemed to Valeria as if they fled through hell, guided by a lank-haired goblin.

Through dim-lit chambers and winding corridors they moved swift and silent, until Conan halted them.

"You think some of your enemies may be ahead of us, intending to ambush us?" he said.

"They prowl through these halls at all hours," answered Techotl. "As do we. The chambers and corridors between Techuhltli and Xecalanc are a hunting ground owned by no man. Why do you ask?"

"Because men are in the chambers ahead of us," answered Conan. "I heard steel clink against stone."

Again a shaking seized Techotl and he clenched his teeth to keep them from chattering.

"Perhaps they are your friends," suggested Valeria.

"We can not chance it," he answered, and moved with frenzied activity. He wheeled aside and led them down a winding stair to a dark corridor. Into it he plunged recklessly.

"It may be a trick to draw us into it," he hissed, great beads of perspiration standing out on his brow. "But we must chance it that they have laid their ambush in the rooms above! Come swiftly, now!"

They groped their way along the black corridor and were presently galvanized by the sound of a door opening softly behind them. Men had come into the corridor behind them.

"Swiftly!" panted Techotl, a note of hysteria in his voice, and fled away down the corridor. Conan and Valeria followed him, Conan keeping to the rear, while the swift patter of flying feet drew closer and closer. Their pursuers knew the corridor better than he did. He wheeled suddenly and smote savagely in the dark, felt his blade jar home and heard some thing groan and fall. The next instant the corridor was flooded with light as Techotl threw open a door. Conan followed the Tecuhltli and the girl through the door, and Techotl slammed it and shot a bolt across it – the first Conan had seen on any door.

Then he turned and ran across the chamber, while behind them the door groaned and strained inward under heavy pressure violently applied. Conan and Valeria followed their guide through a series of well-lighted chambers, and up a winding stair and along a broad hall. They paused at a powerful bronze door, and Techotl said: "This is Tecuhltli!"

CHAPTER

He knocked cautiously and then stepped back and waited. Conan decided that the people on the other side of the door had some way of seeing whoever stood before it. Presently the door swung noiselessly back, revealing a heavy chain across the entrance. Spear heads bristled and a fierce countenance regarded them suspiciously before the chain was removed.

Techotl led the way in and as soon as Conan and Valeria were inside, the door was closed, heavy bolts drawn, and the chain locked into place. Four men stood there, of the same lank-haired, dark-skinned breed as Techotl, with spears in their hands and swords at their hips. They regarded the strangers with amazement, but asked no questions.

They had come into a square chamber that opened into a broad hall. One of the four guards opened the door and they entered the hall which, like the guard-chamber, was lighted from above with a narrow slot-like skylight on each side of which winked the green fire-gems.

"I will take you to Olmec, who is prince of Tecuhltli," said Techotl, and straightaway led them down the hall and into a broad chamber where some thirty men and women lounged on satin-covered couches. These sat up and stared in wonder. The men were of the same type as Techotl, all except one, and the women were equally dark and strange-eyed, but were not unbeautiful in a weird dark way. They wore sandals, gold breast-plates, and scanty silk skirts supported by gem-crusted girdles, and their black manes, cut square at their shoulders, were confined by silver circlets.

On a wide ivory seat on a jade dais sat a man and a woman who differed subtly from the others. He was a giant – as tall as the Cimmerian and heavier, with an enormous sweep of breast and the shoulders of a bull. Unlike the others he was bearded, with a thick, blue-black beard which fell almost to his broad girdle. He wore a robe of purple silk which reflected sheens of changing color with his every motion, and one wide sleeve, drawn back to his elbow, revealed a forearm massive with corded muscles. The band which confined his thick black locks was set with sparkling jewels.

The woman, who sprang to her feet with a startled exclamation at the sight of Valeria, was tall and lithe, by far the most beautiful woman in the room. She was clad evenly more scantily than the others, for instead of a skirt, she wore merely a broad strip of gilt-worked cloth fastened to the middle of her girdle, which fell below her knees. Another at the back of her girdle completed that part of her costume. Her breast-plates and the circlet about her temples were adorned with jewels.

She sprang to her feet as the strangers entered. Her eyes, passing over Conan, fixed themselves with burning intensity on Valeria. The people in the chamber rose and stared. There were youngsters among them, but the strangers saw no children.

"Prince Olmec," spoke Techotl, bowing low, with arms outspread and palms turned upward, "I bring allies from the outer world. In the Hall of Tezcoti the Living Skull slew Chicmec, my companion –"

"The Living Skull!" the people breathed fearfully.

"Aye! Then came I, and found Chicmec lying with his throat cut. Before I could flee the Living Skull came upon me and when I met the glare of his eyes I became as one paralyzed. I could not move. I could only await the stroke. Then came this white-skinned woman and struck him down, and lo, it was only a dog of Xecalanc with white paint upon his skin and a masque upon his head! We have trembled in fear of him, deeming him a fiend the magic of the Xecalancas had invoked from the catacombs. But he was only a man, and now he is a dead man!"

An indescribably fierce exultation edged the last sentence, and was echoed in the low, savage exclamations from the crowding people.

"But wait!" exclaimed Techotl. "There is more! While I talked with the woman, four Xecalancas came upon us – one I slew – there is a stab in my thigh to prove how desperate was the fight. Two the woman killed. But we were hard pressed when this man came into the fray and split the skull of the fourth! Aye! Five crimson nails there are to be driven into the pillar of vengeance!"

He pointed to a black column of ebony which stood behind the dais. Hundreds of red dots showed there – the bright scarlet heads of heavy nails driven into the black wood.

"One red nail for a Xecalanc life!" exulted Techotl, and the faces of the listeners were contorted with horrible exultation.

"Who are these people?" asked Olmec, and his voice was like the deep, low rumble of a bull. None of the people of Xuchotl spoke loudly. It was as if they had taken into their souls the silence of the empty halls and deserted chambers.

"I am Conan, a Cimmerian," answered the barbarian briefly. "This woman is Valeria of the Red Brotherhood. We deserted from an army on the Darfar border, far to the north, and are trying to reach the coast."

The woman on the dais spoke hastily; her burning eyes had never left Valeria's face.

"You can never reach the coast! You must spend the rest of your lives in Xuchotl! There is no escape!"

"What do you mean?" growled Conan, clapping his hand to his hilt and stepping about so as to face both dais and the rest of the room at the same time. "Are you saying that we're prisoners?"

"She did not mean that," interposed Olmec. "We are your friends. We would not restrain you against your will. But I fear other circumstances will make it impossible for you to leave Xuchotl." His eyes also rested on Valeria, and he lowered them quickly.

"This woman is Tascela," he said. "She is princess of Tecuhltli. But let food and drink be brought our guests. Doubtless they are hungry and weary from travel."

He indicated the ivory table, and Conan and Valeria seated themselves, while Techotl placed himself on hand to attend them. He seemed to consider it a privilege and honor to see after their needs. The other men and women hastened to bring food and drink in gold vessels and dishes, and Olmec sat in silence on his ivory seat, watching them from under his broad black brows. Tascela sat beside him, chin cupped in her hands and her elbows resting on her knees. Her dark, enigmatic eyes, burning with a cryptic light, did not leave the supple figure of Valeria.

The food was unfamiliar to the wanderers, some sort of fruit but palatable, and the drink was a light crimson wine that had a heady tang.

"How you won through the forest is a wonder to me," quoth Olmec. "In bygone days a thousand fighting men were not too many to carve a way through its perils."

"We encountered a bench-legged monstrosity about the size of a mastodon," said Conan carelessly, holding out his wine goblet which Techotl filled with evident pleasure. "But when we'd killed it we had no farther trouble."

The wine vessel slipped from Techotl's hand to crash on the floor. His dusky skin went ashy. Olmec started to his feet, an image of dumbfounded amazement, and from the others breathed up a low gasp of awe or terror. Conan glared about him in bewilderment.

"What's the matter? What are you all gaping about?"

"You – slew the dragon?" stammered Olmec.

"Why not? It was trying to eat us. There's no law against killing a dragon, is there?"

"But dragons are immortal!" exclaimed Olmec. "No man ever killed a dragon! No man ever could! The thousand fighting men of our ancestors who fought their way to Xuchotl could not prevail against them! Their swords broke like twigs against their scales!"

"If your ancestors had thought to dip their spears in the poisonous juice of Derketa's Apples," quoth Conan, with his mouthful, "and jab them in the eyes or the mouth or somewhere like that, they'd have seen that dragons are no more immortal than anything else. The carcass lies at the edge of the trees, east of the city. If you don't believe me, go and look for yourself."

Olmec shook his head, hardly seeming able to credit his own ears.

"It was because of the dragons that our ancestors took refuge in Xuchotl," said he. "They dared not plunge into the forest again. Scores of them were slain and devoured by the monsters before they could reach the city?"

"Then your ancestors did not build Xuchotl?" asked Valeria.

"It was ancient when they first came into the land. How long it had stood here, not even its degenerate inhabitants knew."

"Your people came from Lake Zuad?" questioned Conan.

"Aye. Half a century ago part of the tribe of Tlazitlans rebelled against the Stygian kings and being defeated in battle, fled southward. For many weeks they wandered over desert, grasslands and hills, and at last came into the great forest, a thousand fighting men with their women and children.

"It was in the forest that the dragons fell upon them and slew and devoured many, so the people fled in a frenzy of fear before them, and at last came into the plain and saw the city of Xuchotl in the midst of it.

"They camped before the city, not daring to plunge into the forest beyond, for the night was made hideous with the noise of the battling monsters who made war upon each other incessantly. But they remained in the forest.

"The people of the city shut the gates and shot arrows at them from the walls.

The Tlazitlans were imprisoned on the plain, as if the ring of forest had been a great wall. For to venture into the woods would have been suicide.

"Then there came secretly to their camp one of their own blood, who, with a band of exploring soldiers had wandered into the forest long before when he was a young man. The dragons had slain all but him, and he had been admitted into the city. His name was Tolkemec –" a flame lighted the dark eyes at the mention of the name, and some of the people muttered under their breath and spat. "He agreed to open the gates to the warriors. He asked but that all captives taken be delivered into his hands.

"That night he opened the gates. The warriors swarmed in and the halls of Xuchotl ran red. Only a few hundred folk dwelt here, decaying remnants of a once great race. Tolkemec said they came from the east, from Old Kosala, when the ancestors of the Kosalans came up from the south and drove them out. They came westward and built a city here in the plain. Then after centuries, the climate changed, a forest grew where grasslands had rolled, and the dragons came in bellowing herds up from the southern swamps to hem the people of the city in the ring of open plain, even as we are now hemmed.

"Well, our fathers slew the people of Xuchotl, all except a hundred which were given living into the hands of Tolkemec, who had been a slave among them, and for many days and nights the halls re-echoed to their screams under the agony of his torturing.

"So our fathers dwelt here, for awhile in peace. Tolkemec took a girl of the tribe to wife, and, because he had opened the gates, and because he knew the art of making the Xuchotl wine, and of cultivating the fruit they ate – fruit which obtains its nourishment out of the air and is not planted in soil – he shared the rule of the tribe with the brothers who led the rebellion and the flight – Xotalanc and Tecuhltli.

"For a few years they dwelt in peace within the city. Then –" Olmec's eyes rested briefly on the silent woman at his side – "Tecuhltli took a woman to wife. Xotalanc desired her, and Tolkemec, who hated Xotalanc, aided Tecuhltli to steal her. Aye, she came willingly enough. Xotalanc demanded her back, and the council of the tribe decided that the matter should be left to the woman. She chose to remain with Tecuhltli. But Xotalanc was not satisfied. There was fighting, and gradually the tribe broke up into three factions – the people of Teculhtli and the people of Xotalanc. Already they had divided the city between them. Tecuhltli had the southern part of the city, Xotalanc the northern part, and Tolkemec dwelt with his family by the western gate.

"The factions fought bitterly, and Tolkemec aided first one side and then the other, betraying each faction as it pleased him. At last each faction retired to a place it could defend well. The people of Tecuhltli who had their dwellings in the chambers and halls in the southern end of the city, blocked up all doors except one on each tier, which could be easily defended. Xotalanc did the same, and so likewise did Tolkemec. But we of Tecuhltli fell on Tolkemec one night and butchered all his clan. Tolkemec we tortured for many days, and finally cast him into a dungeon to die. Somehow he managed to escape, and drag himself into the catacombs which lie beneath the city, and where lie the bodies of all the people, Xuchotlan or Tlazitlan, who ever died in the city. There without doubt, he died, and the superstitious among us swear that his ghost haunts the catacombs to this day, wailing among the bones of the dead.

"Fifty years ago the feud began. I was born in it. All in this chamber, except Tascela, were born in it. Most have died in it. We are a perishing race. There were hundreds in each faction when it began. Now we number but some forty men and women. How many Xotalancas there are we do not know, but I doubt if they are more numerous than we. For fifteen years no children have been born to us, and since we have slain no children among the Xotalancas, I think it is the same with them.

"We are dying, but before we die, we hope to finish the ancient feud, and to wipe out the remnants of our enemies."

And with his weird eyes blazing, Olmec told the story of that grisly feud, fought out in silent chambers and dim halls under the gleam of green fire-jewels, on floors smoldering with the flames of hell. Xotalanc was dead long ago, slain in a grim battle on an ivory stair. Tecuhltli was dead, flayed alive by the maddened Xotalancas who had captured him.

Olmec told of horrible battles fought in black corridors, of bloody fights waged under the gleam of the fire-jewels, of ambushes, treachery, cruelties, of tortures inflicted by both factions on helpless captives, men and women, tortures so ghastly that even the barbarous Cimmerian shrugged his shoulders. No wonder Techotl had trembled with the terror of capture.

Valeria listened spell-bound, to the tale of that hideous feud. The people of Xuchotl were obsessed with it. It was their only reason for existence. It filled their whole lives. Each expected to die in it. They remained within their barricaded quarter, occasionally stealing forth into the disputed land of empty corridors and chambers that lay between the opposite ends of the city. Sometimes they returned with frantic captives, or with grim tokens of victory in fight. Or perhaps they did not return at all, or returned only as severed heads cast down before the bolted bronze doors. It was particularly ghastly, these people, shut off from the rest of the world, caught together like rabid rats in a trap, butchering each other through the years, crouching and creeping through the sunless corridors to maim and murder.

And while Olmec talked Valeria felt the blazing eyes of the woman Tascela fixed for ever upon her.

"And we can never leave the city," said Olmec. "For fifty years no one has stepped outside the gate, except the victims bound and thrown forth for the dragon. And of late years even that has been discontinued. Once the dragon came from the forest to bellow about the wall. We who were born and raised here would fear to leave it, even were the dragon not there."

"Well," grunted Conan, "with your leave, we'll take our chance with the dragons. This feud is none of our business, and we don't care to get mixed up in it. If you'll show us the south gate, we'll be on our way."

Tascela's hands clenched and she started to speak, but Olmec interrupted her: "It is nearly nightfall. Wait at least until morning. If you wander forth into the plain tonight, you will certainly fall prey to the dragons."

"We crossed it last night without seeing any," answered Conan. "But perhaps it would be better to wait until morning. But no later than that. We wish to reach the west coast, and it's a march of many weeks, even if we had horses."

"We have jewels," offered Olmec.

"Well, listen," said Conan. "Suppose we do this: we'll help you clean out those Xotalancas, and then we'll all see what we can do about wiping out the dragons in the forest."

They were showed into ornate chambers, lighted by the slot-like skylights.

"Why don't the Xotalancas come over the roofs and shatter the glass?" Conan demanded.

"It can not be broken," answered Techotl, who had accompanied him into his chamber. "Besides the roofs would be hard to clamber over. They are mostly spires and domes and steep ridges."

"Who is this Tascela?" Conan asked. "Olmec's wife?"

Techotl shuddered and glanced about him before answering.

"No. She is – Tascela! She was the wife of Xotalanc – the woman about which the feud began."

"What are you saying?" demanded Conan. "That woman is young and beautiful. Are you trying to tell me that she was a wife fifty years ago?"

"Aye! She was a full-grown woman when the Tlazitlans journeyed from Lake Zuad. She is a witch, who possesses the knowledge of perpetual youth – but a grisly knowledge it is. I dare not say more."

And with his finger at his lips, he glided from the chamber.

Valeria awoke suddenly on her couch. There were no fire-gems in the room, but illumination was supplied by a jewel. In the weird dusky glow of the fire-gems she saw a shadowy figure bending over her. She was aware of a delicious, sensuous langour stealing over her that was not like natural sleep. Something had touched her face, awakening her.

The sight of the dim figure roused her instantly. Even as she recognized the

349

figure as the sullen Yasala, Tascela's maid, she was on her feet. Yasala whirled lithely, but before she could run, Valeria caught her wrist and wrenched her around to face.

"What the devil were you doing bending over me? What's that in your hand?"

The woman made no reply, but sought to cast the object away. Valeria twisted her arm in front of her and the thing fell to the floor – a great black exotic blossom on a jade green stem.

"The black lotus!" said Valeria between her teeth. "You were trying to drug me – if you hadn't accidentally awkened me by touching my face with that blossom – why did you do it? What's your game?"

Yasala maintained a sulky silence, and with an oath Valeria whirled her around, forced her to her knees and twisted her arm up behind her back.

"Tell me, or I'll tear your arm out of the socket."

Yasala squirmed in anguish as her arm was forced excruciatingly up between her shoulder blades, but a violent shaking of her head was the only answer she made.

"Slut!" Valeria cast her from her to sprawl on the floor. The pirate bent over her prostrate figure, her eyes blazing. Fear and the memory of Tascela's burning eyes stirred in her, rousing all her ruthless anger and tigerish instinct of self-preservation. The chambers were as silent as if Xuchotl were in reality a deserted city. A thrill of panic throbbed through Valeria, rendering her merciless.

"You came here for no good reason," she muttered, her eyes smoldering as it rested on the sullen figure with its lowered head. "There's some foul mystery here – treason or intrigue. Did Tascela send you? Does Olmec know you came?"

No answer. Valeria cursed venomously and slapped the woman first on one side and then the other. The blows resounded in the room.

Valeria turned and tore a handful of cords from a nearby hanging.

"You stubborn bitch!" she said between her teeth. "I'm going to strip you naked and tie you across that couch, and whip you with my sword-belt until you tell me what you were doing here."

"Why don't you scream?" she asked sardonically. "Who do you fear? Tascela or Olmec, or Conan?"

"Mercy," whispered the woman presently. "I will tell."

Valeria released her. Yasala was quivering, her limbs and body.

"Wine," she begged, indicating the vessel on the ivory table with a trembling hand. "Let me drink – then I will tell you." She rose unsteadily as Valeria picked up the vessel. She took it, raised it to her lips – and then dashed the contents full into the Aquilonian's face. Valeria reeled backward, shaking and clawing the stinging liquid out of her eyes, and her misty sight cleared enough to let her see Yasala dart across the room, fling back a bolt, throw open the door and run down the hall. The pirate was after her instantly, sword out and murder in her heart.

The woman turned a corner in the corridor and when Valeria reached it, she only an empty hall, and an open door that gaped blackly. A damp moldy scent reeked up from it, and Valeria shivered. That must be the door that led to the catacombs. Yasala had taken refuge there.

Valeria advanced to the door and looked down the flight of steps that vanished quickly into utter blackness. She shivered slightly at the thought of the thousands of corpses lying in their stone nitches down there, wrapped in their moldering cloths. She had no intention of groping her way down. Yasala doubtless knew every turn and twist of the subterranean passages. Valeria was drawing back, baffled, when a sobbing cry welled up from the blackness. Faintly human words were distinguishable, and the voice was that of a woman: "Oh, help! Help, in Set's name! Ahhh!" It trailed away and Valeria thought she heard the echo of a fiendish tittering.

Valeria felt her skin crawl. What had happened to Yasala down there in the thick blackness? That it had been she who cried out, the pirate did not doubt. But what peril could have befallen her? Was one of the Xotalancas lurking down there? Olmec had assured them that the south end of the catacombs were walled off from the rest, too securely for their enemies to break through from that direction. Besides that tittering had not sounded like a human being at all – Valeria closed the door and hurried back down the corridor. She regained her chamber and shot the bolt behind her. She was determined to make her way to Conan's room, and urge him to join her in an attempt to fight their way out of that city of devils. But even as she reached the door, a long-drawn scream of agony rang through the halls.

CHAPTER

It was the yelling of men and the clang of steel that   brought Conan bounding from his couch, broadsword in hand and wide awake. In an instant he had reached the door and flung it open, even as Techotl rushed in, eyes blazing, sword dripping and blood streaming from a gash in the neck.

"The Yotalancas!" he croaked, his voice hardly human. "They are within the doors!"

Conan thrust past him and ran down the narrow corridors, even as Valeria emerged from her chamber.

"What the devil is it?" she called.

"Techotl says the Xotalancas are in," he answered hurriedly. "That racket sounds like it."

They ran into the throne-room and burst upon a wild scene of blood. Some twenty men and women, their black hair streaming, and the white skulls gleaming on their breasts, were locked in combat with a somewhat larger number of Tecuhltli. The women on both sides fought as madly as the men. Already the room was strewn with corpses, the greater number of which were Tecuhltli.

351

Olmec, without his robe and naked but for a breech-clout, was fighting before his throne, and as Conan and Valeria entered, Tascela ran from an inner chamber, with a sword in her hand.

The rest was a whirling nightmare of steel. The feud came to a bloody end there. The losses of the Xotalancas had been greater, their position more desperate than the Tecuhltli had realized. Driven to frenzy by the word, gasped by a dying man, that mysterious white-skinned allies had joined their enemies, they had cast all in one furious onslaught. Though how they gained entrance into Tecuhltli remained a mystery until after the battle.

It was long and savage. The surprize had aided the Xotalancas and seven of the Tecuhltli were down before they knew their foes were on them. But still they outnumbered the Xotalancas, and they too were fired by the realization that it was the death-grip at last, and heartened by the presence of their allies.

In a melee of this sort no three Tlazitlans were a match for Conan. Taller, stronger and quicker than they, he moved through the whirling mass with the surety and devastating force of a hurricane. Valeria was as strong as a man, and her quickness and ferocity outmatched any that opposed her.

Only five women were with the Xotalancas and they were down and their throats cut before Conan and Valeria reached the fighting. And presently only Tecuhltli and their allies lived in the great throne room, and the staggering, blood-stained living set up a mad howling of triumph.

"How came they in Tecuhltli?" roared Olmec, brandishing his sword.

"It was Xatmec," stammered a warrior, wiping blood from a great gash across his shoulder. "He heard a noise and placed his ear against the door while I went to the mirrors to look. I saw the Xotalancas outside the door and one played on a pipe — Xatmec leaned frozen against the door, as if paralyzed by the strains of music that whispered through the panels.

"Then suddenly the music changed to a shrill keening and Xatmec screamed like one in agony and like a madman he tore opened the door and rushed out, with his sword lifted. A dozen blades struck him down and over his body the Xotalancas surged into the guard-room."

"The pipes of madness," muttered Olmec. "They were hidden in the city — old Tolkemec used to speak of them. The dogs found them, somehow. There is great magic hidden in this city — if we could only find it."

"Are these all of them?" demanded Conan.

Olmec shrugged his shoulders. Only thirty of his people were left. Men were driving twenty new crimson nails into the ebony column.

"I do not know."

"I'll go to Xotalanc and see," said Conan. "No, you won't, either," his to

Valeria. "You've got a stab in your leg. You'll stay here and get it bandaged. Shut up, will you? Who'll go and guide me?"

Techotl limped out.

"I'll go!"

"No, you won't. You're wounded."

A man volunteered and Olmec ordered another to go with the Cimmerian. Their names were Yanath and Topal. They led Conan through silent chambers and halls until they came to the bronze door that marked the boundary of Xotalanc. They tried it gingerly and it opened under their fingers. Awedly they stared into the green-lit chambers. For fifty years no man of Teculhtli had entered those halls save as a prisoner going to a hideous doom.

Conan strode in and they followed. They found no living men, but they found evidences of the feud.

In a chamber there stood rows of glass-like cases. And in these cases were human heads, perfectly preserved – scores of them.

Yanath stood staring at them, a wild light in his wild eyes.

"There is my brother's head," he murmured. "And my sister's son, and my father's brother!"

Suddenly he went mad. The sanity of all the Tlazitlans hung on a hair trigger. Howling and frothing he turned and drove his sword to the hilt in Topal's body. Topal went down and Yanath turned on Conan. The Cimmerian saw the man was hopelessly mad so he side-stepped and as the maniac went past, he swung a cut that severed shoulder bone and breast, and dropped the man dead beside his dying victim.

Conan knelt beside Topal and then caught the man's wrist as, with a dying effort, he drove a dagger at the Cimmerian's breast.

"Crom!" swore Conan. "Are you mad, too?"

"Olmec ordered it," gasped the dying man. "He bade me slay you while returning to Teculhtli –" and with the name of his clan on his lips, Topal died.

Conan rose, scowling. Then he turned and hurried back through the halls and chambers, toward Tecuhltli. His primitive sense of direction led him unerringly back the way they had come.

And as he approached Tecuhltli he was aware of someone ahead of him – someone who gasped and panted and advanced with a floundering noise. Conan sprang forward and saw Techotl crawling toward him. The man was bleeding from a deep gash in his breast.

"Conan!" he cried. "Olmec has taken the yellow-haired woman! I sought to stay him, but he struck me down. He thought he had slain me! Slay Olmec, take her and go! He lied to you! There was but one dragon in all the forest, and if you slew it, there is no fear but you can win through to the coast! For many years we worshipped it as a god, and offered up victims to it! Haste! Olmec has taken her to the —"

His head slumped down and he died.

Conan sprang up, his eyes like live coals. So that was why Olmec gave orders to Topal that he should be slain! He might have known what was going on in that black-bearded degenerate's mind. He raced recklessly, counting his opponents in his mind. There could not be more than fourteen or fifteen of them. In his rage he felt able to account for the whole clan single-handed.

But craft conquered, or rather controlled, his berserk rage. He would not attack through the door by which the Xotalancas had come. He would strike from a higher or a lower level. Doubtless half a century of habit would cause all the doors to be locked and bolted, anyway. When Topal and Yanath did not return, it might rouse fears that some of the Xotalancas still survived.

He went down a winding stair, and heard a low groan ahead of him. Entering cautiously he saw a giant figure strapped to a rack-like frame. A heavy iron ball was poised over his breast. His head rested on a bed of iron spikes. When this became unbearable the wretch lifted his head — and a strap fastened to his head worked the iron ball. Each time he lifted his head, the ball descended a few inches toward his hairy breast. Eventually it would crush him to a pulp. The man was gagged, but Conan recognized him. It was Olmec, prince of Teculhtli.

When Valeria retired into the chamber indicated by Olmec, a woman followed her and bandaged the stab in the calf of her leg. Silently that woman retired and as a shadow fell across her, Valeria looked up, to see Olmec staring down at her. She had laid her blood-stained sword on the couch.

"She has done a clumsy job," criticised the prince of Teculhtli, bending over the bandage. "Let me see —"

With a quickness amazing in one of his bulk, he snatched her sword and threw it across the chamber. His next move was to catch her in his giant arms.

Quick as he was, she almost matched him, for even as he grabbed her her dirk was in her hand and she stabbed murderous at his throat. Somehow he caught her wrist and then began a savage wrestling match, in which his superior strength and weight finally told. She was crushed down on a couch, disarmed and panting, her eyes blazing up at him like the eyes of a trapped tigress.

Though prince of Teculhtli, Olmec moved in haste and silence. He gagged and bound her and carried her along corridors and hallways to a secret chamber. There, before he could have his will of her, came Tascela. He hid the girl, and he had a clash of wits with Tascela, in which she persuaded him to drink wine with her. He did so and was instantly paralyzed. She dragged him into a torture room and stretched him on the rack where Conan found him.

Then she carried Valeria back to the throne-chamber where the survivors were gathered, after having carried the bodies of the slain into the catcombs. Four had failed to return and men whispered of the ghost of Tolkemec. She prepared to suck the blood from Valeria's heart to retain her own youth.

Meanwhile Conan had released Olmec, who swore to unite forces with him. Olmec led the way up a winding stair, where he struck Conan from behind. As they rolled down the stair Conan lost his sword, but strangled the prince with his bare hands.

Conan's leg was broken, but he hobbled to the throne room where he stumbled into a trap set for him. Then from the catacombs came old Tolkemec, who slew all the Tecuhltli with his magic and while he was so

[Draft stops here; the fifty-second — and probably last — page of the typescript is apparently lost.]

Ephemera

Letter to P. Schuyler Miller

Lock Box 313
Cross Plains, Texas
March 10, 1936

Dear Mr. Miller :

I feel indeed honored that you and Dr. Clark should be so interested in Conan as to work out an outline of his career and a map of his environs. Both are surprisingly accurate, considering the vagueness of the data you had to work with. I have the original map--that is, the one I drew up when I first started writing about Conan--around here somewhere and I'll see if I can't find it and let you have a look at it. It includes only the countries west of Vilayet and north of Kush. I've never attempted to map the southern and eastern kingdoms, though I have a fairly clear outline of their geography in my mind. However, in writing about them I feel a certain amount of license, since the inhabitants of the western Hyborian nations were about as ignorant concerning the peoples and countries of the south and east as the people of medieval Europe were ignorant of Africa and Asia. In writing about the western Hyborian nations I feel confined within the limits of known and inflexible boundaries and territories, but in fictionizing the rest of the world, I feel able to give my imagination freer play. That is, having adopted a certain conception of geography and ethnology, I feel compelled to abide by it, in the interests of consistency. My conception of the east and south is not so definite or so arbitrary.

Concerning Kush, however, it is one of the black kingdoms south of Stygia, the northern-most, in fact, and has given its name to the whole southern coast. Thus, when an Hyborian speaks of Kush, he is generally speaking of not the kingdom itself, one of many such kingdoms, but of the Black Coast in general. And he is likely to speak of any black man as a Kushite, whether he happens to be a Keshani, Darfari, Puntan, or Kushite proper. This is natural, since the Kushites were the first black men with whom the Hyborians came in contact--Barachan pirates trafficking with and raiding them.

As for Conan's eventual fate--frankly I can't predict it. In writing these yarns I've always felt less as creating them than as if I were simply chronicling his adventures as he told them to me. That's why they skip about so much, without following a regular order. The average adventurer, telling tales of a wild life at random, seldom follows any ordered plan, but narrates episodes widely separated by space and years, as they occur to him.

Your outline follows his career as I have visualized it pretty closely. The differences are minor. As you deduct, Conan was about seventeen when he was introduced to the public in "The Tower of the Elephant." While not fully matured, he was riper than the average civilized youth at that age. He was born on a battlefield, during a fight between his tribe and a horde of raiding Vanir. The country claimed by and roved over by his clan lay in the northwest of Cimmeria, but Conan was of mixed blood, although a purebred Cimmerian. His grandfather was a member of a southern tribe who had fled from his own people because of a blood-feud and after long wanderings, eventually taken refuge with the people of the north. He had taken part in many raids into the Hyborian nations in his youth, before his flight, and perhaps it was the tales he told of those softer countries which roused in Conan, as a child, a desire to see them. There are many things concerning Conan's life of which I am not certain myself. I do not know, for instance, when he got his first sight of civilized people. It might have been at Vanarium, or he might have made a peaceable visit to some frontier town before that. At Vanarium he was already a formidable antagonist, though only fifteen. He stood six feet and weighed 180 pounds, though he lacked much of having his full growth.

There was the space of about a year between Vanarium and his entrance into the thief-city of Zamora. During this time he returned to the northern territories of his tribe, and made his first journey beyond the boundaries of Cimmeria. This, strange to say, was north instead of south. Why or how, I am not certain, but he spent some months among a tribe of the Æsir, fighting with the Vanir and the Hyperboreans, and developing a hate for the latter which lasted all his life and later affected his policies as king of Aquilonia. Captured by them, he escaped southward and came into Zamora in time to make his debut in print.

I am not sure that the adventure chronicled in "Rogues in the House" occurred in Zamora. The presence of opposing factions of politics would seem to indicate otherwise, since Zamora was an absolute despotism where differing political opinions were not tolerated. I am of the opinion that the city was one of the small city-states lying just west of Zamora, and into which Conan had wandered after leaving Zamora. Shortly after this he returned for a brief period to Cimmeria, and there were other returns to his native land from time to time. The chronological order of his adventures is about as you have worked it out, except that they covered a little more time. Conan was about forty when he seized the crown of Aquilonia, and was about forty-four or forty-five at the time of "The Hour of the Dragon." He had no male heir at that time, because he had never bothered to formally make some woman his queen, and the sons of concubines, of which he had a goodly number, were not recognized as heirs to the throne.

He was, I think, king of Aquilonia for many years, in a turbulent and unquiet reign, when the Hyborian civilization had reached its most magnificent high-tide, and every king had imperial ambitions. At first he fought on the defensive, but I am of the opinion that at last he was forced into wars of aggression as a matter of self-preservation. Whether he succeeded in conquering a world-wide empire, or perished in the attempt, I do not know.

He travelled widely, not only before his kingship, but after he was king. He travelled to Khitai and Hyrkania, and to the even less known regions north of the latter and south of the former. He even visited a nameless continent in the western hemisphere, and roamed among the islands adjacent to it. How much of this roaming will get into print, I can not foretell with any accuracy. I was much interested in your remarks concerning findings on the Yamal Peninsula, the first time I had heard anything about that. Doubtless Conan had first-hand acquaintance with the people who evolved the culture described, or their ancestors, at least.

Hope you find "The Hyborian Age" interesting. I'm enclosing a copy of the original map. Yes, Napoli's done very well with Conan, though at times he seems to give him a sort of Latin cast of the countenance which isn't according to type, as I conceive it. However, that isn't enough to kick about.

Hope the enclosed data answers your questions satisfactorily; I'd be delighted to discuss any other phases you might wish, or go into more details about any point of Conan's career or Hyborian history or geography you might desire. Thanks again for your interest, and best wishes, for yourself and Dr. Clark.

Cordially,

Robert E. Howard.

P.S. You didn't mention whether you wanted the map and chronology returned, so I'm taking the liberty of retaining them to show to some friends; if you want them back, please let me know.

Map of the Hyborian Age

The following map was originally enclosed with Howard's letter of March 10, 1936, to P. Schuyler Miller. It is, as Howard states, a copy of the original map of the Hyborian Age, which the Texan had prepared in March 1932 (see *The Coming of Conan the Cimmerian*). However, as can readily be seen by comparing the different versions, Howard updated his map during the copying process, adding several cities and countries mentioned in the tales.

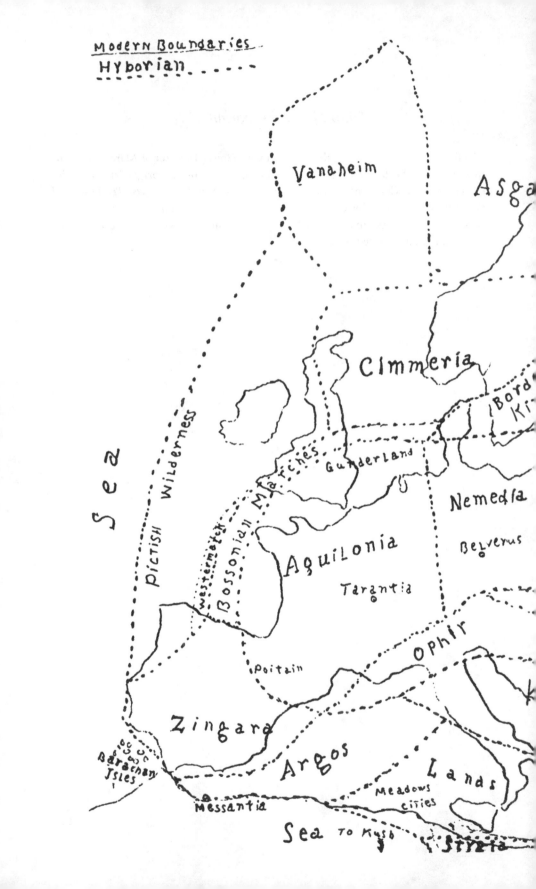

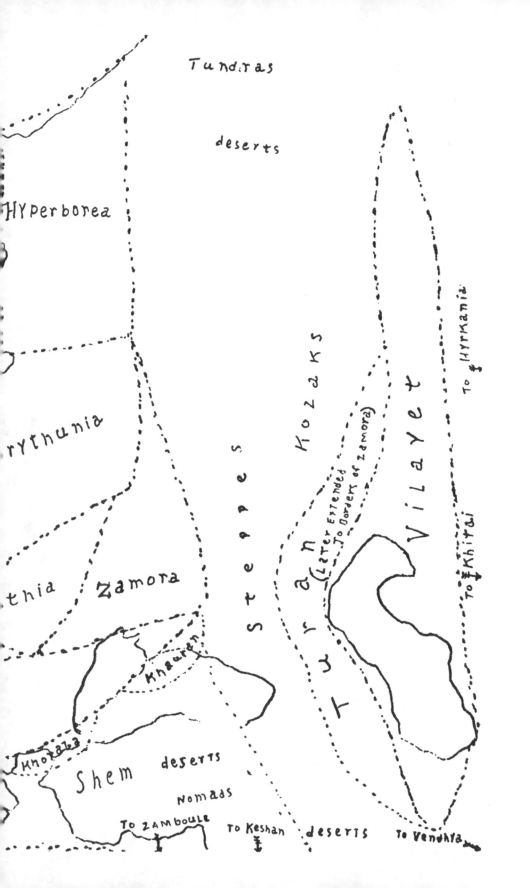

Appendices

HYBORIAN GENESIS PART III
Notes on the Creation of the Conan Stories
by Patrice Louinet

As he was completing *A Witch Shall Be Born*, Robert E. Howard probably felt that he could sell almost any Conan story he submitted to Weird Tales. By 1934, after several years of hardship, including two years early in his career during which he did not sell a single story, Howard had become one of the stars of the magazine. *Witch* was, according to editor Farnsworth Wright, the "best" of the Conan stories submitted to date; praise for Howard and his Conan stories could be found in the letter column of almost every issue of Weird Tales, and, by far the most revealing factor, the Texan was present in ten of the twelve issues published in 1934, eight of these featuring Conan, with the last four winning cover privilege, an impressive record.

Howard had been immersed in Conan for months: *People of the Black Circle* had been written in February and March; *The Hour of the Dragon* was begun just afterward and sent to its intended British publisher on May 20; and *A Witch Shall Be Born* had been completed by early June. Howard's sole respite during those months was the short visit of his colleague E. Hoffmann Price in April. Early in June, then, Howard took his first vacation in a long time. He later informed his correspondent August Derleth that he had "completed several weeks of steady work," and told him that "a friend and I took a brief trip into southern New Mexico and extreme western Texas; saw the Carlsbad Caverns, a spectacle not to [be] duplicated on this planet, and spent a short time in El Paso. First time I'd ever been there...."

The friend in question was Truett Vinson, one of Howard's best friends since high school, about whom more later. The two men left Cross Plains, Howard's hometown, in early June and were gone for a week. That the trip proved enjoyable is attested by mentions of it in almost all of Howard's letters of the following weeks, with the visit to the Carlsbad Caverns in New Mexico as the high point of the short holidays. Howard was particularly impressed by these natural wonders and waxed at length about them to his correspondents, notably H. P. Lovecraft:

> I can not describe the fantastic wonders of that great cavern. You must see it yourself to appreciate it. It lies high up among the mountains, and I never saw skies so blue and clear as those that arch titanically above those winding trails up which the traveller must labor to reach the entrance of the Cavern. They are of a peculiarly deep hue beggaring attempts at description. The entrance of the Cavern is gigantic, but it is dwarfed by the dimensions of the interior. One descends seemingly

endlessly by winding ramps, for some seven hundred feet. We entered at ten thirty o'clock, and emerged about four. The English language is too weak to describe the Cavern. The pictures do not give a good idea; for one thing they exaggerate the colors; the coloring is really subdued, somber rather than sparkling. But they do not give a proper idea of the size, of the intricate patterns carved in the limestone throughout the millenniums.... In the Cavern natural laws seem suspended; it is Nature gone mad in a riot of fantasy. Hundreds of feet above arched the great stone roof, smoky in the mist that eternally rises. Huge stalactites hung from the roof in every conceivable shape, in shafts, in domes, in translucent sheets, like tapestries of ice. Water dripped, building gigantic columns through the ages, pools of water gleamed green and weird here and there.... We moved through a wonderland of fantastic giants whose immemorial antiquity was appalling to contemplate.

Shortly upon his return to Cross Plains, Howard set out to write yet another Conan story, *The Servants of Bit-Yakin*. The story is not a particularly memorable one, with a rather unconvincing plot and insipid heroine, but it has a setting markedly different from the other Conan tales, taking place entirely in a vast natural wonder, filled with caves and subterranean rivers, which was evidently greatly inspired by Howard's visit to the Carlsbad Caverns. As he concluded to Lovecraft: "God, what a story you could write after such an exploration!... *Anything* seemed possible in that monstrous twilight underworld, seven hundred and fifty feet below the earth. If some animate monster had risen horrifically from among the dimness of the columns and spread his taloned anthropomorphic hands above the throng, I do not believe that anyone would have been particularly surprised." Howard probably decided he could write the tale himself, after all.

The result is not quite satisfying, but it was paving the way for greater things to come: for the first time in the series, Howard was weaving elements of his own country into his Conan tales. It was a timid first step to be sure, but an important one nonetheless. The story is not mentioned in any of the extant Howard letters and no record of submission survives. It was accepted by Farnsworth Wright for $155, payable on publication, and published in the March 1935 issue of Weird Tales. Some confusion exists as to Howard's original title for the tale. The story first appeared in Weird Tales under the title *Jewels of Gwahlur*. Howard wrote three drafts: the first is untitled, while the second and third are titled *The Servants of Bit-Yakin*. The third draft has come to us as a carbon of the version sent to Weird Tales, hence the definitive one. A third title, *Teeth of Gwahlur*, appears in a listing found among Howard's papers long after his death (from which the information on the price paid by the magazine comes). This listing was not prepared by Howard himself, though evidently derived from either an original Howard document or series of documents. From internal evidence, it appears that this page was prepared well after the story was published and was very probably intended as a listing of stories sold to Weird Tales to establish what was owed to Howard's estate by the magazine, following his death. In his listings of sales, Howard, as a general rule, would always give the published version's title rather than his own, which is the case in this document (*The Slithering Shadow* over *Xuthal of the Dusk*, *Shadows in the Moonlight* over *Iron Shadows in the Moon*). It seems quite probable, then, that *Teeth* was simply an error: perhaps Howard himself, in giving the title, was remembering the name of the necklace in the story, and the later transcription carried forward the error.

In the weeks that followed, Howard once again decided to experiment with his Conan stories. The attempt itself did not result in a complete story, but it led to a major evolution in the series. If *The Servants of Bit-Yakin* timidly borrowed from a place Howard had visited, this time the Texan opted for a definitely American setting, at the price of an eviction of the Cimmerian himself from his Hyborian world.

In the second part of 1934, it was possible to detect a growing distancing of Howard from his Cimmerian creation, notably in the conversations he had with Novalyne Price, whom he began dating in August. In October, he confided to her that he was "getting a little tired of Conan.... This country needs to be written about. There are all kinds of stories around here."

The author to whom Howard looked when it came to finding inspiration for this new tale was one of his favorites: Robert W. Chambers. Howard's library included three of this author's novels dealing with the American Revolution: *The Maid-at-Arms* (1902), *The Little Red Foot* (1921) and *America, or the Sacrifice* (1924). These novels were to provide the background and inspiration for Howard's next tale of the Hyborian Age, *Wolves Beyond the Border*. A lot of confusing and erroneous information on Howard's use of the Chambers material had appeared over the years until Howard scholar Rusty Burke set the record straight. All the conclusions on the exact degree of that influence originate with Burke's research or are derived from his pioneering efforts.

As he had done in 1932 when he made the decision to write *The Hyborian Age* to give more coherence to his Hyborian world, Howard first proceeded to jot down a series of notes that would help him feel more at ease with the events and locale he was to write about (see page 285). There can be no doubt at all that Chambers' novels were very much in Howard's mind when he wrote this. Almost all the names are taken nearly verbatim from the novels: Schohira for Schoharie, Oriskany for Oriskonie, Caughnawaga for Conawaga, etc. The situation and events Howard describes in his document also clearly evoke Chambers' dramatization of the

American Revolution. More names derived from Chambers would find their way into *Wolves Beyond the Border*.

Wolves is one of the most intriguing Conan fragments precisely because it is not, strictly speaking, a Conan story. It was not the first time Howard had attempted to do something different with Conan and, as we are about to see, not the first time he experimented with another character because he was starting to feel "out of contact" with one of his creations.

Shortly before he wrote his novel *The Hour of the Dragon*, Howard had attempted another story in which Conan is only an off-stage presence for a significant part of the tale. In that case, however, Conan's absence was confined to the first chapters of a story which was envisioned as a novel; as the synopsis for the complete story attests, the Cimmerian was intended as a prominent character, if not actually the protagonist of the story. The situation can be seen as a parallel to that of *A Witch Shall Be Born*, in which the Cimmerian acts mostly off-stage. But in the case of *Wolves Beyond the Border*, the situation is markedly different, most notably due to the fact that this is a first-person narrative, in which Conan makes no appearance, though he is mentioned several times in the course of the story.

A very similar situation had arisen a few years earlier in Howard's career, and makes for an interesting comparison. In 1926, Howard created Kull the Atlantean, his first epic fantasy character, about whom the Texan wrote or began a dozen tales. In 1928, however, Howard apparently started to lose interest in his character. He then began – but never completed – a very intriguing fragment in which the major character was not Kull, who was relegated to a minor role, but his friend Brule, the Pictish warrior, whose characteristics were markedly different in that tale than in his previous appearances. Kull was apparently becoming merely a supporting character in his own series, in quite the same fashion Conan seems to be in *Wolves Beyond the Border*. Howard never completed the fragment, but from that moment on the character of Kull underwent a drastic evolution. It is quite striking to see that in those two fragments, the off-stage characters are barbarians who have become or are becoming kings of civilized countries. And in both fragments, the sentiments of the new protagonists when it comes to politics are about the same. Compare the following:

> The people of Conajohara scattered throughout the Westermarck, in Schohira, Conawaga, or Oriskawny, but many of them went southward and settled near Fort Thandara.... There they were later joined by other settlers for whom the older provinces were too thickly inhabited, and presently there grew up the district known as the Free Province of Thandara, because it was not like the other provinces, royal grants to great lords east of the marches and settled by them, but cut out of the

wilderness by the pioneers themselves without aid of the Aquilonian nobility. We paid no taxes to any baron. Our governor was not appointed by any lord, but we elected him ourselves, from our own people, and he was responsible only to the king. We manned and built our forts ourselves, and sustained ourselves in war as in peace. And Mitra knows war was a constant state of affairs, for there was never peace between us and our savage neighbors, the wild Panther, Alligator and Otter tribes of Picts. (from *Wolves Beyond the Border*)

"We of The Islands are all one blood, but of many tribes, and each tribe has customs and traditions peculiar to itself alone. We all acknowledge Nial of the Tatheli as over-king but his rule is loose. He does not interfere with our affairs among ourselves, nor does he levy tribute or taxes.... [H]e takes no toll of my tribe, the Borni, nor of any other tribe. Neither does he interfere when two tribes go to war – unless some tribe encroaches on the three who pay tribute.... And when the Lemurians or the Celts or any foreign nation or band of reavers come against us, he sends forth for all tribes to put aside their quarrels and fight side by side. Which is a good thing. He might be a supreme tyrant if he liked, for his own tribe is very strong, and with the aid of Valusia he might do as he liked – but he knows that though he might, with his tribes and their allies, crush all the other tribes, there would never be peace again...." (from the untitled Kull fragment)

Here are more than passing resemblances. In both instances, the peculiar political turmoil can also be read as a mirror of a similar turmoil taking place in Howard's psyche, connected to the social situation of his regular protagonists: Kull the king of Valusia and Conan the soon-to-be king of Aquilonia. In both instances, the Picts – only mentioned once so far in the Conan series (in *The Phoenix on the Sword*) – appear as the necessary catalysts for the change: Brule is a Pict, and the threat they pose to the Aquilonian settlement triggers the events of *Wolves Beyond the Border*. The Picts – the savages forever present in Howard's universe – force the Howardian characters to reveal their true nature.

As was the case with the Kull fragment then, Howard did not complete *Wolves Beyond the Border*. His first draft diminished to part-story, part-synopsis, while the second was simply abandoned. The tale was probably at the same time too derivative of Chambers and too much a necessary exercise before Howard could fully tackle this new phase of his character's evolution.

To say that *Beyond the Black River* was born on the ashes of *Wolves Beyond the Border* would be belaboring the obvious. This time, however, Howard got rid almost entirely of the Chambers influence. There is no plot element in *Black River* which can be traced back to Chambers, and only a few names still show the initial connection (for instance, Conajohara was carried on from *Wolves* and "Balthus" was derived from the "Baltus" of *The Little Red Foot*). *Beyond the Black River* is pure Howard.

The tale was particularly dear to Howard. To August Derleth he remarked that he "wanted to see if [he] could write an interesting Conan yarn without sex interest." He was a little more explicit with Lovecraft, writing that his latest sale to Weird Tales was "a two-part Conan serial: 'Beyond the Black River' – a frontier story... In the Conan story I've attempted a new style and setting entirely – abandoned the exotic settings of lost cities, decaying civilizations, golden domes, marble palaces, silk-clad dancing girls, etc., and thrown my story against a background of forests and rivers, log cabins, frontier outposts, buckskin-clad settlers, and painted tribesmen."

It was to Novalyne Price that Howard fully bared his sentiments toward that story:

> Bob began to talk. But he was not berating civilization; instead, he was praising the simple things that civilization had to offer: standing on street corners, talking with friends; walking with the warmth of the sun on your back, a faithful dog by your side; hunting cactus with your best girl.
>
> [...]
>
> "I sold Wright a yarn like that a few months ago." He turned and looked at me, his eyes turbulent. "I'm damned surprised he took it. It's different from my other Conan yarns...no sex...only men fighting against the savagery and bestiality about to engulf them. I want you to read it when it comes out. It's filled with the important little things of civilization, little things that make men think civilization's worth living and dying for."
>
> [...]
>
> He was excited about it because it was about this country and it sold! He had a honing to write more about this country, not an ordinary cowboy yarn, or a wild west shoot 'em up, though God knew this country was alive with yarns like that waiting to be written. But in his heart, he wanted to say more than that. He wanted to tell the simple story of this country and the hardships the settlers had suffered, pitted against a frightened, semi-barbaric people – the Indians, who were trying to hold on to a way of life and a country they loved.... But a novel depicting the settlers' fear as they tried to carve out a new life, and the Indians' fear as they tried to hold on to a doomed country; why, girl, all that would make the best damn novel ever written about frontier life in the Southwest.

[…]
"I tried that yarn out to see what Wright would do about it. I was afraid he wouldn't take it, but he did! By God, he took it! "

Beyond the Black River is considered by many Howard scholars to be his best story, encapsulating the essence of his philosophy: "Barbarism is the natural state of mankind.... Civilization is unnatural. It is a whim of circumstance. And barbarism must always ultimately triumph."

Indeed, all the characters who are not barbarians meet their doom in the tale: Tiberias the merchant, presented as the epitome of civilized decadence, is of course the first example, portrayed with evident scorn as a man unwilling or unable to adjust his civilized ways to life on the Frontier. But even the woodsmen, born to civilization but having lived their lives on the frontier, can not hope to prevail: "They were sons of civilization, reverted to a semi-barbarism. [Conan] was a barbarian of a thousand generations of barbarians. They had acquired stealth and craft, but he had been born to these things. He excelled them even in lithe economy of motion. They were wolves, but he was a tiger." The frontiersmen, Balthus, and Valannus all died because of this, and Howard's genius was not to sacrifice his story for the sake of the usual conventions of the genre.

Much has been written about the exact signification of the last paragraph of the story. Many erroneously credit the statement to Conan, as if it were his sentiment, but it is not Conan but an unnamed forester who utters these words. That the barbarians always ultimately triumph is a simple report of what has just transpired: only Conan and the Picts have survived the ordeal, because it was their nature to survive. That Conan had in fact more in common with the Picts he was fighting than with the Aquilonians had been made clear by Howard earlier in the story:

"But some day a man will rise and unite thirty or forty clans [of the Picts], just as was done among the Cimmerians, when the Gundermen tried to push the border northward, years ago. They tried to colonize the southern marches of Cimmeria: destroyed a few small clans, built a fort-town, Venarium, – you've heard the tale."

"So I have indeed," replied Balthus, wincing.... "My uncle was at Venarium when the Cimmerians swarmed over the walls.... The barbarians swept out of the hills in a ravening horde, without warning, and stormed Venarium with such fury none could stand before them. Men, women and children were butchered. Venarium was reduced to a mass of charred ruins, as it is to this day. The Aquilonians were driven back across the marches, and have never since tried to colonize the

Cimmerian country. But you speak of Venarium familiarly. Perhaps you were there?"

"I was," grunted the other. "I was one of the horde that swarmed over the walls...."

[...]

"Then you, too, are a barbarian!" he exclaimed involuntarily.

The other nodded, without taking offense.

"I am Conan, a Cimmerian."

The import of this passage was not merely to give some additional biographical information on the Cimmerian, but rather to make explicit the connection between Conan and the Picts. Conan is a barbarian "as ferocious as the Picts, and much more intelligent" and this is why he will survive. The insistence on Conan's elemental nature, much more marked than in any of the previous tales of the Cimmerian, very probably provoked the emergence of Balthus as the character readers – and Howard himself – could relate to. Critic George Scithers once noted that Howard had undoubtedly projected himself and his dog Patches into this story under the guise of Balthus and Slasher. As a civilized man himself, Howard could no more hope to prevail in the Hyborian Age than his civilized characters.

It was a rare thing indeed in pulp fiction to see a tale concluding with so bleak an ending, in which most of the characters die and the situation is worse at the end of the story than it was at its beginning. Howard was here trying to deliver a message much more than to simply add another Conan story to his bibliography.

Beyond the Black River was bought by Farnsworth Wright in early October 1934. It was published as a serial in the May and June 1935 issues of Weird Tales, but without the honors of the cover. Either Wright wanted to add some variety to his covers (he hadn't granted *The Servants of Bit-Yakin* cover privilege either), or the lack of a semi-naked heroine prevented him from doing that. The cover for the May 1935 issue did not feature an undressed woman, though, so that question must remain unanswered.

In the months of October and November 1934 Howard was apparently too much occupied with his romance with Novalyne Price to devote any time to writing new Conan tales. At about the time *Beyond the Black River* was accepted, though, Howard received bad news from England: "Just got a letter informing me that the English company which had promised to bring out my book [the Conan novel *The Hour of the Dragon*] had gone into the hands of the receiver. Just my luck. The yarn's in the hands of the company which bought up the assets, but I haven't heard from them." The novel was, however, soon returned. Howard very probably touched it up very slightly, sent it to Weird Tales later in the year, and soon received news that it was accepted, probably in early January 1935. Wright was apparently satisfied that Howard was returning to less experimental tales: "Wright says it's my best Conan story so far."

In December, as he was informing Lovecraft of the sale of *Beyond the Black River* and commenting on its unusual tone, he added: "Some day I'm going to try my hand at a longer yarn of the same style, a serial of four or five parts."

It appears that Howard didn't wait very long before writing this serial. *The Black Stranger* is one of those Howard stories for which we have no information regarding composition, but the writing date can be estimated around January and/or February 1935 thanks to the partial drafts of other stories found on the backs of the pages of several drafts. On the back of *The Black Stranger* are found several pages for stories composed in December 1934 and early 1935. It seems reasonable enough to suppose that Howard began work on that serial after his revision – and the acceptance – of *The Hour of the Dragon.*

The Black Stranger was evidently conceived as a follow-up of sorts to *Beyond the Black River* featuring once again Conan opposed to the Picts, and once again it was a very experimental tale, as the Cimmerian isn't introduced until halfway through the novelette-length story. (He is, of course, featured in the first chapter, but his identity is not revealed to the reader.)

The Black Stranger has never received the critical attention it is due, primarily because it was not published in its original form until 1987, when Karl Edward Wagner included it in an anthology. In all its previous appearances, the story had been mercilessly butchered. The tale is simple enough on its surface, mixing elements of piratical adventure and Indian warfare, but should definitely not be dismissed in a cavalier way, as has been done sometimes. *The Black Stranger* is an extremely complex tale once one has understood that it is replete, consciously or unconsciously, with autobiographical elements, much more so than any of the stories Howard had written to date.

The story is set on the coasts of the Hyborian Age's equivalent of the United States, at a time which would roughly correspond to our seventeenth century. It is the tale of early settlers – of a sort – on a continent that is still largely dominated by wild tribes, the Hyborian Age equivalent of Native Americans. A child is prominently featured, a rare occurrence in a Howard tale. Tina is quite a mystery to the reader: she is presented as a "pitiful waif... taken away from a brutal master encountered on that long voyage up from the southern coasts." What few children appear in Howard's fiction all share an unhappy youth; all are orphans or have been abandoned by their parents, and Tina is no exception. In this case, however, Belesa has apparently adopted the child as her own. A mysterious Black Man is hiding in the forest around the settlers' stockade.

"Art thou like the Black Man that haunts the forest round about us?" asks the heroine of Nathaniel Hawthorne's *The Scarlet Letter* of her husband, Roger

Chillingworth. Hawthorne's novel, published in 1850, presents points of remarkable resemblance to Howard's tale. Both stories are centered around a woman and her child (real or adopted), forced to live in a hostile environment, victims of the scorn of the men around them. The time frame and settings are remarkably similar, and Pearl, the young heroine of Hawthorne's novel, is a child as strange and fey as Tina. In both stories, the child is frightened by a mysterious Black Man almost always offstage. There is too much similarity to consider this a simple matter of coincidence. Hawthorne was not represented in Howard's library, and he is never mentioned by Howard in any of the surviving papers. That he had read Hawthorne, perhaps as part of his schooling, seems more than probable, though: *The Scarlet Letter* seems to have furnished a lot of background for *The Black Stranger*, even though the events themselves have nothing in common.

All this invites a different reading of the tale, in which Tina may be seen as a fatherless child, particularly sensitive to the presence of the Black Man. Readers familiar with Howard's biography will be even more startled, for in Hawthorne's novel Pearl's mother is named Hester, and the father she does not know, counterpart to Tina's Black Man, is the blue-eyed physician Roger Chillingworth. Howard's mother's name was Hester, and she was married to a blue-eyed physician.

The Black Stranger apparently failed to sell to Weird Tales, though no record for this survives. Wright was perhaps irritated by Howard's experimental forays, and, probably around February or March 1935, for the first time in many months rejected a Conan tale. Howard decided to salvage what he could, and rewrote the story. He invented a new character – Terence Vulmea, an Irish pirate – to replace Conan, got rid of all the Hyborian references, and submitted the new story, rechristened *Swords of the Red Brotherhood*, to his agent Otis Adelbert Kline in late May 1935. The new version was circulated for several years, and was sold in 1938, but the magazine which was to publish it folded, so this version didn't see print until 1976.

The next Conan tale would be anything but experimental. *The Man-Eaters of Zamboula* was apparently written around March 1935, judging from the stories found on the back of the draft pages. It is a routine Conan story, similar in quality to those Howard had been forced to write when he was in dire need of money. Surrounded by such masterpieces as *Beyond the Black River*, *The Black Stranger* and the future *Red Nails*, it more than pales in comparison. It seems that Howard borrowed the settings from the various Middle Eastern adventures he was writing at the same time (featuring his characters Kirby O'Donnell and Francis Xavier Gordon), while borrowing some of the premises of an unsold detective story, *Guests of the Hoodoo Room*, which very likely preceded the Conan story by a few months. *Guests* also featured cannibals capturing poor wretches by way of a rigged hotel room. The plot is rather unconvincing, but Howard probably knew this wouldn't prevent Wright from accepting the story. The scene in which Zabibi/Nafertari dances naked amid the snakes seems to have been written with only one goal to mind: to win the cover spot. Brundage's cover illustration for that story is indeed a remarkable one. That it does not feature the Cimmerian was something Howard was growing accustomed to: of the nine Weird Tales covers illustrating a Conan story, the Cimmerian himself was portrayed in only three.

On December 22, 1934, Howard presented Novalyne Price with a most surprising Christmas present: expecting a history book, she was presented instead with a copy of *The Complete Works of Pierre Louÿs*:

"A history?" I asked bewildered.

He shifted his weight in his chair and grinned. "Well,... Yeah. It's a kind of history."

[...]

Then Bob said the book described very vividly our "rotting civilization."

[...]

After Bob left, I sat down, unwrapped the book, and began to look at it very carefully. I read the inscription again, trying to make sense out of it : "The French have one gift – the ability to guild decay and change the maggots of corruption to the humming birds of poetry – as demonstrated by this volume."

Some time later, Novalyne was questioning Howard about this very peculiar present:

"Bob, why did you give me that book by Pierre Louÿs?"

He whirled and looked at me. "Didn't you like it?"

"It was a little too strong for my blood," I said defensively. "I didn't read too much of it."

"Read it.... You lead a sheltered life. You don't know what's going on in the world."

That irritated me. "I don't care to know things like that," I said hotly. "It seems to me knowing about them doesn't make the world a better place; it only makes you a silent partner."

"You're a silent partner, whether you like it or not." He was getting warmed up now. "You see, girl, when a civilization begins to decay and die, the only thing men or women think about is the gratification of their body's desires. They become preoccupied with sex. It colors their thinking, their laws, their religion – every aspect of their lives.

[...]

"That's what I'm trying to tell you girl. Men quit reading fiction, because they only want true stories of men's sexual exploits.... A few years ago, I had a hard time selling yarns ... about sex. Now, I'm going to have to work to catch up with the market.... Damn it to hell, girl, sex will be in everything you see and hear. It's the way it was when Rome fell."

[...]

"Girl, I'm working on a yarn like that now – a Conan yarn. Listen to me. When you have a dying civilization, the normal, accepted life style ain't strong enough to satisfy the damned insatiable appetites of the courtesans and, finally, of all the people. They turn to Lesbianism and things like that to satisfy their desires.... I am going to call it "The Red Flame of Passion.""

The Red Flame of Passion was quite evidently the story that was to become *Red Nails*, but Howard wasn't yet ready to commit his idea to paper. A few months later, around late April or May 1935, Howard had another conversation on the subject with Novalyne:

Bob volunteered that he wasn't through writing Conan stories. I was sorry about that, for I don't care much for Conan, what little I've scanned through.

Bob said he had an idea for a Conan yarn that was about to jell. Hadn't got to the place where he was ready to write it. All he'd done so far was make a few notes, put it aside to let it lie there in his subconsciousness till it was fully built up.

"What's this one about?" I asked.

"I think this time I'm going to make it one of the sexiest, goriest yarns I've ever written. I don't think you'd care for it."

"Not if it's gory." I looked at him a little puzzled. "What do you mean 'sexy stories'?"

"My God. My Conan yarns are filled with sex."

[...]

I couldn't see that the Conan yarns Bob had brought me to read had any sex in them. Gore, yes. Sex, no.

"You have sex in the Conan yarns?" I said unbelievingly.

"Hell, yes. That's what he did – drinking, whoring, fighting. What else was there in life?"

Red Nails was still not to be written for another few weeks, though.

One reason was Weird Tales' shaky financial situation. On May 6, 1935, Howard wrote to Farnsworth Wright: "I always hate to write a letter like this, but dire necessity forces me to. It is, in short, an urgent plea for money.... As you know it has been six months since *The People of the Black Circle* (the story the check for which is now due me) appeared in Weird Tales. Weird Tales owes me over eight hundred dollars for stories already published and supposed to be paid for on publication – enough to pay all my debts and get me back on my feet again if I could receive it all at once. Perhaps this is impossible. I have no wish to be unreasonable; I know times are hard for everybody. But I don't believe I am being unreasonable in asking you to pay me a check each month until the accounts are squared. Honestly, at the rate we're going now, I'll be an old man before I get paid up! And my need for money now is urgent." Howard's need for money was real, as his mother's health was declining at an alarming rate and the medical expenses to care for her were soaring.

It took yet another serious incident in Howard's life to make the story jell: early in the summer, Novalyne Price began dating one of Howard's best friends, Truett Vinson, without telling him. Howard discovered this a few weeks later, just as he and Truett were about to take a trip together to New Mexico. Vinson and Howard were gone a week, and we can only imagine Howard's state of mind during those few days.

The high-point of the visit was Lincoln, home of the famous "Bloody Lincoln County War." It was during this visit that Howard found the last elements he needed to write *Red Nails*: for all their pseudo-Aztec names, Xuchotl and its inhabitants found their origin not in Lake Zuad, but in the little New Mexican town. The following passage from Howard's July 23, 1935, letter to Lovecraft is a lengthy one, but it is indispensable to understanding what Howard was trying to do in *Red Nails*.

[Vinson and I] came to the ancient village of Lincoln, dreaming amidst its gaunt mountains like the ghost of a blood-stained past. Of Lincoln Walter Noble Burns, author of The Saga of Billy the Kid has said: "The village went to sleep at the close of Lincoln County war and has never awakened again. If a railroad never comes to link it with the far-away world, it may slumber on for a thousand years. You will find Lincoln now just as it was when Murphy and McSween and Billy the Kid knew it. The village is an anachronism, a sort of mummy town...."

I can offer no better description. A mummy town. Nowhere have I ever come face to face with the past more vividly; nowhere has that past become so realistic, so understandable. It was like stepping out of my own age, into the fragment of an elder age, that has somehow survived.... Lincoln is a haunted place; it is a dead town; yet it lives with a life that died fifty years ago.... The descendants of old enemies live peacefully side

381

by side in the little village; yet I found myself wondering if the old feud were really dead, or if the embers only smoldered, and might be blown to flame by a careless breath.

[...]

I have never felt anywhere the exact sensations Lincoln aroused in me — a sort of horror predominating. If there is a haunted spot on this hemisphere, then Lincoln is haunted. I felt that if I slept the night there, the ghosts of the slain would stalk through my dreams. The town itself seemed like a bleached, grinning skull. There was a feel of skeletons in the earth underfoot. And that, I understand, is no flight of fancy. Every now and then somebody ploughs up a human skull. So many men died in Lincoln.

[...]

Lincoln is a haunted town — yet it is not merely the fact of knowing so many men died there that makes it haunted, to me. I have visited many spots where death was dealt whole-sale....But none of these places ever affected me just as Lincoln did. My conception of them was not tinged with a definite horror as in Lincoln. I think I know why. Burns, in his splendid book that narrates the feud, missed one dominant element entirely; and this is the geographical, or perhaps I should say topographical effect on the inhabitants. I think geography is the reason for the unusually savage and bloodthirsty manner in which the feud was fought out, a savagery that has impressed everyone who has ever made an intelligent study of the feud and the psychology behind it. The valley in which Lincoln lies is isolated from the rest of the world. Vast expanses of desert and mountains separate it from the rest of humanity — deserts too barren to support human life. The people in Lincoln lost touch with the world. Isolated as they were, their own affairs, their relationship with one another, took on an importance and significance out of proportion to their actual meaning. Thrown together too much, jealousies and resentments rankled and grew, feeding upon themselves, until they reached monstrous proportions and culminated in those bloody atrocities which startled even the tough West of that day. Visualize that narrow valley, hidden away among the barren hills, isolated from the world, where its inhabitants inescapably dwelt side by side, hated and being hated, and at last killing and being killed. In such restricted, isolated spots, human passions smolder and burn, feeding on the impulses which give them birth, until they reached a point that can hardly be conceived by dwellers in more fortunate spots. It was with a horror I frankly confess that I visualized the reign of terror that stalked that blood-drenched valley; day and night was a tense waiting, waiting until the thunder of the sudden guns broke the tension for a moment and men died like flies – and then silence followed, and the tension shut down again. No man who valued his life dared speak; when a shot rang out at night and a human being cried out in agony, no one dared open the door and see who had fallen. I visualized people caught together like rats, fighting in terror and agony and bloodshed; going about their work by day with a shut mouth and an averted eye, momentarily expecting a bullet in the back; and at night lying shuddering behind locked doors, trembling in expectation of the stealthy footstep, the hand on the bolt, the sudden blast of lead through the windows. Feuds in Texas were generally fought out in the open, over wide expanses of country. But the nature of the Bonito Valley determined the nature of the feud – narrow, concentrated, horrible. I have heard of people going mad in isolated places; I believe the Lincoln County War was tinged with madness.

Upon returning to Cross Plains, in late June 1935, Howard at last sat down to write the story which had been germinating in his mind for so many months. If the Bloody Lincoln County War, his handling of sex in the Conan stories, the particularly strained situation between Novalyne, Vinson and himself, and his mother's rapidly deteriorating health furnished the immediate background to the new Conan story, several prototypes also helped give form to the tale.

More than two years earlier, he had completed the Conan story *Xuthal of the Dusk*, which has justly been considered a precursor of sorts to *Red Nails*. The arrival of Conan and a woman in a city cut off from the rest of the Hyborian world, in which they have to face an evil woman and decadent inhabitants, is the basic framework common to both stories. *Xuthal of the Dusk* is a rather inferior Conan tale, probably because Howard was not yet an accomplished enough writer to give it the treatment he felt it deserved. The heroine was insipid and the story was clearly exploitative. However, Howard commented to Clark Ashton Smith that "it really isn't as exclusively devoted to sword-slashing as the announcement might seem to imply."

Among Howard's papers was also found a synopsis for a Steve Harrison detective story that bears strong similarities to the Conan tale. The synopsis is undated, but was probably written only a few months before the Conan story: "[T]here had been an old feud between the Wiltshaws and the Richardsons, of which the present sets were the last of each line. Another family, the Barwells, had been mixed up in the feud until, harried by both Richardsons and Wiltshaws, the last of that line, a grim, gaunt woman, had gone away with her infant son, thirty-five years before, swearing vengeance on both clans.... Eventually [Harrison] discovered that Doctor Ellis was really Joe Barwell, who had returned and lived in the town ten years to consummate his vengeance...."

Howard had no problem amalgamating the two Barwells of the Harrison synopsis into Tolkemec. Another character in the Harrison synopsis, Esau, "a tall, gangling man of great awkward strength...a neurotic, really strong as a bull," was a probable inspiration for Olmec, "a giant, with an enormous sweep of breast and the shoulders of a bull," with the Biblical association of Esau's name reinforcing the connection to the hairy Olmec.

Red Nails is the counterpart to *Beyond the Black River*. With the latter, Howard wrote his ultimate "Barbarism versus Civilization" tale, with the conclusion that "barbarism must always ultimately triumph." He also stated that "Civilization is unnatural." *Red Nails* was the story in which he would expand on that theme. In all the stories he had written on the subject, the decadent and decaying phase of his civilizations, kingdoms, countries, or cities was never allowed to be carried out in its entirety: once divided and thus weakened, the civilized people were systematically wiped out by hordes of barbarians waiting at the gates. In *Beyond the Black River*, the Picts played that part; in *The Gods of Bal-Sagoth*, a 1930 tale whose construction is quite similar to that of *Red Nails*, the "red people" carried out the destruction. *Red Nails* would be different in the sense that no tribe of barbarians would be lurking at the gates of Xuchotl. For the first time in Howard's fiction, the civilizing process, with its decadent and decaying phases, is carried out to its inevitable end. Xuchotl is an "unnatural" city, in the sense implied in *Beyond the Black River*. To be civilized is to be entirely removed from nature and its forces. This is the reason why the city is not only cut off from the rest of the Hyborian world and its barbarian tribes, it is also, and equally importantly, cut off from nature itself: Xuchotl is completely paved, walled and roofed; the light is artificial and so is the food: the Xutchotlans eat "fruit which is not planted in soil, but obtains its nourishment out of the air." As to the Xutchotlans themselves, all – save Tascela – were born in the city. Xuchotl is the epitome of a decayed civilization as Howard conceived it. It is the place where, as he had it, "the abnormal becomes normal." Given these premises, the outcome of the story is not a surprise. As had been the case with *Beyond the Black River*, Howard had a message to deliver and he was ready to follow his assigned course right to the end.

Red Nails is so rich a story that we can't hope to explore it in detail within the scope of this essay; a lot could be said about the relationship between Conan and Valeria, for instance, in which it is quite tempting to see a parallel with that of Howard and Novalyne Price, who had quite a temper; Valeria of the Red Brotherhood is indeed a welcome change from some of Howard's more passive female characters. (He had, however, portrayed strong and interesting women characters before Valeria, and his meeting with Novalyne, such as Bêlit [in *Queen of the Black Coast*] and Sonya of Rogatino [in the historical adventure *The Shadow of the Vulture*].) In Tascela, the female vampire who refuses to die, feeding on younger women, fighting for the attentions of Conan, and thus jealous of Valeria, it is more than tempting to see a fictional representation of Howard's mother, who always was hostile toward Novalyne Price. Olmec could then be seen as Howard's father, and the whole story an allegorical tale, in which Howard and Novalyne set foot in the decayed universe that has become the Howard house....

Howard sent *Red Nails* to Farnsworth Wright on July 22, 1935. The next day he wrote Clark Ashton Smith: "Sent a three-part serial to Wright yesterday: 'Red Nails,' which I devoutly hope he'll like. A Conan yarn, and the grimmest, bloodiest and most merciless story of the series so far. Too much raw meat, maybe, but I merely portrayed what I honestly believe would be the reactions of certain types of people in the situations on which the plot of the story hung." To Lovecraft, he later commented: "The last yarn I sold to Weird Tales – and it well may be the last fantasy I'll ever write – was a three-part Conan serial which was the bloodiest and most sexy weird story I ever wrote. I have been dissatisfied with my handling of decaying races in stories, for the reason that degeneracy is so prevalent in such races that even in fiction it can not be ignored as a motive and as a fact if the fiction is to have any claim to realism. I have ignored it in all other stories, as one of the taboos, but I did not ignore it in this story. When, or if, you ever read it, I'd like to know how you like my handling of the subject of lesbianism." (One wonders if "lesbianism" was indeed the central theme of *Red Nails* to Howard. The story only touches on the subject because of the vampiric nature of Tascela, but this was nothing new after Le Fanu's *Carmilla*.)

As Howard mentions, the story was accepted by Weird Tales, which began its serialization a few days after Howard's suicide and ended it as news of his death was announced in the magazine. It was the last Conan story.

Howard's interests – and output – in the last year of his life were increasingly western-oriented, and he didn't write a fantasy story in that period. A few short weeks before his death, he wrote that he was contemplating writing a fantasy. Two drafts for that unfinished weird story – set in sixteenth-century America – were found among his papers after his death, proof that he had not entirely abandoned the idea of writing fantasy tales. Whether he would have eventually returned to Conan after some time is a question that must remain unanswered.

In 1935, Howard sent several stories to England via his agent Otis Adelbert Kline. The stories, sent to Weird Tales' representative in the United Kingdom, included several Conan tales, which were sent on 25 September: *Beyond the Black River*, *A Witch Shall Be Born*, and *The Servants of Bit-Yakin*. It seems probable Howard had no real hopes for these, as he had tear-sheets of Weird Tales pages sent, not actual typescripts. Anyway, nothing ever came out of this.

Howard's last work on Conan occurred in March 1936, when two fans, John D.

Clark and P. Schuyler Miller, sent him a letter in which they attempted to establish the chronology of the Conan tales. Howard's letter, reproduced in this volume, is essential to the reader interested in Conan's "biography," though Howard was perhaps having some fun with the two fans. For instance, he wrote that Conan "made his first journey beyond the boundaries of Cimmeria. This, strange to say, was north instead of south. Why or how, I am not certain, but he spent some months among a tribe of the Æsir, fighting with the Vanir and the Hyperboreans." Clark and Miller couldn't possibly know that Howard was referring here to *The Frost-Giant's Daughter*, the second-written Conan tale, which had been rejected by Wright and was still unpublished in its original form. With his reply, Howard included a map, expanded from the very rough ones he had prepared in 1932; it was to be the last work he would do on Conan.

Robert E. Howard committed suicide on June 11, 1936. Conan the Cimmerian, however, is still with us. In spite of some difficult years, he has managed to survive, and shows no signs of weakness.

The barbarian's longevity wouldn't have surprised Howard.

The barbarian must always ultimately triumph.

NOTES ON THE CONAN TYPESCRIPTS AND THE CHRONOLOGY
By Patrice Louinet

LIST OF THE EXTANT CONAN TYPESCRIPTS (*July 1934–July 1935*)
The final drafts of the stories published in Weird Tales were probably destroyed after the story was typeset, and thus are no longer extant.

Regarding the terminology used: a draft is "incomplete" when we are missing at least one page; it is "unfinished" when Howard didn't finish the draft. Sometimes Howard would write a draft and rewrite only a portion of it; such drafts are subdivided with numerals (i.e., draft b2 recycles pages from draft b1). All drafts have been examined for the preparation of this volume unless noted.

The Servants of Bit-Yakin
– draft a, untitled, 32 pgs. (numbered 1–5, 7–33 in error)
– draft b, 48 pgs.
– draft c, (final Weird Tales version), survives as carbon, 56 pgs.

Beyond the Black River
– draft a, untitled, 56 pgs.
– draft b, (final Weird Tales version), survives as untitled carbon, 69 pgs.

The Black Stranger
– synopsis a, untitled, single-spaced, 2 pgs.
– draft a, untitled, dwindling to a synopsis, 64 pgs.
– draft b1, incomplete, pgs. 47–81 of 81 pgs.
– draft b2, incomplete, pgs. 47–93 of 93 pgs., (numbered 47–59, 59–93) (pages 79–81 are perhaps missing; they were not located in time for this edition)
– draft c, final version, 98 pgs., (plus discarded pg. 35) (also survives as a carbon)
– in addition to his final draft, Howard wrote a two-page synopsis of the first part of this story, conceived as a serial; undoubtedly this would have appeared in Weird Tales—had the story been accepted—at the beginning of the second installment.

The Man-Eaters of Zamboula
– synopsis, 1 pg.
– draft a, dwindling to a synopsis, 24 pgs.
– draft b, 33 pgs.
– draft c, (final Weird Tales version), survives as carbon, 40 pgs. (page 32 is perhaps lost; it was not located in time for this edition)

Red Nails
– draft a, untitled and incomplete, pgs 1–52 of 53?, dwindling to a synopsis, (probably lacking the final page only)
– draft b, incomplete, pgs. 27–91 of 91, dwindling to a synopsis
– draft c1, partial, pgs. 97–100, (draft for last few pgs. of c2)
– draft c2, (final Weird Tales version), survives as incomplete carbon, pgs. 17–102 of 102 (pages 44–45, 47–51, 53, 56–77 are perhaps lost; they were not located in time for this edition)

Untitled Notes (The Westermarck . . .)
– single-spaced page

Wolves Beyond the Border
– draft a, unfinished and dwindling to a synopsis, 15 pgs.
– draft b, unfinished, 25 pgs.

NOTES ON THE ORIGINAL HOWARD TEXTS

The texts for this edition of *The Conquering Sword of Conan* were prepared by Patrice Louinet, Rusty Burke, and Dave Gentzel, with assistance from Glenn Lord. The stories have been checked either against Howard's original typescripts, copies of which were furnished by Glenn Lord and the Cross Plains Public Library, or the first published appearance if a typescript was unavailable. Drafts of Howard's stories, when extant, have also been checked to ensure the greatest accuracy. Every effort has been made to present the work of Robert E. Howard as faithfully as possible. Deviations from the original sources are detailed in these textual notes. In the following, page, line, and word numbers are given as follows: 57.2.9, indicating page 57, second line, ninth word. Story titles, chapter numbers and titles, and breaks before and after chapter headings, titles, and illustrations are not counted. The page/line number will be followed by the reading in the original source, or a statement indicating the type of change made.

The Servants of Bit-Yakin
Text taken from Howard's carbon, provided by Glenn Lord. (Page 53 of the carbon was in such bad shape that it had to be retyped by Glenn Lord, respecting Howard's layout and eventual mistakes.) The carbon has no title for the first chapter; it was either added by Howard directly on the typescript or added by the Weird Tales editor. 4.6.17: reach; 4.10.4: crossed-legged; 4.17.2: invistigation; 4.25.13: ampiteater; 4.30.3: exaled; 6.2.8: sacret; 6.28.9: indiscretly; 6.33.8: "stood" absent from original and taken from Weird Tales text; 6.35.8: "with within" in original; 8.9.3: lapus-lazuli; 8.17.8: "be" absent from original; 8.33.9: freizes; 9.3.2: preversed; 9.3.8: effected; 9.40.5: established; 10.12.8: Pains-takingingly (hyphenated); 10.28.9: period after "characters"; 10.36.10: this page of the carbon is damaged and the following words or phrases up to and including 10.39.5 are taken from Weird Tales text: 10.36.10: "script"; 10.37.2: "familiar,"; 10.37.9: "been modified"; 10.38.1: "nomad"; 10.38.6: "baffled him. He"; 10.38.13: "recurrent"; 10.39.5: "as a proper name. Bit-Yakin. He gathered"; 11.2.4: mauscript; 11.32.11: posssessed; 14.7.15: carefull; 14.32.9: the last three letters of "immemorial" are unreadable on the carbon; 16.6.10: contemptously; 16.14.11: "forget" absent from original and taken from Weird Tales text; 16.33.6: space before "watching"; 17.5.15: caves; 17.21.17: of; 17.23.2: no period and quotation mark after "immediately" (typed to right edge of paper); 17.24.9: Zembawans; 18.10.5: explict; 18.35.12: "if" absent from original; 18.38.1: squaked; 18.39.6: freizes; 19.17.13: Conan's; 19.36.2: tense; 20.4.6: straining; 20.11.2: holloweed; 21.6.3: "not" absent from original; 21.7.5: Obvious; 22.38.1: Gawlur; 23.23.11: "cry" absent from original and taken from Weird Tales text; 24.32.11: "not" repeated; 25.2.4: "this" repeated (This this); 25.22.14: "the"

absent from original; 27.1.9: instantly; 27.9.1: through; 28.14.7: difficukty; 29.3.14: where; 29.11.2: the that; 30.2.10: phosphorous; 31.3.8: prophesy; 31.6.11: descrated; 31.37.9: yards; 32.3.7: "a" absent from original; 32.9.11: escounced; 32.14.10: phosphorous; 32.25.15: the first three letters of "cavern" are unreadable on the carbon; 32.29.2: set; 34.20.16: the; 34.21.5: chainting; 34.38.15: phosphorous; 35.2.5: is; 36.1.8: grassped; 36.24.3: "glow" absent from original and taken from Weird Tales text; 39.15.10: hyphen instead of comma after "grey"; 40.3.5: blood; 40.14.5: down downward; 40.14.13: nervelss; 41.9.4: jems; 41.16.11: the line: "like you. There's no use going back to Keshia. There's nothing in Keshan" didn't register on the carbon. The text is taken from the Weird Tales text.

Beyond the Black River
Text taken from Howard's carbon, provided by Glenn Lord. (Pages 1 and 65 of the carbon were in such bad shape that they had to be retyped by Glenn Lord, respecting Howard's layout and eventual mistakes.) The chapters are untitled in the carbon, except for the first one. A blank line in the ts. below each new chapter suggests Howard intended to add titles; these may have been present on the ts. sent to Weird Tales. It is also possible that these were added by the Weird Tales editor. 45.7.6: "a" before "soft" in original; 45.13.9: cabin; 46.37.14: "been" absent from original; 48.7.1: "and" absent from original; 50.10.13: quotation mark before "Conan"; 52.14.4: the words "straying" and "strayed" appear on the carbon, one typed over the other, though it is not clear which was Howard's final choice; 52.21.1: accomodate; 52.25.12: "of" absent from original; 52.35.8: blunder; 56.22.6: pythong; 56.39.14: no space between "know" and em-dash; 59.13.2: breek; 59.14.1: sword; 60.40.13: touched; 64.10.3: coifures; 65.22.1: "four of" in original; 65.31.12: accomodated; 65.37.2: of; 67.15.13: shoudders; 67.17.9: that; 67.26.1: beast; 67.40.9: thew; 68.20.2: futiley; 68.29.13: "in" unreadable due to a crease on the carbon; 68.39.7: ancient; 74.17.2: avoiding; 74.22.13: cubs; 74.25.6: "and" absent from original; 76.5.6: carnivora; 76.21.3ff: "looking for us" unreadable due to a crease on the carbon and taken from Weird Tales text; 76.23.12: "to" absent from original; 76.33.13: doesn' (typed to right edge of paper); 77.26.7: villave; 78.15.9: "with" after "trade" in original; 79.8.12: laying; 79.20.4: "the" absent from original; 80.13.7: "a" absent from original; 83.14.12: "yards" absent from original and taken from Weird Tales text; 84.4.3: furious; 84.7.6: no comma after "Cimmerian"; 84.31.6: accrosst; 84.36.12: broast; 86.1.4: glancing; 88.7.13: "and" unreadable due to a crease on the carbon; 88.29.13: hideous; 88.29.14: slashdd; 88.38.12: "was" instead of "no"; 88.40.14: growl; 91.28.10: pleasur (typed to right edge of paper); 93.1.6: "shoulders" absent from original and taken from Weird Tales text; 93.28.12: "blood" instead of "wound" in original; 93.34.2: boths; 96.7.7: slepp; 96.11.10: comma after "blazed"; 98.2.16:

settlers'; 100.1.1ff: the carbon is torn here and the first two words ("No; Conajohara) are unreadable; text taken from Weird Tales text.

The Black Stranger

Text taken from Howard's typescript, in the holdings of the Cross Plains Public Library. The original has a number of annotations in pencil, some of which are from Howard's hand. We have ignored these since they correspond to the changes Howard introduced when he rewrote the story as a Terence Vulmea tale: as was customary, Howard's corrections for the Conan version of the typescript were typed rather than penciled. Interested readers are invited to consult the facsimile edition of "The Black Stranger," published in 2002 by Wandering Star. 104.19.13: statue; 106.23.7: agily; 107.27.7: nitched; 109.6.1: repellant; 109.14.12: cerulian; 112.22.10: neice; 112.23.1: protege; 116.3.5: Storm's; 120.15.8: roasing; 120.22.11: silene; 120.36.12: It's; 121.6.8: neice; 122.27.3: fixidly; 122.38.10: no period after "intentions"; 125.33.11: "in" absent from original; 126.17.4: neice; 126.35.15: curtisied; 128.12.3: comma after "Curse"; 128.26.12: "a" repeated; 129.10.11: neice; 133.21.14: randy; 133.22.1: "the" absent from original; 136.32.2: "the" repeated (the *The Red Hand*); 136.34.12: adaptibility; 138.11.8: surveilance; 140.35.3: every; 140.35.5: eaves dropping; 143.27.8: appeares; 145.11.14: no quotation mark after "years!" in original; 146.26.2: "is" absent from original; 147.6.7: neice; 147.10.16: "w ill" (extra space); 147.35.5: "of" absent from original; 148.22.6: rogue's; 148.26.10: potents; 149.18.15: venmous; 149.24.5: "on" absent from original; 149.39.1: seem; 150.11.13: crew; 152.1.2: paroxism; 153.23.10: "it" absent from original; 153.40.4: dirction; 154.26.13: quotation mark before "he" rather than after "Eagle-Picts,"; 156.7.11: "the" absent from original; 156.40.13: nitched; 158.38.1: jamb; 159.19.5: "for" absent from original; 160.40.7: clapsed; 161.35.8: "cloak-wrapped" not hyphenated ("cloak wrapped"); 162.9.6: resplendant; 163.1.9: no comma after "strand"; 164.40.1: question mark rather than period after "help"; 165.34.5: when; 168.35.6: And; 170.10.1: no comma after "glare"; 171.3.8: headlong; 172.15.11: irrelevency; 172.21.5: consumated; 172.32.6: no space between the quotation mark and "she."

The Man-Eaters of Zamboula

Text taken from Howard's carbon, provided by Glenn Lord. (Page 32 of the carbon is supposedly extant but was not located in time for the preparation of this volume; the text for this page [from 200.35.14: when, to 201.19.3: another] was taken from the Weird Tales appearance). 177.9.2: flambouyant; 179.17.7: heterogenous; 179.38.3: carving; 180.2.14: wounded; 180.5.7: by; 180.28.8: "a" absent from original; 180.28.14: no comma after "suk"; 180.36.6: no quotation mark after "thieves" (typed to right edge of paper); 183.20.14: "there" repeated; 184.4.3: "a" absent from original; 184.17.5: visullized; 184.35.11: a; 185.19.3: "the" absent from original; 185.29.6: "eastern-most" hyphenated at line break; 185.36.5: unsatieted; 185.40.5: no period after "escaped" (typed to right edge of paper); 186.32.12: no period after "streets" (typed to right edge of paper); 186.33.2: "me" absent from original; 189.8.2: black; 189.8.4: no comma after "past"; 189.8.8: scruffing; 189.11.4: "the" inserted in original ("the Aram's death-house"); 189.20.6: unforseen; 189.39.2: quotation mark before "she" rather than after em-dash; 190.1.11: no quotation mark after "name" (typed to right edge of paper); 191.5.5: comma rather than period after "him"; 192.19.10: "A" absent from original (probably didn't register on the carbon); 193.23.12: she; 194.5.10: one; 194.17.9: "help" absent from original; 195.3.6: "under" repeated; 195.10.14: of; 195.13.2: "the" absent from original; 195.36.2: filiaments; 195.40.11: no comma after "tugging" (typed to right edge of paper); 196.17.13: "a" absent from original; 196.27.10: "and" absent from original; 196.29.8: deafeningl (typed to right edge of paper); 198.10.4: breasts; 198.20.13: no period after "corridor" (typed to right edge of paper); 199.15.4: discernable; 200.14.12: no period after "dissemble" (typed to right edge of paper); 201.24.11: monster; 201.30.5: rythm; 201.32.8: tarrantella; 203.1.13: "mad-dog" in original; 203.21.9: plotte (typed to right edge of paper); 203.35.14: quarte (typed to right edge of paper); 207.5.12: grasping; 207.29.5: saw.

Red Nails

Text taken from Weird Tales, July, August–September, and October 1936 (three-part serial). The incomplete surviving carbon has been consulted for the preparation of this edition: variations within the printed text are minimal, mostly corrections of typographical errors. 224.21.1: Sailor's; 227.17.9: period rather than comma after "girl"; 228.34.1: "plowshare" hyphenated at line break; 231.17.1: "love-making" hyphenated at line break; 234.18.5: has; 235.1.7: Science (Howard's carbon has "Silence"; cf. 239.7.11); 238.5.3: Xotalancs; 239.23.4: "sword-thrust" hyphenated at line break; 243.34.3: Xotalancs; 248.2.1: "battle-ground" hyphenated at line break; 250.3.5: restorted; 254.13.6: "nearby" hyphenated at line break; 258.38.11: "sword-play" hyphenated at line break; 259.13.7: "throne-room" hyphenated at line break; 260.39.13: "witch-light" hyphenated at line break; 267.24.15: "wrestling-match" hyphenated at line break; 273.17.8: Techultli.

Untitled Notes

Text taken from Howard's original typescript, provided by Glenn Lord. No changes have been made for this edition.

Wolves Beyond the Border, Draft A
Text taken from Howard's original typescript, provided by Glenn Lord. No changes have been made for this edition.

Wolves Beyond the Border, Draft B
Text taken from Howard's original typescript, provided by Glenn Lord. No changes have been made for this edition.

The Black Stranger, Synopsis A
Text taken from Howard's original typescript, provided by Glenn Lord. No changes have been made for this edition.

The Black Stranger, Synopsis B
Text taken from Howard's original typescript, provided by Glenn Lord. No changes have been made for this edition.

The Man-Eaters of Zamboula, Synopsis
Text taken from Howard's original typescript, provided by Glenn Lord. No changes have been made for this edition.

Red Nails, Draft
Text taken from Howard's original typescript, provided by Glenn Lord. 322.7.9: in the double-spaced typescript, the phrase "a skeleton on a shelf" is inserted between the line ending with "neither able to" and the next beginning with "see above or below her." This was evidently added at a later moment and intended to be fleshed out in later drafts; 327.19.6: the phrase "Branches too light for spear handles and vines no thicker than cords." is inserted between lines of the double-spaced typescript with no indication of the intended insertion point.

Letter to P. Schuyler Miller
Text taken from *The Coming of Conan*, Gnome Press, 1950. 360.3.1: "battlefield" hyphenated at line break.

Thanks so much to Jim Keegan and especially Marcelo Anciano for believing in my work and suggesting oil paint rather than black and white. Many thanks to Irene Gallo for her support and wickedly exacting vision! And thanks to Greg and Miko at Gamma One, New York, for such great transparencies of the paintings.

Gregory Manchess

I would like to thank Rusty, Dave, Stuart, and Marcelo for making it happen once again; you are the greatest guys to work with. Without Glenn, these Conan books would never have been what they are; I can never repay you for your help and patience with my never-ending and sometimes weird requests. A thought for Peluche, who was always there to prevent me from working, I miss you. And last, but definitely not least, all my love to Sheila, who accepted the presence of the Cimmerian for so long.

Patrice Louinet

Many thanks to Marcelo, Patrice, Stuart, David, Jim, and Ed – it is an honor and a pleasure to work with such a doughty band of literary warriors. To Glenn Lord, friend and mentor, and Robert E. Howard's mightiest champion. To Greg, Gary, and Mark, for their outstanding depictions of the Cimmerian and his world. To Bill Cavalier, staunchest of Howard purists and most steadfast of friends, even if he is wrong about *The Black Stranger*. To the members of the Robert E. Howard United Press Association, who have inspired me, encouraged me, ticked me off, and pushed me to greater effort for nearly a quarter century. And, with much love, to Shelly, my soul and my heart's inspiration.

Rusty Burke

Thanks to Marcelo, Patrice, and Rusty for being so good at what they do and making my job a lot easier, and to Greg for his breathtaking paintings, *all* of which are fantastic. Thanks also to Mandy, who keeps the home fires burning when I'm doing these; Emma, who gets a kick out of seeing her name in print; Fishburn Hedges Design for the extracurricular use of their studio; and, finally, to Simon Thorpe, magician with pen, pencil, brush, and Wacom tablet – an inspiration and a great friend – *even though I find your almost total recall somewhat unnerving!*

Stuart Williams

I would like to thank Jack and Barbara Baum and Steve Saffel for their belief in a united Robert E. Howard library. Thanks also to Jim and Ruth Keegan, Stuart, Ed Waterman, and Rusty for their support and special thanks to Nancy Delia for her sterling work on the book. And to Graziana, just because…

Marcelo Anciano